SHOOT FIRST

AN INGRID SKYBERG THRILLER

EVA HUDSON

First published 2015 by Two Pies Press.
This version published by Venatrix 2020.

978-1-9160195-4-6

For the Gorman-Strongs: a quadruple threat

SHOOT FIRST

PROLOGUE

D*ecember 24th, 2012*

"Where are we going?"

"You're not scared are you?"

Like she was going to admit it if she was. Dion swerved, taking the corner past Verhoeven's Yard far too quickly, then accelerated down behind the warehouses that backed onto the river.

"This ain't the way, D," she said.

"It won't take long. I promised Odell I wouldn't turn up empty-handed."

She looked across at him. "Really? You want to *score*? Down here?" They were surrounded by derelict buildings in territory owned by Sutcliffe's people. All the street lights had been deliberately broken. "Lopez is going to blow your head off. Are you crazy?"

"Hey," he held her eye contact far too long for someone in control of a moving vehicle, "it's Christmas Eve. We're going to a party, right?"

"Lopez not selling what you need these days?" She knew

there'd be a helluva fight if Lopez found out D was buying off the Kings. "Why ain't you buying from Lopez? Tell me."

"Let's just say me and him had a little falling-out." Dion slowed the car and started looking carefully at the buildings. "It's round here someplace."

She shivered. It was five below zero and she was dressed to be indoors, in a nice warm house full of warm bodies drinking whiskey and rum, not in Dion's dilapidated tin can with a hole in the floor. She should have waited for Nolan to pick her up, but her sister had wanted the place to herself. Maybe knowing she wasn't going to wait around for him might make Nolan treat her with a bit more respect.

"See, I told ya. This is the place."

She looked up at the warehouse just as a light on the second floor was switched off. "Really? You think *that,*" she pointed at the decaying hulk of a building, "is a good idea. You are one crazy sonofa—"

"Hey, you don't gotta come in with me."

"You ain't leaving me out here on my own." She opened the car door and placed her stiletto carefully in a patch of water, avoiding the crust of snow. She wasn't even wearing pantyhose. "Don't you dare run off," she shouted. "You can damn well help me walk in these goddamn stupid shoes."

"Why didn't you just wear sneakers?"

"Like you say, we're going to a party."

They carefully crossed a junkyard where car parts were stacked to varying heights under an even capping of snow. She was hoping she might see something useful, something she could share with Nolan. Something she could use the next time she needed to trade. Dion pushed against a heavy curtain of PVC strips and they found themselves in what must have once been a kitchen. Or a slaughter-house. Steel countertops, concrete floor, a bank of refrigerators with their doors hanging open. It wasn't any warmer than Dion's car.

"You sure about this?"

"Come on," Dion said. "It's down this way."

"You been here before?"

"Vinny told me where to go."

"So now Vinny's buying from the Kings too?" There wasn't going to be a fight; there was going to be a war.

She followed Dion down a wide corridor lit by a single bulb. Textured glass panels had been installed at ceiling height, but most were broken and shards and splinters crunched under their feet. A series of open doors revealed one abandoned office after the other, some still had furniture, most were empty.

"This ain't a good idea, D."

"Relax." Dion was too laid-back for his own good. "This is how it works. They be watching us, making sure we not cops." He turned back and looked at her, his head darkened against the white light of the bare bulb. "And if we cops, they got time to tidy up. See? It makes sense. This is how they do things. Smart people."

This might be where they make it, she thought, but it sure as hell ain't where they sell it. No way.

At the end of the corridor, Dion turned right. Down the hallway, light came through one of the high glass panels.

"Trust me now?" Dion asked.

"You do know that if anything happens to me Nolan will drop your dick into a meat grinder and then feed you the pie, right?"

"Nolan ain't all that, you know."

You won't be thinking that when you're eating dick pie. Dion was right though: Nolan wasn't much, but Aurora hadn't been invaded by an army of Ryan Goslings who knew how to treat a girl. She knew she could do better, and one day she promised herself she would. She'd get out of Aurora, out of Illinois, maybe start a business. Make something of herself.

She hung back. Dion knocked on the door beneath the illuminated glass.

"Hey, manito," he said through the door, "you want to conduct a little transaction?"

There was no answer. Dion tried the handle: it was locked.

"Come on, D," she said. "This is a stupid idea. Give me your money and I'll buy what you want from Lopez. Let's just get to Odell's, OK?"

The boy didn't want to lose face. "Nah. They're here. They must be."

At the end of the hallway was a pair of large oak doors with square windows of wired glass. They reminded her of high school, like the doors that led into the gym. A dim light crept through the glass.

"See, they're in here," Dion said.

She joined him at the doors and peered into a large machine room big enough to hide a church. About twenty yards inside the door were four men, two in beanie hats and snow gear, one in a suit, the fourth had a shaved scalp. It was Vinny. Had to be. No one else had an X-ray of a skull tattooed on the back of their head.

Vinny was working with the Kings? He was Sutcliffe's guy now? She puffed out her cheeks in disbelief. Nolan and Lopez were going to have something to say about that.

The four men stood in a tight circle, arguing. The heavy doors blocked out the sound. Probably lead-lined or something. One of the men was holding a pistol, another some kind of machete. Her breath steamed up the glass. She wiped it away to see better.

"Maybe we should go," Dion said quietly. "See Lopez, like you said."

One of the men, the one in the suit, was Sutcliffe. She was absolutely sure of it. A sighting of Sutcliffe was the kind of information Nolan could use. Dion tugged at the collar of her mohair wrap, but she couldn't take her eyes off the men on the other side of the door. She wanted to hear what they were saying. She leaned all her weight against the door, prying it open an inch. The men didn't notice.

"Come on," Dion whispered.

She raised a finger to her mouth and dared him to make a sound.

She could hear voices, but not actual words. Then a flash of light. A bang. One of the men dropped to the floor, clutching his knee.

"You fucker," she heard him say. African accent. "You will fucking—"

The second bullet was aimed straight at his forehead. It took him a second or two to fall onto the concrete floor.

"Shit," Dion said.

One of the men turned. "Who's there?"

"Run," she said to Dion, "run!"

He pelted away down the hallway, toward the corridor that led back to the kitchen. She followed but her stupid shoes meant she was slow, awkward. She wasn't going to make it. She could hear footsteps from the other side of the door. She looked left. Right. She chose right, down another corridor lined with doors and high-level glass panels, into the shadowy darkness. She opened the first door she came to and stepped inside, closing it just as she heard the lead-lined doors slam shut.

Shit, shit, shit, *shit*. What a goddamned stupid thing to do. She stood with her back to the door, waiting for the sound of footsteps. Her heart was pumping like a dance floor. Even her fingertips were pulsating.

Voices out in the corridor. Then footsteps. Angry footsteps. She looked down at the door handle. Beneath it was a lock. There was a key in the lock. Was she imagining it? She stretched out a hand and tried the key. It was real and it moved. It *clunked*. Locked. Exhale.

She could hear movement in the corridor outside. Inhale. She felt someone standing on the other side of the door. The handle rattled, but the door didn't open. The footsteps receded. More shouting. Much more shouting. Had they found D? Is that what they were saying? He wouldn't spill, would he? He might. She was Nolan's girl, after all. That might be useful to them.

She looked round the barely-lit room. Another abandoned office. Maybe the old payroll department, or personnel. She could make out two dust-covered metal desks attended by two metal chairs with rat-eaten upholstery. File cabinets. A broken clock on the wall. Nowhere to hide.

She was going to die in there. Either they were going to find her and shoot her. Or she was going to freeze to death. Her jaw started to tremble, then her teeth began to chatter.

She reached into her purse and curled her fingers around her cell. It was 9:35 p.m. She switched it to silent and worked out who she could call. Not Kate-Lynn; she'd made it clear she needed some space. Not Nolan; she couldn't risk owing him anything. And besides, she didn't trust him not to storm in and make things worse. Maybe D would come back for her? And maybe it was 105 degrees outside.

Footsteps rolled through the corridor like thunder.

"Where are they?" Sutcliffe's voice. "Where the fuck are they?"

"It's all right, I know who he is." Vinny's voice, all whiny and nasal. "Saw the car drive off. Dion. D. He's no one. I'll talk to him, straighten it all out."

Blood pulsed in her ears.

"OK, you're right." Vinny's voice again. "I'll see to it."

"I want to see the body," Sutcliffe said. "I need to be sure. What about the girl?"

"What girl?"

"There was a girl with him. I saw her through the window."

She pressed her hands against the door, trying to stop herself from slumping onto the floor.

"It's OK, I'll make him talk before I stop him talking, if you know what I mean." Yes sir, sure sir, how high sir. Vinny wanted to impress his new boss. Probably had to. Was on some form of probation.

Silence.

"OK, OK. I'll go now. I'm leaving already."

"Shut this down, Vinny. Tonight."

She heard Vinny run off. She couldn't close her mouth and puffs of breath left her lips like cotton candy.

"What now, boss?" A voice she didn't recognize.

"We get rid of the body."

The next thing she heard was the heavy doors slamming. A few minutes after that, more footsteps, muttering. She waited. Five minutes. Ten.

Was that it? Had they gone?

She didn't know what to do. Couldn't think clearly. Too cold. What was better: open the door now, leave while they were off dumping the body somewhere; or wait? Surely Sutcliffe would send someone back with bleach and acid. *Help me, someone.* But there wasn't anyone. Yet again she was on her own.

Deep breath. Sort it out. Make a decision.

It was too cold to wait. She could die in there. Decision made. Her fingers trembled as she turned the key in the lock. A clunk. No footsteps. She was too scared to step into the hallway. What if he was there with a baseball bat?

This is stupid. You can't stay here.

She stepped out. It was deserted. Silent. Only the sound of her ridiculous shoes crunching on the floor. She had to keep one hand on the wall to support herself. It was hard to walk when you could barely breathe.

She made it to the kitchen. Still no one. A cold wind heaved at the PVC curtain. She looked out into the yard. Empty. She stepped outside. Was that snow? Just what she needed. She made it to the lane and looked back at the warehouse.

On the second floor, the light went back on silhouetting a figure at the window.

Shit.

She ran as fast as she could down the lane. She was leaving footprints in the snow. Footprints that would lead them right to her. She made it past Verhoeven's. Onto the main drag. Christmas lights in every window. She glanced over her shoulder. No one had followed her. She looked again. Definitely no one on her tail. Exhale. She staggered through the slurry on the sidewalk, wondering how late the bus would run on Christmas Eve. She didn't have the money for a cab.

The only places that were open were bars. It would be a few years before she could pass for twenty-one. She carried on walking, not sure if she should try and get to Odell's, or whether she should go home and risk Kate-Lynn shouting at her.

What was that she could smell? Detergent? The laundromat on the other side of the road was open. There wasn't much traffic, she didn't wait for the lights. She pushed open the door into the moist, warm air. Exhale. The gentle hum of the machines against the Christmas songs dribbling out of the single speaker. It was open. It was warm. She stood in front of a dryer. She could thaw out. She could think. She needed to think.

She sat down on the wooden slatted bench and let her head fall into her hands. Fucking stupid Dion. She reached into her purse for her phone. She needed to call someone for help. She needed a plan. She scrolled through her contacts, desperately looking for someone who had a car and no plans on Christmas Eve. Someone who could get her away and keep her safe. She was going to have to disappear. Sutcliffe's boys were going to come looking for her. She felt her throat tighten, like someone was wrapping barb wire around her neck.

She saw the name but didn't instantly make the connection. She flicked through her contacts again and again, hoping to see someone who would come for her. Her heart was thumping and knowing there was only one person she could call made her blood feel thick, sluggish, making her heart beat harder. She scrolled to the name and paused. Other girls had gone the same way, had dialed the same number, so she knew it worked.

Was it too late to call? What was the time difference? Only one way to find out.

She heard the phone ring once, then twice.

"Nancy Gadd." It was a nice voice. Friendly.

"Hi, you don't know me but—"

"Honey, it's Christmas Eve. Can't this wait until the new year?" There were the sounds of a party in the background.

"Please, you've got to help me." She wiped away a tear. "I might be dead by then."

1

Special Agent Ingrid Skyberg climbed carefully out of the black London taxi. The four-inch heels of her new shoes buckled slightly as she stood up: it was three more inches than she was used to. She pulled out a £20 note from her tiny black clutch bag and handed it to the driver.

"Keep the change," she said.

"You sure?"

She knew her generosity made her look like just another American tourist, but the truth was she had selected the items in her clutch very carefully—a credit card, house keys, security pass, two cell phones, a penknife, her Oyster card and £100 in notes—and she didn't want the loose change clanking around.

"You have a good evening," the driver said and pulled away.

Before the cab had driven ten yards down the street, the paparazzi fired off a flurry of shots until they realized Ingrid was not the actress they thought she was. She rearranged the folds of her gray silk dress, brushed out the creases it had acquired during transit—how did attendees at the Oscars get to the Kodak auditorium without getting crumpled?—and crossed the street toward the gallery. An ear-piercing whistle made her stop as she reached the white dotted line in the middle of the road.

"Ingrid!"

She turned to see her boss standing to one side of the photographers. Sol Franklin was waving to her with one hand while the other held tightly to the dying butt of a cigarette. A car—sleek, low, black, expensive—traveling far too fast for Mayfair streets screeched its tires as it swerved to avoid Ingrid before she tottered carefully to the curb.

"You look wonderful," Sol said as he crunched his cigarette under his patent leather loafer. "We should get dressed up more often."

"Thank you," Ingrid said. "You're looking pretty dapper yourself." The penguin suit was a big improvement on the corduroy and cardigans Sol usually wore. He had even trimmed his salt-and-pepper beard.

"Pretty dapper? You're talking like a true Londoner." He handed her an invite, a cream card, embossed with dark gray type, like a large old-fashioned calling card from a black and white movie. Understated, elegant and unmistakably classy.

Tom Kerrison
Emergent
Neuwirth & Ball Gallery
Burlington Gardens
Tuesday September 3rd 2013, 7pm
R.S.V.P.

"Have you seen Shevkenko arrive?" Ingrid took Sol's arm to help her balance as they climbed the stone steps to the gallery's entrance.

"No, but Rybkin is here. Should be a good chance for you to observe the Russian oligarch in his natural habitat." Ingrid was hoping to encounter some of the super-rich Russians who had been turning parts of the capital into a mini-Moscow. Some were investing in London property while others were taking over British companies, but they were all competing with one another in the galleries and auction houses, pushing up the price of art regardless of whether it was created by an old master or a kid with a spray can.

"And the ambassador didn't mind giving up her invite?"

"I imagine she minds very much, but she's still in Estonia."

When they reached the top of the stairs, the photographers on the sidewalk unleashed a frenzy of flashlights and hollers. A driver opened the rear door of his limousine.

"Is that Keira Knightley?" Ingrid asked.

"Or Natalie Portman? I have trouble telling them apart."

"Wow, this event is a really big deal, isn't it?" Ingrid gawked as the movie star posed briefly for the cameras. She thought she had made an effort in her $200 dress and an extra layer of mascara, but she felt like Cinderella in the presence of such sophisticated beauty.

They showed their invites to the doorman whose suit probably cost three times what Sol had paid for his. Or maybe it was just his firm pectorals and youth that made him look like a guest rather than an employee. If it wasn't for the Bluetooth headset and clipboard in his hand, Ingrid wouldn't have been surprised to learn that he was the star of a string of successful teen movies. He looked them up and down, checked their names against his list and waved them through.

The Neuwirth and Ball gallery was in an old—Ingrid had a hard time dating anything earlier than the twentieth century—classical-looking building. While it retained its original stonework and hardwood floor, everything else in the interior of the vast space was immaculately whitewashed. In front of them, a stone staircase curved up inside a rotunda lined with a succession of enormous, muted canvases.

"Wow," she said again.

"I told you'd like it," Sol said. "Bet you never went to anything like this when you worked in the Cleveland field office."

A waitress carrying a tray of champagne flutes walked past and Ingrid grabbed a couple of glasses, swiftly handing one to her boss. She took a sip, then a gulp. "Actually, that was the last time I went to an art show. A graffiti artist we had under surveillance during a meth factory bust." Ingrid looked down at her dress. "It was a sneakers-and-hoodie sort of a night."

"Well, I bet you looked good in a hoodie too."

They both sensed Sol had said something inappropriate. A fifty-something male commenting on a thirty-something subordinate's attire, however complimentary, was the sort of small talk that could see him breach the FBI's code of conduct if it weren't for the fact that Ingrid knew Sol was about as far from a sleazeball as it was possible to be. They had worked together at the US embassy in London for nearly a year, and Ingrid had formed the opinion that Sol was short for solid: her boss was one of the good guys. So good, in fact, that he knew when he was crossing a line and backed away into embarrassed silence. Ingrid became aware of the sounds of a cello drifting over the chatter of the glittering guests.

"So, if this Tom Kerrison is such a big shot artist, how come I've never heard of him?" Ingrid placed her empty glass on a passing tray and picked up another.

"That stuff is meant to be savored," Sol said.

"I'll savor this one," Ingrid smiled and took a sip.

"You really haven't heard of him?"

"You have?"

"He's a fashion designer. He's the big guy at Gucci, or Yves Saint Laurent or Chanel, or… I don't really know. Famous for shoes, I believe, and he made that documentary a few years ago. Got nominated for some award in Cannes. You must have heard of him?"

"I'm more surprised that you have."

"I have teenage daughters," Sol said by way of explanation.

"So he's a fashion designer, a filmmaker *and* an artist?"

Sol nodded.

"And he's brilliant at all three?"

"And that's why I can't believe you haven't heard of him."

"Hey," Ingrid said, knocking back another glug, "I'm just a simple farm girl."

"Well consider tonight part of your cultural education."

Not for the first time, Ingrid wished she had grown up in a

big city rather than rural Minnesota with parents who thought the only culture that mattered was conducted under floodlights. An usher swished past and handed them both a brochure, also printed in a vintage style, featuring a sepia photo of a sculpture of… well, Ingrid wasn't quite sure what. "Is that a woman?" she asked.

"A pregnant woman. It's his signature piece," Sol said. "Apparently it's already been the subject of a bidding war. So, how are you settling back in? I'm sorry we haven't had a chance to talk before now."

Ingrid had been back in London for six days after taking a month's leave. She had been home to attend the funeral of an old school friend. "It's nice to be focusing on work," Ingrid said.

"How was it," Sol asked gently, "back home?"

How was she supposed to answer a question like that? "It was odd."

"I'd thought you would have stayed for Labor Day."

"To be honest, I needed to make sure I left beforehand. That's the most time I have spent with my mother since I was a teenager. It was definitely time to leave."

"But you think it was…," he searched for the right word, "helpful?"

Ingrid considered how to answer. "I think after so long, knowing the truth, however awful, probably is better than knowing nothing." Megan had gone missing when they were fourteen, her body only recently discovered in what the press had labeled a House of Horrors.

"And you're sure you're ready to come back to work?"

Ingrid nodded. "Especially if this oligarch thing gets green-lit."

Sol's phone started to ring in his breast pocket. He fished it out and glanced at the screen. "Louden. Maybe it's the green light."

"You better take it."

Amy Louden was the head of the FBI's Legal Attaché program at the US embassy in London and Sol's boss. She was one of those quietly powerful people who could apply intense pressure without ever leaving finger marks: somehow, she had discovered a way to make pretty much everyone do her bidding. Sol wandered back toward the main door where it was a little quieter to take the call.

Talk of home had triggered memories of Megan's funeral and Ingrid had to quickly blink back the tears. She needed distraction. She headed down a long, wide corridor festooned with what looked like multicolored duct tape. A small card on the wall informed her the title of the piece was *Pride*. The corridor opened out into a darkened space where a large group of people had gathered. She estimated the combined net worth of the assembled would be a ten-figure number. In the middle of the group, illuminated by a warm single spotlight was the sculpture of the pregnant woman. Up close, it was simply breathtaking. Physically, genuinely, breathtaking. Ingrid felt a slight pressure on her solar plexus, not unlike the sensation of attraction, or fear, or loss.

Carved from marble, she saw the woman had been dismembered: the sculpture had all the components of the human form, yet nothing was quite where you expected it, as if body parts had been found in a heap. Ingrid could not tell if the expression on the woman's face was agony or ecstasy. It had all the power of a blow to the head and Ingrid felt side-swiped by it. She wondered who in the room had bought it, and if it had sold for seven figures or eight.

"*Dobriy vyecher*, Agent Skyberg."

Ingrid recognized the voice at her shoulder instantly. The smell of his cologne made her cringe: Nick Angelis, London's leading private security consultant.

"Hello Nick." She turned to face him and was a little annoyed at how good he looked in a tuxedo. The tan, the pompadour, the confidence, the 100-watt smile: how she wished she had resisted his obvious charms a little harder. "Who let you in?"

"Ow. And may I say how stunning you look tonight." His hand reached up to her neckline and he adjusted the way the silk draped over her left shoulder. "Your, um, scar," he whispered. "Wouldn't want anyone to see."

Ingrid flamed inside as his fingers brushed against her skin:

she hated that Nick knew about her scar, hated that they had spent the night together, but mostly she hated that she had enjoyed it so much.

"How long have you been back in London?" Nick's accent—upper crust, clipped—was an affectation: Nick Angelis, the greatest actor never to step on a stage. Though probably he had done that too.

"You mean you no longer have me under surveillance?"

"That was an unfortunate oversight. It won't happen again. And I believe I have apologized enough for that."

Yes, but not for anything else.

"You here on business or pleasure?" she asked.

"The former."

Ingrid glanced around the room to see who might be employing the skills of Fortnum Security Services. She identified a senior vice president of the World Bank, an American actor who had been a member of the eighties Brat Pack, a Saudi prince and the wife of one of the more prominent Russian oligarchs who called London home. "I'm guessing you're here to look after Mrs Ivanov?"

"I couldn't possibly comment."

"No, but you haven't let her out of your sight the whole time we've been talking. Is she the buyer?"

"I couldn't possibly comment." He grabbed two glasses of bubbly from a passing waiter's tray onto which Ingrid placed her empty glass. He handed her a flute of champagne.

"*Za vashe zdorovye.*"

"*Zdorovye.*"

"You know, if you came and worked for us, there'd be many more nights like this. The Met, the Bolshoi, private views in the Hermitage," Nick said. "The remuneration might not buy you a Tom Kerrison original, but it'll add a zero to whatever the FBI is paying you."

"Nice as that would be, it would mean working with you."

"Your words cut me to the quick, agent. Is that really such a terrible prospect?"

It was, Ingrid thought, it truly was. Her brain tried to dismiss the circling memories of their lone night together, but she found herself looking at his shirt just at the spot where she knew, behind the pressed, pleated cotton, was a medallion he refused to ever take off. She pictured it: a silver figure of Aphrodite resting against his firm, waxed chest. Nick might play the part of James Bond, but underneath the shirt were the tattooed reminders of his days working in restaurants and the military before his employment by MI6. Her knowledge of his tattoos, and of their intimacy, created a feeling of pressure at the base of her throat, and she suppressed the urge to retch. "Some of us choose to serve," she said, trying to salvage her dignity. "If I was interested in money I would never have joined the Bureau."

"Maybe not tonight, but some day." Was he talking about the job, or another liaison? He spotted something over her shoulder. "If you will excuse me."

Nick's hand brushed lightly over Ingrid's waist as he moved purposefully to follow someone—the prince or the wife, Ingrid wasn't entirely sure—out of the room and she flinched at his touch. Nick was good-looking, charming, a gentleman even, but his pursuit of Ingrid had possessed an arrogance, a certainty, and a persistence that had made him repulsive to her… until that one night when a combination of alcohol and low self-esteem had defeated her resolve.

She felt a sudden need for air and found her way into a small, overlooked courtyard. In the middle of it was a bronze fountain spewing a plume of golden spray as the water caught the sodium rays of the original gas lighting. Ingrid followed a limestone path through lush foliage. It was so warm it almost felt tropical. In places, the overgrown shrubs and trees cut out the weak light creating patches of total darkness. She spotted a bench, sat down and immediately removed her shoes placing the soles of her feet on the cold stone slabs.

"Are they new?"

Ingrid looked in the direction of the voice. American accent. East Coast. Male. She couldn't see anyone.

"Your shoes? Are they new?"

The man leaned forward, and out of the shadows, and smiled

at her.

"Is it that obvious?"

"May I?" He stepped toward her and gestured to the bench.

"Be my guest."

His bow tie was untied and his top button was undone. He looked like a high rolling gambler who had just lost at the casino. Forties, maybe fifties, rugged, like one of those models in an aftershave commercial that airs in the run-up to Father's Day.

"You're not outside for a smoke," he said, "so... you must be hiding from someone?"

Ingrid didn't like it when other people played detective, but there was something so warm, so likable about this man, that she decided to play along. She nodded.

"A man?" He offered her a cigarette. She declined.

"Embarrassingly, you're right. One of many bad choices I've made recently."

A playful smile stretched across his lips. "Perhaps you should try girls."

Ingrid stopped rubbing her sore feet and stared at him. "I did." What was she doing confessing to a stranger? "Once. Wasn't for me."

"I think you should try everything at least once. My problem is that I never stop at once." He lit his cigarette and inhaled deeply. "Even when something is patently bad for me."

"So who are you hiding from out here?"

"Oh, pretty much everyone," he sighed. "You know, a little talcum powder would make a difference."

"Pardon?"

"With your shoes. Stops the rubbing. Well, reduces it anyway." He fished a silver flask from the inside pocket of his jacket and took a slug.

"Thanks for the tip. How on earth did you find that out?"

He looked perplexed, as if she had suddenly started speaking in another language.

"I'm in the trade," he said deliberately.

"Oh my word." Ingrid suddenly felt herself prickle with sweat. "You're not, are you? You're Tom Kerrison. This is your show! I'm, uh, I'm such an idiot." She felt herself blush. "Shouldn't you be inside?"

He nodded slowly. "I'm not very good with all of that. More of a back-room boy."

"Ingrid Skyberg," she said, extending her hand. "Your sculpture… the one of the pregnant woman, it's incredible. Truly."

He shook her hand, gently but firmly. "Thank you. I am about to become a father. It's a very personal piece."

"Congratulations. On the baby," she said nervously, "as well as the show."

His eyes narrowed as he scrutinized Ingrid. "Have we met before?"

"Not unless you've committed a major crime, and I think I'd remember if that were the case. I work for the FBI."

"Really? Now that's exciting. Are you… what's the word? *Tailing* someone? Is there a scoop I should know about?"

"I'd be pretty bad at my job if that were the case," she nodded to the otherwise empty courtyard. "No, I work out of the US embassy. I'm here with my boss."

"Frankie?" There was genuine excitement in his voice. "Is Frankie here?"

"Who's Frankie?"

He wrinkled his nose at her and exhaled two perfect plumes of dragon smoke. "Frances?" Ingrid obviously looked none the wiser. "Byrne-Williams?"

Ingrid laughed. "Ah. To you she might be Frankie, but to me she's Madam Ambassador. How do you know her?"

There was a clatter of footsteps and an usher from the gallery's staff ran out into the courtyard. "Mr Kerrison? Are you out here?"

Tom waved his cigarette in the air. "Over here."

The young man rushed toward them. "Mr Kerrison, sir." He was nervous, the anxiety in his voice was palpable. "Sir, you need to come with me."

Scared, Tom looked at Ingrid, unsure how to respond. "If you'll excuse me," he said falteringly. He stood up.

"This way," the usher said. "It's about the baby."

2

Ingrid checked her watch: 8:24 a.m. That meant it had taken thirty-four minutes to run five miles. Far too long. Before the trip back to Minnesota, she had run from her apartment in Maida Vale to the embassy in Grosvenor Square, incorporating a methodically measured loop round Hyde Park, in less than thirty-one minutes. She was out of shape. Another reason why the trip back home had been a mistake.

She swiped her security pass and pushed through the turnstile. As she waited for an elevator, twenty or more embassy employees arrived to start their working day. She was far too sweaty to share an enclosed space with anyone, so she opted for the stairs and ran up three flights to the offices of the Legal Attaché program. Between ten and twenty FBI agents worked at the embassy at any one time, depending on where the latest intelligence and budget constraints required them to be deployed. The other agents all worked in counter-terrorism and counter-intelligence; Ingrid was the only investigator in the criminal division and led a small team of civilian staff.

Like the rest of the building, Ingrid's office looked tired and so dated it could almost be called vintage. Everything from the furniture to the ceiling tiles looked like it had come from the consulate of a small nation in receipt of international aid. Ever since the decision had been made to build a new embassy on the south side of the Thames, all investment in the Grosvenor Square building had stopped, leaving Ingrid and her colleagues dealing with a succession of leaks, drafts, infestations and compromises.

"Good morning," Jennifer Rocharde said without even looking up from her screen, a telephone receiver clamped between cheek and shoulder. Jennifer was the division's recently promoted senior clerk and was on a mission to show everyone at the embassy she had earned her promotion. Her eyes were bright, her tail was bushy.

"Morning, Agent Skyberg."

"Morning..." Damn, Ingrid couldn't remember the poor guy's name. It was only his third day. It was one of those boring names, the kind of name a man in his fifties would have, not a twenty-three-year-old who hadn't quite outgrown his acne. Trevor? Martin? "Morning, Don."

Ingrid gave Jennifer a wave as she sat at her desk, sweat making her leggings slide over her skin as her behind hit the seat.

"Good run?" Don asked, nervously trying to make small talk with his new boss.

"Yup," Ingrid said abruptly; she was distracted by the messages Jennifer had left on her desk. Her month's absence from the division had meant a backlog of cases to be reported on, filed and closed. Pressed against her computer screen was a row of Post-It notes, stuck in an arc to resemble bunting. Three of them told her that Ralph Mills had phoned. Again.

Ingrid ripped the Velcro fastener of the pouch strapped against her right bicep, then tore off an identical pouch from her other arm. She retrieved a cell phone from one and her wallet and locker key from the second. She scrolled through the missed calls on her phone: there were three of them; surprisingly only one was from Ralph. She'd been back a week and they hadn't spoken. She stared at the small illuminated screen, breathing deeply as she recovered from her run. She thought for a moment about just calling him there and then. Getting it over with. Getting the embarrassment out of the way. Her finger hovered over the call-back option. But she couldn't. She just couldn't. Not after what had happened in Minnesota. In fact, she wasn't at all sure she could ever face Ralph again.

"OK," Jennifer said to Don, "Shaun from the visa team says he can get, like, three. Agent Simmons and Agent Ryan are in. How many more do we need?"

"How many have we got now?" Don asked. His voice was baritone deep: Ingrid wondered how such an impressive sound could come out of such a puny chest.

Jennifer tapped her pen down a list on her pad. "Seven."

"Then we need another two; another four ideally in case of no-shows."

"Ingrid?" Jennifer turned to her boss. "Do you want to play?"

"Play what?"

"Softball. Regent's Park. On Friday. After work."

Ingrid hoped her face disguised the surprise she felt: Jennifer Rocharde was not the kind of girl you expected to be indulging in outdoor pursuits. The twenty-five-year-old tended to get out of breath just bringing coffee up from the canteen. "Who's playing?"

"US of A against the Republic of France."

"Excuse me?" Ingrid turned her computer on.

"The French embassy is getting a team together."

"Wouldn't they rather play rugby? Or boules?"

"Oh come on!" Jennifer said, her cheeks flushing slightly. "You'll be our secret weapon. You're, like, the best at sports."

"I haven't played softball since Quantico."

"And I bet you were excellent at it. Can I put you down? Say yes." Sometimes—often, in fact—Jennifer's eagerness resembled a puppy's.

Ingrid didn't like the idea of spending her free time with Simmons or Ryan from the counter-terrorism team, but it would look bad if Jennifer could get them to play and not her. "I guess. Sure."

Out of the corner of her eye, Ingrid was pretty sure she saw Jennifer perform a fist pump. Ingrid's screen blinked into life. She keyed in her password and opened her emails while Jennifer got back on the phone and tried to recruit additional team members.

How had Jennifer made quite so many friends? She had only been in London a few months longer than Ingrid and yet she was always meeting people from work, or telling tales about a speakeasy in Shoreditch or an Ethiopian restaurant in Kentish Town. Now that Ingrid wasn't speaking to Ralph, she could count the number of friends she had in England on one finger. Not for the first time in the past week, Ingrid wondered why she had come back to London at all.

Don approached Ingrid's desk. "You want me to run through your appointments today?" he asked.

"So long as my first task is taking a shower, sure. Pull up a seat." Ingrid didn't like being anyone's boss—delegation and trust were two concepts she had trouble with—but she knew she had to be kind and encouraging to the new recruit.

"OK," he said, pulling up the calendar on his iPad. "Your first—"

Ingrid's desk phone started to ring.

"You want me to answer that for you?" Don asked.

Ingrid picked up the receiver. She could answer her own damn phone.

"Agent Skyberg"

"Please stand by," the voice said. "I have the ambassador for you."

Ingrid's heart instantly pumped harder. The ambassador? She had never called Ingrid before. They had barely even met. A series of whirrs and clicks came down the line: the ambassador was obviously still in Estonia.

"Agent Skyberg, this is Frances Byrne-Williams."

"Good morning, ma'am." The words came with a little difficulty due to the tightness in her throat.

"I need you to do a favor for me."

"Of course, ma'am."

"I need you to get to Truman Cooper's house right away. You know who he is, don't you?"

"Of course." He was the Brat Pack actor Ingrid had seen at the gallery the night before. "My assistant will give you the address. He's a very dear friend of mine and he seems to be in the most terrible trouble. He's distraught."

"What kind of trouble?"

"I'll let him tell you himself." The ambassador put her hand over the receiver and proceeded, as far as Ingrid could make out, to talk to someone in German. She removed her hand. "You still there?"

"Of course, ma'am."

"Truman is probably the highest-profile American living in the UK at the moment, so I want you to offer whatever support he needs. No press, no local cops. Discreet, that's what I'm asking for."

"Of course, ma'am."

"Thank you, agent. I'm going to hand the phone to Felix, he has the details you need."

Once Ingrid had written down the address of a residence in Wapping, east London, Ingrid returned the receiver to the cradle and exhaled.

"Everything OK?" Don asked.

"Sure." Ingrid picked up the locker key from her desk.

"You want me to continue?"

"Whatever is in my diary for today, I think you better cancel it."

Ingrid opened her locker and pulled out her suit and her washbag.

"New assignment?"

"Looks that way." Ingrid stared at her suit. It was three years old and had been packed in so many suitcases and traveled so many miles it looked like it had come from a thrift shop. Even she knew that bootcut pants were no longer in style. She peered into the bottom of her locker.

"Jennifer?"

"Yes?"

"Have you seen my shoes?"

"You took them home last night. You said you wanted a backup pair for that thing Sol took you to."

"Really? I did that?" Ingrid looked down at her sneakers. "Well, I guess I'll be wearing these all day."

"Want me to go to Oxford Street for you?" Jennifer offered. "Size seven, right?"

Ingrid looked over at the eager clerk: she was starting to understand why she had so many friends. "You know I would normally tell you not to bother, but I have a feeling you'd make a better choice than me anyway."

"Black. Something you can wear with pants or a skirt?"

Ingrid nodded. "You're a star. And I'm going to need a car to take me to a place called Wapping in about half an hour."

"It'll be waiting for you in the garage."

Ingrid swiped her washbag and headed for the door.

"Before you go," Jennifer said. "Sol says he needs you to do target practice. Today if possible."

Ingrid was halfway out of the office before she'd worked out what Jennifer had said. She popped her head back round the door.

"Target practice? He does know you can't carry a gun in the UK?"

"Like, duh. He says you need an up-to-date certificate or something."

"Did he say why?"

"Nope. Just that you're going to need it."

3

The embassy driver followed the Thames east. Between the buildings there were glimpses of Tower Bridge and St Paul's Cathedral, but Ingrid was beyond the tourist stage and didn't look out of the window. She scrolled through Truman Cooper's IMDb listing on her phone as the black sedan inched through the London traffic. Ingrid had seen more of his films than she had realized, mostly on VHS at friends' birthday parties when she was a teenager, by which time his films had already been ten years old.

He'd become a star at nineteen, a proper dreamboat pin-up, on the back of a movie called *Slow Dance* and between 1983 and 1986 he'd made a string of films starring opposite his fellow Brat Pack members Demi Moore, Molly Ringwald, Rob Lowe and Emilio Estevez. He'd played a dancer, a soldier, an athlete, a Wall Street trader and a public defender, but the all-American boy's Hollywood career was over by the time Ingrid had started elementary school.

Her cell started to vibrate in her purse. She looked at the screen: it was Ralph. She let it go to her messaging service. She knew she had to speak to him at some point, but that point definitely wasn't right now. She switched her attention to Truman Cooper's Wikipedia entry which revealed that he had continued to act in theater, directed a few plays, taken the occasional guest role in TV series, acquired a stalker and won an early series of *Celebrity MasterChef.* Two years ago, he had relocated from his Montana ranch to London to star in a new TV series, an Edwardian period drama in which he played a fading American playboy who had unexpectedly inherited a distant relative's stately home. *The Belgravia Set* was the most successful imported TV drama in American history, according to *USA Today*.

Her phone rang again. It was a number she didn't recognize. She swiped to answer.

"Special Agent Ingrid Skyberg."

"So you are ignoring my calls, then." Ingrid felt a sudden pressure in her stomach: it was Ralph's voice. A hot flame flashed over her skin, whether due to guilt or embarrassment she wasn't sure.

"It's been hectic," she lied. "I didn't want to call until I had time to talk properly. I'm sorry, I should have found a moment but—"

"It's OK." She could tell from his voice that it wasn't. Detective Constable Ralph Mills was more sensitive than any other police officer she'd known, his heart worn prominently on his sleeve.

"Listen—"

"Yes?" He sounded a little too eager. Which made what she was about to say even harder.

"We should meet." Ingrid hoped Ralph had some contacts she could use in her new role profiling Russians in London. At least she hoped it was her new role, if Louden would just add her rubber stamp. As well as billionaire art buyers, Ingrid needed to get access to the fixers and enforcers further down the income scale, the kind of men who cooled hot rubles into kosher currency or made sure beluga caviar escaped customs tariffs. The kind of crooks a copper like Ralph probably ran into every month, if not every week.

"I'd like that."

She felt awful. She knew he was anticipating a different kind of conversation.

"How about lunch later?" he said.

"I don't know."

"Oh." His disappointment was audible.

"No, it's not like that. I just got a new assignment. I really don't know how the next few hours are going to pan out."

"Well," he took a deep breath, "I'll be at Borough Market from twelve-thirty until I have to leave for my shift. You know the stall that sells those burgers everyone's going on about?"

"Yes, yes I do."

"They're as good as everyone says. Come if you can?"

She didn't want to promise anything, but felt she had to offer him a crumb. "I will."

Ingrid stared at her phone as it faded into standby mode. *Well,* she said to herself, *that wasn't the conversation I'd expected to have with him.* They had spent one night together, a night Ingrid had anticipated would be the first of many. But then she had gone to Minnesota. An uncomfortable memory from a motel near the Wisconsin border forced its way into her thoughts. She really didn't know if she could see Ralph, not after what she'd done.

"Do you want me to wait for you?" the driver asked as he parked the car.

Ordinarily, Ingrid wouldn't have taken an embassy car in the first place, but as she didn't yet know what kind of trouble Truman Cooper had gotten himself into, she asked the driver to stay outside. A getaway vehicle might be required.

Ingrid checked the address she had written down to make sure she was standing in front of the right building. All she could see were the enormous wooden gates of an industrial goods yard. To one side was a brushed stainless steel intercom panel. When she approached it, she heard the whirr of a security camera swinging into action. She looked up into its lens and pressed the button.

"Hello." It was a woman's voice. Ingrid couldn't make out her accent from just two syllables. Italian? Romanian?

"This is Special Agent Ingrid Skyberg. From the US embassy."

The intercom buzzed, there was a solid clank as a lock was released and one of the huge wooden gates slid behind the other. Once Ingrid had passed through the gap, the gate immediately closed behind her. She found herself trapped inside a newly cobbled courtyard, accessorized with mature olive trees, a brand-new Range Rover and a decidedly covetable Triumph Thunderbird. In front of her was a restored warehouse that faded lettering told her had once been the premises of the Dunedin Trading Co. A large steel door opened. A dark-haired woman in her twenties appeared at the threshold in the kind of understated woolen black dress that Ingrid suspected cost over $1,000.

"I am Manuela." There was no emotion on her features, no inflection in her voice.

"Special Agent Ingrid Skyberg."

Manuela opened the door a little wider and indicated that Ingrid should step inside. A faint sneer appeared on her face suggesting she thought Ingrid was from a lesser sartorial species. Ingrid was led through a hallway dominated by a heavily riveted cast-iron staircase and into an open-plan space which, despite the high ceilings and exposed beams, felt inviting as well as impressive.

"Sit," Manuela said. "The gentlemen will be with you shortly."

Gentlemen? Manuela's grammar lacked the precision of her couture. Ingrid didn't like having mean thoughts—English was obviously her second language—but the housekeeper's demeanor had been so contemptuous of Ingrid that she couldn't help but score a tiny, silent point against the woman. Manuela gestured toward a group of three Corbusier couches arranged in a horseshoe around a coffee table made from a single piece of wood and some kind of salvaged machinery that could have been found in the building by the renovators, or alternatively bought in a Belgravia antiques shop for more than Ingrid earned in a month.

Manuela's heels clacked across the worn wooden floorboards back into the hallway. Instead of sitting, Ingrid walked over to the huge casement windows and immediately gasped: Truman Cooper's back yard was the Thames. The house was right on the river. "Wow," she couldn't help saying out loud. She stood at the window for a few moments staring at the view. To the west she could see Tower Bridge and the colossal new Shard tower behind it. To the east, the broad river curved south in front of a cluster of skyscrapers at Canary Wharf.

An expertly assembled collection of rugs, throws, cushions and art made the industrial room feel like a home. Ingrid thought about her own apartment; furnished simply and cheaply by her landlord, the only personal touches she had added were the vodka in the freezer and the free weights beneath the bed. She knew comparing her home to that of a millionaire actor was ridiculous, but she nevertheless felt a twinge of panic: the emptiness of her apartment was an indication of just how rootless she felt. In the space of a few months she had broken off her engagement to Marshall, been more promiscuous than at any other time in her life, and now Megan had finally been buried, the fire that had compelled her to join the FBI had been extinguished. The certainties of marriage, morals and career had crumbled, and Ingrid didn't really know who she was anymore.

"Agent Skyberg. Thank you for coming."

The man she had spoken to in the courtyard the previous night was striding toward her.

"Mr Kerrison," she said, extending her hand to shake his. "I wasn't expecting to see you."

"You weren't?"

"No, I was told to come and meet Truman Coop—"

"Truman will be up in a moment. I should warn you that he's in a terrible state. Distraught. He just needs a moment."

"What's happened?" Ingrid asked. "Why does he need the Bureau's help?"

"It's our son," Kerrison said. "He's disappeared."

4

"Your son?" Ingrid was confused. "Didn't you say last night that you were *about* to become a father?"

"Frankie didn't tell you what's going on?"

Ingrid pursed her lips. "No, the *ambassador* only asked me to get here as soon as possible."

Manuela reappeared with a tray bearing an iced bottle of water and three glasses. She set it down on the coffee table and retreated.

"Manuela, darling," Kerrison said, "can you tell Truman that Agent Skyberg is here?"

She shrugged. "He knows."

"I swear," Kerrison said conspiratorially, "that woman is actually a robot. We call her Siri. Please, take a seat."

Ingrid eased herself onto the designer couch, all too aware that her attire was the tawdriest thing in the room. The shoes Jennifer had bought for her were far too good for her tired suit: she desperately needed some new clothes. She glanced enviously at Kerrison's light blue shirt. The material, the stitching and the fit suggested it had been tailored for him. His jeans, though soft and worn, were almost certainly also bespoke.

"Tell me about your son. When did you last see him?"

Tom Kerrison raised an eyebrow, his pale blue eyes betraying signs of disbelief. "You really don't know, do you?"

"Don't know what?"

"And there's me convinced that everyone already knows." He poured them both a glass of water, his hand trembling. "We must be doing a better job of keeping things private than I realized."

"Mr Kerrison, please, you're going to have to explain."

There was a loud clatter and an enormous Old English sheepdog cantered toward them, his tail wagging. Kerrison's face softened and he leaned forward to nuzzle the excited dog.

"What's the dog's name?"

"Cully." Kerrison tickled the dog behind his ears. "As in cuddly."

"He's certainly that." Ingrid smiled at the dog. Out in the hallway, Ingrid could hear heavy footsteps on the staircase. A familiar figure entered the room and she stood to greet him, the dampness of her palms confirming that she was nervous.

Truman Cooper was taller in real life than she had imagined from his movies. Still boyish and tanned at forty-nine, the costume designers on *The Belgravia Set* had to pad him out and gray his hair for him to play the aging cad. He was wearing sweatpants and a tight-fitting black tee that revealed he kept in shape. His hair was wet.

"Did that help?" Kerrison asked him.

Cooper shook his head.

"We have a pool in the basement," Kerrison explained to Ingrid. "Sometimes a work-out can—"

"Well it hasn't, all right." Cooper was almost shouting. He leaned over and poured himself a glass of water and sat down on the empty couch. "Are you from the embassy?"

"Special Agent Ingrid Skyberg." She stood up and extended her hand. He didn't. "I'd say it's a pleasure to meet you, but it's obviously a very difficult time for you."

Cooper's face was stern, his jaw clenched. He took a slug of water and eyed her intently. "So can you find him?"

Ingrid sat back down. "I'm very sorry, Mr Cooper, but I really don't know what has happened. Would you like to start at the beginning?" She was trying to sound sympathetic and soothing.

Cooper turned to Kerrison. "Really? This is who Frankie sent?

A fucking idiot?" He fell back against the couch, his legs spread, his arms outstretched, taking up as much space as possible. The dog looked obediently up at him as he stared at Ingrid, daring her to look away. He wasn't going to apologize, and she sure as hell wasn't going to let it show that his insult had hurt her.

"I understand your son is missing," she said calmly. "When did you last see him?"

"Wow," he said. "You really are a waste of space."

"Would you like me to leave?" Ingrid asked, straining to keep the irritation from her voice. She was grateful she had asked the driver to stay.

"No," Kerrison interjected. "We wouldn't, would we?" He reached out and placed a firm hand on Cooper's knee. Cooper shrugged.

Kerrison turned to Ingrid. "Last night we received a phone call. While we were at the gallery."

"Yes, I remember," Ingrid said.

"It was from the surrogacy agency. The woman who is carrying our unborn child has gone missing."

"Ah, I'm starting to understand." She hadn't even known that Truman Cooper was gay, let alone that he was in a relationship with Kerrison. Perhaps if she read the gossip magazines she would have had the appropriate intel.

"She is eight months pregnant," Kerrison explained, "and Truman… *we*… are very worried about the wellbeing and whereabouts of our baby."

Ingrid switched her attention to Truman, his angular features barely able to contain his anger.

"It'll be the press. They'll have offered her money." The dog, sensing his owner's discomfort, placed his head affectionately on the couch. Cooper pushed the animal sharply away causing Kerrison to flinch.

Ingrid reached into her purse and pulled out a pen and her notepad. "Well, I'll take some details, make some calls and see what I can find out for you."

"Thank you," Kerrison said. He was definitely the calmer of the two, though his hands were constantly in motion, tapping his knee, stroking the dog, playing with his cuffs. A man in need of a cigarette.

Ingrid turned to a blank page. "What is your surrogate's name?"

"Kate-Lynn Bowers," Tom Kerrison said.

"And how long has she been missing?"

Kerrison looked at his Philippe Patek watch. "With the time difference, I'd say nineteen hours."

"Time difference? She's not in London?"

Truman Cooper inhaled sharply. "She's in California." His tone made it clear he thought Ingrid was stupid.

"The surrogacy laws in California allow us both to be on the birth certificate," Kerrison explained.

California? This was a waste of her time, but she took a deep breath and decided to play nice. "I presume you've already called the authorities in California?"

"The surrogacy agency did," Kerrison said.

"And they were told, I'm guessing, that an adult who has been missing for less than twenty-four hours isn't going to be assigned any law enforcement resources?"

"And that," Cooper said slowly, "is why we asked for your help. She's eight months pregnant. That must change things?"

Ingrid ran her hands through her short hair. "I'm afraid not, Mr Cooper. Unless she's a minor, and I'm guessing you wouldn't be allowed to use a surrogate under eighteen, or unless there are clear reasons to suspect she's in danger, there won't be anything official I can do."

"Then why—"

"But *unofficially*," Ingrid carried on, mindful that Frances Byrne-Williams had personally asked her to help, "I'll see what I can find out, but I'm going to need as much information as you have. Is Miss Bowers a resident of California?"

"She has been for the past nine months. It's a condition of the contract: she has to remain at the facility in Los Angeles."

"Facility?"

"It's a baby farm," Cooper said, his exasperation evident in every syllable. "A luxury holiday camp for pregnant women.

Nine months of spa days and macro-fucking-biotic meals with a check for twenty-five thousand dollars when they're discharged."

Ingrid suspected the reality might be more like an extended stay at the YWCA. "And before her pregnancy, where did she live?"

"Iowa, I think," Kerrison said.

Cooper muttered something.

"What was that honey?"

"It's Illinois. Aurora, Illinois." He seemed very certain.

"Manuela!" Kerrison called out. "Manuela would you mind coming here?"

Almost instantly Ingrid heard the sound of the housekeeper's ominous footsteps moving at an unhurried pace toward them.

"Yes?" she said, standing in the doorway.

"Would you print out the documents we have from Nuestra Señora for Agent Skyberg?"

"Yes," she said solemnly and promptly disappeared. She was the embodiment of unflappable; a sullen if efficient automaton.

"I can check some databases, but you might also want to hire a private investigator in Los Angeles. I can ask a colleague to recommend one if you like?" Ingrid offered.

Truman Cooper shook his head. "The more people who know, the more danger the baby is in."

"Why do you say that?"

He inhaled so sharply he practically snorted. "Kidnapping. Frank Sinatra Jr. Michael Douglas. The Beckhams. There's a damn good reason why Brad and Angelina have their own security arrangements."

He was sounding paranoid. "I understand your need for privacy, Mr Cooper."

"The hell you do. Do you know what'd happen if this gets into the magazines? Do you?"

Ingrid decided it was a rhetorical question.

"Our lives will be a circus and our son would be the chief freak. I'll be outed—"

"You're not already out?" Ingrid was perplexed. "I mean *I*

didn't know you were gay, but then I don't read those magazines —I couldn't even pick a Kardashian out of a line-up—but from the way you were talking, from the way you are with one another, I assumed… Being gay isn't really such a big deal anymore, is it?"

The dog made a whining sound. Tom Kerrison patted the couch and the dog came to sit beside him. "Can you name any out actors?"

Celebrity tittle-tattle wasn't something Ingrid knew much about, but she felt sure someone like Jennifer could rattle off an entire list. Maybe not a long list, but a list nonetheless.

"You're right," Cooper said. "Being gay is no longer such a big issue. Being closeted for thirty years is. I'll be the jerk who was too ashamed to be honest when everyone else was spilling their life stories to Oprah. I'll be the self-hating, paranoid idiot that didn't come out when he should have done. That's the fucking story now, not that I'm gay but that I never came out."

"And now you feel like you can't?"

"Not now I have a son to protect. I won't have his life becoming a shit storm of a tabloid mess before he's even born, do you understand?"

It was the first reasonable thing Truman Cooper had said since she'd arrived. "I think I do."

Manuela reappeared clutching several sheets of paper and handed them to Ingrid. "This is her application to the agency?" Ingrid asked.

"Yes, that's all her personal details," Kerrison said.

"Is this the best photo you have of her?" The girl was slim, long mid-brown hair, pale skin. She'd be pretty if she smiled.

"No, we have others." Kerrison turned to Manuela. "Would you print those out too?"

She nodded and disappeared.

"So your housekeeper knows all about the surrogacy?"

"Housekeeper?"

"Manuela."

"She is Truman's assistant," Kerrison explained, "and, yes, she knows all the details."

"And you obviously trust her," Ingrid said.

"Obviously," Cooper thundered. "Besides, she's signed a non-disclosure that means she needs my permission to get out of bed."

Ingrid sensed the actor's fuse was about to blow. It was time to leave. "OK, this looks like a lot of good information here," she said. "I'll make some calls, run it through some databases, see if I can't find Kate-Lynn for you." She stood up. "I'll be in touch later in the day."

"I'll show you out," Kerrison said. The moment he got to his feet, the dog went to sit next to Truman Cooper, desperate for its owner's affection. She wondered if any hearts would be broken by the revelation that Truman Cooper was gay, and how many more would be shattered by the knowledge he was such an ass.

"Is there some reason," Ingrid asked Tom Kerrison as they walked toward the front door, "why the agency believe Miss Bowers is missing? How do they know she hasn't just stayed with a friend, or gone to see her folks?"

"Apparently," he said in hushed tones, "she left everything in her room. Her phone, her pocket book, her medication, her clothes."

That didn't sound good but Ingrid wanted to offer reassurance. "You know, in ninety per cent of cases like this, it just turns out she met a friend in a bar and got talking and..."

"The girls aren't allowed to leave the compound. That's part of the deal. It's how the agency guarantees that your child won't have fetal alcohol syndrome, or be born with an addiction."

"You make it sound like prison," Ingrid said.

"From what I understand, for most of those girls it's more like heaven. No abusive boyfriends, no dealers, no pimps for nine months. They get clean, they get sober and then they get paid. Win, win, win."

"You think Miss Bowers has a history of addiction?"

"Listen, we're not naive, we know a girl only chooses to be a surrogate when she doesn't have many options, but she passed the medical, she seems like a bright girl, it's why we chose her."

"You've met her?"

"We've Skyped."

"She knows whose baby she's carrying?"

Tom Kerrison peered at Ingrid, not quite sure how to answer. "If you're asking whether she knows that Truman is famous, then yes, but I doubt she's ever seen him in anything, she's only twenty. And it's not like she'd ever have been in one of my boutiques. What impresses her is that we are rich."

Now Ingrid peered back at him. "You think her disappearance is about money? You think she's, what, kidnapped herself? For a higher payment?"

He crossed his arms and exhaled. "I wouldn't be surprised. Why make twenty-five thousand dollars when you can emotionally blackmail your client into doubling your fee?"

Ingrid became aware that Manuela was standing in the hallway, observing them.

"Photos."

"Thank you, Manuela," Kerrison said.

The black-clad assistant handed the photos to Ingrid then opened the front door.

"I'll be in touch," Ingrid said.

Tom Kerrison fished out a business card from his back pocket and Ingrid nodded her thanks.

"Nice shoes, by the way," he said as she stepped back out into the courtyard. He smiled broadly, revealing a broken tooth.

If Ingrid didn't know better, she might have thought he was flirting with her.

5

"You can just drop me here," Ingrid said to the driver as they crossed London Bridge. "You don't want to drive into the market. You may never make it out."

"Need me to wait?"

"No, you can head back to base."

Ingrid picked her way through four lanes of traffic toward a steep flight of steps that led from the bridge down to the street below. She dialed as she walked.

"Jennifer, it's me."

"Hi, Ingrid."

"I know it's lunchtime, but could you check a name against all the usual databases for me?"

"Of course."

Ingrid stood to one side when she reached the bottom of the steps and retrieved the print-outs from her bag. When she had conveyed Kate-Lynn Bowers' age, address and description, Ingrid put the phone in her rear pants pocket and returned the paperwork to her bag. She steeled herself: in about two hundred yards she would risk seeing Ralph. *How difficult can it be? We're both adults.*

The pathway snaked under the train viaducts and into Borough Market. It had once been a traditional produce market, but was now famous for selling everything from artisan breads, to empanadas, purple carrots and gourmet take-out. Ingrid followed the smell of grilling meat, letting it lead her past chattering coworkers and overwhelmed tourists.

Her breath stalled when she saw him. Tall, skinny, leaning against a pillar, scrolling through his phone trying to look nonchalant in his tight jeans and a vintage *Star Wars* tee-shirt. He pushed a hand through his collar length brown hair and looked up. When they made eye contact he smiled.

Not the smile. It turned Ralph into the spitting image of her schoolgirl crush, Clark Swanson. And right now Clark was the last person Ingrid wanted to think about. She blinked away her memories from the motel and smiled back. She slowed her pace, subconsciously extending the moments before she would have to acknowledge what had happened and confess her sins.

"Hi," he said.

"Hi."

He leaned in. For a moment she thought he was going to kiss her on the lips, but his greeting found her cheek. He hadn't shaved, just like the last time they had kissed when they'd said a hopeful goodbye at the airport.

"It's, um, nice to see you."

"You too." This was already excruciating.

"You want to eat?"

"That's why I'm here." As soon as the words left her lips she regretted them. "Obviously it's not the *only* reason I'm here, but let's get in the line. This place is popular."

The burger stall had recently won praise from the *Evening News*, London's leading paper, beating Michelin-starred restaurants to the award for the best meal in town.

"As soon as I got here, I thought it was a dumb choice."

"You want to leave it to the tourists? There are plenty of other places to eat."

He smiled. "An excellent idea. Pick a cuisine, any cuisine."

Ingrid gave it some thought. She fancied Italian but that was way too ordinary. French was too easy, Mexican too obvious. "Brazilian?"

"That shouldn't be too hard."

They wandered through the maze of market stalls and concessions looking for somewhere selling espetinhos or feijoada. "Listen, I'm sorry I didn't call."

"I'm guessing you had a lot to deal with. The funeral can't have been easy. Sorry," he said, "you don't have to talk about it. I don't want to intrude."

Out of nowhere, a man in his twenties shoved past them running at Usain Bolt speeds. His clothes and his pace suggested he was running away from something. They both looked in the direction he had come from: no one was giving chase. "We don't need to follow him, do we?"

"Hey, it's not my jurisdiction."

"Nor, technically, mine. This is Southwark. And they wouldn't want my big Lewisham boots stepping all over one of their collars."

"We didn't see anything anyway."

"Maybe he's just late for work."

They carried on strolling until they stumbled across a Uruguayan restaurant.

"What about this place?" Ralph asked.

"You promised me Brazil."

"We can always come back if we don't find anything better. So," he cleared his throat nervously, "how come you stayed in Minnesota so long?"

Ingrid braced herself for a confession. "It wasn't the plan, as you know. I thought I'd only be gone a week, but the funeral took longer to arrange than expected. The authorities took a long time to release Megan's remains for obvious reasons, and then, once it was over, I just felt I needed a little time."

Ralph didn't look convinced.

"I called Sol. He cleared it, so I hung around for a bit, trying to figure a few things out and spend some time with Megan's mom." Every word Ingrid spoke was true but each one felt like a lie. If she didn't tell him about Clark, about what she'd done, then omission was the same as deception. "Plus I had to sort things in DC. Signed over my lease… Sold the Harley."

"So that means you're staying? In London?" He was unable to keep the excitement from his voice.

She hadn't meant to give him hope and made sure her answer sounded downbeat, non-committal. "For the time being."

"And how were things with your own mom?" He emphasized the American pronunciation.

"My mother?" Ingrid was surprised at the question. "Well, let's just say it's possible Svetlana isn't the complete dragon I may have portrayed her as. At times I'd go as far as to say she even displayed emotions the rest of us might recognize as sensitivity."

"You know I Googled her while you were away. She sounds remarkable."

"Normally, people say 'formidable'."

"She's certainly got a story to tell. Does she ever talk about it?"

Ingrid stopped walking and stared hard at Ralph for a moment. "You mean the Olympics? No, but her medals are still in the house. I always used to think they were there to chastise me, to tell me that I wasn't good enough. But I think that's all she ever heard from her parents too. Took me years to realize that's why she defected; not to get out of the Soviet Union, but to get away from her father."

"Thankfully she didn't win gold. She'd have been impossible." Ralph pulled a contrite face, just in case making fun of Ingrid's mother was a step too far.

Ingrid smiled: "You're not the first person to say that."

They started walking again. Why was talking to Ralph so damn easy? Seeing him again was meant to be hard.

"If we don't make a decision soon, we'll be back at the burger stall. What about this place?" he asked. They were standing outside a pizza restaurant, a long thin establishment inside a railway arch. He started reading the menu. "Seems pretty good. We can share if you like."

Ingrid shrugged. "Italy's way too far from Brazil. We've got to be able to get closer than that."

Ralph shoved his hands into his pockets and followed Ingrid.

"There's definitely a Mexican place down here somewhere. Will that do?"

"Let's give it a go."

They found the Adobe Hut, sat on stools at the bar and ordered two sodas while they waited for their food.

"So." Now they were sitting down, eye contact had become harder.

"So."

"I'm glad you called," she said.

"Why wouldn't I have called?"

"You know." She was not handling this at all well.

"You mean, after…"

They were acting like teenagers.

"Well, I just want you to know this isn't at all awkward for me."

"Me either."

"A little uncomfortable, maybe. If the dial goes up to excruciating, I'd say it's hovering just below the embarrassing mark."

"To be honest, I thought it would be more uncomfortable."

A waiter placed their paper-wrapped burritos and their check on the counter. "Can I get you anything else?" he asked.

Ralph answered for both of them: "We're good, thanks."

"Shall we just forget about it?" she said.

"About what happened? Cos I have to say it was pretty memorable."

"No! The embarrassment."

Ralph took a bite of his burrito, leaving a drip of sauce on his chin. Ingrid reached out to wipe it away but checked herself.

"You have a little…" she said.

He grabbed a napkin and wiped away the sauce. "Thanks."

"Listen, there's something I wanted to talk to you about." Ingrid hoped her cheeks weren't flushing too obviously. She should have prepared something. At least the first few words. She couldn't just blurt it out. *Oh, by the way, I slept with someone else…* She had to tell him gently.

"OK. Shoot."

"I was wondering…"

"Yes?"

"If you… If you know anyone working the Russian cases." She dug her fingers into her thigh, furious at herself for ducking the issue.

"Oh. You want to talk about work?"

She bit into her lunch, grateful to be filling her mouth with something other than stupid words.

"You mean the murders?" In the past couple of years, several prominent Russians in London had mysteriously fallen off balconies, or been sold cars with inadequate brakes or employed housekeepers who couldn't tell the difference between rat poison and salt.

"So they are homicides?"

"Officially, no." Ralph looked at his watch.

"When do you need to leave?"

"I'm cycling so… in about twenty minutes."

Ingrid looked around for a bag of gear, but Ralph didn't have a helmet or even a jacket.

"Boris bike," he explained. "Changed my life."

Ingrid hadn't yet tried London's cycle hire scheme: she preferred her Triumph Tiger 800 to pedal power.

"But unofficially?"

"Unofficially the investigations are still open, as far as I know."

"Anyone you can put me in touch with?"

"I can ask around. Can you tell me what you're working on?"

She spread her fingers on the countertop. "I'd love to. Maybe in a couple of days. Just waiting for the green light on something."

"Sounds exciting."

"Potentially, it is."

He dropped a crumpled napkin onto the counter. He had finished his burrito in less than four bites. "So maybe if you get this green light you could tell me about it over dinner?" Was he asking her out on a date? Ingrid's throat tightened: she had to tell him about Minnesota. If they were to stand a chance, she needed to be honest with him.

Ralph pulled out a £20 note and placed it on top of their check. "It's on me," he said.

"You're doing me a massive favor, so I'll get this one." She reached down for her purse in search of her own £20 note.

"Take it." She held it in front of him, her eyes daring him not to grasp it.

"Don't be daft."

She gave him her best Jedi stare.

He took the note. "Just so long as you know I'm not happy about it." He smiled and his face briefly merged with Clark Swanson's, making Ingrid's heart miss a beat.

"I—" Her cell started buzzing in her back pocket. She looked at the screen: it was Jennifer. "I really ought to take this."

"Go ahead," he said.

Ingrid stood up and walked toward the restaurant door. "Hey, Jen. What have you got for me?"

"That girl you asked me to look up?"

"Kate-Lynn Bowers?"

"She boarded a plane at LAX seven hours ago."

"Know where she's headed?"

"London. Due in at Heathrow in about two hours' time."

6

Jennifer had left three Post-Its on Ingrid's screen. The pink one was a reminder about target practice, the yellow one told her to call Ralph Mills and the green one was asking if the money for the shoes should go on the office spreadsheet under 'sundries' or 'entertainment'. Ingrid presumed it was a test of her honesty.

"I'll get some cash out later and reimburse you."

"OK, I just thought, you know, seeing as you needed them for work..."

Ingrid stared at the clerk. "Really? You think shoes would be an 'allowable expense'?"

"Hey," Jennifer said, "they can always say no, but if you don't even try..."

Ingrid couldn't quite tell if Jennifer was joking, or if she was just trying to look cool in front of Don. She was an excitable California girl who often seemed young for her age. Was she lacking in life experience, or morals; or was Ingrid a fool for playing by the rules? She fired up her computer and dialed Ralph's number.

"Hey."

"Hi."

"So, you found something out?"

"Uh-huh." He sounded more unsure than usual.

"Bad time to talk?" Ralph's squad room was noisy. She

thought she could hear her friend Natasha McKittrick barking orders in the background.

"No, that's not it." Sometimes, Ingrid wanted to play her conversations with Ralph at double speed.

"Spill."

"Well, OK. You can make your own assessment." She certainly could. "My contact on the organized crime team was very forthcoming. Too forthcoming, if you ask me."

"What did he say?"

"*She* said they're reviewing the deaths of three Russians on the assumption they're linked."

"Which ones?"

"Um…" He checked his notes. "Bazarov. Nikolaev. Yuditsky."

"And the link?" She grabbed a pen and started to make notes.

"Certainly not cause of death. Bazarov choked to death on an olive in the Beaufort Club. Nikolaev had a heart attack. Yuditsky rather carelessly tripped and fell in front of a lorry on Park Lane."

Ingrid entered her password and logged onto the system. "So why the case review?"

"Sorry. It's hard to hear you. It's full-on here."

"Why the case review?"

"Ah. Seems they'd all been in contact with the same person in the weeks leading up to their deaths."

Intriguing. "Who?"

"Her name is Irina Markova."

Ingrid shoved the phone under her chin and typed the name into Google. Too many returns to be useful. "And who is she?"

He paused. "See, this is why you should worry. No one in organized crime ever gives out info this easily. Apparently she used to be married to someone in the KGB or whatever they call it now."

"The SVR. And where is this mysterious Mrs Markova now?"

There was a commotion in the corridor outside the criminal division's office. A scurrying of feet, a crescendo of voices.

"Most recent info had her working as a barmaid at a pub in Pimlico."

A uniformed Marine entered the room, scanned their vintage computers and chipped furniture before carefully making eye contact with all three of them. Ingrid instinctively stood up, the phone still clamped to her ear. "What's the name of the pub?"

"The Queen Mary. But don't go alone. I think I should come with you." Was he pushing for a date? "I used to work at the Belgravia station. I know the place a little."

"It's clear," the Marine said firmly.

Ingrid stilled her breath. "Ralph, I really have to go."

"So—"

"Right now."

The sound of clipped, purposeful footsteps were followed by the arrival of a diminutive figure in the doorway. In a pillar-box red dress and looking more like Jackie Onassis than ever was the ambassador, Frances Byrne-Williams.

"Ma'am," Ingrid said, putting down her phone.

Don and Jennifer both got to their feet.

"Agent, I just wanted to say thank you."

"For what?"

"For racing to Truman's side."

"Thanks aren't necessary, ma'am."

"Truman's such a good friend, and I know how desperate he can get when he's stressed—"

Ingrid remembered the actor's foul temper. "I was happy to help out."

The ambassador took a step toward Ingrid. "Excellent. He's a good person to have on our side. Always useful in the soft power stakes, especially at the moment. Great at functions. You know that show is popular all over the world? Five hundred million people watch it in China. Unbelievable."

"So I hear."

"Were you able to help him?"

Ingrid nodded. "You've not spoken to him then?"

"No, I've just got in from Tallinn."

"It was a straightforward missing person. It was Jennifer who tracked her down. I passed all the details on to Manuela."

Frances Byrne-Williams smiled at Jennifer. "Thank you."

"Actually," Jennifer said nervously, "it was Don who ran the searches."

Don looked at the ambassador, his cheeks blowing in and out like a fish. He was finding standing in such exalted company difficult.

"Looks like you're running an excellent team here, agent."

"Thank you, ma'am."

"Right," the ambassador said, "calls to make, wars to end."

"Thank you for dropping in. It's appreciated."

Ingrid was aware that her hands were sweating but she was relieved not to have made a fool of herself in front of Byrne-Williams. When they had met previously, Ingrid had felt like a thirteen-year-old at a New Kids On The Block concert.

"So that's where you went this morning? Truman Cooper's place? Like, for real?" Jennifer was sounding every inch the Valley girl. She stood in front of Ingrid's desk. "Seriously?"

Ingrid was taken aback by just how impressed Jennifer seemed to be by this. "He's just an actor," she said, entering her password sequence into the system. "How did you even know which Truman she meant?"

"Like, dah."

"OK, so it's an unusual name but there's got to be more than one of them in London."

Jennifer was standing with her hands on her hips, mouth slightly open in what appeared to be genuine shock.

"What?" Ingrid said.

"You really don't know, do you?"

"Don't know what?"

Jennifer's freckled face broke into a huge smile. "Oh my God, you really don't know."

Ingrid looked up at her. "You're right, I have no idea what you're talking about."

"Oh. My. God." She skipped back to her desk and pulled up YouTube in her browser. "You are going to love this. Like, totally love it."

Ingrid got to her feet and stood behind Jennifer as she typed

'*Slow Dance* moonlight swim' into the search field. She scrolled through the results. "This is the one."

She clicked on it and within seconds a slimmer, younger Truman Cooper was on her screen. Shirtless and sitting on a pontoon dock jutting out into a New England lake, the moonlight catching the well-defined muscles covering his arms and torso. Ingrid remembered the scene: his character, Brandon, was brooding after his dance partner had dropped him for another guy.

"What's this got to do with the ambassador?" Ingrid asked.

"You mean you still don't know? Like, really?"

"Yup, still clueless."

"I'm going to fast-forward." Jennifer dragged the slider and the video jumped over the skinny-dipping scene that Truman Cooper would always be remembered for. She released the cursor at the point when Cooper, filmed from the waist up, emerged from the water, tossing his hair so that the droplets became illuminated by the moon.

"Oh, hi," he says, "how long have you been there?"

The camera then cuts to his point of view and we see who he's looking at: a short, brunette girl whose brown eyes and full lips made her look like a young Jackie Kennedy.

"Oh my God," Ingrid said, instantly realizing she was sounding like Jennifer.

"Oh, wow," Don said. "It's her, isn't it?"

"It totally is. She played the big sister. Remember now?"

"Of course it's her," Ingrid said. "How did I not know this?"

The three of them carried on watching the scene in which Brandon suggests a casual night of fun under the stars. Even though Frances Byrne-Williams' Betty has fancied him for the entire length of the movie, she tells him that he only just broke up with her friend and there are rules about that sort of thing.

"You know, when she becomes secretary of state the news channels are going to have this on a loop," Jennifer said.

"Thank God she didn't do a sex scene," Don said, "then she could never run for president."

Ingrid wondered how many sex scenes Ronald Reagan had

filmed and flinched at the thought. She sat back down at her desk as Jennifer explained that Frances Byrne-Williams, or Frankie Byrne as she appeared in the credits, lived next door to the director and had been a last-minute replacement for Andie MacDowell.

Ingrid glanced at the target practice reminder and then at the clock on her computer. It was 3:10pm. She may as well get it over and done with. "When does the shooting range shut?"

Jennifer looked up from her desk. "You don't know?"

"That's why I'm asking."

"I mean, you don't know it's closed? They're deciding whether or not to refit it before they shut this place down." Jennifer's phone started to ring.

"And until they do, where am I supposed to do this target practice refresher?"

Jennifer picked up her phone. "Hello. FBI Legal Attaché program."

Don piped up. "There's a facility not far from here." He rifled through some papers on Jennifer's desk while she took down extensive notes from whoever she was talking to. "Here you go," he said, handing Ingrid a piece of paper. "Bayswater Road."

"And how, legally, am I supposed to get my Glock from here to there?"

"You mean you can't carry a gun here?"

"Please tell me you haven't been—"

"Me? No! Never held a gun in my life. Not my thing."

Ingrid thought that was just as well: Don's arms didn't look like they were strong enough to handle the spark from a cigarette lighter let alone the recoil from a Glock 23. She looked at the sheet of paper: the place was a twenty-minute walk, five minutes on the bike. If she took the gun there in a locked flight case, who would ever know? She crossed the room and knelt in front of the safe. She entered her security PIN. It was the first time she'd used the code since Megan's funeral: the date her friend had disappeared, the date she would never forget. The door popped open and Ingrid reached in for the pistol.

"Right," Jennifer said. "That's going to have to wait. You know Congressman Whitford?"

"Represents the 3rd district in Nebraska," Don said, attempting to be helpful.

"Well, his wife just got arrested for shoplifting. A boutique in Notting Hill." Jennifer handed Ingrid the notes she had just made. "She has requested consular assistance and the call desk has assigned the task to you, Agent Skyberg."

Ingrid kicked the safe shut and sighed. She hated these Rich-American-In-Peril gigs. "Well, isn't it my lucky day."

7

Ingrid stood in the wood-paneled corridor outside Sol's office on the fifth floor. She couldn't think of any good reason why she was feeling so nervous. She remembered a night in a bar near Quantico, sinking beers with an instructor, and asking her what the most frightening part of the job was. She'd answered: it doesn't matter how much armor you wear, it doesn't matter what weapon you carry, walking through the door is always the scariest part.

Ingrid knocked.

"Come in. Good run this morning?" Sol asked.

"I came on the bike. You wanted to see me?"

"I did indeed. Come, have a seat."

Sol's office was one of several rooms on the fifth floor that hadn't been remodeled since the embassy had opened in 1960. Blond wood mixed with molded concrete and a view out over Grosvenor Square, it was one of the nicest spots in the entire building. However, Sol, as a forty-a-day man, would rather have had something nearer the front door or the roof. A packet of Marlboro lay next to his keyboard: this was the first meeting Ingrid had had with Sol in a long time that hadn't coincided with a nicotine fix. He crossed the room and closed the door.

"So," he said, and cleared his throat, "Louden's been in touch about your new role."

"You're not making it sound good."

He sat back down behind his enormous steel and oak desk. It was probably a collector's item. What were the designers calling it these days? Mid-Century Modern. The embassy was finally hip and they were abandoning it for a place on the other side of the river. "She's been going through your files."

"Uh-huh."

He moved a mouse on his desk and his computer screen flashed into life. He started reading from a document. "Recruited as a language specialist after serving with the Jackson County sheriff's department. Graduated cum laude, naturally, from UIC. You speak three fluently, conversational in another two. But you didn't ever do international work, did you? Until now, that is."

Ingrid was a little worried about the data the Bureau had compiled on her. "No, I wanted to specialize in child protection. It's why I joined the VCAC. What's Louden seen in my file?"

Sol ignored her question. "Get to use your languages in Violent Crimes Against Children?"

"No, not much. Came in handy with a people-smuggling gang once." She was trying to sound relaxed, but she desperately wanted Sol to tell her what Louden's problem was.

Sol looked away from his screen and directly at Ingrid. "Let me guess, it was your Russian that was required, not the Italian or the French."

"Correct."

He placed his palms on the desk and spread his fingers. Behind his steel-rimmed glasses, his eyes narrowed. "And how are your languages now?"

"I imagine the French and Italian would benefit from a long vacation, but the Russian is kind of embedded."

Sol inhaled deeply, and a rattling noise emanated from his chest. It was only a couple of months since he'd almost been killed in a brutal attack: Ingrid wondered if his chest trouble was part of the healing process, or a sign that the smoking was going to achieve what a serial killer had failed to do. "So that brings us neatly on to your mother." He clicked his mouse and started scanning a new document. "Svetlana Kashlikova. Grew up in

Leningrad, recruited into the Soviet gymnastics program aged seven, competed at the Montreal Olympics in 1976, won two bronzes, one for the vault, one for the beam—"

"Sol," Ingrid interrupted. "I do know all this. She is my mother."

For a moment he looked surprised and pushed his glasses higher up the bridge of his nose. "Of course you do. It's just that, well… she might be the fly in your ointment."

It wouldn't be the first time.

"Look," he said, his hands once again spread out on his desk, his little finger gently nudging the carton of smokes, "there are a couple of problems we need to address before we can officially make you our oligarch POC, our oligal, if you like—"

"I don't."

"Didn't think you would."

"The problems?" Ingrid's rising frustration made her want to stand and pace, but she knew she had to stay calm and seated. Now wasn't the time to let Svetlana ruin things by showing her exasperation.

"First we need to get you armed. Islamic extremists might get the resources, but the statistics since 2005 tell us you're in greater danger infiltrating the Russian underworld than an al-Qaeda cell."

Ingrid thought about the intel Ralph had given her. "Jennifer's already booked me in for target practice."

"That's just the first step. Once you get the certificate from us, you'll have to get a license from the Met. And if you want to use your Glock, we need to file for special permission with the home secretary."

"I'm going to need the Glock. It's kind of hard to conceal a rifle."

Sol nodded. "So, we'll get that ball rolling, then—"

There was a knock on the door.

"Yes?" Sol looked over Ingrid's shoulder to the security guard in the doorway.

"We need to do a sweep."

"Now?"

"Yes, sir."

"But you only searched this place two days ago."

"Got the anniversary coming up," the guard said.

In six days' time it would be September 11th. Security was always raised as a precaution in the week before. Sol logged out of the system and grabbed his cigarettes. "Shall we take this outside?"

A few minutes later they were walking down one of the streets at the back of the embassy where the low fall sun hadn't yet warmed the air. Sol inhaled on his cigarette like he was planning on swimming a length underwater. "We should be careful," he said, "that no one overhears us."

Ingrid glanced round. The proximity to the embassy meant the street was one of the most scrutinized addresses in the world. More security cameras than residents, given how many of the apartments were empty. There were probably listening devices too.

"How's your Italian?" Ingrid asked.

"About as good as my Swahili. I was recruited as a data specialist."

"I never knew that. Well then," Ingrid said, "we'll just have to whisper. Do you want to walk and talk, or just talk?"

They perched on a low red-brick wall that marked the perimeter of one of the most luxurious apartment buildings in London. Even a ground floor studio would be over a million dollars.

"So what are the other problems?"

"We need clear boundaries between you and the counter-terrorism team. No overlap."

"There's bound to be overlap."

"Then we need to agree procedures."

"We absolutely do. Agent Simmons isn't going to play nice."

"He's an ass."

"Aren't you his boss too?"

"And that's why you didn't just hear me say that. We'll iron everything out with him. After that, it's just your mother." Twin vortices of smoke billowed from his nostrils.

Ingrid sat with her legs apart and leaned forward so her elbows were on her knees. Svetlana had never made anything easy. "You're seriously worried that the daughter of a defector will… what? Be a double agent?" Ingrid stood up and moved to the other side of Sol in an attempt to get upwind of the smoke.

Sol pushed his glasses onto the top of his head and rubbed the bridge of his nose. "God no," he whispered. "With your pedigree you've been more closely monitored than most agents."

"My *pedigree*?" It was hard to sound indignant while whispering but Ingrid was giving it a good try.

"Look, it can't be a surprise to you that someone with your background was seen as a risk. You were monitored. You proved yourself. That's how it works."

Ingrid looked up to see two armed officers from the Diplomatic Protection Group patrolling the street. There were security barriers at both ends of the street. Did proximity to the embassy make residents a target, or immeasurably safer than people living a few blocks away?

"So what's the problem?"

Sol ground his cigarette beneath his scuffed lace-up shoe and turned to face Ingrid square-on. "We don't have a problem with you, we're just wondering how the Russians will feel about your past. Some of them will see your mother as a hero, others as a traitor."

Ingrid pressed her fingers into her knees in a subconscious attempt to expel the anger from her voice. There had been so many occasions during her FBI career when rooms had gone quiet when she'd walked into them, or invites had got lost in the internal post. Her current security-level clearance was way below where it should be: was this all because of Svetlana. *Still*? She took a deep breath to steady the quiver in her voice. "And how would they know who my mother was? Surely I'll have a cover story?"

"Well," Sol said, turning the carton of Marlboro over and over in his hands, "that's what we have to work out. An agreed identity. You'll need documents."

Ingrid considered helping herself to one of Sol's cigarettes: it would do her less harm than punching a wall. "You know, it's not nice hearing that my mom's defection nearly forty years ago, before I was born, means I've got a permanent mark on my record. My dad was born in Minnesota. *I* was born in Minnesota, and you have never seen anyone celebrate the 4th of July like Svetlana Skyberg. Has the FBI also been monitoring my family links to Sweden? I believe I have some third cousins there."

"Take it easy, agent. It's how things work."

Her fingers dug a little tighter into her thighs. She didn't like it when Sol called her 'agent' instead of using her name. It wasn't as if she needed a reminder of her place in the hierarchy. "Well, how would you like it?"

"You have noticed I'm Jewish? You think I haven't been on some internal Zionist watch list the whole of my career? Who knows, maybe it's why I report to someone ten years my junior. It happens to us all. Don't take it personally."

"Guess we should just be relieved they let the pinko and the yid work together."

Sol stood up. "This wall is cold. They must have finished checking my office by now."

Ingrid followed him back toward the embassy. If she was going to take on a new role, she wondered if it was the right moment to bring up her other duties. "You know, if I'm going to do this Russian gig, I really can't be bailing out tourists who break the law. I spent three hours yesterday with some private security firm persuading them they didn't need to call the cops."

"Ah, that. I hope you gave the embassy's regards to Mrs Whitford and explained what an honor it was to be able to help her?"

"Sol, I'm serious. It's not a good use of my time." They showed their security passes to the guards at the rear entrance and filed back into the building.

"Doesn't help your case that just yesterday Louden got a note from Byrne-Williams praising your professionalism. You're stuck with the criminal division. I'm sure you'll find a way to make it work."

Ingrid's cell buzzed in her pocket. "I better take this."

Sol nodded and made his way toward the elevators. Ingrid stepped back outside.

"Special Agent Ingrid Skyberg. Legal Attaché program."

"Thank God you're there." It was a man's voice. East Coast accent.

"Mr Kerrison?"

"Can you come over right away?" In the background she could hear Truman Cooper spewing expletives.

"What's going on over there? What's happened?"

"It's Kate-Lynn. She's gone missing."

"Again?"

8

The gate slammed behind her and Ingrid was once again trapped inside the courtyard of Truman Cooper's impressive riverside home. She stopped to admire the Triumph Thunderbird. It only had 575 miles on the odometer. *What a waste.* Having just sold her Harley Fat Boy, she lingered more in regret than envy. The Triumph Tiger 800 she had parked outside might have been a practical choice for the city, but it was hardly the kind of bike you grow up dreaming about. Ahead of her, the steel door opened. Manuela stood at the threshold; even though she was wearing an A-line tunic of gray utilitarian felt, she still managed to look like a supermodel.

"You are here." Her manner had not softened since the last time they'd met.

"I am indeed," Ingrid said. Before she had even stepped into the hallway she could hear Truman Cooper sounding as angry as a Mob boss who'd just found out the money was missing.

"Upstairs," Manuela said, her conversational skills as simple as her attire.

Ingrid climbed the cast-iron stairs but Manuela did not follow. With each step, Truman Cooper's tirade became a little more decipherable. Someone with such anger issues was not a great candidate for parenthood. An image of a toddler cowering in a corner popped into her mind.

"... well I won't be there... I don't damn well care... you'll just have to make it work without me. Give my lines to Woodbridge... how many times do I have to tell you... I do not fucking care!" Truman Cooper slammed his cell phone down onto a granite kitchen worktop just as Ingrid entered the room. The shattered battery casing skidded along the surface. "You? What are you doing here?"

"I called her." Tom Kerrison was sitting on a stool behind a counter that divided the kitchen area from a large vaulted dining space. He pushed his MacBook Pro to one side and got to his feet. He was wearing zipper-covered jeans and a grubby tee, revealing arms covered with faded tattoos. It was hard to square his disheveled appearance with the tuxedoed charmer she'd met at the gallery. Truman was still in his pajamas. Neither of them looked like they had showered.

"Why?" Truman shouted.

"Because I can help," Ingrid said, her training kicking into action. Calm voice, affirmative message, cool things down, even if you have to tell a lie. Truman Cooper's rage was instantly downgraded to fury. "Let's take a moment, tell me what's happened and we'll see what can be done."

Tom Kerrison opened the refrigerator and pulled out a half-liter bottle of water. "Would you like one?"

"Please," Ingrid said.

"Truman? How about you?"

Truman shook his head. His backless phone started ringing. He looked to see who was calling. "Oh for fuck's sake!" He strutted over to the sink, dropped the phone in and turned on the faucet. He was a child in a forty-nine-year-old's body. The phone kept ringing. "Manuela!"

Although she had run up the stairs at some speed, Manuela entered the kitchen with neither a hair nor a seam out of place. "Yes?"

"Take that damned phone away from me. And the next time they call, tell them I quit."

"Yes," she said, "of course." She turned off the faucet, picked up the device and retreated from the kitchen. Ingrid wished she could do the same.

"Let's talk about Kate-Lynn, shall we?" She took a seat on a stool and placed her notebook and bottle of water on the counter. She reminded herself that Frances Byrne-Williams might be secretary of state someday and it would be nice to have a friend in such a high place. "Let's see if I can help."

Tom sat down opposite her as his laptop pinged with a new mail alert. Truman stayed on his feet.

"What happened?" she asked. "I assumed when I told you she was headed for London that she was on her way to see you two."

Truman turned away and began pacing in front of the enormous casement windows, completely ignoring the magnificent view of the river beyond.

"She came here last night," Tom began. He found it difficult to wrench his eyes from the screen. "After you called us, we rushed out to the airport, brought her here."

"How was she?"

"Surprised, mostly. Didn't understand how we knew she was on the plane."

"How did you explain that to her?"

"Told her we'd used our contacts, told her it was because we were worried." A succession of delicate bells rang on his laptop as emails continued to arrive. He reached out to the keyboard, and Ingrid noticed a deep scar on his left wrist incorporated into a tattoo of the Brooklyn Bridge.

"So she hadn't planned to see you? That wasn't why she was coming to London?"

"No, actually it was. She claimed she wanted to see where the baby would live. I guess we saved her the cab fare from the airport." Tom Kerrison looked a decade older than the night they had met at the gallery.

"As if she'd have got a cab," Truman butted in.

"And she had your address?" Ingrid's phone vibrated in her pants pocket. She did her best to ignore it.

Tom wasn't sure how to answer. "You know, I don't know. Honey, would she have had this address?"

"How the hell am I supposed to know that?" Ingrid looked over at Truman: was it really possible he was the same man as the beautiful young skinny-dipper in the YouTube clip?

"Then how was she planning on finding you?" Ingrid asked.

Tom rubbed his stubble and glanced over at Truman then stared at his screen, momentarily perturbed either by the volume or nature of his correspondence. The man had a business to run and a new exhibition to monitor. He returned his attention to Ingrid and blinked as he remembered what her question had been. "Um, Truman's not hard to find. Every fan site will tell you they film at Elstree, or that square in Islington. There are hundreds of fans about whenever they're on location." He ran his fingers over his hair, smoothing down some of his bed-head cowlicks. "Or she could have come to my store, though to be fair if someone walked into the boutique and asked for me the assistants might not know how to locate me... But she's smart, you know. She'd have found us."

"She seemed confident?"

Tom thought before answering. "She was exhausted, but the kid's got mettle."

"It's good she can handle herself." Ingrid looked at her notebook. She daren't write down what she was really thinking in case Tom could read her scrawl upside down. "Did she explain why she left the... facility?"

Tom bit the inside of his bottom lip. "Second thoughts, she said. She only wanted to see where her baby would grow up—"

"It's not her fucking baby," Truman shouted.

"It isn't?"

Tom took a deep breath. "The legal term is 'gestational carrier'. The biological mother is a Wall Street trader, Harvard graduate; at least according to her profile."

Ingrid suddenly imagined the two of them swiping through a list of donors and carriers on a website: making babies, twenty-first century style.

"And the father?" Ingrid asked.

The two men looked at each other. "Um, we've asked not to be informed," Tom said. Another image, less savory than the last, involving a small plastic cup, lodged in Ingrid's brain. "Apparently the non-biological parent can have difficulty bonding. If we don't know which of us is the father, the theory is we'll make a stronger family unit." Tom scratched his forearms, a nervous tic.

Truman walked over to the counter and stood behind his partner. "If this leaks," he said to Ingrid, "you will have a lawsuit to deal with that's bigger than fucking Texas, you understand?"

"Though of course," Tom said in conciliation, "if the baby comes out cursing we'll instantly know whose he is, won't we darling?"

Ingrid wondered how many times Tom had excused Truman's awful behavior and language over the years. She took a second before continuing. "So, you brought Kate-Lynn here from the airport. Then what happened?"

Tom took a swig from the Evian bottle. "She was exhausted. Eight months pregnant and a ten-hour flight. She had a lie-down, then we had some supper."

"Here, or did you go out?"

Truman's face expressed his frustration with Ingrid's questions. "How is this finding her? How is this finding my son?"

"Sir," Ingrid said, "I appreciate that this situation is awful for you, but a couple of days ago you asked for my help and I was able to locate Kate-Lynn. For the next five minutes, can we please assume that I know what I'm doing and that I'll achieve the same outcome?"

Truman Cooper pursed his lips. It was obviously a long time since anyone had spoken to him like that. He turned sharply away. If Ingrid was being unkind, she'd have described it as a flounce. Tom tried to suppress a grin.

"We stayed in for supper," Tom said. "Truman is an excellent cook."

Ah yes, *Celebrity MasterChef*. Was that why Tom stayed with such a monster? A combination of firm pecs and advanced culinary skills?

"And how was it? I'm not talking about the food, obviously."

Tom placed his hands on the counter and leaned back on the stool. He stole a glance at Truman. "It wasn't easy, I'll be honest. When we explained to Kate-Lynn that she had to return to California, like, today—"

"Two ten-hour flights in two days? When you're eight months pregnant?"

Tom sighed. "The baby needs to be born in California."

Ingrid raised her eyebrows: "Why? The hospitals here are excellent."

"I'm sure they are, but it's a legal thing. California lets us both be on the birth certificate. If she gives birth here, she becomes the legal parent." He paused, the strain of the situation beginning to take its toll. "So you see our concern?"

Ingrid nodded, even though it seemed to her their priorities needed reordering. "Of course, though right now I'm sure your focus is just on finding her and making sure Kate-Lynn and the baby are OK. I should tell you, if you don't already know, it's possible no airline will let her fly now until after she's given birth. You might have to prepare yourselves for a formal adoption process after the baby is born."

"United let her fly yesterday? Why not tomorrow?" Truman demanded.

"My understanding is that women who are that close to giving birth need medical approval to fly. They don't want to have to divert to Reykjavik when her water breaks."

"We can always charter something privately," Tom said, as if hiring a plane was no more extravagant than ordering take-out. Truly, Ingrid thought, it might be the same planet but they lived in a different world.

"So tell me, what did you do next? What happened after dinner?"

Tom scratched his arms again. "Not much. Answered some emails, did the dishes. Domestic stuff. She went to bed soon afterwards, we stayed up and finished the wine, then we went to bed too. Fast-forward to six this morning and she's gone. We got up, I came downstairs to make us all breakfast when I heard a scream from upstairs."

"A scream?"

"Oh, it was just Truman being theatrical."

Ingrid shifted her attention to the actor. "Mr Cooper? What happened? You knocked on her door this morning and didn't get an answer?"

"I am not," he said in tones reminiscent of a witness on the stand in a 1940s melodrama, "in the habit of opening young ladies' bedroom doors. It was already open."

Ingrid's eyes followed him as he walked up and down. His deliberate, controlled movements were a reminder that he had trained as a dancer. "And she hadn't said she would leave? How were things between the three of you when she went to bed?"

Truman Cooper shoved his hands under his armpits, stretching the cotton of his pajama top tight across his pectorals. "Oh fuck," he said. "Fuck, fuck, fuck."

"Sir?" She turned to Tom, the more reasonable of the two, for interpretation.

"She was upset," he explained. "We told her she had broken the terms of the contract, that she wouldn't get paid. She seemed pretty desperate. To be honest, we were all in a state."

"But she didn't say anything about leaving?"

The two men looked at one another. "No," Tom said. "In fact, she said she wanted to stay with us until the baby is born. We just weren't prepared—"

"Prepared? In what way?"

Tom Kerrison wasn't quite sure how to answer. "Our plan was to collect him when he's born and bring him home. Our schedules have been planned around his due date." His laptop trilled with a new round of emails as if to emphasize how overloaded their diaries were.

"But you have the space. You can afford a midwife." Ingrid didn't mean to sound quite so combative, but for deep-seated reasons too uncomfortable to explore, her tone was veering toward aggressive. She knew she had to sound more sympathetic: confrontation wasn't going to achieve anything.

"Ah, that's not really the point. We have paid Nuestra Señora. That's the service they provide," Tom said, his own tone somewhere between defensive and diplomatic. "We did not agree to have a stranger live with us while she is pregnant. Whatever your views are on our arrangement—"

"I really don't have a view." When the words left her lips, Ingrid was surprised to discover that she did indeed have a view, and appalled to discover how traditional her opinions were. She supposed she had seen enough of children being treated as commodities in her work with the VCAC.

Tom nodded. "So we told her that if she went back to LA, we'd make sure she got paid, even if we had to pay her in addition to the money we've already given the agency. The baby absolutely has to be born in California."

Truman looked like he wanted to hit something. If he hadn't been in bare feet, the trash can was a likely candidate for a punt down to the far end of the steel dining table. No wonder the dog and Manuela were hiding in another part of the house. "She's stolen my baby, don't you get that?" He leaned over the counter, his face just a couple inches from Ingrid's. "Do you fucking understand? It's kidnapping. It's theft. I want to see some fucking action." His spittle sprayed Ingrid's face. His hand reached forward.

"Get any closer and you're committing a crime." She slowly and deliberately wiped her face. "Take a seat, Mr Cooper." She turned to Kerrison, who was clearly embarrassed by his partner's behavior. "From what you've told me so far, Kate-Lynn's done nothing criminal. Sure, she's breached her contract with you, but that's a matter for your attorney. All you're telling me is that an adult woman has gone for a walk. There won't be much I can do for you." *And to be honest, there's not a damn thing I'm inclined to do for you.*

"Can't you trace her credit cards? Her cell phone? Surely—" He pointed to his laptop as another batch of emails announced their arrival in his inbox. "She's got to be leaving some kind of digital trail?"

"Mr Kerrison," she raised a hand. "Those are the kind of measures we are authorized to use when a crime is suspected. There's no crime here. It was already a huge invasion of her privacy for me to access the flight manifest for you. I have no reason to use those resources unless I think someone is in immediate danger. Anyway, didn't you say she'd left her cards and phone in California?"

Truman Cooper pushed himself away from the countertop with such force that it moved. "Our son is in danger!"

Calmly, Ingrid reached out for her bottle of water, slowly unscrewed the lid and took a long drink. A few seconds later, she placed the bottle back on the counter. "You don't know that."

"Really?" Tom said. "She breaches her contract, she crosses the Atlantic because she's having 'second thoughts'; she's clearly unstable and she's eight months pregnant. She no doubt has a chaotic history. I'd say that baby is pretty vulnerable." Desperation was finally creeping into his voice.

"I understand, but there are thresholds that have to be met before I can throw the FBI's resources into tracking her down. But please, we're not done here yet. There's a lot of information I don't have, and I'm sure there'll be something I can do. She's twenty years old: she'll reveal something on Facebook or get in trouble for running out on a hotel bill. She'll surface. They always do. Now, does one of you want to put that coffee machine on?"

9

Tom Kerrison placed a mug of coffee down on the long steel dining table in front of Ingrid. She had suggested a change of location in the hope that sitting formally at a table would aid a more rational conversation and help her get the information she needed.

"Thank you."

"I think when Truman comes out of the shower he'll be calmer. He finds these situations very hard." He pulled out the chair opposite Ingrid and sat down.

"These situations?"

"Stressful situations."

"It must be stressful for you both," Ingrid said, observing that yet again he was scratching his forearms. A control mechanism. Truman let his anger out, Tom stored his up.

He took a sip. "You live on the streets for a couple of years, you get a different perspective on what's stressful."

Ingrid's research on Tom Kerrison had revealed his first business—a shoe store on the Lower East Side—had gone bust leaving him with crippling debts. A few years living on the streets followed, as did addiction and an overdose. Reading between the lines he had probably turned a few tricks. The scar on his wrist was likely evidence of a suicide attempt. He'd served eight months in Rikers when he was twenty-five, and on his release made a living with a spray can, creating interiors for bars and backgrounds for hip hop videos. It was, according to some of the cuttings she'd read, a chance encounter with an old client in a back room of a Greenwich Village club that led to him getting a job at Versini and his rehabilitation in fashion.

"OK, let's start with the basics. Kate-Lynn left here before six. Can you be any more precise?"

"We went to bed around eleven. So, some time after that. I guess."

"And her bed has definitely been slept in?"

"I can show you if you like."

"That would be helpful. Might reveal something."

"You want to come upstairs?"

Ingrid took a large gulp of coffee, put the mug back on the table and followed Kerrison out into the hallway. "Where's your dog today?"

"The veterinarian has him." He paused at the bottom of the staircase. "Cully's an old dog. Spends half his life there."

"How old?"

"Not entirely sure. He's a Battersea dog. You heard of Battersea Dogs Home?" He led the way up the industrial iron stairs. "It's this candy shop of abandoned dogs, all with faces sadder than the last saying 'Take me, please, please kind sir, take me and love me.' We were lucky to get out of there with just the one dog."

They reached a broad landing decorated with an enormous abstract oil painting.

"One of yours?" Ingrid asked.

"You like it?" Sounds of running water could be heard from beyond the open door behind him. Truman was taking a long shower. Hopefully it would have a therapeutic effect.

"It's kind of stunning," she said, "like this entire house."

"You didn't say if you liked it."

"You noticed, huh?"

"I'll take that as a 'no' then," he said as he started up another flight of stairs. "Which is fine because it's not one of mine. Truman bought it at an auction just to show off."

"You got anything from the Gardner heist?" she asked. All federal agents fantasized about discovering the stolen masterpieces that had eluded the Art Crime Team for decades. "After all, you are originally from Boston, aren't you?"

"We don't put those on display. Never know when a Fed is going to swing by for coffee."

They reached another landing which had five doors leading off it. "It's in here," Kerrison said.

Ingrid walked into the large room. Exposed brick walls, steel girders, dark wood floors: it looked like something from a realtor's catalogue except for the fact that the shades were down. Kerrison started to open them.

"Stop."

"Won't it be easier to see with a little light?"

"Sure, but first I want to look at the room as Kate-Lynn left it."

Kerrison let go of the cord pull. The room was furnished with a queen-sized bed that, like the clothes rack, had been made out of scaffold poles. The bedside tables were old cable reels and the galvanized steel light fittings looked like they'd been salvaged from the kind of barge that might have once delivered goods to the Dunedin Trading Co before the warehouse had become their home. An open door led into an en-suite bathroom, covered in subway tiles, and a small desk made out of trestle legs and an old door completed the room. The bedclothes, white Egyptian cotton, were pushed to one side. On the floor was a discarded newspaper.

"You can open the shades now."

Light burst into the room as Ingrid stepped into the en-suite. A wet towel was on the floor. When she returned to the bedroom she saw an unlit neon sign on the wall that said NOT VACANT. She assumed that, when switched on, the NOT would flash. Ingrid didn't want to make too many assumptions about the kind of woman who chooses to become a surrogate, but she'd be willing to bet a chunk of change this would be one of the nicest rooms Kate-Lynn Bowers had ever slept in: it was the sort of place you'd think twice about running away from.

"What did she have with her when you picked her up at the airport?" Ingrid asked. "Did she bring a lot of stuff?"

"Hardly anything. A small backpack, the kind of thing you take on a picnic not a transatlantic flight. I don't think she even had a jacket."

"And yet she planned to stay until the baby was born?"

"It doesn't sound good, does it?"

She didn't want to agree with him, but it didn't. "As far as you can tell, she's taken all her possessions with her?"

"Yes, it's just a hanging rail in here, no walk-in closet. We didn't want to encourage guests to outstay their welcome."

Ingrid inspected the sheets. They had definitely been slept in, so that probably put Kate-Lynn's departure closer to 6am than 11pm. "You said she'd left her phone at the... I don't know what to call it... the compound? The place she was staying at in Los Angeles."

Tom rubbed a hand over his stubble. "That's why they were so concerned. Her phone, her wallet, they said everything was still in her room."

"Which begs the question of how she paid for her plane fare. Or rather who paid for it." Ingrid crouched down and opened one of the bedside cabinets. It was empty apart from a stack of glossy magazines. "These are yours, I take it?"

"We figured they were more likely to get read than a copy of the Bible."

She examined the newspaper on the floor. By the look of it, every page had been read and reread on Kate-Lynn's long flight.

"Should you be touching that?" Kerrison asked, the alarm raising his pitch slightly.

Ingrid looked up and gave him a smile. "This isn't a crime scene."

"It isn't?"

"I realize that's how it must feel to you right now, but unless you think someone came in and took Kate-Lynn, this is just the room she slept in last night." Ingrid picked up the newspaper. "Interesting."

"What is?"

"It's the *Chicago Sun Times.* Didn't you say she was from Illinois?"

"I think so."

"Guess she picked up a familiar paper when she boarded the plane."

The sound of footsteps thundered up the iron staircase. Moments later, Manuela was standing in the doorway with Truman Cooper's damaged phone in her hand.

"Mr Kerrison, it is Mr Duncan. He says he is sending someone. Right now." There was just the slightest trace of emotion in her voice. She was human after all.

"Have you told Truman?"

"He is in the shower."

"Still?" Tom Kerrison planted a hand on one hip while the other held his head. "Well, when they get here, just don't let them in, OK?"

"OK." Manuela backed away.

"Don't even answer the bell," he shouted after her. Tom Kerrison turned to Ingrid who was still crouched beside the bed. "The producer," he explained, "of Truman's show. They're filming the Christmas special and he's kinda central to the big festive storyline."

Ingrid folded the newspaper and looked at the front page. It was the Labor Day edition: it was two days old. "He doesn't seem like he'd be much use to the production today," she said, a little distracted by the headlines about the White Sox and Mayor Emmanuel.

"Oh, he'll be all right in an hour or so. He gets angry quick, but he gets nice quick too."

Ingrid raised an eyebrow. "Really?"

Tom Kerrison shrugged. "You really haven't seen the best of him. He's not always like this." A tiny smile brightened his weathered face. "Come, I want to show you something."

He led Ingrid back out into the hallway and pointed at one of the other doors. "Open it."

Ingrid twisted the doorknob. The first thing she noticed was birdsong and as the door widened she saw the room was decorated like a jungle. Fake fronds descended from the ceiling, and she had to move huge plastic banana leaves to see further into the room. She could hear running water. "Is there a fountain in here?"

"It's a fish tank. You'll come to it in a moment."

The room even smelt of wet foliage. She felt like Dorothy stepping out into a Technicolor Munchkinland. "This is incredible," she said. Ahead of her was a crib made of lashed-together bamboo.

"Truman did it all. By himself. He wanted to create an amazing bedroom for the baby."

"Well, he's succeeded," Ingrid said. She really couldn't believe the attention to detail. Huge fabric butterflies and cute plastic frogs poked out from between the leaves. "He's absolutely succeeded. It's like being in an episode of *Tarzan*."

"Don't say that. Truman will only want to get a chimpanzee."

She looked around the room in awe. There were cartons of diapers and formula stacked against a crate that was stenciled with the name of a fake shipping company. On a shelf was every parenting book written in the past half-century. They were prepared. She was about to say that the baby was very lucky but stopped herself: right now, the boy's future was wildly uncertain.

"I just wanted you to see he's not always like, well, like he's been today. He's passionate, he's creative, he's actually very patient; he'll be a wonderful father."

That instant, Truman Cooper burst into the room making Ingrid flinch. "It's gone," he said. "The fucking money's gone."

10

"What money?" Kerrison asked.

"The cash I got out at Heathrow. She would have seen me put it in my jacket pocket." Truman Cooper held up his jacket. "Five hundred pounds."

"Are you sure you didn't put it somewhere?" Kerrison asked.

"Damn sure. It went straight in this pocket and I never took it out."

Tom Kerrison turned to Ingrid. "Is this now a crime scene? Now is there something for you to investigate?"

Ingrid shoved her hands in her pockets and bit her bottom lip. "I'm happy to call the local cops for you, but I am an FBI special agent and this isn't a federal crime."

Truman Cooper pushed his wet hair out of his eyes and inhaled so deeply his chest expanded by several inches. He exhaled, and Ingrid prepared herself for a tirade of expletives. "An American citizen has just robbed another American citizen, isn't that of interest to the *embassy*?" His emphasis on 'embassy' showed what he really meant was 'ambassador'.

It took Ingrid a second to realize she hadn't been drenched in f-words. "Look, Mr Cooper, sir, I'll do what I can for you, check some databases, but this is something for the Metropolitan Police though I doubt—"

"I don't want the cops involved," Cooper said firmly.

Ingrid stared at him. "Really? They could help."

"They could also leak something to the press. No cops, OK? I'm not having my son born in Holloway prison."

Ingrid nodded. "They probably wouldn't do anything anyway. To be honest, the missing money is a good sign: it means Kate-Lynn can buy herself some food or a couple nights in a hotel." She looked hard into his pale blue eyes. "It means she's taking care of herself, and that means she's taking care of your baby too."

Both men relaxed slightly, reassured by Ingrid's analysis.

"It's only been a few hours. It's entirely possible she's still on LA time, got up, went for a walk and got lost. I know you're anxious, but let's stay positive," Ingrid said. "I mean, if she has come to London to reassure herself that you're going to be good parents, she must have been thrilled when she saw this room."

For the first time, Ingrid saw Truman Cooper smile. "You like it?" he asked, boyishly.

"Not half as much as your son will." Ingrid walked over to the bamboo crib. "What did Kate-Lynn say about all of this?"

"I think she was overwhelmed, to be honest," Truman said, clearly proud of his work. "She absolutely loved the crib."

"I'm not surprised. This is really, really wonderful. It must have taken you ages." She reached out and stroked a vivid orange flower dangling over the crib. "Where did you even get this stuff?"

Truman Cooper put the emptied jacket over an arm, instantly striking a more relaxed pose. *He gets nice quick too.* "Most of it came from the set of a film I made earlier this year. Cheaper than shooting in an actual jungle." He carried on talking but Ingrid didn't hear what he said. She had peered into the crib and was staring at a bullet.

What the hell?

A bullet. A single, solitary bullet, lying on top of the brand-new mattress like a jewel in Tiffany's window, or a tooth left out for the fairies. Ingrid felt a pressure in her sternum, forcing her heart to beat harder. Aluminum casing, lead nose. Her best guess was a .38 special. She glanced up at the two me: Tom was now holding Truman's arm as he continued his story. All Ingrid could hear was the sound of blood pulsing through her ears. She could tell from their faces that they had no idea what was in the crib. She looked again at the bullet.

This is Britain, not even the cops carry guns.

The rushing sound in her ears became louder. Why would someone put a bullet in a crib? To warn someone. Kate-Lynn? Truman? Did someone mean them harm? Or the baby? Ingrid straightened herself up and found herself nodding to whatever it was Truman Cooper was saying. "Let's go back downstairs," she said, managing to keep any trace of alarm from her voice. "I'm assuming you have CCTV in the house?"

Tom and Truman looked at each other. "Yes," Tom said, "we have a camera at the front door."

"Is there s-some way I can take a look at the footage?" When she started to stutter, she knew she was stressed. She put her hands in her pockets in an attempt to steady herself.

Tom shook his head. "I have no idea how it works."

"Manuela will know how to do it," Truman said.

"Let's find out. If nothing else it should tell us what time she left this morning."

Truman puffed out his cheeks. "Why didn't we think of that?"

Ingrid followed the men down the stairs, her brain crunching through the gears and into overdrive.

First question: was the bullet theirs or Kate-Lynn's? If it was theirs, what kind of trouble was Kate-Lynn really in? No wonder they didn't want the cops involved. But if it was Kate-Lynn's, then how the hell did it make it through airport security? And what kind of message was she sending Truman and Tom? Was it a bargaining chip? Was she sliding a pawn across the board, making an opening move in a game of kidnap? Ingrid stopped on the next landing and called down to Tom.

"You two sleep on this floor?"

Tom looked up at her. "Yes."

"You both do?"

"I don't want to scare you honey, but we share the same bed."

"Just checking. People have all sorts of sleeping arrangements."

Tom climbed the stairs to join her. Below, Truman started shouting for Manuela.

"Which is your room?" Ingrid asked. Tom looked alarmed. "It's OK, I don't have to go in it."

"That one." He pointed to a room on the river side of the house.

"So not underneath the room Kate-Lynn was staying in. You wouldn't have heard her move around up there?"

Tom kicked the wooden floor. "Beneath this is about a yard of brick. It'd take an atom bomb to hear anything."

Ingrid hadn't heard anyone say the phrase 'atom bomb' in over a decade. "And no one else stayed here last night?"

"Like who?"

"I'm just trying to get all the facts. Does Manuela stay here?"

"Good God, no! Not a chance. She lives somewhere on the other side of the river," he said, pointing in the vague direction of south.

"You have no live-in help?"

"No." Tom Kerrison managed to squeeze several syllables into his reply. "We have a housekeeper who comes in most days but no one lives with us. As you may have noticed, we value our privacy too much to want to share it."

When they walked down the stairs, their footsteps ricocheted off the cast-iron treads. "I take it you didn't hear Kate-Lynn come down the stairs?"

"I think," Tom said, pausing for a moment outside the kitchen "we might have mentioned that. Do you want your coffee?"

"Thanks."

"Keep going down as far as you can. I just need to find a tray."

Ingrid clanked down the iron stairs to the ground floor, then found a stone staircase at the back of the hallway that stretched down into the basement, the smell of chlorine wafting up to meet her.

The corridor in the basement was narrow, claustrophobic. A

doorway opened onto a long, thin, windowless room. At the far end, Manuela sat at a computer with Truman standing behind her. On one wall was an enormous flat-screen television showing Bloomberg on mute. Two couches covered in blankets, which in turn were covered in dog hairs, bordered a coffee table laden with magazines. At a quick glance, every single one of them featured Truman Cooper on the cover. Tom entered the room behind her, placing Truman's coffee mug on the desk next to a paper cup and flattened bag covered in pastry flakes: evidently Manuela brought her breakfast in with her from home.

"Come on!" Truman said through gritted teeth. "Come on!"

"I am doing as fast as possible." Manuela refused to be irritated by her boss's impatience.

"Come on!" he said again, picking up the coffee mug.

"Here. It is here," Manuela said and pushed back in the chair.

The three of them stood behind Manuela looking at the monitor and watched a good-quality image of the inside of the front door.

"What speed are you playing it at?" Ingrid asked.

Manuela shrugged.

"May I?"

Manuela stood up to let Ingrid sit down. She picked up the mouse and clicked twice on an icon that doubled the playback speed. It didn't make any difference to the image on screen: the lack of activity meant they were effectively looking at a photograph. Ingrid clicked the icon a third time.

Just as the image started to lighten, there was movement. A figure flashed across the screen, the door opened for a millisecond and then they were back to watching a still image.

"Go back!" Truman said.

Ingrid clicked rewind, pressing play when the figure had reversed out of the shot. The four of them watched in silence as Kate-Lynn re-entered. The camera was facing the door: perfect for seeing who is arriving, not so good to study whoever is leaving.

"Who made this coffee?" Truman's voice was so loud it made Ingrid flinch. "Who made this fucking mug of shit?"

"Honey?"

"How many fucking times have I told you to use the filtered water?"

Ingrid swiveled the seat and looked at the actor. He was quaking with rage. "Please, sir, just put the cup down. You don't want it spilling on the computer."

Truman's gaze was lasered onto Tom. You'd think he'd made the coffee with formaldehyde. Deliberately. "How many fucking times? How many?"

Tom stared back, daring Truman to throw the mug at him.

Ingrid stood up, pushed the chair back sharply and took the coffee from Truman's grasp. She put the mug on the desk, gave the two men her best schoolmarm look of disapproval and then returned to the computer. Manuela's expression had not changed throughout: an outburst from Truman was no more a significant event in her working life than signing for deliveries or making restaurant reservations. Ingrid didn't know how she put up with it.

"Shall we?" Ingrid said, pressing play on the footage.

Kate-Lynn was wearing a floral summer dress and sandals. Her hair was pulled into a ponytail, and a small canvas backpack was slung over one shoulder. It didn't look like it had much in it. Kate-Lynn stopped momentarily and turned, her face briefly visible, and bent down. She stood up, stretched a hand across her extended belly and reached for the door handle. Her left hand was clenched as if she was holding something. She tugged the handle with her right hand and stepped out into the weak early morning light and didn't look back. The time code in the bottom right-hand corner of the screen said 05:14.

"Rewind!" Truman shouted.

They watched the footage again, this time in slow motion. Ingrid now noticed that Kate-Lynn's hair was wet and remembered the towel on the en-suite floor. Generally, if someone is fleeing a violent situation—being confronted by a man with a loaded gun, for example—they don't bother to take a shower before they run. She paused the footage at the moment where Kate-Lynn almost faces the camera.

Her face was a little puffy-looking, which could either be pregnancy or air travel, or both, but there was something pinched about her features as if she'd spent her whole life scowling. Ingrid looked for a mole or a scar or some other distinguishing mark, but Kate-Lynn Bowers could best be described as plain. If Ingrid hadn't known Kate-Lynn was twenty, based on looks alone she'd have put her age at fourteen. She reminded Ingrid of a fallow deer, caught in a hunter's gunsights. Far, far too young to be pregnant.

Ingrid thought of all the vulnerable girls she had worked with in VCAC. She thought of Megan and knew that the girl on the screen was someone else's Megan. No matter what the protocol of this particular case, looking after young girls in trouble was why Ingrid had joined the FBI. She thought about the bullet in the crib. There was no way Ingrid could walk away from this, or from Kate-Lynn, now.

She tapped play and they watched as Kate-Lynn bent down, her head disappearing out of shot, before standing, turning, stroking her belly and reaching for the door. Ingrid was no expert, but she'd have said Kate-Lynn was either pregnant with twins or closer to nine months than eight. She stared closely at the girl's left hand. Something was dangling from her clenched fist. Was it a necklace? A rosary? A few seconds later, Kate-Lynn was outside and the door had closed behind her.

"That's my baby," Truman said. "My baby just walked out the door." His voice was so soft, and in such contrast to the fury he had just displayed. Manuela took hold of Truman's hand. She was human after all.

Ingrid stood up. "That was helpful," she said, trying to sound businesslike. "We have a time for her departure." Truman and Tom were still staring at the computer screen, as if watching their baby recede over the horizon. "It wasn't just helpful, guys; it was *hopeful*."

They wrenched their eyes from the screen and looked at her, their expressions asking for more.

"Look, she didn't appear anxious, she wasn't crying, she wasn't running, she wasn't bleeding, or limping, or…" she ran out of things to say. "Trust me, that was encouraging. We know she's not in distress, we think she's got sufficient cash for the next few hours and days. Things could be a lot worse."

Truman nodded, tears spilling out of his eyes. "OK, I believe you." He squeezed Manuela's hand tightly.

"So what happens next?" Tom asked.

"I put some calls in, run a few checks, and—"

Ingrid was interrupted by the doorbell ringing.

"Oh fuck, *fuck*. They've fucking sent a car for me, haven't they?"

Manuela and Tom exchanged a nervous glance.

"We don't have to open the door," Tom said.

The four of them stood in silence as the bell rang again. And again. Ingrid spoke first: "In my experience, this will be much easier if you all get on with your days as normal. I just have a couple more questions and then, if you can, go to work, let routine get you a couple of hours into the future and I'll call when I find something out."

The bell rang again.

Truman took a deep breath. "Tell them I'll be with them in ten minutes."

Manuela nodded and walked briskly out of the office.

"You're sure this is a good idea?" Tom asked.

Ingrid shrugged. "I know hanging around here going crazy is a bad idea."

"You're right," Truman said.

"Before you go," Ingrid said, "I need a bit more information from you."

"Yes?"

"Where did you leave your jacket last night? Did you take it into the bedroom with you?"

He nodded. "Yes."

"So, if Kate-Lynn did take the cash she either snuck into your room while you were sleeping or she took it before she went to bed."

"I guess. But it would have to be the latter. One of us would have woken up, surely?"

"You'd be surprised what people have slept through. Was there anything else in your jacket that's missing? A phone? Keys? Wallet?"

Truman shook his head. "No, it was just the cash."

"And the bills, sorry, *notes*," Ingrid corrected herself, "they were twenty-pound notes, presumably, if they were from an ATM?"

Truman nodded.

"Shame. A fifty-pound note is a little more memorable if she tried to spend it."

"Any more questions?"

"Uh-huh." Deep breath. "Do you have any weapons in the house?"

The two men looked shocked at the question.

"Wow, no." Truman was aghast.

"I guess there are knives in the kitchen," Tom said. "You think she might have taken one?"

"It's always worth checking."

"Then I will." He moved toward the office door.

"What about other weapons?" Ingrid asked. "Either of you have a gun license? Or a gun?"

Truman spluttered. "You're seriously asking two gay men if they keep a gun? In *England*?"

"Hey, I'm an equal opportunity investigator."

"Well, no," Tom said. "We don't have guns. We don't even vote Republican. Anything else?"

Ingrid nodded. "I just want to take another look upstairs, if that's OK?"

"Of course."

While Truman prepared to leave for work and Tom checked their kitchen drawers, Ingrid sprinted up to the top floor of the house. She ran into the nursery, pushing giant fake fronds out of her way to reach the crib. When she looked inside, the bullet was gone.

11

Ingrid reached in, pushing her hand between the collection of stuffed toys. There was no small metal object. The brand-new mattress was bare. There was no sheet or coverlet for anything to get caught up in. She felt around the edge of the mattress to check the bullet hadn't got lodged against the bamboo frame. But it wasn't there. For a second she thought she might have imagined it, but it *had* been there. It had *absolutely* been there.

She glanced round the room. The window was closed, so no gust of wind could have moved it. The sound of burbling water meant it was hard to hear anything going on outside the room, to know if Truman and Tom, or possibly Manuela, were discussing the fact that Ingrid had returned to the nursery. One of them had to know about the bullet. Ingrid walked over to the fish tank. "If only you guys could remember things for more than a few seconds. And could speak, of course."

She stepped back out onto the landing. There were five doors leading off it and she had only been in two of the rooms. She opened the door next to the nursery. It was a closet, stacked with a well-ordered array of cleaning materials and folded linens. She tried the next door. Locked. It was the room above Tom and Truman's bedroom. Ingrid knelt down to look under the door. It was an old building: the floors weren't true and the doors were warped. There was a half-inch gap. Ingrid grabbed her phone, held it flush with the floor and pushed the camera lens into the gap.

She stood up and looked at the image she'd just taken. Eighty per cent of the photo was the door, with an isosceles triangle of blurred light accounting for the rest. As good as useless.

The next room was the one Kate-Lynn had slept in, so Ingrid moved on to the final door. It opened into another bedroom, neatly folded towels on the foot of the bed suggested it was another guest room. Ingrid slipped into Kate-Lynn's room. As far as she could tell, whoever had removed the bullet hadn't touched anything in there. She stepped into the bathroom and pulled the cord to turn on the light. An extractor fan immediately purred into life.

On the tiled ledge there was a toothbrush. In the trash can, Ingrid saw the discarded packaging from the toothbrush. So when Kate-Lynn had left LA she hadn't even packed a toothbrush. Nor had she taken it with her now: did that mean she hadn't planned to leave? Had she just gone for a jet-lag induced walk and simply not made it back yet? The other toiletries were the miniature kind found in hotel rooms: the Cooper-Kerrisons might not like house guests but they sure knew how to take care of them. Nervously, she picked up the wet towel from the floor and inspected it. No blood. That was something.

Back in the main room, Ingrid checked to see what she might have missed. The only trace of Kate-Lynn was the discarded newspaper. Over at the window, Ingrid looked at the view out over the yard to the cobbled street beyond. On the other side of the road was a small park, the kind where rich Londoners walk miniature dogs while poor Londoners deal drugs. Wapping was a borough that still had some gentrification to do. Beyond the park was a railway viaduct.

Ingrid couldn't be sure how much would have been visible to Kate-Lynn at night, but even if she had seen the view in daylight, it wasn't the kind of sight that inspires you to go exploring. No famous buildings were visible, no reassuring landmarks. Ingrid tried to put herself in Kate-Lynn's place. Twenty years old, about as pregnant as it's possible to get, in a strange town having just fled both a place of safety and a $25,000 payday. Add in the disappearing bullet and Ingrid was truly scared for her.

She stepped over to the bed and lifted the cover, just to make sure she hadn't left something, anything, behind that might offer some idea of where she was headed. Nothing. Ingrid sat down on the bed and picked up the *Sun Times*. She put the paper on top of the bedclothes and started flicking through it. Maybe Kate-Lynn had torn something out, or underlined something: Ingrid was desperate for anything that could help. She flicked through all the way to the sports pages, but nothing stood out. Until she reached the penultimate page. The headline read: Cubs Defense Lac. That was it. Cubs Defense Lac: the page opposite was missing.

Hurriedly, Ingrid turned to the front of the paper. Page three was also missing. Kate-Lynn had removed one sheet of paper, corresponding to four pages of the *Sun Times*: there had to have been something on either page three, four, 155 or 156 that had meant something to her. It wasn't much, but it was somewhere to start.

Ingrid called Jennifer. "It's me."

"What do you need?"

"Three things. First, the girl I asked about yesterday, the one on the flight from LA."

"Kate-Lynn somebody?"

"That's right. Is there any way you can find out how her ticket was paid for? Or who paid for it? Is that kind of information available without raising too many flags?"

"Dunno, but leave it with me. Next?"

"Send Don down to the research department. I need to see a copy of the Labor Day edition of the *Chicago Sun Times*."

"And the other thing?"

"I need you to call around the London hospitals. See if she's visited the ER. Or been admitted to a maternity unit."

"She's pregnant?"

"Very."

"OK. We're on it."

By the time Ingrid got back downstairs, Truman Cooper had already left for the studio, accompanied by Manuela. She found Tom Kerrison back at the counter in the kitchen poring over his laptop, which continued to emit a series of alerts telling him he had yet more mail.

"You find anything helpful?" Tom asked.

"She had a shower before she left, that's another good sign."

"It is?"

"Trust me: a woman on the verge of doing something reckless doesn't put daily grooming high up on her list of things to do. What about the knives?"

"All present and correct."

"Another good sign."

Tom's head dropped into his hands and a long, low moan escaped from his mouth.

"Chances are, this will all be over in a few hours. She'll be in a greasy spoon round the corner eating for two."

He looked up at her. "It's not Kate-Lynn: it's work. It's just hell at the moment. I took time out to handle the exhibition and things have completely fallen apart at the atelier."

"You've got a lot on your plate," Ingrid tried to sound sympathetic. "Focus on work and leave Kate-Lynn to me. I'll be in touch."

She scooped up her notebook and threw it into her bag.

"I'll show you out," Tom said.

"No need."

But he was already on his feet and heading for the stairs. When they reached the bottom, Ingrid turned to look where the camera was and thought again about Kate-Lynn's departure. Tom opened the door.

"If you haven't heard from me by two o'clock, give me a call," she said, shaking his hand.

"Thank you," he said, "not least for getting Truman out of the house."

Ingrid stepped out into the courtyard and stroked the Thunderbird on her way to the gate.

"You ride?" Tom asked.

Ingrid turned back to him and pointed at her boots. "I'm surprised you haven't mentioned my footwear today. I've got a Tiger 800 outside."

"I have no idea what that means. The bike is Truman's."

"Well, he has fabulous taste in bikes."

The gate clicked and slid open. She waved to Tom and stepped out onto the sidewalk. Moments later, the gate clunked shut behind her. Ingrid slung her bag over her shoulder and stood there for a while. Five and a half hours earlier Kate-Lynn Bowers had stood in the same spot and had made a decision. Did she choose left, right, or straight ahead?

To the left, were several other former warehouses, though judging by their size and the number of recently added balconies they had been converted into apartments. That increased the likelihood of finding witnesses to Kate-Lynn's departure. If this was a police investigation, if there was sufficient manpower, then house-to-house inquiries might find one of those witnesses. But this wasn't a police matter—so far, no crime had been committed—and the only resources Ingrid had were her time and her guile.

To the right, about fifty yards down the street, was a small pub that presumably also backed onto the Thames. It would have been closed at a quarter after five in the morning. Maybe there would have been a postman, or someone delivering papers or milk, but finding them would be too time-consuming on her own.

Ahead, beyond the tightly packed cars, was the park she'd seen from Kate-Lynn's window. Close up it looked more dealer than dog walker. Not a place to linger.

Ingrid tried to imagine being heavily pregnant, jet-lagged and alone in a strange city. What would her next move have been? Would she have done if she were Kate-Lynn? In the distance she heard a rumbling. It grew louder. She looked up at the railway viaduct to see a Docklands Light Railway train glide past and begin to slow down: the nearest station couldn't be far away.

That's what she would have done: Kate-Lynn would have headed for the train.

12

Ingrid set off, marching past the Tiger 800 and vowing to upgrade to something closer to a Thunderbird when the lease was up for renewal in a few months' time. Ahead of her, running down one side of the dog-walkers' park, was a narrow cobbled lane heading underneath the viaduct. A notice on the park railings said it was open from 7:30 a.m. till dusk, so it would have been closed when Kate-Lynn left the house. That didn't necessarily mean it was empty: the railings were only waist-high.

Ingrid continued beneath the railway as a train went overhead. On the other side of the viaduct was a gas station. The signage told her it was open twenty-four hours. She felt a tiny surge of adrenaline raise her alert levels, making her feel energized. Someone would have been around at 5:15 a.m., and that meant she had a shot at finding a witness. She rushed into the gas station and up to the counter. She laid her ID card down next to the display of chewing gum.

"FBI? It's all right, love, you don't need fake ID to buy cigarettes from me." The guy was Asian, around twenty and spoke with London accent.

"It's not fake," Ingrid stared hard at him, "and I don't smoke."

Her accent made him take notice. He looked down at the ID, looked back up at Ingrid and smiled. "I ain't al-Qaeda."

"Right now I wouldn't give a damn if you were. I only want to know who was on shift here between five and five-thirty this morning."

He looked over her shoulder to a customer. "Number six, yeah?" he said to the driver as Ingrid stepped to one side. The driver shoved his credit card into the reader. "Between five and five-thirty you say?"

Ingrid nodded.

"Well, it's your lucky day, innit. Thanks, mate," he said to the driver and handed him his receipt. "Cos it was me."

"I don't suppose, by any chance, you remember a heavily pregnant woman coming in? She's twenty years old, wearing a flowery sundress?"

He sucked his teeth and shook his head. "Nah, pretty sure I'd remember."

"You got cameras here?"

"Smile," he said, "you're being recorded from about six different angles right now."

"Any of them cover the street?"

He shook his head. "Nah, they're on the pumps and the counter. That's it."

"None of them even catch a bit of the road?"

He thought about it for a second. "S'possible the one on pump six does. You wouldn't see much though."

"How easy would it be to check?"

He shrugged. "Dunno. No one's ever asked before."

"Anyone else here who might know?"

"Tariq starts his shift at twelve. I can ask him."

Ingrid didn't have the luxury of time or manpower. She reached inside her jacket and pulled out a calling card. "If you can, find someone to take a look, and if they see a pregnant woman walking past between five-fifteen and six—"

"Thought you said five-thirty?"

"Nice to know you were paying attention. If someone can

look at the footage up until six, that'd help. If you see her—floral dress, out to here—call me."

The clerk took Ingrid's card. "What if I just want to take you for a drink?"

She smiled at him. "Well, you've got my number." They both knew he was never going to ask. "One more favor. Which way is the nearest station?"

He pointed east. "Westferry, two minutes that way."

"I owe you."

Ingrid brushed past another motorist on her way out of the shop and broke into a jog as she crossed the forecourt. She was at Westferry station in less than a minute. When she got there, she discovered that the station was at the same level as the viaduct; about fifty feet in the air. She looked around for an elevator. There were two entrances to Westferry station on either side of the viaduct: it was a confusing place for someone who had never been there before. When she did find the elevator she also found a notice that said it was out of order. Ingrid looked up at the steps: would a woman who was eight months pregnant take on the climb? At twenty years old, she could probably manage it. Ingrid ran up the steps, taking them three at a time.

When she reached platform level she found the station almost empty, just a lone passenger on the opposite platform. There was no ticket hall, no staff to ask, just a machine where you could top up your Oyster card. She figured the place would have been equally deserted at a quarter after five in the morning. She punched the ticket machine: her investigation had run aground after less than five minutes. There were cameras, but she'd need a reason to request access to the footage, as well as the time to review it.

On the ticket machine she noticed a large 'help' button above a round speaker. It had to be worth a try. She pressed it. A few seconds later, a garbled voice spoke to her. So garbled, she couldn't work out what was being said.

"Er, hi," she said, leaning toward the intercom, "I'm a—" Explaining who she worked for was too complicated. "I work with the police. I want to speak to anyone from London Transport who was working at Westferry station this morning."

The metallic voice—male, African—rattled the speaker.

"I'm sorry, I couldn't make that out. Could you repeat that please?"

More unintelligible sounds.

"Thanks for your help." Ingrid walked back toward the exit. She sprinted down the stairs to street level knowing her best bet for finding Kate-Lynn without witnesses was to hit the phones instead of the sidewalk. At the bottom of the staircase, Ingrid saw something she hadn't noticed on her way up: beneath the steelwork was a pile of cardboard and clothes. She reached into her bag and felt around for her wallet and pulled out a £10 note.

"Hi," she said to the pile of clothes. "I'm sorry to disturb you." The pile of clothes didn't move. She crouched down and gently grabbed a dirty, worn sneaker and shook it gently. "Hi," she said again. "Hi, I really need your help."

The homeless person started to move.

"I'm so sorry to disturb you."

A young, dirty face, eyes blinking in the light. It was a woman, no older than Kate-Lynn. Ingrid held out the £10 note. The young woman eyed her suspiciously.

"I'm looking for someone," Ingrid said. "She's about your age. Eight, maybe nine months pregnant. She's gone missing, but she was here this morning. I'm just wondering if you saw her."

"You're American," the woman said.

"And by the sounds of things you're Scottish." It was one of the few regional dialects Ingrid was confident of identifying correctly. "I'm sorry I had to wake you."

The woman was staring at the £10 note.

"Take it," Ingrid said.

The girl extended her arm and snatched it from Ingrid's grasp. "What was it you were asking?"

"Were you here this morning, just after five?"

She nodded.

"Did you see a pregnant woman. Your age. Wearing a summer dress?"

"Yeah, I saw her." Her eyes, now adapted to the light, darted left and right. "I'd just got here. Even this time of year, even this far south, it's too fucking cold to sleep at night."

Ingrid knew it wasn't just warmth that kept girls like her on their feet at night: it was safer to sleep during the day and be alert during darkness.

"You alone?" Ingrid asked.

The girl shook her head. It was only then that Ingrid saw another body lying under the clothes.

"Boyfriend?" Ingrid asked.

"No, just a mate. You got another one of those tenners?"

Ingrid pulled out her wallet and looked inside. "I do. If I give it to you, what am I going to get in return?"

"I can tell you where she went, your friend."

There were several beer cans lying by the cardboard mattresses. Ingrid knew exactly what her money would be spent on: a piece of her wanted to give the girl enough for a room for the night. She handed over the note.

"I spoke to her," the girl said.

"How did she seem?"

"What do you mean?"

"Was she scared? Anxious?"

"No, just lost. She wanted to know how to get to Vauxhall. I told her I had no fucking idea but that the trains would start running in a bit and she could ask someone on the train."

"Vauxhall? You're sure?"

"Aye."

"And did she get on a train?"

"Took her five bloody minutes to get up those stairs."

Ingrid studied the girl's features, assessing whether or not she was telling the truth or just what she wanted to hear. She looked up at the stairs above their heads then back at the girl. "Thanks for your help."

"No problem."

Ingrid ran straight back up the steps, tapped her Oyster card onto the automatic reader and waited for a train. She'd have to come back for the Triumph. The departure board said the next train was to Bank station, and the one after that to Tower Hill: which route would Kate-Lynn have taken? Ingrid studied the Tube map on the station wall. It was no longer as confusing to her as it had been when she'd first arrived in London, but it took a while to find Vauxhall station on the Victoria line.

The electric train glided along the viaduct, passing between buildings and affording her glimpses into apartments and offices. Electronic announcements mixed with the tssh-tssh coming from other passengers' headphones and a distant phone conversation from the other end of the coach. Ingrid tuned it all out and focused on Kate-Lynn Bowers.

She made a mental list of all the things she knew about the girl. She was from Illinois, but had joined a surrogacy program in California. She had escaped Nuestra Señora, leaving behind her phone and her wallet yet somehow managed to keep hold of her passport. This bothered Ingrid: from what Tom and Truman had told her about Nuestra Señora, it sounded like the kind of institution that would keep hold of their clients' passports. In fact, Ingrid realized, that wasn't the only thing that troubled her about the passport: in her experience, the kind of girl who's desperate enough to become a surrogate isn't generally the same kind of girl who even has a passport. Something wasn't fitting together.

Ingrid had to figure that, nine months ago, Kate-Lynn Bowers had been so desperate about something that she chose surrogacy, but in the very recent past something worse had happened to make her flee—she didn't even pack a toothbrush—and board a transatlantic flight. She needed to arrange for an agent from the LA field office to collect the girl's phone. If she couldn't find the girl quickly, retrieving data from her phone was the obvious next step.

Ingrid tried to imagine how frightening the prospect of giving birth must be for someone so young, especially in a strange country. It had to be a terrifying prospect for Kate-Lynn. Yet the threat of being forced to return to California had seen her walk out of the safest place in England she could have been with people who cared deeply—in the short term, at least—about her wellbeing.

When she pieced together what she knew, Ingrid was forming a picture of a scared, vulnerable but strong-headed young woman.

And then, of course, there was the bullet.

The good news, however, was that it seemed Kate-Lynn Bowers wasn't totally alone in London: she had to know someone in Vauxhall. It wasn't like she asked for directions to Buckingham Palace or King's Cross station. Vauxhall was the kind of place you only went to if you had a damn good reason to go there. All Ingrid had to do was work out what the hell that was.

On the seat next to Ingrid was a discarded copy of the previous day's *Evening News*. She was just about to pick it up and see what stories her old adversary Angela Tate was reporting on when her phone started to buzz in her pocket. She got it out and looked at the screen. *That is not possible. That is simply not possible.* She swiped to answer.

"How the hell did you know I was just thinking about you?"

"Call it journalistic instinct if you like. Honed over decades."

"You're not on the train, are you?" Ingrid looked around the coach, searching for a woman with temperamental hair and a penchant for leopard print.

"No," Angela Tate said, "I'm at the office, and I've got a slightly more pressing question for you, Agent Skyberg."

Ingrid got the distinct impression she was about to be ambushed by the most astute journalist in the city. She took a deep breath. "Go ahead."

"What were you doing at Truman Cooper's house this morning?"

13

Ingrid clipped the security pass to her lapel and hit the button for the 23rd floor.

The trip to Vauxhall hadn't been worth it. It wasn't so much a dead end as a Hydra's head of infinite ends. She'd emerged out of the Tube station to be confronted by one of the busiest intersections in London. As well as the Tube, there was also a railway station and a bus station, not to mention a four-lane roundabout. If Kate-Lynn had indeed gone to Vauxhall there was no way of finding out easily where she had headed next. Sure, there were probably as many security cameras as there were traffic lights—the area was home to the headquarters of MI6—but getting the warrants and the manpower to obtain and study the footage would take days. Ingrid had conducted a brief tour of the place, and apart from a large motorcycle dealership with a seductive array of Bonnevilles and Thunderbirds, Vauxhall's main attractions appeared to be a petting zoo, a collection of gay bars and an unusually dense concentration of Portuguese restaurants. There was no maternity unit, no café catering to recently arrived American tourists, no obvious reason for Kate-Lynn to go there. Assuming she had got to Vauxhall around 6 a.m., it would have been busy with early commuters and finding witnesses would require the assistance of the Met. And for that, Ingrid would need an actual crime to have been committed. As the elevator doors opened, Ingrid remembered the bullet. If it hadn't disappeared, it was the kind of evidence that could get her the backup she so desperately needed.

She stepped out into the vast open-plan office of the *Evening News* and looked for someone who could help her. Everyone was so focused on their work that no one even registered her presence. "Wow," she said out loud, noticing the view. *How does anyone get any work done here?* The 23rd floor of Docklands' tallest tower offered astonishing views back toward the City and West End of London. Ingrid walked over to a window, and made out a few of the obvious landmarks: the Gherkin, the London Eye, the gleaming new Shard.

"Agent Skyberg."

Angela Tate, hands on hips, was dressed in a leopard print dress and her trademark patent leather boots. Her wild frizzy hair had slightly more gray than when they'd last met, something Angela was compensating for with a brighter shade of lipstick.

"Angela," she said, "nice to see you." Five words Ingrid never thought she'd say to the *Evening News*'s chief reporter.

"Come this way." Ingrid followed as Angela Tate navigated her way between banks of desks. "Excuse the mess. Actually, I have no idea why I'm saying that. I don't really care about the mess. Reminds me of home."

The office looked like it was doubling up as a warehouse, with stacks of boxes and crates at the end of each bank of desks. "Are you moving offices?" Ingrid asked.

"Bloody hope not. We've not unpacked since the last move. Got taken over by Ivanov's lot, moved us out here. Consolidation with their other titles. Probably be sold to the Saudis next." She stopped momentarily and turned. "They'd only move us out to Osterley or some other suburban hell. So, could be worse."

"What's the scoop of the day?" Ingrid asked, stepping over a stack of magazines.

"Something I couldn't get past the lawyers. Right," Angela's pace slowed as she maneuvered through a narrow gap between tall gray file cabinets, "this is the picture desk. Danny?"

A man in his twenties with geek specs, an Elvis hairstyle and a buttoned-up gingham shirt turned round.

"Danny is our deputy picture editor. Danny, I'd like you to meet Charlize Theron."

"Ah," he said, getting to his feet. He looked Ingrid up and down. "You don't actually look that much like her."

"I look *nothing* like her," Ingrid said.

"Oh, come off it," Angela said, "you must get it all the time."

Ingrid had heard it before, though not often. She ran her hand through her hair nervously. "She's got to be a lot taller than me."

"Well, you created quite a stir this morning when the pics came through."

"Can I see them?" Ingrid asked.

Danny nodded and entered a flurry of keystrokes into a search field on his computer.

"If I hadn't been coming to see Danny about something else—can't say what, obviously—and spotted you on his screen, the showbiz desk was getting ready to run a tease on the big Hollywood star who was joining the cast of *The Belgravia Set*."

A series of images fluttered onto Danny's enormous flat-screen monitor like the flipped pages of an animation book. All of them featured Ingrid at microsecond intervals climbing off her Triumph Tiger 800 outside Truman Cooper's Wapping residence.

"Actually," Danny said, "her publicist said she was filming in Cambodia, or Thailand, or somewhere, but for a few minutes we thought we might bid for exclusivity."

Ingrid stared at the screen. "Really? Isn't a movie star more likely to be climbing out of a limo, or a cab?"

"All the stars ride bikes," Danny said. "Only way they can be anonymous."

Ingrid nodded. "So who took them?"

Danny clicked on the top left corner of the image to reveal a pop-up window. "The G-Whizz Agency. Snapper called Emil Ali."

"Is he someone you work with a lot?" Ingrid asked.

"The agency, yes. Buy stuff from them all the time. The actual photographer?" Danny shrugged. "Never met him but his name crops up every now and then. The kind of pap that sends a courier package just to get a celeb to answer the door in their undies."

"Nice." Ingrid said. "He must have been sitting in a car on the opposite side of the road. I didn't see him."

"The lenses they've got, he could have been miles away," Angela said.

Probably somewhere in the dog park.

"So what I need to see," Ingrid said, peering at the screen, "is everything else he took this morning."

Danny turned back toward his computer. Angela Tate held her hand out. "Before you do that, Danny my boy, Agent Skyberg and I have a little negotiation to carry out."

"We do?" Of course they did. Somewhere on Angela Tate's body there had to be a tattoo that said 'Quid Pro Quo'. "Sure."

Angela led Ingrid toward a small kitchen area where *Evening News* employees who knew how to operate a kettle made tea for themselves. The only beverages Ingrid could recall Angela drinking were of the alcoholic variety. Ingrid suspected her domestic skills didn't extend much further than paying the cleaner and ordering take-out.

Outside the busy kitchen was a small seating area with hard foam couches that were showing their age. Angela sat down heavily on one of them and indicated Ingrid should join her. On the wall above them was a framed photograph of Karlos Ivanov holding up an edition of the paper. Ingrid couldn't work out why it was capturing her attention so much.

"So," the veteran journalist said, "we both know you didn't come here to look at pictures of yourself."

"True." Ingrid sat down and noticed a run in Angela's pantyhose stretching over one knee, rising out of her boot and disappearing under her dress. She wasn't sure if she should mention it.

"And I know you're not dumb enough to think I'd let you out of here without telling me why Truman Cooper needed the help of the FBI this morning."

"Also true."

Angela pursed her lips together, forming a craquelure of creases. "So, why are you really here, Agent Skyberg?"

Ingrid was drawn again to the photograph and stood up to take a closer look.

"Agent?"

The caption beneath the image read: 'A real Londoner. New proprietor Karlos Ivanov celebrates the acquisition of the *Evening News* with a pint in his local pub.'

It was the Queen Mary public house in Pimlico.

14

Something moved out of the corner of her eye and Ingrid turned instantly toward it. *Please God no.* A plane was outside the window, no more than five hundred yards away. It was so close she could see it was a Lufthansa jet. No one else seemed to notice.

Angela stared up at Ingrid, then followed her gaze out the window. "Ah, probably should have warned you about that. It always freaks out the Yanks."

Ingrid couldn't answer: it was as if she had seized up, a hundred years of rust accumulating in just a few seconds.

"London City airport," Angela said. "Sometimes they do get awfully close. Although I am reliably informed they are always further away than you think."

Ingrid's pulse deepened as she watched the jet continue past the building and behind the adjacent HSBC tower.

"When this place was first built it was the only tower for several miles," Angela said. "You got a complete three-sixty. Had a friend who worked on the *Mirror* at the time, said they lost hundreds of man-hours watching planes land and take off."

Ingrid's heart rate still hadn't returned to normal.

"Agent?"

"Yes?"

"You were about to tell me the real reason you schlepped out to Canary Wharf."

"Ah." Ingrid looked again at the photo of Ivanov, buying herself a little time. She needed to throw Angela a bone. A juicy, distracting, irrelevant bone. "Wouldn't I be better off speaking to one of your colleagues on the showbiz team? I'd have thought a story about an actor was a bit beneath your pay grade."

"Flattery won't work." Angela leaned in. "If it requires the FBI, it's news. So?"

Ingrid recoiled slightly, retreating from Angela's aroma of Camel cigarettes. "It's really not that big of a deal."

"I'll be the judge of that."

"He's an old friend of the ambassador. I was just relaying some information to him, passing on a message."

Angela's mouth crinkled, her lips forming a vermillion slash. "So that explains why you went to his house—not an adequate explanation, by the way—but it doesn't tell me why you came here to see whatever photos Danny's got on his computer. Oh bugger," Angela looked down at her knee. "I appear to have laddered my tights. That'll teach me for climbing over fences."

Ingrid knew nothing would stop Angela Tate's pursuit of a story, and certainly not the combination of a leopard print dress and a fence. She was like one of those old-fashioned kids' toys with a curved base that couldn't be knocked over. Ingrid struggled to remember what they were called. A *Weeble*. Angela Tate was a journalistic Weeble.

"Agent, what were you hoping to see?"

Ingrid had to give her something. "If I tell you, you can't print it. Not yet, anyway."

"That's usually how this works. You promise to give me the story—exclusively—at a date in the very near future so I don't go digging for it in the present. So what is it?"

Ingrid bit her bottom lip. "You know that Truman Cooper has a stalker?"

"I didn't."

"It's on Wikipedia, it's not a secret. Well, we have reason to believe an individual who has been obsessed with him for several years is in London."

Ingrid was pretty pleased with her lie. Plausible, vague, and with the promise of juice to come. But Angela blinked hard. She wasn't buying it. Negotiating with her was like playing chess, the hack was always thinking one move ahead while only sacrificing pieces she knew she could live without. Ingrid feared she'd let too much slip.

"And that's a federal matter?" Suspicion raised Angela's pitch incrementally.

Not the response Ingrid had hoped for. "Well, it certainly crosses state lines."

"A stalker? That's it? Every bloody celebrity has one. For Christ's sake, *I've* had stalkers. I was rather hoping for more."

Ingrid knew not to embellish any further. If Angela Tate wasn't tempted by the bait, that was just fine. "What can I tell you, being an FBI agent isn't as exciting as everyone thinks. It's been weeks since I got to scramble over anybody's fence."

The journalist thought for a few seconds, then took a deep breath. "When can I run it?"

"I thought you said it wasn't a story."

"Not much of one, but it'll fill a few inches."

"As soon as we've got the stalker in custody, you'll be the second person to know."

"Second?"

"After Mr Cooper. Now, can I take a look at those photos?"

A couple minutes later, Angela and Ingrid were standing in front of the deputy picture editor's monitor looking at a screen full of thumbnail images taken outside Truman Cooper's Wapping warehouse.

"What's the earliest one taken today?" Ingrid asked.

"This one." Danny pointed to a picture of Ingrid parking her bike.

"There's nothing from before I got there?" It was too much to expect a shot of Kate-Lynn leaving at sunrise, but Ingrid had hoped she might find something out, even if it was just who took the dog to the veterinary practice.

"No, that's it."

"What about other photographers? Might there have been a few of them lurking there this morning?"

"God! It's not like he's Tom bloody Cruise," Angela said.

Danny searched for all photos submitted by picture agencies of Truman Cooper in the previous twenty-four hours. Thumbnail images started popping up on his monitor, arranged like stamps in an album.

"Makes me feel sorry for him. Everywhere he goes there are paparazzi." She peered at the screen. There was him leaving his house at the wheel of the Range Rover, him walking down a tree-lined street, him stepping out of a shop.

"Don't," Angela said. "He wouldn't get paid nearly so well if we didn't give him so much attention."

"Scroll down," Ingrid said to Danny.

Even more images appeared on his screen. None had been taken outside the house. There wasn't going to be a shot of Kate-Lynn being followed by a sinister-looking man wearing a distinctive sweatshirt that she could track down by the end of the day. The prospect of a nice, big, fat, juicy lead receded with each swipe of Danny's mouse.

"Stop! That one. Show me that one," Ingrid said.

Danny clicked on it to display it at almost full screen. It showed Truman Cooper walking down a corridor next to Tom Kerrison. They appeared to be having a massive argument.

"You have any more from this location?"

"Sure." A sequence of photos appeared on Danny's screen in which the two men were gesticulating and shouting, apparently at each other and not at the photographer. "They were taken at Heathrow airport yesterday afternoon. Time stamp says 14:33 on that one."

Ingrid sensed Angela inhale deeply. "So, why, Agent Skyberg, are you so interested in these photographs in particular? It can't be that you're shocked Truman Cooper is… I was going to say bent, but that's really rather not the thing to say anymore. Everyone knows he's been in a relationship with Kerrison for years."

"They do?"

"Everyone," Danny confirmed. "They met in a bar in Greenwich Village sometime in the nineties"

"Then why's no one printed it?" Ingrid asked.

"We only print what's news."

So, for all these years Truman Cooper hadn't come out of the closet because he feared looking like a fool for not doing it earlier… meanwhile, no news organization was willing to say that he was gay for fear of… not reporting it earlier. It made Ingrid smile. "Is there any way of finding out if these photos have been published anywhere?" she asked.

"Let's see." Danny drilled down into reference numbers and authorization codes.

"So you're interested in these particular photos because…?" Angela asked.

Without any backup from the embassy or support from the Met, tempting Angela Tate to start sniffing around the story might just provide another avenue to tracking Kate-Lynn down. Ingrid knew it wouldn't take Angela long to work out why she was really interested in the Heathrow photos. "Timing, mostly," Ingrid lied. "Really helps us piece together Truman Cooper's movements over the past twenty-four hours."

"Doesn't he have a diary, or an assistant who can give you that kind of information?"

Angela was too smart to let anything go unchallenged. "This is independent. Much more admissible if anything goes to court."

Danny turned round. "There you go. TMZ, Page Six, *Daily Mail*… it's been in loads of places."

Ingrid took another look at the images. Walking several paces behind Truman and Tom was a young pregnant woman wearing a floral dress. *So that's why Kate-Lynn left.* Someone must have seen those photos. Someone had found out where she was.

15

Ingrid took the Docklands Light Railway two stops from Canary Wharf and found herself at Westferry station for the second time that day. She ran down the steps to street level, pulled the phone from her pocket and listened to her messages. Among them was a short, downbeat request from her friend—just about her only real friend in London—Natasha McKittrick to take her out and get her drunk. She sounded like she was in a bad way. Ingrid knew she had better call her, but Kate-Lynn had to take priority. As a detective inspector in the Metropolitan Police, Natasha would understand. Ingrid dialed her assistant at the embassy.

"Jennifer, hi, it's me."

"Hey, Ingrid. Look, I haven't got the payment info you asked for. United say the financial records require an official request before they can tell you who paid for… ticket. The passenger manifest is, like, well not exactly public… but it's not covered by, you know, corporate…"

"You're cutting out." Ingrid walked quickly toward Truman Cooper's house.

"I can… you fine."

Ingrid glanced at her phone: her battery was down to the red zone. Reception always started to cut out when power got low. "I'm going to call you right back."

She threw her iPhone into her bag and rummaged around for her Nokia. It was her US cell: she'd gotten in the habit of always taking it with her in case someone called about Megan.

"Damn." She stopped walking: Jennifer's number wasn't programed into the Nokia. She reached into her bag for the iPhone. She felt her wallet, her umbrella, a notebook, keys, penknife... "Oh, come on," she shouted in frustration. She didn't have time for this. A homeless person—possibly the man she'd seen with the Scottish girl earlier—turned sharply to see who was making the noise. *Finally*. She scrolled through the contacts on the iPhone, found Jennifer's number and hurriedly keyed in the details, correcting herself after every other tap. *Less haste*, she reminded herself. The phone started to ring, and she exhaled.

"Hi, is this better?"

"It was totally fine for me anyway. So, United Airlines—"

"Hey, Jen, I trust you to stay on top of it. You don't need to give me status updates." Ingrid started walking again: had she really just said that? She *trusted* someone else. Had she just learnt the art of delegation? "I need something else from you."

"OK. Fire away."

"Kate-Lynn Bowers."

"Yup."

"I need you to find her Facebook page, her Twitter feed, Instagram, the whole lot—"

"Already done."

"What?"

"Yesterday, when you asked me to find out what I could, I like totally checked her out online."

"And?" Up ahead, Ingrid could see her much-photographed Tiger Triumph still parked where she'd left it.

"And... I'm just flicking through my notes... Right, so... Facebook hasn't been updated for almost two years; as far as I can tell she isn't on Twitter, and her last Instagram post was from a Christmas party. She's twenty. She's probably all over Snapchat and, as far as I know, there is like no way of tracing her on that."

"So—"

"So, that Christmas party... There were a couple of names in the caption. I found them on Facebook and then, like, Don and me, we set up a fake account. Apparently he does it all the time when he's checking out new guys—"

"Don's gay?"

"Like, duh. Anyway, we made up a kid who went to elementary school with them but moved away and is, like, now making contact with old friends. We sent a zillion friend requests and now Marcia Harding is Facebook friends with seven or eight people from Aurora."

Ingrid was so surprised she had stopped walking. "You did that?"

"Sure."

"I mean, you can do that?"

"Like, totally. And then we found them on Twitter and Reddit so, you know, if this Kate-Lynn is in contact with one of them, maybe they'll tweet a picture of their milkshake and she'll be in the background and you can buy me and Don a beer."

"Jennifer, if this pays off I'm taking you for tequila shots." Ingrid scratched her head. She knew Jennifer was good, she just hadn't realized how good. She started walking again, patting her pockets in search of her bike keys.

"Just hit a few home runs tomorrow night, that's all the payment I ask for. You hadn't forgotten, had you?"

She had. "Of course not. Hyde Park."

"Regent's Park. You will be there, won't you?"

"Absolutely. So you'll let me know the minute you find out any tiny little thing about Kate-Lynn?"

"Sure. It might help if you tell me why you're interested in her. Is she, like, Truman Cooper's secret love child or something?"

Ingrid inhaled: she couldn't risk telling Jennifer about Kate-Lynn's real connection to Truman Cooper. The girl was good, but she was also young and liked to gossip. "Hey, if I tell ya, I'd have to shoot ya."

"Talking of which, I just went ahead and, like, booked you that target practice."

Ingrid jingled her bike keys. "When for?"

"Eight tomorrow morning. Hope that's OK?" It was fine, especially as she'd already told Sol it was booked.

The bike seemed to be unmolested. No dents, no scratches; not that Ingrid much cared: as soon as her lease agreement was up she was definitely handing it back to the dealership. "That's fine."

"Cool, it's already in your iCal. Should sync with your phone."

Talk of target practice reminded her of the .38 that had magically disappeared inside the house she was standing in front of. Someone in that building had placed a bullet in an unborn baby's crib. That wasn't the behavior of a sane, rational person. So who did it? The obvious candidate was Kate-Lynn, literally leaving a warning shot as a prelude to a ransom request. But if that was the case, why did someone else remove it? Why wasn't Tom, or Truman or Manuela screaming in her face that they'd found a bullet? Ingrid wanted to believe the .38 was just another prop from Cooper's jungle movie, but she couldn't shake the feeling it meant Kate-Lynn Bowers was in grave danger.

"Jen?"

"Uh-huh."

"I need one more thing from you."

"Name it."

"Can you find out who manufactures .38 caliber bullets with aluminum casings."

"Sure. Why?"

"And then see if anyone sells them in London."

"Sure. You heading back to base soon?"

"I'm on my way."

"Then I should probably warn you Agent Simmons is on the warpath."

Ingrid had a pretty good idea what he wanted to pick a fight about.

Just as she was buckling up her helmet, her iPhone started to ring. She pulled it out of her bag and saw it was McKittrick.

"Hey."

"You get my message?" She sounded awful and it wasn't just because the line was cutting in and out.

"I did, sorry. What's up?"

"Any chance you can meet for lunch?"

Ingrid calculated if she had the time. "Sure. I know just the place. Can you get to the Queen Mary pub in Pimlico?"

16

Anonymity wasn't the primary benefit of riding a bike: less than fifteen minutes later Ingrid was parking up in a side street in Pimlico. Hemmed in by its more famous neighbors, Westminster and Chelsea, Pimlico had all the attributes of an up-market neighborhood but none of the swagger. It had nice houses and nice cars, but no chauffeurs or full-time dog walkers.

The Queen Mary occupied a prominent corner position at a residential intersection where an imposing row of white-painted houses with porches and black railings faced a five-story housing project. Ingrid wondered which of the local clientele the pub was going to cater to. It didn't look like the drinking den of billionaires, but neither was it an obvious pick as a gangland hangout where hits could be ordered in exchange for manila envelopes of cash. It was just a regular neighborhood pub with leadlight windows, hanging floral baskets and a couple of benches outside.

She was about to lock her helmet in the top box but had second thoughts: carried the right way, a crash helmet could be a useful offensive weapon. Given Ralph's concerns about why he'd been given the information so easily, it was a sensible precaution.

While she waited for McKittrick to arrive, Ingrid walked round the exterior of the building. She spotted a second entrance to the bar, and toward the rear was a gate that presumably led into a yard. She tried the gate. Locked. As she walked back toward the main entrance, she noticed the trapdoors in the sidewalk which allowed barrels to be delivered straight to the cellar. So two doors, a gate and a cellar. If the Queen Mary really was as dangerous as Ralph had implied, she shouldn't have any problem making her escape.

She heard a faint bleep emanating from her bag. It wasn't a huge surprise to read McKittrick's text.

Sorry, not going to make it. Just crazy here. Explain when I see you.

The iPhone was almost out of power. She needed to get a new battery for it. She dropped it back into her bag, gripped the chin guard of her helmet in her right hand, and shouldered open the double doors to the pub.

Several large TV screens were showing a soccer match; a repeat, presumably, considering the time of day. The audio was muted and the only sounds were the electronic bells and dings from a bank of gaming machines that blinked and winked into the empty room. Chairs and tables had been cleared out to reveal a dark, patterned carpet. A long trestle table set for a buffet offered up the remnants of stroganoff, knishes and dumplings. Russian food. The only movement came from a foil 'Good Luck' sign that fluttered as the door closed behind her. The place was completely deserted. What could possibly have happened to cause a party to be abandoned so quickly that no one had even had time to lock the door?

"Hello? Anyone here?"

Ingrid placed the back of her hand against the tureen of stroganoff. It was still warm: whoever had been there had only just left. On the far side of the bar were two doors: one to the kitchen and another to the restrooms. Next to the counter was a door marked 'private'. She pushed it open and saw a narrow staircase leading up to the landlord's apartment. Her iPhone bleeped in her pocket. She ignored it in case she needed the battery power to call to the emergency services.

Clutching her chin guard tightly, she opened the door into the kitchen, immediately smelling the stale oil from the deep-fat fryers. The oven was still warm but had been turned off. A packet of frozen pierogi had been left in the sink to defrost. Someone had recently been there. She looked at the large freezer chests, unsure if they were more likely to contain crimes against health and safety, or body parts from unsolved murders. She didn't like this place one little bit. It gave her the creeps.

A sudden gust of wind blew open the kitchen door, forcing an involuntary gasp from her throat. It wasn't like her to be so easily spooked. Slowly, she stepped toward the open door and the sounds of the housing project—screaming kids, shouting mothers, the revving engines of souped-up street cars—invaded her ears.

"Hey," she said, aware for the first time just how hard her heart was beating. "Anyone here?" She switched the helmet to her left hand so she could wipe the sweat from her right palm on her jeans. She reached the rear door and stepped out into a small yard. Concrete floor, six-foot fence, empty barrels, trash cans, a bicycle wheel and a scattering of cigarette butts that resembled fallen petals.

She turned back into the kitchen. A loud thud. It had to have come from the barroom. She snuck a glance through the small square glass panel in the kitchen door to see the double doors from the street swing shut. She had company.

Nervously, she stepped into the main barroom. She couldn't hear any movement in the building. Her instincts told her to get out—the place was abandoned for a reason—but if the angel on one shoulder told her to go, the devil on the other shoulder wanted to find out what was going on.

She pushed open the door to the restrooms, instantly smelling air freshener with undertones of dampness. The short corridor had three doors leading from it: the men's room, the women's room and, she presumed, the cellar.

She opened the door to the women's room. The cubicles were empty. A faucet was gushing water. Pink, sodden toilet paper was strewn across the floor.

Next, Ingrid knocked on the door to the men's room.

"Anyone in there?"

No reply. She leaned against the door, opening it slowly. A constant stream of water emptied into the urinal. The solitary stall was empty. She caught sight of herself in the dull mirror and noticed it was splattered with blood. The basin too was blood-stained. Drips from a wound and spray from a punch. Her hand reached for her phone: it was time to call the cops.

Heavy footsteps clattered down the corridor outside. Ingrid flung herself into the stall. She held her breath, but whoever it was didn't enter. Another thud: the door into the barroom closing. She moved the helmet back to her right hand and pulled the door into the corridor open a crack. Was that a man's voice she could make out? She needed to get out. She glanced down the corridor at the cellar door, her alternative exit.

Breathing deeply, she tried the handle. It opened easily. Too easily. She nearly lost her footing at the top of a steep ladder down into the basement. In her first week at Quantico, new recruits were given a screening of *The Silence of the Lambs*. "And the moral of that story," her instructor had said, "is that an FBI agent should never go down into a cellar alone." She closed the door and in the distance she heard a police siren.

There was another thud from the barroom. The double doors to the street slamming shut. Her tee-shirt was starting to stick to her back. Gripping the helmet firmly, she opened the door into the bar.

"Hello? Who's there?"

The only noise came from the street and the gaming machines. Whoever it was had gone. She glanced over the bar: the till drawers were both open, and had both been emptied.

The sound of the siren grew louder. Through the mottled glass in the leaded windows she saw blue flashing lights.

Stay or run?

She pushed against the kitchen door, ran out into the yard and scaled the wooden gate before dropping down onto the sidewalk.

17

Ingrid headed for the escalator, ducking and weaving past store assistants in Selfridges perfume department like they were combatants on the Quantico assault course. Every one of them had their arms outstretched, wielding bottles of noxious fluids and offensive fake smiles. Emerging on the second floor more or less unscathed, Ingrid headed directly to the personal shopping department. After the incident at the Queen Mary and a run-in with Agent Simmons, the last thing she felt like doing was browsing for clothes.

Eugene Simmons, a former Navy SEAL and now orthodox G-Man complete with pressed white shirt and slicked-back hair, was so furious about her new assignment to gather background on Russians in London, that he was actually spitting as he shouted at her. Cornering Ingrid in the corridor alongside the bullpen he accused her of compromising his counter-terrorism sources, of endangering the lives of American citizens because he'd no longer be able to extract intel from assets because she was—obviously—going to screw everything up. "You work with kiddies and shoplifters," he'd sneered. Ingrid had taken some pleasure in responding in Russian—a childhood with Svetlana had supplied her with some particularly venomous expletives—but she was still liable to shove anyone who looked at her the wrong way.

While waiting for her appointment, Ingrid flicked through one of the nearby sales racks. She was inspecting the ticket on a gray pants suit when two hangers rapidly shifted apart to reveal Natasha McKittrick's face staring through the gap.

"What on earth are we doing meeting here?" the detective inspector asked. "I thought you feared shopping more than wisdom tooth extraction." She straightened up and peered at Ingrid over the top of the hanging rail.

"I need a go-bag. For the office."

"A what?"

"For unexpected assignments. It's supposed to have everything and anything you might need for a couple of nights away. Toiletries, a change of clothes, smart shoes, a cocktail dress, nightwear, underwear..."

"Back up a second. Cocktail dress? What kind of assignments are you likely to go on?"

"Well, this week I've been to a gallery opening in a dress that was falling off my shoulders and in shoes that doubled as instruments of torture."

"Beats my trip to the morgue."

"Actually, the dress was probably the high point, sartorially speaking. The rest of the time I've either been in a suit that makes me look like a matron from a nineties TV show or I've been dressed like a motorcycle messenger. I need clothes," Ingrid said, pulling an A-line skirt from the rack. "I've needed them ever since I came to London. I thought I was only going to be here for four days, remember?"

"Well that sure as hell doesn't suit you. Put it back and step away." McKittrick sighed. "How long is this going to take? I really—and I mean *really*—need a drink."

Ingrid checked her phone. It was 6:30 p.m. "Reckon we can be at the bar in forty-five minutes. I can't shop for longer than that anyway."

"Miss Skyberg?"

Both women turned toward the sales assistant. Forties, tanned, trim with a neglectful paunch just above the belt and beard that was unmistakably dyed: Christopher took longer to get ready in the morning than Ingrid and McKittrick combined.

"That's me," Ingrid said. "And this is my second opinion."

"Natasha," McKittrick said, extending her hand.

"And are you shopping too?" Christopher asked.

"Not today. Brassic."

"Well, if you would both like to come with me."

Christopher led them through a doorway into a salon with cream leather sofas, a coffee table laden with glossy magazines and a bank of noticeably generous changing rooms. To McKittrick's evident delight, it also sported a fridge. "Would you ladies like a glass of champagne?"

"Too bloody right." McKittrick turned to Ingrid. "Maybe this won't be so bad after all."

Christopher failed to keep a look of disapproval from his features, but nonetheless opened the fridge and pulled out a bottle of what was clearly prosecco.

"You realize this will get added to your bill?" McKittrick said.

"Well, we'd be paying for it in a bar; at least here we're not getting hit on by stag parties."

McKittrick glanced at Christopher. "Nope, no chance of that."

Ingrid was so grateful that McKittrick had agreed to come with her. Not only did she hate shopping for clothes—for some reason, buying books, CDs, gadgets and almost anything else didn't induce the same feelings of insecurity and panic—but she would have found Christopher's scrutiny deeply uncomfortable without McKittrick there as a foil. Natasha was really her only friend in London and would be the one person she could really talk to about what had happened in Minnesota if it weren't for the fact that she was also Ralph's boss.

A reassuring 'pop' was followed by a gentle hiss as Christopher poured out two flutes of fizz. "Ladies," he said, handing them both a glass.

"Thank you," Ingrid said.

"Cheers," McKittrick added.

Christopher sat down on the couch next to Ingrid. "So, what are you looking for today?"

Ingrid shrugged. "Pretty much everything."

Christopher's shoulders raised and his mouth tightened. Ingrid's card had just been marked as a difficult customer. "OK, and what sort of budget do you have?"

Ingrid shot a look at McKittrick. She hadn't given it any thought. Jennifer had suggested a personal shopper, and given her appalling track record in clothes-buying she'd accepted it was a good idea, but she hadn't had a chance to think it through before Jen had made the appointment. "I, er, I've never used a personal shopper," Ingrid said. "I really don't know what to expect."

Clearly, this was a situation Christopher had encountered before. He gave her a smile. "OK, let's take it another way. How much would you normally spend, say, on a pair of jeans?"

Ingrid thought back to when she had last bought denim. "A hundred bucks, I guess. Seventy pounds or so."

Christopher nodded. "And how much on a pair of boots?"

"Maybe a couple of hundred dollars, but they were for the bike."

"The bike?"

"Motorcycle. They have armor at the ankles, protection up the shins. Maybe they were closer to two-fifty. If we're talking fashion shoes—"

Christopher exhaled. "Tell me more about the bike. Do you ride every day?"

Less than ten minutes later, Christopher's skillful questioning had ascertained the key components of the average Skyberg day: a five-mile run, parkour, a motorcycle ride, several meetings with clients and superiors, representing her employer in a good light, constantly meeting new people while always trying to create the right impression. He'd also established her discomfort with heels that were too high, necklines that were too revealing and the importance of pockets.

"And what size do you normally wear?"

"Um," Ingrid was suddenly a little embarrassed to be having this conversation in front of McKittrick. "In the US, a six, I guess," she said, knowing that McKittrick was more like a ten or a twelve. "What's that in the UK?"

"For you, honey, it's the wrong size. You need something more fitted if you want to look smart." Christopher got to his feet. "Right, leave it with me. Help yourself to more champagne and I'll be back in around twenty minutes when I've pulled together some options for you."

He had barely left the salon when McKittrick got to her feet and opened the fridge door. She retrieved the prosecco and didn't ask Ingrid if she wanted a refill. "I'll get a taxi home," Ingrid said, "the bike can stay in the embassy garage."

McKittrick took a long draft. "Your life is far too glamorous. Cocktail dresses, gallery openings, personal shoppers and *underground parking*. You're like a character from *The Good Wife*."

Another TV show Ingrid had never seen.

"I better not tell you about the case I'm working then. It's all very A-list and millionaire riverside mansions."

McKittrick flopped back on the couch. "Just don't. I'm up to my arse in a random stabbing outside a pub in Deptford. It's why I bailed on you at lunch. Poor fucking bastard. Mistaken identity. He was just having a drink with colleagues after work when this gang of the nastiest eight men in London set on him."

"Christ."

"Didn't stand a chance. Bled out before the ambulance got there."

"Poor guy."

"Wife, three kids. He was thirty-nine." The two friends sat in silence for a moment. McKittrick took another glug. "So I gather you met Ralphy-boy for lunch yesterday. It's back on, then? You and him?"

"I, er—"

"It's fine, you don't have to tell me. Probably better if I don't know the details." McKittrick downed her second glass. She was —even for her—in a tremendous hurry to get drunk. She filled up her champagne flute and settled back on the couch. "So, oh glamorous one, distract me. Tell me about your A-lister. I promise not to get jealous. No, before you do that, tell me about Minnesota. How were things back home?"

"Well—"

Their conversation was interrupted by the arrival in the salon of a loud, overweight, flamboyantly dressed middle-aged woman shouting at her teenage daughter in Arabic. Behind them, two exasperated assistants were carrying armfuls of clothes. The teenager slumped on the couch opposite Ingrid and McKittrick without looking at either of them and promptly took her phone out of her bag. Ingrid let out an enormous sigh of relief: this wasn't the moment for a quiet talk about Megan's funeral, or indeed her night of shame with Clark Swanson.

18

"What do you think Christopher is going to come up with for me?"

"Oh, a diamante-encrusted denim onesie, I imagine."

"Paired with stiletto heels." For a few minutes, Ingrid had forgotten why she was drinking fizz with her mate, and the sheer terror of what lay ahead had abated. Now that she had remembered where they were, her intestines constricted. What had she let herself in for? "So," she said, wanting to think about something else, "why are you so hellbent on getting drunk tonight?"

McKittrick drained her glass and put it down on top of a copy of *Vogue*. "Remember I told you I was being investigated?"

Ingrid had forgotten. Her only friend in the country and she hadn't even remembered that she was navigating her own circle of hell. "Of course."

"I have my misconduct hearing tomorrow, hence the determination to drink alcohol tonight," she said, pouring herself another.

"Have they given you any idea what they're going to say?"

"If the averted eyes and silent treatment are anything to go by, I'd say I'm about to be relieved of my duties."

"Really? Natasha, I'm so sorry. What will happen?"

McKittrick kept her eyes on her champagne flute. "They'll

bring in another DI to run the case, but the career? Not so straightforward. Guess it kind of depends if they think I'm guilty."

Ingrid couldn't believe what she was about to say. "And are you?"

McKittrick took another mouthful.

Ingrid tried to recall anything Natasha had told her about the investigation. She'd been so evasive, so opaque, that there wasn't much to go on. To pry now would only make it clear she hadn't paid enough attention in the past. It had something to do with prescription drugs; not just taking them, but taking them from a crime scene.

"Won't they just, you know, refer you to rehab or something?"

McKittrick exhaled. "God, that'd be worse than losing my job."

"You don't mean that."

"Can you really see me in group therapy?"

It was true—Detective Inspector Natasha McKittrick was not someone you could accuse of over-sharing.

"What'll you do?" Ingrid asked.

"Ladies!" Christopher reappeared in the doorway. Ingrid had been very ready to dislike Christopher when she first met him—anyone who dyes their beard deserves a certain level of mistrust—but she had already accepted her initial judgment had been harsh. He had asked intelligent questions, been thoroughly professional and, judging by the boots he was holding, he might even be very good at his job. "Won't be a moment," he said, and disappeared once more onto the shop floor.

Ingrid got up and walked over to pick up the boots. Black leather, low-heeled calf-huggers without a tassel, buckle or other unnecessary adornment. Good choice. She turned one of them upside down.

"Stop!" McKittrick said, loud enough to attract the attention of the teenage phone addict. "Don't you *dare* look at the price. That will totally ruin the fun."

Ingrid was taken aback by her friend's level of insistence.

"Put it down. Step away from the boots. That's a good girl."

"OK, OK."

Christopher wheeled in a hanging rack bearing a modest selection of clothes. "Do you like them?" he asked.

"You know, I think I do."

"Don't sound so surprised. This is what I do. Now," he said firmly, "try these on."

He proffered a pair of skinny black pants.

"I'll never fit into those."

"Oh, just do what the man says," McKittrick said.

Ingrid took the pants into one of the changing cubicles. She looked at herself in the mirror. She hadn't realized how filthy her jeans were, or how battered her boots looked. Or how badly she needed a haircut. She sat down on the stool, unzipped her boots and slipped out of her jeans.

"How are you getting on in there?" McKittrick asked.

"Give me a chance."

"But I need entertaining!" The alcohol was taking effect.

Ingrid unclipped the black trousers from their hanger. They were soft and the stitching detail suggested an Italian atelier rather than a Bangladeshi sweatshop. She checked the label, just in case they happened to have been designed by Tom Kerrison. She couldn't help but see the price tag: £195. *Three hundred bucks for a pair of pants?* Spending a little money wouldn't be the most reckless thing she'd done in recent history, but that was a lot of dough. She slid one foot in and then the other and pulled them up. A little snug, but they'd give. She pulled back the curtain.

"What do you think?" she asked.

"More importantly, what do *you* think?" Christopher asked.

"I, er, I like them I think."

"Good. They're a hybrid material. They have a Kevlar lining so should offer some protection if you come off the bike. And the stitching here," he pointed to the knees, "is reinforced. They're actually from our equestrian range." He handed her the boots, which she could now see were also inspired by riding gear. She sat down next to McKittrick and levered them on. Then she looked at herself in the mirror.

"Wow," McKittrick said. "You are skinny."

"I think I'm thinner than I realized," Ingrid said. The past few months hadn't contained much in the way of proper meals or adequate nutrition. One of the many ways in which she had not been taking care of herself. "What size are these pants?"

"They're an eight," Christopher said.

"What? They can't be."

"A US size four."

"A four, really?" She hadn't been a size four since high school.

"Well, it suits you," McKittrick said. "If I could find trousers that fitted me that well I'd buy a pair for every day of the week."

You haven't seen the price tag.

"So, a good start?" Christopher asked, knowing full well from Ingrid and McKittrick's faces that he'd ticked the right boxes. "I have to say, selecting for someone of your proportions does make my job much easier. I imagine you could rock the proverbial potato sack."

Ingrid pulled a face.

"That's a compliment," he reassured. "Now, I've brought a selection of tops for you to try on. I've avoided shirts—they're lovely of course, make much more of a statement, but they wouldn't survive five minutes under a leather jacket. So these are all mixed-fiber pieces that won't crumple easily." He handed Ingrid a gray tank.

"I can't even work out which is the front," she said, handing it back to him for guidance. He slipped it off the hanger and returned it to her facing the right way. She'd pulled off her tee before she'd considered the tattered state of her bra. For someone who used the showers at the embassy most days, the privacy of the cubicle seemed unnecessary.

"Oh my God," McKittrick said, a little too loudly. Instantly, Ingrid knew her friend wasn't alarmed at her less than glamorous underwear. "Is that what it looks like?"

Ingrid hurriedly pulled the tank on to cover up her scar. She adjusted the fabric and looked at her reflection. It was not something she would normally wear. It had a ruffle for Chrissakes.

"It's the sort of thing," Christopher explained, "that can go from daytime to night-time with the addition of accessories. I've brought some scarves and some—"

"You can stop right there, mister," McKittrick said. "Asking Ingrid to accessorize is like asking a dolphin to climb a tree. It ain't going to happen." McKittrick widened her eyes at her. "Well I'm right, aren't I? The only accessory I've ever seen you wear was your engagement ring, and that didn't hang around for long."

She had a point. Ingrid looked in the mirror. She wondered what Marshall would make of her spending $300 on a pair of pants. Just imagining his outrage all but sealed the deal. She was going to have them, and maybe the tank too.

"What else have you got on your rack?" she asked Christopher.

He handed her a black leather jacket. It wasn't her usual style. It was longer, almost covering her buttocks, and belted, with a high collar that brushed her jaw.

"I look like a spy," Ingrid said softly. She couldn't quite believe she was looking at herself. She wanted two of everything.

"Obviously it doesn't offer the same sort of protection a proper biker jacket would give you, but it's well-made and, in and around the city, it'll probably do the job."

"Sounds like you ride," Ingrid said.

"I have an absolutely gorgeous Aprilia Habana Custom. Just a 125cc."

"Oh, but they're beautiful bikes," Ingrid said. "A blue one or a black one?"

"One of the blue ones."

"A classic." Christopher was growing on Ingrid. She turned to McKittrick: "What do you think?"

"I think Ralph Mills would go a little wobbly if he could see you now. You look amazing. Question is, how much does that ensemble come to?"

Ten minutes later, Ingrid handed over her credit card to purchase two pairs of the pants, the jacket, the boots and three of the tops Christopher had selected. She was more than a little surprised to discover that spending so much money on so few items of clothing didn't feel reckless after all: it felt fabulous.

Christopher offered to find out if the in-store salon could fit her in for a haircut. It was a not-so-subtle way of saying her hair also needed an overhaul—just about his only indiscretion—but she had promised Natasha a drink and their next stop had to be a bar.

They found a quiet corner in a place just off Duke Street, and Ingrid gave McKittrick strict instructions to keep a close eye on her purchases while she went to the bar. McKittrick was drunk, but not incapable. When Ingrid returned to their table with a bottle of Sauvignon Blanc and two glasses, McKittrick didn't waste any time in getting the first question in.

"So, how did you get that bullet wound?"

19

Ingrid closed McKittrick's bedroom door and walked through into her friend's kitchen. It had been a long time since she'd had to take a drunken friend home—not since college—but Natasha had almost passed out in the wine bar, and so Ingrid called them a cab and gave the driver the address of McKittrick's Kentish Town apartment. She figured she had a change of clothes in the yellow Selfridges bags, so she'd spend the night on McKittrick's couch, make sure her friend got to her misconduct hearing in the morning and would then head straight to work from Kentish Town.

Ingrid had stayed at McKittrick's before. A few months previously, Ingrid had been in the hospital and the doctors wouldn't discharge her unless she could be looked after by a responsible adult. Ingrid glanced at McKittrick's bedroom door and wondered just how responsible the detective inspector really was. They'd been out drinking on several occasions, and many times they'd got drunk enough to be a little shamefaced the next morning, but Natasha had never collapsed like she'd done tonight.

Ingrid let the faucet run until the water was cold and filled a glass. She'd had nearly a bottle of wine herself, but it was only a little after ten, and with enough water she might be able to sober up enough to avert a hangover. She'd tried to get McKittrick to drink something non-alcoholic, but just getting her undressed and into bed was enough of a challenge. Her make-up would be all over her pillow in the morning: Ingrid wasn't great at taking it off her own face, let alone someone else's, especially when the someone else was incapable of cooperating.

The cell phone in Natasha's bag started ringing again. She must have had six missed calls since they'd left the wine bar, so Ingrid delved into her friend's purse and pulled out her phone. Marcus was calling. *Who the heck was Marcus?* McKittrick had never mentioned a Marcus. Ingrid swiped at the screen, but she didn't have the knack of operating Natasha's Samsung and the call went to voicemail. Before the screen died, it revealed she had five missed calls from Marcus, whoever the hell he was.

Ingrid sat down at the kitchen table and got out her own phone. She had twenty new emails, including one from Jennifer with the subject line: Kate-Lynn Bowers. She tapped to open it.

It contained the log-in details for the fake Facebook account in case she wanted to monitor it herself, as well as confirmation that none of the maternity units in central London had admitted a woman matching Kate-Lynn's description. There was also a reminder that she had target practice at 8am. Damn. Ingrid had forgotten. Hopefully McKittrick would be capable of getting herself ready in the morning. Ingrid set an alarm to remind her to get to the firing range so she didn't forget again.

She tapped the Facebook app but as soon as it opened she closed it down again. Megan's funeral had sparked a lot of new communication between her old school mates, and just seeing some of their faces made her feel uncomfortable. She detested the fact that out of a list of familiar names, the one her eyes lasered in on was Clark Swanson's. At least she wasn't as drunk tonight as she had been when she'd gone to the motel with him. She opened Google and typed in Kate-Lynn's name.

Natasha's phone rang again. It was the mysterious but persistent Marcus.

"Natasha's phone."

"Who's this?"

"Ingrid."

"Ah, of course! The accent. Hi, this is Marcus." He certainly seemed to know who she was. "Where's Natasha?"

"She's gone to bed. She wasn't feeling well."

"I've been a bit worried about her for a while," he said. Ingrid couldn't make out his accent. Birmingham? Manchester? "I think she might need to see a doctor, see if she's deficient in something, you know? Good that you're there again. Are you there for long?"

"Um, just tonight. Can I give her a message?"

"Oh, the usual. Just tell her I love her and I'll see her at the weekend."

Ingrid was too stunned to speak for a second. "Right. Of course. I will."

"Nice to talk to you, Ingrid. I've heard so much about you."

"Nice to speak to you too." Ingrid hung up and almost dropped the phone. *Tell her that I love her?* Is that really what he said? McKittrick had a boyfriend? A secret boyfriend? How come that had never been mentioned? Not even a hint. Ingrid looked down the hallway at the closed bedroom door. You sly old devil. She took a long drink of water and started to feel a little more sober. She put it down to shock.

Ingrid slipped McKittrick's phone back into her shoulder bag and as she did so she noticed a blister pack of pills. Temazepam. An anxiety drug. As she dropped them back into McKittrick's bag she saw another blister pack. Oxycodone.

Christ, Natasha, that's what junkies use.

Ingrid wondered how she'd never noticed her friend had such a serious habit and scoured her memory for evidence. Natasha was moody, that was for sure, and there had been times when they had been working together on a murder investigation when she had even been hostile. Was that the drugs? Something lurched in Ingrid's stomach: how many investigations might have been compromised?

She tapped her own phone back into life and instantly sobered up: the Google returns on her Kate-Lynn Bowers search included a news report from the *Aurora Bugle*. The headline read: 'Boy, 2, Left Alone With Mother's Body For 3 Days'. She tapped on the link, scanning the article as quickly as she could, looking for the reason why this awful case was linked to her investigation. The facts were as sparse as they were horrific. The victim had been shot in the head. Local police were working on the assumption the killer hadn't known there was a toddler in the house. Then Ingrid came to relevant sentences. She had to reread them several times.

...Local police have named the victim as 20-year-old Auroran Kate-Lynn Bowers. Her son has been taken into protective custody...

How many twenty-year-old women called Kate-Lynn Bowers could there be from Aurora, Illinois? She zoomed in on the photo of the victim. She knew she wasn't entirely sober, but she also knew she wasn't drunk enough for her faculties to be completely unreliable. She was damn sure the woman who had been killed in Illinois three days ago looked just like the woman she'd seen on CCTV footage at Truman Cooper's house that morning.

20

"Aurora Police Department."

"Can you please put me through to the detective leading the Kate-Lynn Bowers inquiry?" Ingrid said.

"Please hold."

Ingrid's head was spinning, but not through alcohol. If Kate-Lynn Bowers had been dead for three days, who on earth was the woman who had spent last night at Truman Cooper's house? An impostor with a cushion shoved up her dress? Were Cooper and Kerrison being targeted in an elaborate con?

"Detective Merrison, how can I help you?"

"I'd like to speak to the detective leading the Kate-Lynn Bowers investigation."

"If you have relevant information, you can speak to me."

"I'd really like to speak to the detective in charge."

Detective Merrison inhaled audibly. "May I ask why you're calling?"

Ingrid got to her feet and started pacing round McKittrick's kitchen. "I'm Special Agent Ingrid Skyberg, I need to speak to the detective leading the investigation."

Merrison took a beat before replying. "Ma'am, all due respect, but your call is registering as 'international'."

Dumb, obstructive local cop: the bane of a federal investigator's career. "That's because I work at the embassy in London. Will you please put me through to your superior, detective?"

The phone line went dead. Had Merrison hung up on her? She tapped her phone back into life and reread the *Bugle* piece again. There was a quote from a Sergeant Mavis Tillbrook. She was just about to hang up and redial and ask for the sergeant directly, when the phone line whirred back into life.

"Sergeant Tillbrook." The woman sounded like she had inhaled helium.

"Good evening—"

"Good afternoon," Tillbrook corrected.

Well, it's evening here. Ingrid checked her temper, and her tone. "Good afternoon. I'm Special Agent Ingrid Skyberg, I work at the FBI's Legal Attaché program at the embassy here in London."

"Good afternoon, agent."

"I need some more information about your investigation into the murder of Kate-Lynn Bowers." Ingrid took a sip of water: her mouth was unexpectedly dry.

"May I ask why you're interested? You're an awful long way away."

Ingrid took a deep breath. "I'm working on a misper. A Kate-Lynn Bowers, twenty years old, from Aurora, Illinois was reported missing here in London this morning."

"Well, that can't be—"

"I've seen the photo of the woman you found in Aurora," Ingrid interrupted. She was keen for Sergeant Tillbrook to take the connection seriously. "And she looks just like the woman who was seen in London yesterday. Now either I can help your investigation, sergeant, or you can help mine, but I hope by the end of this conversation we'll be helping each other."

"Please hold the line."

What? She put her on hold? How dare she. Ingrid punched the fridge, rattling the contents. Contents which sounded like a lot of bottles knocking into one another. She yanked open the door. Nestled between several bottles of wine were several smaller bottles of beer. She pulled one out. There was also a pot of hummus which suddenly seemed deeply appealing. In the vegetable crisper there was a bag of carrots. She pulled one out but it was bendy like silicone. She put it back and closed the door.

With the phone clamped between her ear and shoulder, Ingrid rummaged through Natasha's drawers looking for a bottle opener. There was a noise coming from the bedroom: she had disturbed McKittrick. Ingrid slowed down her search, rolling over utensils as quietly as she could looking for an implement to open the beer.

"Agent?" Tillbrook's squeaky voice came back on the line. "I'm at my desk now, how can I help you?"

So that's why she'd been put on hold. Ingrid was rushing too quickly to judge people lately; it was something she needed to keep in check. She found a bottle opener and pried the metal cap off the Corona. She started exploring McKittrick's cabinets, hoping to find some corn chips or pita bread to dip into the hummus.

"What can you tell me about the victim?"

She heard a sound of a fingers tapping on a keyboard. "OK, let's see what we have. Victim is Caucasian, five feet three, around one-twenty pounds. Long mid-brown hair, blue eyes, um..." more taps on the keyboard. "Several tattoos, mostly on her lower abdomen. Twenty years old."

Ingrid took a swig from the bottle of beer. "Family? Lifestyle? What do you know about her?"

"She was a mom. Lived on welfare. Her apartment is in a block that is notorious round here. Dealers, hookers, cockroaches. I'm sure you know the kind of place."

"Was she a hooker?"

"If she was, she's never been arrested. None of the johns we spoke to knew her, so I'd say not. Doesn't mean she wouldn't give head to score a joint, you know what I mean."

Ingrid found a stale loaf of bread in a cupboard. If she could toast it she was on her way to a half-decent midnight snack. She returned to the utensil drawer in search of a breadknife. "In the paper it said she'd been shot in the head."

"Back of the neck, in actual fact."

"Sounds like an execution."

"It was. Face down, muzzle against her spine and boom."

"Face down? What about the baby?"

"Um," Sergeant Tillbrook returned to her computer. "He's been placed with local services—"

"No, not the toddler. The baby. Kate-Lynn Bowers is, or was, eight months pregnant. She couldn't have been lying face down. And the baby couldn't have survived inside her for three days."

"Excuse me?"

Ingrid found a breadknife, inducing a small sensation of achievement. "Well, I wouldn't be able to lie face down if I was eight months pregnant."

"The victim wasn't pregnant. I'm looking at the autopsy report. I mean, she wasn't even a few weeks pregnant. No fetus."

Ingrid didn't know what to say.

"Agent?"

"Um..." Ingrid willed the cogs in her brain to turn. "Any other family?"

"I believe her mother's dead. Father disappeared decades ago."

Sergeant Tillbrook was painting a depressingly familiar picture. Pity welled up inside Ingrid: it's why she'd worked in child protection for so long, to try to help young women to break cycles, to not live and die like Kate-Lynn Bowers. "You have a suspect?"

"Uh-huh. Latin Kings."

"In Aurora?"

"People round here like to think we're a city, but really we're just a suburb of Chicago. Workers commute in, gangs commute out."

"So the Kings are active in Aurora?"

"Not like they were, but a hit like this, killing a young mom, *executing* her, it's got to be someone who's killed before."

Ingrid dropped a slice of bread into McKittrick's toaster. "Who raised the alarm?"

There were more keyboard sounds as Tillbrook located the

correct information. "Landlord looking for his rent. And you know why he called? He just wanted the place cleaned up so he could get another tenant."

"He see anything? Anyone see anything."

"It really wouldn't matter if they had; if we're dealing with the Kings, ain't nobody gonna say nothing to us any old how."

"You got phone records? A computer? Do you know who the last person Kate-Lynn spoke to before she was killed?"

Sergeant Tillbrook sighed. "You breathe some clean air up there at the FBI, dontcha? You think there was anything left of value in that apartment before we got the call? They would have taken the clothes off her corpse if there hadn't been flies and blood everywhere."

Suddenly, Ingrid could picture Kate-Lynn Bowers apartment painfully clearly.

"So, you want to tell me about this girl you've got in London?"

The bread popped out of the toaster. Ingrid grabbed at it with the tips of her forefinger and thumb, dropping it on the counter quickly it was so hot. "She arrived in London around 2 p.m. local time yesterday, went AWOL sometime overnight. She doesn't know anyone in the city, she doesn't have a phone, or even a coat. She has about seven hundred and fifty dollars in cash but no access to credit. And she's eight months pregnant."

"What is she doing in London?"

What could Ingrid tell her? "I'm afraid I can't share that with anyone at this stage. But, apart from the baby bump, she's a perfect match for your victim."

"So what are you thinking, agent?"

Ingrid's brain was firing on all cylinders: she was having too many thoughts to properly process them. It couldn't be a coincidence, could it: two girls with the same name from the same place, matching the same description, and one goes missing at almost the exact same time the other winds up dead. Had the girl who came to London been the target? Did she run because she knew someone was after her? Hell, was that why she joined the surrogacy program nine months ago? To disappear? Ingrid's heart was beating hard and fast.

"Agent?"

"I'm thinking that they can't both be Kate-Lynn Bowers. I'm going to double check the ID of my girl. Are you sure you've got the real Kate-Lynn Bowers? Did you see her driver's license, or a passport?"

Sergeant Tillbrook whistled. "I don't suppose this girl ever even saw the ocean. We didn't find a passport, but we didn't look for one either: girl like her is about as likely to travel overseas as she is to travel through time."

"Look, I'm going to send you a photo of the girl who disappeared here this morning. When you see what she looks like, perhaps you'll understand the need to check again." Ingrid broke a piece of toast and scooped up a dollop of hummus. "Is there anything else you can tell me?"

Ingrid heard the sound of Mavis Tillbrook's fingers hammering at a keyboard. "Nope, I think that's it… Wait…we're waiting for ballistics and forensics and… no, that's all I got for you."

"But you've had an autopsy?"

"Yes."

"So you know what bullet was used?" Ingrid felt a chill cover her skin as she asked the question.

"Hold on. Yes, here it is. A .38 special."

The same as the bullet she had seen in the crib.

21

"You're not coming in."

"Look, this is my card—"

"You already showed me your card—"

"This is my badge."

"I have no way of knowing if this is for real."

"Listen, I just need to speak to Mr Cooper."

"As does everyone else here." The security guard crossed his arms and stared hard at Ingrid. "You're not coming in. Not you. Not anyone."

One of the fans tapped Ingrid on the shoulder. "If you're a stalker, and you stab Truman Cooper, or like just cut off a lock of his hair and like totally ruin continuity, he'll be in trouble."

Ingrid looked around at the wall of faces daring her to ask again for access to the set. Fans had come from all over the world to get a glimpse of filming. A Japanese family in matching outfits, a couple from South America with faces like stone carvings, a man in a White Sox shirt with a baseball cap pulled low over his forehead, and a couple of plus-sized women in clothes that were too small for them with Canadian maple leaves pinned to their lapels. All with their smartphones in hand, all ready to snap any actor they recognized.

"Besides, honey," said another, an American tourist in a pink leisure suit, "if he lets you in there'll be a stampede. I mean, we all want a piece of him, don't we ladies?"

A chorus of 'oh yeahs' and 'you bets' drifted through the group hemming the security cordon at one end of a Georgian square in Islington, north London. Even though Ingrid had never been there before, it was instantly familiar: it must have been used in countless period dramas before *The Belgravia Set* had started filming there.

She tried calling Tom Kerrison's number again, just in case, but it went straight to voicemail like all the previous times she'd called. While making Natasha breakfast, Ingrid had even tried the Versini offices in the hope of tracking him down that way, but his assistant had been about as helpful as a lettuce. She'd also called Truman Cooper's agent and the production company, but in the end she'd had to do what everyone else standing at the cordon had done, and found the leaked filming schedule on a fan site. Ingrid scrolled through the contacts on her phone and dialed a familiar number.

"Sol Franklin, Legal Attaché program."

"It's Skyberg."

"Agent Skyberg!" His voice was unusually bright. "What kind of trouble are you in now?"

"Hey, that's not nice, but I do need a favor."

"Uh-huh." The Assistant Special Agent in Charge's habitual gruffness had returned.

"Could you ask the ambassador to call me."

"What? Why?"

Ingrid explained that she was helping out a friend of Frances Byrne-Williams and was hoping the ambassador would be able to call him on her behalf. "I know if I go through the switchboard she'll never get my message. Could you, you know, just pop your head round her door."

"Sure! No problem!" He was layering on the sarcasm pretty thick.

"Or slip a note to her secretary?"

"Look, I'm only one step up the food chain from you, but I'll see what I can do. And perhaps you could return the favor by actually turning up for your target practice."

"Oh." *Damn*. "Sol, I'm sorry. I had a crazy morning." A vision of trying to wake McKittrick, make-up all over her face, drool stains on her pillow, popped into Ingrid's head. "I'll do it this afternoon. I'll call Jennifer now and get her to rebook."

"Louden's given you the approval. You need to step up on this Russian thing."

"That's fantastic news. You can tell her I'm already on it. Got a good lead from my Met liaison." That was one way to describe the name of a pub given to her by a man she'd had a one-night stand with. "I'm making a start."

"So, all the more reason to get you tooled up."

"I'll do it this afternoon, I promise."

She ended the call and opened her alarm app. She had set the time, but hadn't programmed it to go off: maybe she had been a little more drunk than she'd realized. Ingrid started tapping a text message to Jennifer when she heard a familiar voice and looked up.

"Manuela!"

Truman Cooper's assistant was surprised to see her.

"Hi, Manuela. I need to speak to Truman. Will you tell him I'm here, and tell him it's urgent."

Manuela's face softened slightly. Perhaps there was even a hint of a smile before she turned to the security guard. "It's OK. She can come."

"You're sure?" he asked.

Manuela nodded.

"OK, then."

Ingrid had to sign several documents in which she agreed not to reveal anything about the set, plot, costumes, script, or any behind-the-scenes details to any third party. She had to switch her phones to flight mode in case their signals interfered with the camera equipment and once her bag had been inspected she was allowed to enter the square. Had she done the target practice, and obtained the relevant permissions, she wondered if someone carrying a Glock 23 would have been allowed on set.

"Nice jacket," Manuela said. She was carrying a cardboard tray from Starbucks. The scrawled names on the cups said 'Mickey' and 'Minnie'.

It didn't matter that Manuela had said it without smiling, or emotion, or eye contact. Manuela, the ice maiden of personal assistants, had complimented Ingrid's new jacket. She couldn't have been more thrilled if someone had said: "You've just won Olympic gold." Every penny—every pound—had been well spent and Ingrid started walking with more confidence, her back a little straighter, all trace of a hangover blown away.

"Agent Skyberg!" Truman Cooper, dressed in a tweed suit with a mustache glued to his face, got up from his chair and threw down his script. He looked at Ingrid with such expectation. "Have you found her?"

Ingrid pulled what she hoped was a sympathetic face. "No, but I do have news. I can see that you are busy, but do you have five minutes for me? I tried to get hold of Mr Kerrison but he's not returning my calls."

Manuela handed him a cardboard cup. "For you, I'd fake a heart attack and get the whole fucking place shut down for the day. This way." He stretched out an arm and gently placed it on Ingrid's shoulder to guide her away from the make-up people, the hair people, the lighting people and the countless other professions that cluttered the set. "They haven't even brought the horses round yet, so we've got five at least."

He ushered her to a cobbled alleyway that led beyond the black brick houses of the square to a mews behind where the row of two-story cottages would once have been the servants' quarters, or the stables, or the garages. Now, of course, they were highly desirable residences. Except on days when the place was cordoned off for filming.

"That's a very nice jacket, by the way," he said. He pulled off the plastic lid of his coffee and took a sip, the foam sticking to his fake mustache.

"Thank you," she said, rummaging inside her bag for her phone. She looked up at him: he looked so different from the man who had been fuming and cursing in his pajamas twenty-four hours previously.

"Would you hold this?" He handed her his coffee and proceeded to unbutton his gloves. "It's supposed to be November. They've put Nancy in a fur coat. A real one! I'm just grateful it's a bit overcast today, but not nearly as grateful as the DP." He looked down at Ingrid. "I'm sorry, I'm rambling. Nervous. What have you got for me?"

Ingrid could handle a nervous Truman Cooper a whole lot more easily than the belligerent version she'd dealt with the day before. "Please take a look at this photo." She handed him her phone and showed him the portrait of the Chicago murder victim. "It's not a great image, but is this Kate-Lynn Bowers?"

"Oh my God. You've found her, haven't you?" His hand started shaking; Ingrid thought he might spill his coffee. "Is she dead? Is my son dead?"

"Mr Cooper, no, I haven't found her, and I have no reason to think that your baby is in danger. Please, just take a look at the photo and tell me if it's Kate-Lynn."

His eyes were wet with tears. He nodded and took a huge breath. He closed his eyes, held very still for a moment, then opened them and exhaled, his face transformed. It was as if Ingrid had said 'Action!' and he was now playing the part of a capable adult. He looked at the photo.

Ingrid couldn't tell from his expression if he recognized her or not. "Well?"

"It could be her. It certainly looks a hell of a lot like her." He raised his gaze and stared at Ingrid. "Who is this woman?"

"That's what I'm trying to find out." She lowered her voice: "Is she your surrogate?"

He looked again at the image on the phone and shook his head. "How recent is this photo?"

"Um, I don't know."

"Because Kate-Lynn doesn't look like this right now. She's got preg face, you know what I mean?"

"I think so."

"She's kind of ballooned up, not just here," he said, holding his coffee in front of his own padded belly.

Ingrid switched her weight onto her other foot, dropping her left hip: the new boots were taking a little getting used to. She leaned against the wall as a man on a penny-farthing bicycle rode past. She wasn't sure what vintage a penny-farthing was, but suspected it was older than the Roaring Twenties *The Belgravia Set* depicted. "This may sound like an odd question, but the girl who stayed at your house the other night, she was definitely pregnant?"

"Pardon?"

She inhaled sharply, knowing full well that her next question sounded ridiculous. "There's no way she could have had a cushion up her dress?"

Truman Cooper's eyes widened. "What kind of a question is that?"

Ingrid didn't answer.

"No, no way. Absolutely not," he said. "I felt the baby kick. Why would you ask something like that?"

Ingrid closed her eyes, and took a moment to calculate how much information she should share with Truman Cooper. He was much calmer this morning. In fact, he seemed much more like the man Tom Kerrison had described.

"Agent? Why are you asking?"

She took a deep breath, and an enormous risk: "It seems there are two twenty-year-old women called Kate-Lynn Bowers from Aurora, Illinois, and you're looking at one of them."

He looked again and shook his head.

"While looking for the girl who disappeared from your house yesterday I came across this girl, and she is definitely not in London."

"You have a location for her?"

"She's at home in Aurora."

"You're sure she's there, and not here?"

Ingrid wasn't about to tell him she was on a mortuary slab. "Very sure."

"Then they have to be sisters."

"With the same name?"

He handed her the phone. He stroked his mustache, looked down at his shoes and then stared hard into Ingrid's eyes, transformed now into a man of menace. "So where is my son, agent?"

She put the phone back in her bag. "That I can't tell you, not yet. But I have colleagues tracking her social media accounts, I'm still trying to find out who paid for her flight and I have alerts in with all the maternity units in London. When she runs out of that five hundred pounds, she'll surface. She has to."

He seemed reassured by her confidence. "And this woman in Illinois? What's she got to do with my son?"

"Honestly, I'm not sure, but at least you know I'm following up every possible lead." That took the wind out of his sails.

"Mr Cooper? There you are." A young woman in hoodie, jeans, Converse sneakers and headset holding a clipboard walked toward them. "They're ready for you."

"Just a minute," he said to her. He switched his attention back to Ingrid: "What happens now?"

"We both go back to work."

He nodded slowly.

"Listen," Ingrid said, "can I have your number? It took me a long time to track you down this morning when I could have updated you by phone."

They took a few steps down the alley back toward the square. Bright arc lights had been turned on to mimic low winter sun. Truman Cooper handed Ingrid his coffee and started to pull on his gloves. "Manuela will give it to you."

"You don't know it?"

"Not a clue." They reached the end of the alley, and standing just round the corner was the ever-present Manuela. "The very woman."

Had she been listening to their conversation? Truman Cooper asked her to give Ingrid his number.

"I will text it you." Each syllable was uttered with the same weight and pace.

"But your phone is switched off," Ingrid said.

"No," she said simply. "I turn it on. No problem."

The woman with the clipboard led Truman Cooper toward a huddle of activity, and he was soon obscured by a curious mix of women in crinoline skirts and men with beer bellies protruding beneath their Iron Maiden tee-shirts. Ingrid deactivated flight mode on her phone. "You're sure this is OK? It won't interfere with the equipment?"

The implacable Manuela shrugged. "What is your number?"

Ingrid gave it to her and the assistant sent her an SMS.

"It is coming," Manuela said.

"*Gracias.*"

Manuela's eyebrows pinched in the middle. "I am not Spanish." Clearly she was insulted by Ingrid's presumption.

"Oh."

"Portuguese."

"Then, *obrigada.*"

"Very good," Manuela said, the tiniest flicker of a smile surfacing on her plum-colored mouth.

Ingrid's phone buzzed in her hand. It wasn't Manuela's message, but an international caller. She swiped to answer as she walked back toward the cordon.

"Agent Skyberg."

"Hello agent, my name is Benjamin Dilner, Agent Dilner. I work in the Chicago field office."

"Hi," she said, keeping her voice low until she got further away from the filming. "Are you calling about Kate-Lynn Bowers?"

"Sergeant Tillbrook from the APD said you'd been in contact yesterday."

"That's right, I—"

"Well it's now a federal case."

Ingrid reached the security guard and was let back out into the throng of fans.

"Why? What's happened?"

"Ballistics are back. Kate-Lynn Bowers was killed by the same weapon used in a gangland murder on Christmas Eve last year."

22

Ingrid pushed her way past the tourists, bumping into the big guy in the baseball cap in her haste to get away.

"The photo you sent to Sergeant Tillbrook," Agent Dilner continued, "we're pretty sure that's Kate-Lynn's seventeen-year-old sister, Kristyn." Ingrid stopped dead still for a moment. The girl she was looking for was only seventeen? And about to give birth in a foreign city? Her stomach lurched just imagining how scared she must be. "Now," Agent Dilner exhaled loudly, "are you thinking what I'm thinking?"

"I'm pretty sure we're on the same page." Ingrid started walking again, heading down a leafy residential street. In the background, she could hear voices arguing. It wasn't yet 3 a.m. in Chicago. Why was Dilner's office so busy in the middle of the night?

"Actually, I think we might be a chapter or two ahead of you over here," he said. "Kristyn Bowers is the only surviving witness to the murder of Michael Oboloyo, a small-time property developer. The other witness, a school friend of Kristyn's by the name of Dion Paphitis, known as D, always claimed she was there with him, but she hasn't been seen since Oboloyo went down. Until, that is, you sent her photo to Sergeant Tillbrook."

Ingrid reached an intersection, looked both ways and took the street she hoped would lead to a main road and the chance to hail a cab. "What happened to the boy? To this Dino?"

"Dion."

"You said Kristyn was the only surviving witness. So what happened to him?"

"Knifed to death six days ago on the forecourt of a Taco Bell. Now here's the thing," Dilner continued, "Paphitis had been in witness protection. New identity. New location. He was due in court on Monday, three days from now, to testify against the suspect in Oboloyo's murder."

Ingrid's feet started to move as quickly as her thoughts. She instantly knew why Dilner was calling. "And let me guess: if I can't find Kristyn Bowers and get her to testify on Monday, your case falls apart and the killer walks free?" Her skin froze as she spoke. *Please tell me I'm wrong.*

"Damn you're good, agent. No wonder Louden hired you."

Ingrid heard a diesel engine behind her and turned in the hope it would be a black cab. It was a delivery van. She carried on walking, picking up speed. She needed to get to her desk. "You know Louden?"

"She passed through here a couple of years ago. We like to think we were an important step on her career ladder." Amy Louden was a bit like Marshall: they'd both go anywhere and do anything for a promotion.

"Who's the guy on trial? Who killed the property developer, and presumably the kid outside the Taco Bell and Kate-Lynn Bowers?"

Dilner took a beat before answering. "Dennis Sutcliffe."

Ingrid's heart felt heavy, like it was sinking inside her ribcage. "Sooty? He's on trial again?"

"And this time we want the conviction."

Dennis 'Sooty' Sutcliffe was a name Ingrid remembered from her university days in Chicago. A member of the Latin Kings, he'd been on trial in the late nineties for murdering three people. Even though there was DNA evidence, eyewitnesses and CCTV footage that put him at the crime scene just minutes before the shootings, the jury had acquitted him. He was the Illinois version of OJ Simpson, guilty in the media, guilty in the bars and barbershops, but still free to roam the streets. He hadn't been rich enough to bribe the jury, so the suspicion was he'd threatened and intimidated his way to freedom. If Kristyn Bowers could make sure he was finally found guilty, Ingrid would have done a good day's work.

"So when will you be here?" Ingrid asked. "When's the first flight out?"

The cacophony behind him was loud enough to compete with the road noise around her. What was going on in Chicago?

"No can do, agent. We have a big operation going down. Been in the planning for months. All leave has been cancelled. All roles assigned. Believe me, I'd love to take a break in London, but there's no way I can leave the city, not this weekend."

Great.

"You can't be the only agent in London. Can't you pull in help from other cases?"

Fat chance. The idea that CT and CI agents would lend her a few days—even a few hours—to help put away a gangster from the suburbs was somewhere between zero and zilch. Not with the Snowden leaks and Syria kicking off. Up ahead was a set of traffic lights; that meant she had to be approaching a main road. She broke into a run, testing her new boots.

"Agent Dilner," she said, "I'm going to need your help."

"I can't—"

"No, I understand. I'll do the legwork, but I need you to authorize a few things, set a few things in motion. I need intel. If you want Kristyn Bowers in court on Monday, that means I've only got forty-eight hours to find her and get her on a plane. If there are strings you can strum, I need you to start playing a tune."

"Understood."

Ingrid reached a busy high street. Shops, cafés, buses, but no damn taxis. She looked up the road, then down. *Come on.* "So, first things first: do you think Kate-Lynn was killed because they thought she was Kristyn? If they look so much alike, was it mistaken identity?" She kept looking up and down the street, hoping a black cab with an orange light would swing into view.

"It's not clear, but I'd say it's unlikely. Kate-Lynn lived in the kind of apartment building where she'd have been in regular contact with the Kings. Most likely they would have known her." He put his hand over the receiver and said something inaudible to someone in his office. "Sorry about that, we're starting to move out."

"Then talk quick and start emailing me everything I'm going to need. You have background on the Latin Kings?"

"Sure."

"And whatever gang Oboloyo was part of."

"He wasn't a gang member. He was just your regular crooked property developer who stole money from the wrong guy. I'm attaching everything I've got in an email to you now."

A black cab appeared up ahead, but its light wasn't on. Ingrid wondered how close the nearest Tube station was. "So, back to Kate-Lynn. If it's the same gun they used to kill Oboloyo, they were sending a message, right?"

"That's my theory too. They couldn't get to Kristyn but they wanted to send her a message. Why else use the same gun? They wanted her to know if she came out of hiding, if she turns up in that court on Monday, then they got another bullet just for her."

Ingrid's thoughts zoomed in on the nursery in Truman Cooper's house and the .38 caliber. She needed a few moments to piece things together, to make the connections. "Tell me about Kate-Lynn. Tillbrook said it was an assassination."

"Seems she was just home watching TV; it was still on when the cops were called. No sign of forced entry, though it was a dime-store lock. Time of death is pretty broad. Pathology think she'd been there for three days so it's hard to be specific, but there were dinner things in the sink, not breakfast things, and her boy was in his PJs, so we're guessing she'd put the boy to bed, and settled down for the night until someone she knew knocked on, or down, her door."

"Taxi!" Ingrid shouted and stuck her hand out. "Taxi!" The cab swerved toward the sidewalk and slowed down. She exhaled as the driver lowered his window. "Grosvenor Square." She jumped in. "You still there?"

"Still here," Dilner said. "But not for much longer. You got about a minute more of my time."

"Then you have to do one thing. Kristyn Bowers traveled on her sister's passport and I'm guessing she didn't have the kind of money to pay for a flight. She was on a United flight, left LAX two days ago. You need to authorize a warrant to find out who paid for her flight."

"Hang on a sec. You're saying Kristyn Bowers only just went to England? Where's she been for the past nine months?"

"California. It's a long story."

"So who reported her missing?"

"A client of hers."

"She's a hooker?"

She might have been selling her body, but not like that. "Not as far as I know, but who knows what she'll have to do for money now she's on the run. Listen, arrange the warrant, let's find out who paid for the flight, put a lock on Kate-Lynn Bowers' passport and send me that intel."

"Email's on its way. Do you know where to find her, agent?"

The cab was stuck in traffic. Ingrid didn't have time for this. "Not yet, but I do have a lead."

"You do?"

She leaned forward and tapped the glass to speak to the driver. "Change of plan. Take me to Vauxhall."

23

Even though the cab hadn't moved for five minutes, the meter continued to tick over.

"It'll be all right once we're through this junction," the driver said. "After this it's a straight run down to the river."

Ingrid didn't really care. It gave her time to work a few things out. She dialed Jennifer's number.

"Legal Attaché program, criminal division." It was Don's voice.

"It's Skyberg. Where's Jennifer?"

"Oh, hi. Um, she's, ah—"

Cut to the chase. "Don?"

"Agent Simmons asked her to shadow him today." He sounded appropriately sheepish. Everyone knew they'd had a stand-up row the day before.

"And she said 'yes'?"

"He kind of didn't give her a choice."

Ingrid thumped a fist into the fake leather seat. "But she's *my* assistant. She works for the criminal division not Git-Man's counter-terrorism."

Don took a deep breath. "She knows that. She was real uncomfortable about it."

Ingrid was so angry she could spit. Agent Eugene Simmons was a manipulative, unprofessional, bullying piece of shit.

Taking advantage of a keen and eager-to-please girl. Putting her in an awkward position. What had Sol called him? An asshole. And a jerk. And a thug. And a… she didn't have time to be angry, but the next time Ingrid saw him she was going to do a hell of a lot more than swear at him in Russian.

"OK then, Don, whatever it is you're working on, park it," Ingrid said. "Whatever is on your desk, clear it. We've got work to do."

"Oh, OK. Cool."

Cool? Did he really just say 'cool'? "The Kate-Lynn Bowers case is now the Kristyn Bowers case."

"Her younger sister?"

"You know about her?" Ingrid almost gasped. Something inside her leapt at the thought Kristyn was going to be easier to find now they had the right name.

"Only from Facebook. An old post of Kate-Lynn's, years ago."

"Is Kristyn on Facebook?"

"She's only seventeen, isn't she? She's going to want to hang out on Facebook as much as she's going to want to think about her 401k."

"What about elsewhere online? Any trace of her?"

"Not that I remember. I'll check with Jen, but give me a couple of hours and I'll see what I can find. Might help if I knew who she was."

Ingrid looked through the glass at the taxi driver. He would be hanging on every word; eavesdropping was one of the perks of the job, like being paid in cash. She calculated the risk was low: black cab drivers were supposed to be like priests; what gets said in the cab stays in the cab. She inhaled. "You paying attention?"

"Always."

"Kristyn Bowers witnesses a murder late last year. She disappears. No one knows where she is, because she starts using her sister's ID." Ingrid paused as she pieced together the next part of the story. "She enrolls in a surrogate program in California—"

"What?"

"You know, being paid to have someone else's baby."

"I know what surrogacy is. But she's seventeen. That's got to be illegal." Don sounded almost prim.

"So we can assume she used Kate-Lynn's ID for that too." Ingrid had lost her original train of thought and took a moment to grasp the right thread. "So, she's in California… the murder suspect comes to trial, then, in the past couple weeks, the witnesses start getting bumped off. So, I'm guessing Kristyn gets spooked, and uses Kate-Lynn's passport to come to London." Saying things out loud helped clarify matters.

"Is it OK if I ask a question?"

"Fire away."

"Why London?"

"That's where the parents of her unborn baby live." Saying 'parents' felt a little odd, but she guessed that was the best way to describe Tom and Truman. "She must have thought she'd be safer here." The moment she said those words, they troubled Ingrid: why hadn't Kristyn been safe in California? Dilner had said no one knew where she had been since Oboloyo's murder. But something had made her run. "So now she's missing. She's seventeen. She's eight months pregnant and her sister's just been murdered. Don, we have to find her."

The taxi started moving. Finally.

"What do you need me to do?" The guy sounded nervous.

I need you to be Jennifer. "First, call the maternity units again. Then find all her social media accounts and track down someone she knows in London. Hell, someone she knows in *Europe* would be a start. Can you handle that?"

Silence. Not a good sign. "Yup, just making notes."

"I need to know you've got this, Don."

"I'm on it." He knew the right thing to say, but he wasn't saying it with conviction.

"Whatever else you were doing today, cancel it. I need, *we* need, to get this girl on a plane to Chicago within forty-eight hours because she absolutely has to testify at that murder trial. The Bureau's been trying to get this guy in jail for over a decade. We're going to get her on that plane. Got it?" Ingrid caught the taxi driver's eye in the rearview mirror. "Can't you go any faster?"

He stopped looking at her and started paying attention to the traffic.

"Um, Agent Skyberg?" Don said.

"Yes?"

"I'm guessing this is a bad time to mention target practice?"

"Not unless you want to be the target."

Ingrid swiped to end the call, then immediately scrolled through her contacts for Sol.

"Sol Franklin."

"It's Skyberg."

"I'm about to go into a meeting."

"Who with?"

"Since when did you start asking questions like that?"

"Since Agent Dickhead commandeers my assistant without the courtesy of consulting me."

"He ran it by me."

"Sol!" Ingrid was gripping the phone so tight the screen was in danger of cracking. "You didn't even think to mention it!"

"I'm mentioning it now."

Ingrid took a deep, hard breath and filled him in on the basics of the hunt for Kristyn Bowers. "So I need bodies. I need backup. For the next forty-eight hours, I need to pull in a helping hand from counter-terror, or counter-intel and I absolutely need my own goddamned assistant!"

Sol didn't say anything.

"What? Some other secret operation I don't know about?" Ingrid said as the cab drove down a canyon of high-rise blocks in the financial district. "Some big ball Cinderella isn't invited to?"

Sol sighed. "Something like that."

"Then I need you to do something for me because I don't know when I'll be back at my desk. Can you at least file a request for local support for me? I'm going to need to pull in the Met if the Bureau won't help its own."

"Agent," he said—it was never a good sign when Sol called her 'agent'—"you know as well as I do that'll take forty-eight hours to become effective. You've got contacts there. You're our Met liaison for Chrissakes. I suggest you make those calls. Right now, there's a war starting in Syria and I've got to make like a good soldier and get to a meeting."

For a moment, neither of them said anything.

"I'll see what I can do about Jennifer," he said before hanging up.

Ingrid dropped her cell into her lap. She glanced up at the meter. It was already over £25. She didn't know how much cash she had on her. She opened her bag and felt inside for her wallet. She had £40 and some change. "How much longer?" she asked.

"We'll be at the river in a minute. Cut through Elephant and Castle. Should be less than ten," he said.

Ingrid's phone buzzed in her lap. The illuminated screen told her she had a text from Ralph. Use your Met contacts, she heard Sol say. She swiped to read the message.

What are you doing tonight? Drink? Maybe? Perhaps?

She should call him. Even though she didn't have time for a drink, and even though she had to tell him about Minnesota, she should absolutely call him. She flushed at the thought. Maybe later. The Met contact she really wanted to hear from was McKittrick, but right about now she was probably sitting at one end of a long boardroom table, finding out whether or not she still had a job.

Of course, there was one other person Ingrid could dial for help, but Nick Angelis was someone you only called when you had absolutely no other choice.

Ingrid tapped her phone back into life and read the documents Dilner had sent through. The details of Oboloyo's murder were gruesome. His body parts had been sent, one by one, day by day, to his widow: the more she read, the more determined she was that Dennis Sutcliffe had to be put behind bars. And to do that she had to find Kristyn. She just had to find her.

"Where do you want me to drop you?"

Ingrid looked at the meter: £38.80. "Right here, right now."

She opened the door and stepped onto the sidewalk of a busy six lane highway. She handed two £20 notes through the open window to the driver. She resisted saying 'keep the change' and only hoped that, somewhere in the universe, the fact she had over-tipped the night of Tom Kerrison's private view somehow balanced out her penny-pinching this time around.

She walked briskly toward the row of shops she'd seen the previous morning. Vauxhall was little more than an intersection combined with a construction site: the new embassy was being built somewhere nearby. Between six lanes of traffic and the bus, Tube and railway stations, Vauxhall was the sort of neighborhood you passed through. It wasn't a destination. Yet this was the place Kristyn Bowers had asked for directions to. Why? It wasn't anywhere she'd have seen in a movie. It wouldn't have gotten a mention in any guidebook.

The only connection Ingrid could make between a scared seventeen-year-old girl on the run and Vauxhall was the enigmatic Manuela: she was from Portugal and Vauxhall was full of Portuguese restaurants. Someone had to have guided Kristyn's choices. Someone had to be helping her. Ingrid was working on a hunch that Manuela must have given her an address of somewhere she could go, or the name of someone who could get her to safety. It was a long shot, but when you've only got one lead, you follow it.

Ingrid walked past a Portuguese deli, a tapas bar and a specialist Portuguese bakery displaying custard tarts ranging in size from gem-like to gigantic. There were just too many establishments to choose from. Somehow she needed to make the connection between one of them and Manuela. Further down the highway, on the opposite side of the street, she came to Café Porto and something about it was attracting her attention. She crossed the road to take a closer look.

It was more of a sandwich shop than a café and didn't look

like it had been remodeled since the 1960s. Its windows were covered with a film of grime, but Ingrid peered inside as best she could. She looked down and saw the morning's mail was still on the mat: the place hadn't opened for breakfast, and it didn't look like it was preparing to open for lunch. That raised Ingrid's interest: what were the owners of Café Porto doing instead? What urgent mission had taken them away from making the day's profit?

And then she made the connection. Stacked above the coffee machine were leaning towers of cardboard cups, all of which bore the café's logo: a red rooster. She had seen the same cup on Manuela's desk. Adrenaline surged through her blood. Whether the place was owned by Manuela's relatives or she was just a regular customer, she now had a reason why Kristyn had headed for Vauxhall.

Ingrid knocked on the door. She didn't expect anyone to answer: the place had clearly been abandoned for something more important. Like helping a teenage runaway to disappear. She knocked again, waited, then ducked down an alley that led into a yard behind the café. Smelling of urine and barely three feet wide, it was cluttered with crates and trash bags. Ingrid stepped carefully through the obstacles and quickly found herself in what was more of a garden than a yard. Sun-bleached plastic garden furniture was strewn across an overgrown lawn that extended thirty or forty feet toward a broken fence. The next time someone told her that working for the FBI sounded glamorous, she'd tell them about this place.

She looked up at the back of the building. Five stories high, a different kind of drape at each window, many of which were cracked and held together with tape. Weeds were sprouting from the guttering.

Ingrid shoved her shoulder bag so it rested on her behind and planted her hands on her hips. She stood and stared at the building and slowly started shaking her head. This was a wrong turn, a bad move. She thought about how manicured, how perfect, how *precise* Manuela was: it seemed too unlikely that this run-down place would have a connection to Truman Cooper's assistant. The red rooster was a red herring. She needed to leave. Just as she headed for the alleyway, a tall thick-set man emerged from it.

"Who are you?" He was holding a meat cleaver.

"Health and safety."

24

The man was six feet tall and wearing a sports coat over a shirt. Either he hadn't shaved for a few days or he had just trimmed his beard. The greasy hair smoothed over his head suggested it was the former. He looked like he'd slept as much as he'd washed. She'd guess he was forty, but a shave and a shower might take a decade off her estimate.

"You don't look like health and safety," he said.

"I knocked at the front."

"Not open today." His accent was almost identical to Manuela's, though the woman spoke so little it was hard to judge accurately.

"It was a joke. I'd have a clipboard if I was coming to do an inspection," she smiled at him, and took a step toward him. "I'm Sarah. A friend of Manuela's." He looked confused, but moved the cleaver to his left hand and accepted Ingrid's offer of a handshake. "She said you could help me."

He nodded. "Inside."

He fumbled with a large bunch of keys and opened the back door to the café. No amount of training could compensate for the sensation that following a strange, grumpy man holding a meat cleaver into an empty building was a bad idea, but Ingrid nevertheless stepped inside and made her way through a maze of stacks of cardboard boxes and into the kitchen. She was trained to disconnect offenders from their weapons. She could handle it.

The man slammed the cleaver down on the counter. He looked deliberately down at the heavy blade then slowly up at Ingrid. "Who is Manuela?"

"You know Manuela," Ingrid said, trying to sound friendly and casual. "Long dark hair, brown eyes, always dresses real smart?"

He shoved his tongue between his lips and his teeth. He was suspicious of her.

"Anyway, she said you were the one who could help me find Kristyn." Ingrid just hoped that if she kept talking, something would come to her and he'd take his hand away from the meat cleaver.

"I don't have Kristyn. You have bad information."

"But you know where I can find her?" Ingrid's use of the word 'her' seemed to throw him. "I need to find Kristyn. Or Kate-Lynn. Do you know where Kate-Lynn is?"

He shook his head. "You have the wrong guy, wrong place."

"Please! It's important. I have to find her. You have to help me."

The man placed his hand over the handle of the cleaver. He really wanted her to go. Ingrid looked from the blade up to his grubby, serious face. The windows rattled as an articulated truck rumbled past the window, and the ground vibrated beneath her. Or maybe it was just her knees shaking.

"Go. I don't have crystal."

Had she finally heard him right. Crystal? Is that what he'd been saying? The guy was a goddamned meth dealer?

"What about a little," she dabbed at her nose, "you know?" Maybe Manuela picked up a little something extra when she bought her coffee?

His expression didn't change. His hand was still on the meat cleaver. "Go."

Ingrid reached into her purse and pulled out one of her phones. She pressed a few buttons and put the Nokia on silent.

"I'm gonna call Manuela," she said. "She was sure you'd be able to help."

He glowered at her.

"No, silly me. Wrong phone." She could play dumb while acting smart. She grabbed the iPhone from her jacket pocket, dialed the Nokia then answered her own phone. "Jeez, this is confusing. I don't have her number—"

He picked up the cleaver and slammed it onto the counter. Ingrid flinched.

"You go. Now."

"OK. I got bad information, what can I tell you."

He moved toward the street door, an enormous bunch of keys in his hand. While the man fiddled with the lock, she placed the Nokia behind a chair stored upside down on one of the tables. He opened the door. "You go now."

"You really don't know Manuela?" Ingrid asked.

"Go!"

She stepped out onto the noisy sidewalk. She needed to find somewhere quieter, quick. The first door she came to was a betting shop, but she'd attract too much attention in there. She put her finger over the iPhone's microphone and hurried down the street. The motorcycle showroom was up ahead. She ran for it.

The dealership smelt of polish and leather, and when the double-glazed door swung shut behind her, she exhaled: it was like walking into a sound-proofed booth compared to the traffic noise outside. Ingrid clamped her phone to her ear and listened.

Nothing. She checked the screen. The call duration was two minutes and four seconds: she was still connected to the Nokia. She hoped her improvised listening device would tell her whether or not Mr Cleaver really did have anything to do with Kristyn's disappearance.

"Can I help you?" said a smiling woman in her twenties.

Ingrid raised a finger to her mouth.

"Let me know if you need anything."

Ingrid nodded and walked through an archway into another

part of the showroom. She found herself standing in front of a row of Triumphs, but forced herself not to look at the specifications, or the prices. She took her finger off the microphone, put it in her other ear and listened intently. Footsteps. Mr Cleaver was on the move.

The footsteps got louder. He was moving toward the Nokia. Ingrid gulped hard. *Please don't spot it.*

"Still here." He was on the phone, pacing up and down.

Aware she was breathing deeply, Ingrid put her finger back over the microphone.

"Crystal," he said, then after a pause, he said it again. "She kept asking for crystal, but I tell her I don't know what this is… What do you think?" He walked away from the Nokia, making it harder for Ingrid to hear him. "You want to go ahead?" she thought she heard him say. "I don't think she's cop. American. Dressed too nice, you know." Ingrid had to smile a little. "OK," he said, "see you at two." Then there was a loud clatter as if he'd kicked something.

Ingrid hung up. She'd heard enough. He wasn't on the phone to Manuela and he wasn't talking about a runaway. If she'd been recording the call she'd have evidence of a drug deal happening at 2 p.m., but that was something she was going to pretend she'd never heard. Without thinking, her hand stretched out and caressed a chrome headlight on a Thunderbird. She noticed the price tag hanging off the handlebars: £8,999. Worth every penny.

"Thanks very much," she said to the sales assistant and pushed open the double-glazed doors onto the forecourt. She ran back up to Café Porto and knocked on the door. The man turned, saw it was her and gesticulated she should get lost. She knocked again. He slammed a hand against the counter then reluctantly stomped over to the door. He unlocked it.

"I cannot help you."

"Sorry. I think I left my phone." She gave him one of her best smiles. "I think I put it down…" She slid past him and into the empty café. "See, here it is." She waved the Nokia at him. "So glad I realized before I got on the Tube."

Before he could say anything she was back on the sidewalk.

She threw the Nokia in her bag, and opened her contacts on the iPhone.

"Hey," McKittrick said.

"Oh, no, that doesn't sound good," Ingrid said. "I hope that's a hangover I can hear in your voice and not—"

"No, it's unemployment. This is what stupidity sounds like." Ingrid didn't know what to say. It certainly wasn't the right moment to mention a slam-dunk tip about a drug deal. She thought she heard McKittrick sob. "Suspended. At least three months while they investigate further. No third umpire. No review. I'm out and back in the pavilion. Or rather the pub."

Was that a cricketing metaphor? Ingrid carried on down the street looking for other Portuguese businesses. She stopped at a set of traffic lights and waited to cross. "Who's with you?"

"My good friend vodka and her sidekick tonic. Want to join me?"

Ingrid didn't answer. On the other side of the street there was a man in a White Sox shirt. His baseball cap, peak pulled over to the left, was low over his forehead. It was the man from the cordon in Islington.

"Ingrid? Did you hear me?"

She continued to look at the baseball fan on the other side of the street. It was definitely the same guy. What the hell was he doing here? "Natasha, I'm really sorry, I can't. Something just came up."

25

Ingrid stared at the man in the White Sox shirt on the other side of the intersection. He was built like a linebacker, well over six feet tall and the unhealthy side of two hundred and fifty pounds. The four lanes of traffic between them slowed, and one of the beautiful new double-decker Routemaster buses briefly came to a halt at the junction. It was the first time Ingrid had seen one in the flesh and she took a moment to admire its bold curves. When it pulled away, the man had gone. It was as if a magician's cloak had swept in front of him and made him disappear.

Ingrid pushed the hair off her forehead and stood at the traffic lights, mouth agape. Where the hell had he gone? The only option was a side road about twenty yards ahead.

She couldn't wait for the lights to change. She held out her right hand, palm raised, made eye contact with the driver of an oncoming car who slowed as she stepped out in front of him. She'd made it a quarter of the way across. She stood on the dashed white lines, standing between two lanes of free-flowing traffic, looking for a gap. A white van sped past, inches from her face. She spotted her chance and darted onto the traffic island in the middle of the road.

She looked left, raised her left palm to the oncoming traffic and stepped out, daring the driver of a black Mini to run her over, and within seconds she had navigated her way to the sidewalk on the far side and safety.

Immediately and instinctively, Ingrid started to run. She reached the turning and accelerated into the side road, lined on both sides with brick-built two-story row houses. She scanned the road ahead but couldn't see him. Where was he? He was a big guy: there was no way he could have outrun her, and there was nowhere for him to hide either. He had to have taken a different route.

Ingrid dashed back to the busy highway and scanned all the possible exits. There wasn't anywhere he could have reached in the time: he had simply disappeared. Just as Ingrid was starting to think she had imagined him, she caught sight of the red double-decker bus. *That's* how he'd disappeared.

The bus was already a hundred and fifty yards down the road but the traffic was heavy and there were so many traffic lights that Ingrid rated her chances of catching up with it. She started running again, the new boots only hampering her speed a little. Ahead of her, a group of women in hijabs walked four abreast, blocking the sidewalk. Ingrid pumped her arms hard and leapt onto a low concrete wall to bypass them, running at full speed for several paces before bouncing down onto the sidewalk via a wooden bench.

The bus was pulling away from her. It would have to stop soon; all she had to do was keep it in sight. She picked up speed, her shoulder bag slamming into her hip with every stride. Up ahead, two men pushed a cart across the sidewalk, delivering bags of cement to a construction site. Ingrid ran straight for them.

"Hey, watch out!" one of them shouted.

Ingrid vaulted over their cart.

"Not bad," said the other as she sped away from them. It felt good to be on the move and when the burn started to electrify her limbs she smiled: other agents could chase felons, but not many could close in on a moving vehicle.

The bus indicated to turn left and it slowed to make the maneuver. By the time it disappeared from view, Ingrid was only sixty yards behind. She reached the corner ten seconds later, and saw a bus stop in the middle distance. She willed someone to stick out their hand and get the bus to pull over.

She came to a building site. On one side of her were huge constructors' fence panels, while on the other scaffold poles supported overhead workers. It meant the sidewalk narrowed to almost exactly the same width as the double buggy an exasperated mother was pushing toward her. Ingrid flung herself at a scaffold pole, using it to swing out into the road before continuing her run.

The passengers waiting at the bus stop started to shuffle and one of them stretched out an arm to signal to the driver. Ingrid pushed hard, desperate to catch up with the bus. It indicated to pull over. She kept running hard, her lungs starting to hurt a little.

The driver applied the brakes and opened the doors. No one got off, and only one person got on. The doors would close again in just a few seconds, but the new Routemaster buses were open at the back, allowing passengers to jump on and off between stops.

Ingrid started waving, hoping the driver would look in his mirrors before pulling away. She accelerated, her new leather jacket rigid against her muscles, restricting her movement. She was close enough to see the driver in his wing mirror. She urged him to notice her. The doors closed. The indicator was turned on. Ingrid kept running; she was just ten yards away. Then the bus edged forward, pulling out into the road between cars. Ingrid calculated she had twenty yards before the bus would be traveling faster than she could run. Her heels pounded into the sidewalk and she pushed through her toes, her arms scissoring up and down: she was gaining. Four strides, three, two… Ingrid prepared to leap, her arms reaching out for the handrail and for a moment she was airborne. She grabbed the rail, bent her knees and brought her feet down on the footplate.

A woman sitting on the rear seats, shopping bags on her knees, looked at Ingrid who was panting hard. "There's another one right behind," she said.

Ingrid shoved a hand into her bag in search of her Oyster

card. She leaned against the rear stairs and scanned the passengers on the lower deck. He wasn't there. She pulled out her Oyster card and tapped it against the ticket reader, then bounded up to the top deck as the bus headed north over Vauxhall Bridge. She walked forward, aware that beads of sweat were pricking at her hairline: running in leather was a bit like running in 100 per cent humidity. From behind, she could see that no one was wearing a baseball cap. He must have taken it off. But there were only six people on the top deck, and none of them looked like an overgrown American sports fan. She kept walking toward the front, lurching as the bus took a bend too quickly, in case her assessment was wrong. She reached the front staircase and turned to look at the passengers' faces. She had been correct: Mr White Sox wasn't on the top deck. She slumped down onto a seat and took a minute to get her breath back.

The bell rang and the LED display screen switched to 'bus stopping'. Ingrid looked out of the window, not quite sure which bit of London she was now in. The bus pulled over to the curb and Ingrid tried to see a street sign to get her bearings. She couldn't see one, and didn't recognize any landmarks, so she got out her phone and opened Google Maps. The GPS would tell her where she was. By the time the bus started to pull away, her breathing had returned to normal. While the app loaded, she gazed out of the window: standing at the bus stop and looking decidedly lost was Mr White Sox.

Shit. *Shit.*

She rang the bell, leapt out of her seat and shoved her phone in her pocket as she ran to the rear of the bus, then jumped down the stairs two at a time. Below her, the rear of the bus was open to the street. Her momentum was carrying her so fast that she wouldn't be able to stop herself from tumbling out onto the blacktop, and under the wheels of whatever vehicle was behind. Ingrid reached out for the handrail. Her right hand grabbed hard, but she missed with her left. Her legs carried on moving beneath her till they were outside the bus. She reached up with her free hand, grasped the rail, bent her knees and just brought her feet back inside the bus as it accelerated away. A gymnastic display Svetlana would have been proud of.

Ingrid stood in the open doorway, panting heavily, as the Chicago sports fan receded into the distance.

"You need to slow down," the woman with the shopping said. "You'll come a cropper one day."

Ingrid got off at the next stop and checked her phone to find out where she was.

She was in Pimlico. About half a block from the Queen Mary pub.

26

Ingrid saw the reflection of a well-dressed, slim woman in the window of the double doors of the Queen Mary and it took a moment to realize she was looking at herself. She looked so different in her new clothes.

After the strange emptiness and sirens the day before, it wouldn't have been entirely surprising for a bobby to be standing sentry outside, but there was just a man smoking a cigarette. He gave Ingrid the once-over as she walked—a little more tentatively than usual—toward the entrance.

Shoulders back. Stomach in. Smile.

She pushed open the double doors and the smell of beer instantly wrinkled her nose. The place wasn't deserted like it had been the day before, but it was far from full. She strode confidently up to the bar and perched on a stool upholstered in what looked like carpet. The barman was leaning over the counter, reading the sports pages of a tabloid newspaper. She glanced round: not only was she the only woman in the place, she was also the only person under forty. A piece of tape with a strip of the 'Good Luck' sign still attached drifted like a cobweb from the paneling above the counter. It was the only visible sign of yesterday's abandoned party, assuming of course that every trace of blood had been cleaned from the toilets.

"Hi," she said, forcing the barman to look up at her, "I wonder if you can help me?"

He gave her a look that was probably transmitted as a smile but received as a leer. "What you like?" A Muscovite accent.

Ingrid peered over the counter to see what soft drinks were in the chiller cabinets. They had Tarkhun, a soda she hadn't drunk since her semester in St Petersburg. She was tempted, but ordering it would only attract attention.

"Mineral water, please." Though a shot of one of the many vodkas they stocked wasn't completely out of the question. The stack of paired cutlery in rolled-up napkins she'd seen on the buffet table was now on the counter next to the menus. "What time do you start serving lunch?"

He glanced at a clock on the wall next to a chalkboard advertising Russian specialties.

The barman—fifties, pock-marked nose, skinny, balding—stood up a little straighter and eyed her with caution. "In here? You want to eat here?"

"I think I'm in the right place." She took a moment, pursed her lips and decided to leap into the unknown. "My friend Irina told me you do good food here. Real authentic."

She watched his features intently as she mentioned Irina's name. His eyes narrowed almost imperceptibly. She hadn't even used the surname of the woman Ralph had mentioned and it had still got a response.

"I will check with cook." He placed a glass of ice and water on the counter and disappeared into the kitchen.

Ingrid studied the pub's other patrons. There was a pair of workmen in paint-spattered clothes drinking Coke and eating potato chips, staring at their phones on the table as if just looking at them could make them ring. Either waiting for work, or avoiding it. The three single men in the pub all had pints of beer and were presumably avoiding stress at home while cutting to the head of the line to get cirrhosis of the liver. One of the men had a dog at his feet. A pitbull. She made eye contact with the dog owner, who smiled at her. He was missing most of his teeth. Apart from the workmen, Ingrid was confident the beer drinkers were regulars, individuals loyal to their pub in the way other men are wedded to their soccer team.

Ingrid picked up her bag from the floor and put it over her shoulder, the strap lying diagonally across her chest: she didn't personally feel vulnerable—she was confident she could handle herself —but she could easily imagine how her iPhone might end up on eBay by the end of the day if she didn't take precautions.

She tried to picture Karlos Ivanov, the owner of the *Evening News*, sitting where she was now and enjoying a drink. If the Queen Mary really was somewhere he visited, and not just a location chosen by his PR for a photo opportunity, then it was a reminder of who the oligarchs from Russia really were. Their wealth hadn't been inherited. They hadn't spent their summers in the South of France or their schooldays at Eton. They were regular guys who probably grew up in apartment blocks like the one her mother had lived in. Sure, they could afford cocktails and Cristal in Mayfair's bars and clubs, but maybe they felt more at home in a place like the Queen Mary. Profiling them was going to be fascinating.

She scanned the chalkboard menu, deciding if she was in the mood for dumplings or stuffed cabbage leaves. It was only when she saw the prices next to the menu items that she remembered she had spent all her cash on the taxi. The Queen Mary didn't look like the kind of establishment that took cards. Given the residential nature of the neighborhood, she guessed she was a long walk from an ATM.

"You ask about food?"

A short, stocky man in his thirties wearing a stained blue soccer shirt—Chelsea, at a guess—stretched tight across his pot belly was standing behind her. A rope of silver chain was around his neck; his knuckles were encrusted with signet rings. She remembered the blood she had seen in the men's toilets: his jewelry was practically designed for ripping flesh.

"Hi, yes," Ingrid smiled at him. "I was just wondering how long I'd have to wait for lunch?"

The short stocky man turned to the barman. "Who is she?" he said in Russian.

He shrugged his reply: "She knows Irina."

Irina was a fairly common name. If pressed, it would be easy to explain that the imaginary friend who rated their food was a different woman from the Irina they knew.

The man in the soccer shirt scrutinized her. "You looking for work?"

That wasn't a question she'd anticipated. "Um, no. Just an early lunch."

"Food starts twelve-thirty." He turned and went back to the kitchen. It was 11:45 a.m.

Ingrid swallowed several mouthfuls of water, her throat suddenly in need of lubrication. "That's a shame," she said to the barman, who had turned his attention back to his newspaper. "I'm not sure I can wait till then. I'll just have to come back another day." She yawned: her late, drunken night was starting to catch up with her. Her next stop needed to involve caffeine.

Her thoughts returned to the man in the White Sox shirt. She could come up with two possible explanations for his appearance in Vauxhall, three if she was prepared to add in sheer coincidence. The first was that there was some unidentified magnet for American visitors in the neighborhood, something that had been posted on Twitter or Snapchat that explained why both he and Kristyn had made the trip south of the river. It was a reason she might have been prepared to entertain if it wasn't for the way he'd looked at her when they'd locked eyes at the traffic lights. He had panicked. He knew that she had seen him and he ran. So that meant her final explanation was the more likely: he had followed her there.

She yawned again. Her eyes were starting to swim a little and her brain was fogging over. Suddenly startled by the ringing phone of one of the decorators, Ingrid wondered if she'd actually nodded off for a moment. The two men got to their feet and left in a hurry: whatever instructions they'd been waiting for had obviously been delivered. She took another sip of her water and noticed that the ice cubes had melted. She checked the clock: almost midday.

That wasn't right. Couldn't be. It had been a quarter to just a few moments earlier.

The double doors swung open and two young men entered, one white, one black, wearing sweatpants and hoodies. They nodded to the barman who nodded back. "This her?" one of them said.

Ingrid's heart thundered. She shook her head, desperate to make herself wake up.

"You know Irina?" the white man said. London accent. He walked up to her, coming a little too close for comfort.

"Hi." Her throat constricted.

"He asked you a question," the black man said, now standing just two feet away.

Ingrid's forehead puckered. Why was she feeling so dizzy?

"Does she look familiar to you?"

"Yeah," his friend said. "She does."

Not the Charlize thing again.

The white man leaned in. "You look an awful lot like this bird I saw on telly yesterday. You woz running around in an empty house. Nah, I remember now. It wasn't a house, was it? It was a pub. It was *this* pub." Ingrid felt his spittle on her face and followed his gaze toward the CCTV camera above the door. She blinked hard at it, trying to focus. What was happening to her?

The black man took a step toward her and the barman stood a little straighter. Behind her, Ingrid heard a door swing shut. She glanced over her shoulder: the man in the Chelsea shirt had returned from the kitchen and was holding a knife. A sharp, long blade reflecting the twinkling lights of the fruit machines.

Ingrid felt herself wanting to slump over the bar. What the hell had they put in her drink? She had to get out of there. Her eyes drooped shut. Fight it. *Fight it.*

She clenched her teeth and focused on the double doors. Ingrid grabbed a set of cutlery from the pile at her elbow, fell forward off her stool with enough force to make the white man stumble. She carried on falling and as she tumbled into the black man she raised her hand as powerfully as she could, driving the knife and fork hard under his ribcage.

"The bitch stabbed me! The bitch fucking stabbed me."

Ingrid took another step toward the door. The white man grabbed her wrist, she rotated her arm backwards, forcing him to let go. She managed another step toward the doors. The pitbull started barking. The man with the kitchen knife ran at her. She turned, brought an open palm up to his wrist, knocking the blade to the floor.

"Who the fuck are you?" one of them shouted. She could no longer tell who was speaking. Her hearing was fading in and out. She managed another step while the Chelsea fan crouched to retrieve his weapon. The younger white guy moved in front of her.

"No you fucking don't," he said, his hands reaching up to grab Ingrid's shoulders.

She rotated into him, knocking him off balance. She continued her rotation, falling against the doors, before using all her strength to pull them open. On the sidewalk. Run. But something was holding her back. Her bag was trapped between the doors. She shoved both doors as hard as she was able and was rewarded with the sound of wood hitting skulls. She pushed the doors again, releasing her bag, then turned and ran.

She didn't look back. She didn't dare. Just run, she told herself. Just one more step. Her gait was unsteady, her pace was slow. Her lungs hurt. But this was only a jog. Not much more than a stroll. Why did she feel so weak? What drug could work so quickly? Her brain was too sluggish to figure it out. She saw a red London phone booth up ahead. Just get to the booth, then look round. She forced her right foot forward, her left leg dragging along the sidewalk. One more step. *Come on!*

Ingrid fell against the booth just as a wave of nausea rose up from her stomach. Her vomit sprayed down the glass door.

"You all right?" It was a female voice. Something inside Ingrid relaxed. She slumped onto the ground and passed out.

27

Ingrid tried to open her eyes. Some deep part of her brain willed her to open them, but the effort required was too much. She could hear voices, but couldn't tell who was talking or how far away they were. "Pulse sixty-two… back from the lab… under observation… BP one-ten over sixty-five… is that OK?… any allergies or adverse reactions… vending machine down the hallway… just a sharp scratch." Her lids were too heavy; she tried again to open them but couldn't manage. She felt something on her hand. What was it?

"Thanks, Kate." Was that McKittrick's voice?

"You look like you could use it."

She could smell coffee. Ingrid felt the pressure on her hand again. She made her right eyelid flicker. Blurred light. Nothing more. She tried again; this time her eye stayed open longer. A gurney. A hospital. Ingrid tried to move her fingers.

"Hello again," McKittrick said.

Ingrid knew she was meant to say hello back, but her tongue was heavy, pressed against the base of her mouth. With one eye open she looked down at her hand, resting on a light blue ribbed blanket. McKittrick's hand was on top of hers. Ingrid twitched her hand, and McKittrick squeezed it.

"You want some water?" she asked.

Ingrid managed to make her head nod. McKittrick got up,

picked up a plastic beaker from a table and brought it to Ingrid's lips. She took a sip.

"Are you going to stay with us this time?"

What was she talking about?

Ingrid licked her lips.

"More?" McKittrick asked.

Ingrid nodded, and her friend held the cup to her mouth once again. "What…" Ingrid swallowed. Her tongue felt strange, like it wasn't her own. She tried again: "Why are you here?"

"You don't remember?" McKittrick asked. She sat down on the edge of the gurney. "Really?"

Ingrid slowly and gently shook her head.

"Wow. We've been through this several times." McKittrick reached out for a different plastic cup, a beige one, and took a sip. "OK, I'll tell you again, and hope you're going to remember it this time. You were blue-lighted in about four hours ago, and one of the nurses here dialed the most recent number in your history, and it turns out that was me. Aren't you lucky you didn't order pizza for lunch, because the man from Domino's wouldn't have had a spare pair of trousers in just the right size in a Selfridges bag in his living room."

"Four hours?"

"Do you remember what happened?"

Ingrid tried to think. She remembered the man in the White Sox jersey. She remembered being on a bus. The concentration required was too much, she had to give up. Had she been in an accident? "No."

"Ambulance picked you up from Belgrave Road in Pimlico. The woman who dialed 999 said you were running and then collapsed—"

A slightly plump man in his late twenties, red cheeks with prickles of perspiration at his temples and a stethoscope around his neck, appeared at Ingrid's bedside. "DI McKittrick," he said, "I don't think Miss Skyberg is ready for questioning just yet."

"Dr Mullally," she said, "I'm not here for work. Ingrid's my friend."

"Ah, I see," he said, "not much fun that this is where you get to spend your spare time. You're in here enough as it is." He smiled at Ingrid. "How are you feeling?"

Ingrid didn't know how to answer. "What happened? Why am I here?"

He pushed his wire-rimmed spectacles higher on the bridge of his nose. "Do you remember me?" he asked.

"No."

"Not surprising, really. My name is Brendan Mullally; I'm one of the registrars here. Do you know where you are?"

"Hospital."

He smiled. "Well done. Was it the white coats that gave it away, or the smell?" When Ingrid didn't respond, he carried on. "You were brought in by paramedics at lunch time. You were unconscious. We're running a tox screen, but my suspicion is that you were administered a drug like Rohypnol."

Ingrid tried to remember. She could see a red phone booth. Why was that in her brain?

"Do you remember if you were drinking at lunchtime?"

McKittrick locked eyes with Mullally. "Trust me, Ingrid can handle her booze. That isn't it."

"Are you on any medication?" he asked. "Any prescription drugs?"

Prescription drugs? Why did that ring a bell? An image of a blister pack in a handbag popped into her head. Ingrid looked at McKittrick, who conspicuously avoided eye contact. Ingrid remembered about Natasha's misconduct hearing. She had said she'd lost her job, or been suspended… she'd said she was in the pub drowning her sorrows. The morning started to assemble itself in Ingrid's memory. She saw the Queen Mary pub. She felt her hand grip around a napkin filled with cutlery. *Did I stab someone*? She thought she might pass out at the memory. She closed her eyes.

"Ingrid," McKittrick said, "stay with us."

Ingrid took a deep, slow breath and opened her eyes. Did she? Did she really stab someone? She looked down at her right hand, observing it as if it was someone else's and brought it up near her face. She turned it over and looked at her palm. There was a small patch of dried blood. Her hand slumped back down onto the bed, suddenly too heavy to be held aloft.

"What is it?" McKittrick asked.

Panic coiled up from Ingrid's stomach, burning her throat. She looked up at the doctor: "Could you leave us alone for a moment?" she said.

"Of course. Rest. I'll pop back later." He looked at McKittrick: "Come and grab me when she's ready."

Ingrid watched as he walked away and saw the clock on the wall for the first time. Nearly six o'clock. *Six*? She didn't have time to lie in bed. She had to speak to people; she needed to find Kate-Lynn. No, the girl's name wasn't Kate-Lynn, that was the sister, she needed to find… She searched her cloudy memory for the name. *Kristyn*. She had to find Kristyn. She turned to her friend. "Where's my phone?"

McKittrick reached over to the nightstand and handed it to Ingrid.

"I put it on silent. And charged it."

Ingrid looked down at the screen. Fifteen messages. She scrolled through the missed calls and texts. Jennifer, Sol, Ralph, Angelis, several numbers she didn't recognize. She needed to shake the fog. She needed to think clearly.

"Natasha?" she said, not looking up from the screen. "Will you help me?"

"Sure, that's why I'm here. Though if the nurses had called any later I might have had one too many. As it is, I think I've sobered up nicely. What do you need?"

Ingrid took a moment to consider if she should release the words that were forming in her mouth. "I need you to investigate something for me."

"You do remember the bit about me being suspended, right? Cos we just mentioned it."

Ingrid nodded. "Of course," she said softly, "but this is something that I really, really don't want the police to know about." She raised her hand and showed McKittrick her palm. "This isn't my blood."

"Ingrid?" McKittrick leaned in, her voice dropped to a whisper. "What happened? What have you done?"

"That's what I need you to find out. I've remembered what happened to me this afternoon, and I have to know if I… if I might have killed someone." Her jaw started to tremble with the shock.

McKittrick reached out and placed her hand on top of Ingrid's. "Tell me what I need to know."

Ingrid relayed as much information as she could remember.

"Ingrid, you and I both know how hard it is to kill someone with a table knife."

"I have blood on my hand. I broke the skin. I even remember —" She shuddered. "I remember the blade going in. And if he was OK, why didn't his friend run after me?" Ingrid swallowed hard.

McKittrick took a deep breath. "Look around. Do you see him? This hospital is less than a mile from the Queen Mary. If he'd been stabbed, he'd be in here getting stitched up. You didn't kill him. Not unless he just slowly oozes to death and keels over when his blood pressure finally drops too low."

Ingrid stared at her.

"Sorry. No more attempts at humor. Maybe I'm still a bit drunk."

Ingrid pushed the blanket back: she had to get out of there.

"What are you doing?"

"I have to go. I have to find the girl."

"Who's the girl?"

"This missing girl."

"You've not mentioned a missing girl. I thought your current case was A-listers and mansions."

"Same case," Ingrid paused, taking a slow, deliberate breath. She grabbed her phone and swung her legs over the side of the gurney.

"What are you doing? You can use your phone in hospitals these days."

"You can also use them in the back of a cab. Where are my other trousers?"

McKittrick reached down and picked a yellow Selfridges bag up from the floor. "I saw the price tag. One hundred and ninety-five pounds? Two pairs?"

"Thank God I did buy two."

"Fair point. Just try not to throw up over this pair. I sponged the jacket down. It looks OK and mostly it just smells of new leather, so I think you've got away with it. Tiny scratch, no one will notice."

McKittrick drew the cubicle curtain across and Ingrid got dressed, selecting a black sleeveless silk blouse to go with the trousers.

"Here," McKittrick said, snapping off the price tag, "don't want you to look like a shoplifter as well as a murderer."

Ingrid glowered at her.

"Go easy on me, I probably just lost my job, and my pension, and you bring me to A&E, a place where a person with a habit like mine might get a little distracted with all the deliveries arriving from the pharmacy, so cut me some slack."

Ingrid raised her blood-stained palm.

"OK, OK, no more jokes. And no more attempts at lame excuses. Guess it's not a good time to ask again about your scar?"

"Not unless," Ingrid said as she pulled up a boot, "you want to tell me about Marcus."

McKittrick's eyes widened, as did her mouth. "How did you… No, you're right. We can both keep our secrets."

Ingrid slowly got to her feet. "How do I look?"

"We'll leave via the loo. You might want to look in a mirror. You've got a bit of…" McKittrick didn't quite know what to say. She raised a finger to the corner of her mouth. "Just a bit… here and… here."

"Some friend you are! You've let me lie here for four hours and not wiped the vomit off my face! Last night, I should tell you, for the record, *I* wiped vomit off *your* face."

"You did?" McKittrick pulled the curtain back. "Oh, God, Ingrid. I am so sorry about that."

"In a few days' time, you and me are going to have a serious conversation about some of the other things you don't remember about last night." Ingrid took a few steps forward.

"Are you going to be OK?"

"I think so."

Ingrid picked up her bag, checked she hadn't left anything vital behind and stepped out into the corridor as McKittrick strode ahead. The young doctor appeared from another cubicle.

"Ah, you must be feeling better," he said.

"Just visiting the restroom," Ingrid said.

"I'll pop back and see you in five," he said.

Five minutes later, Ingrid was in the back of a cab scrolling through the messages on her phone. A reminder about the softball match from Jennifer, a slightly pathetic suggestion from Ralph that they don't leave it too long and a laconic one from Nick Angelis that simply said 'Beaufort Club'. She came to a number she didn't recognize and tapped to read the message:

Tariq been thru CCTV footage like you asked. No pregnant lady. Cheers, Abdul (petrol station).

Ingrid's brain was still a bit foggy. She couldn't instantly recall who Abdul was. An image of an Asian man in a red quilted vest popped into her head... She smelt donuts... it was coming back to her: the gas station near Truman Cooper's house.

Ingrid remembered seeing a bank of images from CCTV cameras looking out over the pumps to the street beyond, but as the cab crossed the river she couldn't work out why this information was so important. Her instincts told her this was significant. She willed herself to work it out, to disperse the last remnants of the Rohypnol from her brain.

And then it came to her: if Kristyn wasn't on the gas station's CCTV footage, that meant she hadn't walked past the premises. And that was the only route from Truman Cooper's house to the

DLR station. Ingrid slumped back against the taxi's firm upholstery.

If Kristyn hadn't gone to the station, then she hadn't got on a train. Ingrid had simply paid the homeless girl £20 to name the first station that had come into her head. Kristyn had never gone to Vauxhall. Her only lead had turned to dust.

28

The cab pulled over to the curb. "This OK for you?" the driver asked.

Ingrid looked out the window. It definitely wasn't Regent's Park, but the illuminated displays of two ATM machines jogged her clogged and fuzzy brain.

"Great, yes."

She grabbed her bag, and walked over to the ATMs, inserting her card into the one that looked slightly less vandalized. She punched in her PIN, and simultaneously called Sol.

"It's the evening," he said by way of greeting. "It's *Friday* evening. Whatever it is, go home, enjoy your weekend." In the background she could hear voices. It sounded like his daughters were visiting for the weekend.

"Sol, I need you to send my backup request higher up the food chain."

"Ah." The reluctance in his voice was obvious, even over the road noise. "Even if I do, there's still no one at the embassy who can assist. You know that."

"Not even civilian staff?"

"Slow down, Ingrid. Let's stay in the shallow end here. What's the rush?"

Ingrid took her cash from the machine and climbed back into

the taxi. She mouthed 'thank you' to the driver in the rearview mirror. She hoped she was right about the London black cab drivers' code of omertà.

"I just lost an entire afternoon. I got sideswiped, passed out, *knocked out*, woke up in the ER."

"What the hell happened? Are you OK?" His tone sharpened with genuine concern.

"It'd take too long to explain, and yes, I seem to be OK, but I'm hours behind schedule. I've got less than forty-eight hours to find Kristyn and get her on a plane."

"I thought the girl's name was Kate-Lynn."

"It was."

"I don't understand."

"Something else that'd take too long to explain. I've only got forty-eight hours and I need help. Have I at least got my own assistant back?"

"Two days? For you, that's plenty. You can do it."

His positive reinforcement management spiel wasn't what she needed. She took a deep breath. "Can I have your permission to go to Louden with this?"

"Really? You're seriously asking to go over my head?"

"With your permission."

Sol made a low moaning noise, somewhere between a grunt and a sigh. It was his 'I've had enough of this sound'. "Look, Louden knows all about the Bowers case. She asked me to keep her up-to-date."

That was odd. "Why is she taking an interest in it?"

"Didn't say."

"But she won't give me bodies?"

"There aren't any bodies, agent."

"What about you?"

There was a long pause. "Give me a call in the morning, but tonight is sacrosanct."

The Sabbath? Did he mean the Sabbath? He'd worked plenty of Friday nights before. Or had he? Maybe she just hadn't noticed. The next person on her call list was Agent Dilner in the Chicago field office. He'd left two messages asking for an update.

"This is Agent Skyberg."

"Finally. How's it going over there?"

The taxi crawled up Charing Cross Road, navigating its way through the upheaval caused by the construction of a new underground railway.

"I don't have anything for you, but I'm just gathering my team together now to go through all the leads, make sure we concentrate on the right areas. We've got forty-eight hours, give or take. We'll find her." She was inflating both the concept of what constituted a team and her confidence in the outcome. "Any progress on who killed Kate-Lynn?"

He sighed. "It was a hit, which means there's no forensics and no witnesses with working mouths. Plus the decomposition probably means there's some stuff we'll never know. But I do have some information for you."

"Go ahead."

"One of Sutcliffe's associates, a guy named Donaho."

"Yes?"

"He's on a watch list."

"Yes?"

"And he boarded a flight at O'Hare last night. Want to have a guess at his destination?"

Ingrid felt the skin on her neck prickle. "London?"

"Full marks, agent."

"You think it's a coincidence? Has he been to London before?"

"That I don't know. I imagine his international travel is usually to Colombia or Venezuela, if you know what I mean."

The cab broke sharply. "Fucking idiot!"

Ingrid looked up to see a rickshaw driver shake his fist at the cab.

"You unlicensed, unqualified little piece of shit." The driver opened the glass. "Sorry about my language, but these idiots… One day someone's going to get killed."

Ingrid nodded to him. A conversation about the growing menace of rickshaws in London wasn't something she wanted to be drawn into. Still, at least it meant the driver wasn't paying attention to what she was saying. "So, tell me what you do know about this Donaho."

"Avery Donaho. Big guy, Irish, obviously with a name like Donaho. Last photo on file he has a ZZ Top beard, but every time we bring him he looks different—"

"He's got a long rap sheet?"

Dilner paused. "Let's see. Give me a second. His file is… right here. OK. Wow, that's unexpected."

"Agent?"

"He's never been inside. Been arrested fourteen times, charged twice, stood trial once, acquitted."

"What are the arrests for?"

"Assault, assault with a deadly weapon, attempted murder, murder. I can't believe we've never been able to get this guy. Seems his get-out-of-jail card is that he actually has a gun license."

"And the connection to Sutcliffe?"

"Cousin."

"Well, at least he wouldn't have got a gun through airport security. You think he's after Kristyn?"

"I'd figure it was a distinct possibility."

Ingrid shivered. No wonder the girl had disappeared. "Is there a faster route?" she asked the driver.

"Won't be long. Which bit of Regent's Park are you after?"

"Somewhere near the zoo, I think." She hoped she'd remembered right.

"You're going to the zoo?" Dilner asked. "I thought you were going into a meeting."

"I am. First I just need to haul my team out of a softball match."

"At the zoo?"

"The zoo is in the park. Like Central Park."

"Ah, OK."

Neither of them had time for small talk. "What else do I need to know about Donaho, apart from the beard?"

"You won't miss him. He's six feet five, weighs two-fifty, two-sixty, built like a linebacker. His nickname is Shoeless because he has difficulty finding shoes that fit. He's got, like, size twenty feet or something unheard of. Plus, you know, he likes his baseball."

Ingrid's heart thumped hard against her ribs. "What team does he support?" She didn't need to hear what was coming next. She already knew who Shoeless Joe Jackson had played for.

"The White Sox."

29

It was just after 7 p.m. when Ingrid, Jennifer and Don made it back to the embassy. Their corner of the building was unusually quiet: the counter-intelligence and counter-terrorism offices were both empty, with only two assistants manning the bullpen, one of whom was taking a nap at her desk. Normally, the time difference meant there were agents in the office until at least the close of play Pacific standard time.

"Where is everyone?" Ingrid asked the solitary conscious assistant, a preppy charmer with family ties to both fortunes and favors.

"It's Danny's wedding tomorrow. They're all taking him out for a drink. Plus, you know, there's that softball game in the park," he said, his attention instantly returning to the bank of TV screens streaming the major networks.

Ingrid wouldn't have expected an invitation to join them, but still felt a little put out that she didn't even know about the wedding. Could Svetlana really be the reason why she was so isolated in London?

Jennifer and Don were still in their sweatpants. Don managed to look even skinnier in casual clothes. It was possible his waist was so small he had to buy his pants in the boys' section. When Ingrid had first run up to them in Regent's Park they had cheered, assuming she'd come to hit a home run and seal victory over the French. Instead, she'd squared up to Simmons, told him to leave her assistant alone and insisted Jennifer and Don abandon the softball match and return to work. She got the impression they were both secretly pleased: not only had the US team been losing, but Ingrid's insistence had made them seem vital to national interests and had probably elevated their status —and that of the criminal division—among their teammates.

"What's first?" Jennifer asked, her freckled cheeks still a little flushed from exercise.

"First," Ingrid said, "I think we send Don out for some food." She fetched her wallet from her bag and handed him £30. "It's going to be a long night."

He looked a little disappointed at the level of his task. "What do you want?"

"Jennifer? What are you in the mood for?"

"Pizza? McDonald's?"

"Anything with fewer carbs?" Ingrid asked. She really couldn't face the starches that made up the majority of Jennifer's calorie intake.

"There's a Greek place down toward Shepherd Market," Don said. "Souvlaki, spinach pie, that kind of thing."

"Sounds great," Ingrid said. Jennifer was clearly disappointed. "Pick up a salad as well, will you?"

"Sure. Nice coat, by the way."

"Thanks."

When he had left the office, Jennifer turned to Ingrid. "You know, that is a nice coat. You actually went to the personal shopper and you totally bought something." Ingrid looked at her sternly. "OK, I get it. No time for small talk, but you know, if you'd been here at least once today, we wouldn't be in such a rush."

Ingrid filled her in on her unplanned hiatus in the emergency room. It was clear the moment she mentioned getting roofied that it made Jennifer uncomfortable.

"How are you feeling now?" the assistant asked. All the brightness had gone from her voice.

"Not too bad." Ingrid had a flash of the knife going into her assailant's abdomen, and instantly felt nauseous. "If I don't think about it," she added.

"And you're sure nothing..." Jennifer searched for the right words, clearly uneasy about broaching the subject with her boss.

"Nothing happened. Nothing like that."

"Because, you know... at college... it happened a lot."

Ingrid examined Jennifer's features: was she expressing concern or confession? She couldn't be sure. Ingrid laid a hand on the girl's arm: nothing more needed to be said.

"I'm OK," she reiterated. "Let's get to work."

"Let's," Jennifer agreed. "So the first thing you need to know is the email we got back from United about Kate-Lynn, sorry *Kristyn's*, ticket."

Dilner's intervention had produced results. It made a difference now they could finally make use of the Bureau's resources. Ingrid sat down at her desk and turned her computer on. "Before you tell me anything else, the absolute first thing I need you to do is send over an urgent request to Scotland Yard for assistance in locating a man called Avery Donaho. He flew in from O'Hare last night. I doubt he's armed—he wouldn't have got any firearms through security, at least I hope he wouldn't have—but he is extremely dangerous."

"Give me that name again."

"Avery Donaho. He'll have a profile and photo on the database, though he no longer has the beard."

Jennifer finished making a note. "What's the connection to Kristyn?"

Ingrid drummed her fingers on her desk, willing her computer to boot up faster. "I think he wants to kill her."

Jennifer's mouth fell open, her eyes widening with shock. "Seriously?"

"Extremely. He must have spotted me in Islington with Truman Cooper this morning—"

"You met Truman Cooper?" There was nothing in her tone to suggest that this was any less shocking than the fact someone was trying to murder a heavily pregnant young woman.

"He then followed me to Vauxhall," Ingrid continued, "presumably in the hope that I would lead him to her."

"Ah. Of course. The photo."

"What photo?"

"Truman Cooper at Heathrow, with his boyfriend. The designer."

"Where did you see the photo?"

"Can't remember. Plenty of places. I've run a lot of searches on Cooper in the past couple of days. But it's Kate-Lynn, sorry, Kristyn in the background, isn't it? Is she, like, Truman's niece or something?"

"Something like that—"

"So he sees the photo… knows Kristyn is with Cooper… then sees you with Cooper… OK, I get it."

"Good, now tell me about the plane ticket."

Jennifer ran the tip of her pen across the list on her notepad. "It was paid for by a Mrs Irene Bull, from Silver Lake."

"And so you've checked out the generous Mrs Bull, I presume?"

"Ah… yup, though I had to hand it over to Don. There's an email from him here… Mrs Bull reported her bag snatched about ten minutes after the ticket had been purchased. She'd been collecting her son from LAX. So, I'm guessing that's a dead end."

"Sounds like it." It wasn't much of a surprise to learn that a girl with Kristyn's background had acquired the skills of a bag snatcher during a challenging childhood. Ingrid typed in her password and logged onto the embassy's server. She opened Google and searched for the Nuestra Señora facility in Los Angeles.

"There's also a scan here of a doctor's letter declaring her fit to fly."

"The name of the doctor?"

"It's not very high res. Van Der Something. From the Nuestra Señora Center for the Family."

Well that explained why she'd been able to board a plane. "Is it possible she's still using Mrs Bull's phone? It's not like she's going to be worried about the roaming charges."

"Um, no. The police report says the bag was found intact, pocketbook, phone, personal fan… I don't need to go on."

"Is it possible," Ingrid said, her brain in hyperdrive, "that Mrs Silver Lake doesn't even know her card has been used yet? I mean, until she gets the bill… Never mind. Not our problem." She refocused on what mattered: "I don't suppose in anything you've looked into so far you've found out why Kate-Lynn had a passport? The cops in Aurora said they didn't look for one because girls like her never have them."

"You know what, that did come up." Jennifer flicked through her notebook. "Yup, here it is. A Facebook post from a few years ago. There was a photo of her in Hong Kong of all places. Some school sports tour. She was a cheerleader."

An image of a bright, enthusiastic, typical cheerleader popped into Ingrid's head, swiftly followed by a mental picture of a slowly putrefying corpse being clung to by a toddler. She shook her head, trying to erase both images. "What else have you got for me?"

"Um," Jennifer glanced down at her notepad. "You asked about the Labor Day edition of the *Sun Times*?"

"Uh-huh." Ingrid was paying attention to the clerk while navigating Nuestra Señora's website for contact details of its senior personnel.

Jennifer got to her feet and walked over to Don's desk. "Here it is," she said, and deposited it in front of Ingrid, who turned straight to the pages that had been missing from the copy she'd found at Cooper's house. Page three featured a story about a new housing development that at first glance seemed irrelevant. On page four, however, there was a report about the stabbing of a nineteen-year-old male on the forecourt of a Taco Bell in Skokie, Illinois.

"Is that what you were looking for?" Jennifer asked.

"I think so." Ingrid scanned the article. The victim was named as James Earley: there was no mention of him being in the witness protection program, or that he had been due to testify against Sooty Sutcliffe, but everything else matched the information Agent Dilner had told her about Dion Paphitis. Ingrid was aware Jennifer was hovering, keen to move on to the next item on her list. "Give me a second, I just need to read this."

"It's, like, gruesome, isn't it?"

It was appalling. Paphitis hadn't just been stabbed fourteen times—he'd had his lips cut off. Ingrid shuddered. Kristyn would have known why: to send a message that anyone who was thinking of testifying against Sutcliffe would be silenced. When Ingrid looked up at the eager Jennifer, she had to wipe away a tear.

"You OK?" Jennifer asked.

"I'm fine. What else have you got for me?"

"Let's do the ammo dealers next."

Ingrid pushed back in her seat, her attention momentarily grabbed by the image on her screen of the director of Nuestra Señora, a woman called Nancy Gadd who had the face of a plastic surgeon's muse: stretched, symmetrical and scary.

Ingrid had forgotten she'd asked Jennifer about finding the source of the mysterious disappearing bullet. "Fire away," Ingrid said, only realizing the pun as the words left her mouth.

"So .38 caliber, aluminum casing, lead tip. Only match I came up with was the Blazer brand. I wasn't sure if you wanted me to place an order or not?"

"Why would I want .38s?"

"Why did you ask me to find some?"

"Ah." Ingrid had obviously neglected to tell Jennifer. "Long story. Now isn't the time to explain, but good work. Thank you. Next?"

"Um…" Jennifer grabbed a different pad from her desk.

Ingrid clicked on her email client and logged into her account. When the software program loaded, she was surprised to see she only had fifteen unread messages. Even though emails came through to her phone, the embassy's servers didn't mark them as read until they had been viewed in the office.

"OK, so, social media? You want to do that now?" Jennifer asked.

It took Ingrid a moment to register what the clerk had said. "Jen," she said slowly, keen to make sure there was no trace of accusation in her voice, "did you look at my emails during the day?"

Jennifer folded her arms, instantly taking a defensive stance. "I, like, don't even know your password, so, like, no. Totally no."

"Hey, OK, relax. IT must have done something their end." She looked up at Jennifer. "Has anyone else been in here today?"

"I wouldn't know, would I? Been with Simmons and CT. Though Don did mention Louden had come in and introduced herself. I reckon he got all uptight and tongue-tied. Why, is there a problem?"

"I'm probably misremembering..." The lingering traces of Rohypnol meant Ingrid couldn't quite be sure of anything. "OK. Social media. Anything on Kate-Lynn's accounts? Anything on Kristyn's?"

Jennifer took a breath. "A few condolence messages on Kate-Lynn's, but way fewer than you'd expect, like only three or four. You'd kind of expect a deluge, even if people are just saying how sorry they are for her kid."

"Any news on how the little boy's getting on?"

"Local media are saying the authorities are chasing his father."

"And Kristyn? What have you found out about her?"

"OK, so, there are dormant Twitter and Instagram accounts. She was on Bebo when she was, like, twelve or something. She must be using fake names: no seventeen-year-old, unless they live in Tajikistan or somewhere, isn't online. Actually, probably even there. But, ta-dah! We did find something interesting."

"Oh?"

Jennifer stood a little taller, her mouth suppressing a smile. "Kristyn Bowers is a big One Direction fan."

"Really?" Ingrid was intrigued.

"Yup, and she's a shipper."

"What the hell's that?"

"Duh! How old are you?" Ingrid assumed it was a rhetorical question. Admitting that she was just days away from her thirty-second birthday might bring unwanted cakes with candles and impromptu singing. "She was all over the forums, defending Harry and Louis."

Ingrid was just pleased that she knew who One Direction were. Individual band members was information she didn't need to clutter her brain with.

"So, she used the same username in lots of places and if you want I can do you a summary of, like, the sorts of things she's interested in, you know, if that'd help."

"That'd be great." It was actually better than great. People follow patterns and they repeat them: an investigator's job is to spot the pattern and wait for the suspect to revert to type. Profiling wasn't always as effective with people of Kristyn's age as their tastes and habits tended to be more fluid, but with no Facebook and no Instagram to go on, extrapolating from Kristyn's forum comments was potentially the best way of finding her. It wasn't like they had much else.

"And the ta-dah info…" Jennifer's tone indicated she was excited about what they'd found out. "Don says there's a big One Direction thing happening tomorrow. Thousands of fans are planning on camping outside Harry's house in the hope of some, like, big announcement." She looked at Ingrid, clearly hoping for praise, but Ingrid was too busy clicking around the Nuestra Señora site for a contact number.

"So if she's such a big fan, and if she's now lurking in 1D forums rather than posting, and if she's in London, you know, maybe she'll go to Harry's house tomorrow?"

Ingrid ran both hands through her hair and leaned back against the chair. "You know what, it's the only goddamned lead we've got. If we brought in a profiler, they'd probably recommend sending someone. Where is it?"

"North London somewhere. Don's got the address and I can tell you now he's going to be totally up for going."

"He would?"

"You do remember I told you he was gay?"

"Hey, I don't want to presume that just because the guy's gay he's going to be into boy bands."

Jennifer placed a hand on her waist and jutted out a hip. "One Direction aren't just any boy band, Ingrid."

"OK, tomorrow we send Don on a top secret undercover mission. But tonight, what I need from you is..." Ingrid raised her hand and started counting her fingers, "one, a report on Kristyn Bowers' other forum preferences, anything that might tell us what she's into and where she might be, apart from at this Harry's place tomorrow."

Jennifer sat back down at her desk and placed a spiral-bound notebook squarely in front of her. "Done."

"Two. I want a summary of the Latin Kings. I'm sure there'll be an up-to-date file on the Bureau database."

"Latin Kings?"

Ingrid had forgotten that Jennifer's civilian training wouldn't have covered gang culture and history. There was no reason why she should know about the Kings. "They're a gang. Seriously, there'll be a file. Just print off the first two pages. I don't have time to read anything else."

"I'll give that one to Don."

"Three. I want a profile of a guy called Dennis Sutcliffe. Just a couple of pages. His nickname is Sooty. Nasty piece of work."

"He's the defendant, right? At the trial we're trying to save?"

"Correct. And your fourth task," Ingrid said, pulling on her ring finger, "is a background summary on the victim in that trial, a man named Michael Oboloyo. There might just be something, some connection, I'm not seeing."

"And number five?" They both turned to see Don in the doorway holding paper take-out bags in both hands. "Oh my God, that smells *amazing*."

"Number five? It's one for Don."

"Name it," he said, putting the bags down on his desk.

"Call the maternity units again. Maybe widen the circle. Maybe try doulas and freelance midwives."

"But it's nearly eight o'clock," he said, his deep voice rising incrementally.

"Yes, and babies don't get born on a schedule. They should all be answering their phones."

Ingrid picked up a souvlaki that Don had laid out on a flattened bag. "And while you're doing that, I'm going to call Nuestra Señora and find out just how helpful they're going to be when I tell them that they have been using an underage surrogate."

"Let's get to work then," Don said.

"Let's," Jennifer agreed.

Ingrid took a bite of her souvlaki and hoped their diligence paid off. Right now, the criminal division had to operate like a sales team, generating leads and pursuing them until someone bought what they were selling. Because the way things stood, their only hope of finding Kristyn Bowers was a tenuous link to a boy band.

30

Ingrid pushed the fire exit open and stepped out onto the roof terrace. The cigarette butts at her feet told her Sol wasn't the only smoker who used this spot, each obeying the smoker's code to leave the door unlocked. A folded business card jammed near the handle ensured it *looked* locked when the security teams patrolled, but it was simple enough to pry it open when in desperate need of nicotine.

What Ingrid needed, however, was space, so she climbed the steps up onto the roof where the Stars and Stripes moved noisily on an enormous flagpole. She needed to clear her head. Her infuriating conversation with Nancy Gadd at Nuestra Señora revealed the woman didn't just have a frozen face, but nerves of ice. If she felt in any way threatened by the thought of an agent from the LA office turning up on her doorstep to examine the paperwork of their other surrogates, or the prospect of Dr Van Der Veelte being struck off, her voice betrayed no sense of panic or concern. Ingrid had heard about criminals having Botox injections in their armpits to stop them from sweating in an attempt to beat a polygraph: Nancy Gadd, it seemed, had had Botox injected into her soul to cauterize her emotions. Still, she was happy to gather Kristyn's things ready for collection by an agent in the LA field office, although she warned the girl's room had already been cleared and cleaned.

All the leadership courses the Bureau had sent Ingrid on talked about the importance of stepping back, about thinking strategically, about taking stock. She needed to forget about her tumultuous day, about the glamour of *The Belgravia Set*, the grime of Vauxhall, the ER, even the blood on her hand, and focus solely on finding Kristyn Bowers. She put her phone on silent so that the only interruptions would come from the sounds of the city evaporating into the cool evening air.

The setting sun was still just visible above the rooftops and tall trees of Hyde Park. Cranes, spires, ornate pediments and modern angular roofs clawed at the sky, vying for attention. Kristyn was out there somewhere, missing in a city of endless possibilities. *Where had she gone to?* Ingrid closed her eyes and ran through everything she knew about Kristyn Bowers.

Bull's-eye.

She opened her eyes, retrieved her phone from her pocket and dialed downstairs to Jennifer.

"Criminal division."

"It's Skyberg."

"Might have guessed."

"I've got a sixth thing to add to your list."

"Go ahead."

"We know she stole a bag at LAX, that woman from Silver Lake?"

"We do."

"So let's check in with the Met, see if there have been any reports of heavily pregnant bag snatchers in the past forty-eight hours." If they were lucky, there might have been a clutch of them in a particular location. If they were really, really lucky, a pregnant girl in a floral summer dress was in a custody suite somewhere in the city.

"Consider it done," Jennifer said before hanging up.

The flip side of Kristyn's kleptomania was that she had almost limitless access to untraceable cash. She wouldn't be surfacing as soon as Truman's £500 ran out.

Ingrid inhaled, expanding her chest, and kept her arms by her side. She let her gaze settle on the horizon. Mountain pose. Her breathing deepened and slowed, centering her thoughts on finding Kristyn. She recalled her basic training and the procedures to implement when a case runs cold. She was suddenly back in a Quantico classroom, sitting next to Marshall Claybourne, the good-looking overachiever she wished she'd never accepted a piece of gum from, let alone a proposal of marriage. *Go back to the last known sighting,* she heard her instructor say.

She worked backwards. The last confirmed sighting was on Wednesday night, almost forty-eight hours ago, when Kristyn had gone to bed at Tom and Truman's house. But then she had been seen on CCTV footage in their hallway a little after 5 a.m. the following morning. Ingrid tried to remember everything she could about the footage.

She pictured the scene in as much detail as possible. Kristyn's hair was in a ponytail, she was carrying a small canvas backpack and there had been something in her hand as she'd opened the front door. A breeze picked up, reminding Ingrid that—in London as in Minnesota—her birthday marked the beginning of fall. Ingrid thought about the flimsy dress and the small backpack: it didn't look like it contained more than a sweater and a spare pair of underwear. If Kristyn was used to California weather, she had to be feeling the cold by now.

Ingrid focused her mind on the CCTV footage again. What was she missing? She replayed it in her head and saw the back of Kristyn's head as she walked in front of the camera and toward the door. Then the girl had turned round, letting them see the left side of her face, before bending down. Why did she bend down? She wasn't wearing sneakers, so she wasn't tying shoelaces.

It was the dog. She was bending down to pat the dog. Ingrid considered if this was significant. She thought about Cully, a good-natured creature that had wanted Truman's love even when the actor had forcibly pushed him away. What had Tom told her about why the dog wasn't there the following day? The vet's. But the dog hadn't appeared to be in pain or discomfort when she had seen him. Had Tom lied to her? Why?

Something else was bothering her about Tom. She scrolled through her messages to check: not one of them was from Tom even though she'd called him and texted him several times that morning. It was now twelve hours later and he hadn't bothered to get in touch. It was obvious that Truman Cooper was the driving force behind their move into parenthood, but Ingrid had thought Tom Kerrison cared enough about the baby, and about Kristyn, to ask for an update on the investigation.

She focused again on her memories of the footage. What had that been in her hand? Nothing in the research showed she was Catholic, but it did look like a rosary. Might it have been a necklace? Might she have stolen something valuable from Tom and Truman, something that was bankrolling her disappearance?

Not for the first time, Ingrid tried to put herself in Kristyn's shoes—it was five o'clock in the morning, in a strange city, and she was close to giving birth for the first time. She thought again about what Kristyn had left behind when she'd walked out on Tom and Truman: money, a comfortable bed behind high-security gates, hot showers… The shower, that was it, Kristyn had had a shower. She'd had wet hair when she'd left. Surely, if she was planning on walking the streets, she'd have dried her hair? Or not washed it in the first place.

Picturing the footage again, Ingrid finally saw what she'd been missing: Kristyn hadn't looked frightened, or even concerned. Ingrid had never been eight months pregnant, but she imagined the prospect of leaving that comfortable house and wandering the streets with wet hair would not have been a pleasant one for a woman so close to giving birth, yet Kristyn's face didn't show a trace of apprehension.

And that meant one thing: Kristyn Bowers had been picked up.

31

"Criminal division." Jennifer's voice had lost some of its usual sparkle: she was obviously working hard.

"It's me again."

"Hey, Ingrid."

"She was picked up. I'm sure of it. Kristyn was picked up. The question is, who by?"

Ingrid could hear Don in the background calling yet another maternity unit.

"Did you hear me?"

"Yes, I did. I guess I'm just surprised. I mean, she doesn't know anyone in London, at least no one we've found."

A siren drifted up to Ingrid from the streets below. "That's because we've been looking in the wrong place. Have you still got the flight manifest?"

"Um, I must have. It was an attachment to an email. Hold on a moment."

"I'm thinking that, if we can't find a family connection to London, and there are no social media, no commercial, no *anything* ties to London, then the only person she knows in this city is someone she met on the plane." Ingrid's words were running together with excitement. Not even riding country roads at a hundred miles per hour could beat the thrill of prying open a case.

"OK," Jennifer said, "I'm looking at it now. Kate-Lynn, sorry, that's just the name on the list, I do know we're talking about Kristyn here, she was in an aisle seat, 57G. Back of the plane, right-hand side, where there are a few rows with just two seats together. I'm guessing they, like, put the pregnant girl near the restroom."

Ingrid willed her to stop prattling and just tell her who Kristyn was sitting next to.

"And in 57H, so the window seat, is a Gwyneth Jones. How many Gwyneth Joneses do you think there are in London?"

"You're about to find out. And if you don't find one in London, widen the search to the southeast of England. Obviously, a name like that, she might have got on a connecting flight to Wales, but just see what you can find out, will you?"

"Sure thing."

Ingrid was relieved Kristyn had been sitting next to a woman. It made it more likely that she would have said 'if you need anything while you're in town, call me' or that they had talked for hours about birth plans and baby names.

The moment her screen went dark, Ingrid tapped it back into life and scrolled through her contacts until she remembered that she hadn't programed Truman Cooper's number into her phone. She felt her rear pants pockets for the card Manuela had given her in Islington that morning. It wasn't there. *Damn.* Had it fallen out in the back of an ambulance? In the ER? She slipped a hand inside a jacket pocket, it wasn't there either. She tried the other pocket and exhaled as she retrieved a bent business card, blackened at the edges where it had rubbed against the new leather inside her pocket. She looked at the number Manuela had written down and noted the horizontal lines through the sevens in the continental style.

"Who is this?" Truman Cooper's tone was hostile.

"Special Agent Skyberg."

"At fucking last. Where the fuck have you been?" The expletives had returned to his vocabulary.

"Sir," she was tempted to tell him she'd been knocked out, that she'd spent the afternoon unconscious, but calculated it wouldn't elicit sympathy, only accusations of incompetence. "I didn't want to call you until I had news for you."

"Well, you don't sound like you've got any. If you'd have found her, you'd have said so by now."

Ingrid took a deep breath, reminding herself to stay calm in the face of his temper. "My team has been making progress." Ingrid waited for him to say something like 'go ahead' or 'have you', but there was just silence. She looked at the screen to make sure the call hadn't been terminated. "Would you rather I spoke to Mr Kerrison? Do you want to put him on the line?"

"Mr Kerrison," he said through gritted teeth, "is in Milan, or Rome, or I don't fucking know where."

"He's gone away? At a time like this?" Ingrid was shocked. "At least you've got Cully for company."

"The dog? The fucking dog? Fuck knows where the dog is. The vet's, most likely, but I am not paying you to talk to me about my goddamn pet."

"Sir, Mr Cooper, you are not paying me. I am a federal agent." She could almost hear him bristle. He acted as if the entire world was on his payroll, and it was possible that in his world, almost everyone he met was.

"Are you calling to tell me where my son is, or not?"

The conversation was going badly, but she needed to keep him talking. Right now, Truman Cooper was holding the most promising lead in his hand and the last thing Ingrid needed was for the actor to hang up or, worse, drop his phone in the sink and run the faucet. She tipped her head back, looked up at the darkening sky and took a deep, centering breath. "Mr Cooper, I think you are currently holding the key to the case, quite literally. When the cash was taken from your jacket, was your phone also in your pocket?"

"Yes. Yes it was." His tone had changed. She had engaged his curiosity and in doing so had tempered his anger.

"I have good reason to think she was picked up from outside your house. That means it is likely she called someone. We know she left her phone in Los Angeles, so I think she must have used yours."

He didn't say anything. At least he wasn't swearing.

"Can you check the call history? See if your phone was used that night after you went to bed?"

"How the hell am I supposed to do that while I am on the goddamn phone?"

Another calming breath. She wasn't about to become his technology adviser. "If it's easier, hang up, check the call log and then call me back."

The line went dead. Ingrid's relief at no longer being on the receiving end of Truman Cooper's temper was equal to her anxiety that he wouldn't call back. She turned the ringer back on. What if he found a number, called it, and did something reckless? Ingrid puffed out her cheeks and exhaled.

No wonder his career had fallen off a cliff: it was amazing anyone at all was prepared to work with him. Kristyn giving birth in a jurisdiction where Truman and Tom would have to go through a formal adoption procedure wasn't such a terrible idea. At least then Cooper would be subjected to a psych test. She had worked with enough vulnerable children to know the damage a parent with a quicksilver temper could inflict.

Ingrid glanced down at her phone, hoping to see the screen illuminate before she heard it ring. Nothing. *Come on!* Maybe Truman Cooper was so dependent on help that he didn't even know how his phone worked. It had only been a couple of minutes, Ingrid told herself, give him a chance. The wind picked up, ruffling her hair: the weather was definitely turning. She buttoned her jacket, the buttonholes stiff with newness, then belted it.

Her phone lit up.

"Agent Skyberg."

"Four-thirty AM, two-minute call."

Heat surged up through Ingrid's body. At last. "And you have the number?"

"You know, I've played a cop a few times, but I never knew it could be so exciting."

"Mr Cooper. The number?"

"How the hell am I supposed to give you a number while I'm making a goddamn call?"

He was forty-nine, not eighty-nine.

"Hang up, check the number, write it down, call me back."

"Couldn't I just give you the name of the company she called? Wouldn't that do?"

"You called them?"

"No, they're programed into my phone. It's Jupiter Cars. She called a taxi. You were right, agent, she was picked up."

Either the quickening breeze or the breakthrough raised the hairs on Ingrid's skin. "That's your car service?"

"She got a cab." The relief in his voice was palpable. It was just possible that this difficult, rude man might be a decent human when he wasn't tormented about the whereabouts of his unborn child. "They'll tell you where they took her, I'm sure they will. Very discreet, very helpful. She might even be home for breakfast."

She wanted to tell him not to get his hopes up, but this was good news, the best news the investigation had had in two days. "I'm going to call them right now," Ingrid promised. She started walking toward the stairs down onto the roof terrace a floor below. "I'll keep you posted."

Ingrid took the stairs two at a time, eager to get to her desk and move the investigation up a gear. She reached the fire exit and felt for the door handle only to discover that there wasn't one. It only opened from the inside. Which was a problem, because the strategically positioned piece of folded card must have been dislodged by the breeze.

She was trapped.

32

Jen and Don's lines were both constantly busy, which was just as it should be given the work Ingrid had asked them to do. She considered calling the main switchboard, but decided she'd really rather not be known as the FBI agent who locked herself on the roof: her best bet was finding an open window. The roof terrace wrapped right around the top floor of the building. How many windows did that give her access to? Thirty? Fifty, maybe? Statistically that was pretty good odds. It had been a warm day; someone in one of those offices would have left their window ajar.

"Can you give me a number for Jupiter Cars in London, please?" she asked the operator as she tried to open a window into a small office.

"Would you like me to put you through?" the operator asked. "There is an additional charge for this service."

Ingrid couldn't give a damn about the cost. "Yes, please." The window was jammed. She carried on round the roof terrace, turning the corner of the building so that the trees of Grosvenor Square came into view.

"Jupiter Cars, can I have your address please?"

Ingrid explained that she didn't want a car, only information. She told the call handler that she was phoning from the US embassy and that she was involved in helping track down a vulnerable pregnant woman. "You sent a car to Narrow Street in Wapping at five-fifteen yesterday morning. Thursday September 5th. I need to know the address you took the passenger to."

"One moment."

Ingrid peered over the wall down to the square below where there was, as always, a group of protestors with placards. Either they wanted the US to get involved in a conflict, or to get the hell out of one. She thought she could see a couple of them wearing orange jumpsuits: another Guantanamo event. Ingrid reached a window that had been left open a fraction. It moved when she tried to shift it. She peered inside. It was a huge room, like the ballroom on a cruise ship: it was one of the entertaining suites. She opened the window and climbed inside.

"Hello," the call handler said. "Are you still there?"

"Yes I am."

"I spoke to my manager, and she says we cannot give out that sort of information without a warrant. Client privacy, you see." Truman had said they were discreet.

Ingrid stepped gingerly over an enormous geometric rug, keen for her footsteps not to attract attention: she didn't really want to be caught in one of the embassy's prestigious reception rooms without a reason. "Look," she said, keeping her voice low, "I am an FBI agent. I am investigating the disappearance of a vulnerable young woman, and it's not me who needs your help, it's her. If you won't do it for me, do it for her."

"Yes, well, you say you're an FBI agent but, you know, there's nothing to stop me saying I'm Beyoncé, is there?"

Ingrid's heart began to pound with the frustration, but now wasn't the time to get angry. "Please, there is a young woman who is missing. She's extremely vulnerable and she needs your help. If you're not willing to share this vital information with me right now, please hang up, call the US embassy in London and ask to be put through to the FBI's Legal Attaché office. They will connect you to me. My name is Special Agent Ingrid Skyberg. Then will you believe that I am who I say I am?"

"Is this a joke?"

"Please," Ingrid knew she sounded desperate. "Call the embassy, verify my identity and then please, please help me."

"All righty."

Ingrid's jaw was clenched in frustration. The one big, fat, juicy lead, the only way of knowing for sure where Kristyn Bowers had disappeared to, and some operator from a car service was being obstructive. Ingrid gripped her phone so tightly she risked crushing it.

She crept past a grand piano and reached a set of double doors that had to open out into the main corridor. She tried the handle. Locked. She tried both handles together. Still locked. There was another set of double doors at the other end of the room. Ingrid stepped softly past a series of portraits of dead presidents to reach the other exit.

Why hadn't her phone rung? Had the woman at Jupiter Cars not bothered, or had the preppy intern in the bullpen put the call through to her desk even though he knew she wasn't in the office?

She tried the handles. The second set of doors was also locked. Damn. This was getting ridiculous: the only way out was back through the window and onto the roof terrace. Once she was outside again, she checked her phone. She couldn't wait any longer and called them again, this time faking her best Portuguese accent.

"Jupiter Cars, may I have your address please?"

Ingrid was relieved to hear it was a different call handler. "Good evening. This is Manuela, calling for Truman Cooper." Already Ingrid realized she'd made a mistake: Manuela would never bother to say 'good evening'. "He ask me to call."

"Hi, Manuela, this is Sofia. What's your destination?"

"I don't need car, I need your help."

"I'll see what I can do." This conversation was going much better than the last one.

"You sent car here yesterday morning, about five o'clock. He want to know where you drop off passenger." Ingrid feared her Portuguese was veering dangerously northeast toward Russia.

"OK, let me see. Was it cash or account?"

"We don't know."

"Yesterday… Narrow Street… OK, that job was given to Olek… Yup, it was charged to your account… drop off in Victoria. Anything else you need?"

Ingrid was so excited she thought she might yelp. "You have the address?"

"It was Victoria station." All her excitement evaporated. She had hoped for a street name and a house number. Victoria station was one of London's busiest transit hubs.

"Thank you, Sofia."

"Say hi to Truman for me. Tell him we're all waiting for the new series."

Ingrid shoved her phone in her back pocket and leaned heavily against the roof terrace wall. What bad luck. What absolutely terrible luck. Victoria station. With those two words, the strongest lead she'd had since Kristyn went missing had been transformed into multiple, weaker leads: there must be hundreds of train stations reachable from Victoria, and Kristyn could have been headed for any one of them. Ingrid closed her eyes and forced all the air in her lungs out through pursed lips. She needed to find a way to narrow the search. Without help, without more time, she needed to be strategic. She needed to think clearly.

"Put your hands in the air."

Ingrid turned sharply: ten feet further along the roof terrace was a Marine holding a Beretta M9 and pointing it right at her head.

33

It was almost eleven o'clock by the time Ingrid made it to the Beaufort Club. She'd let Jennifer and Don go home around ten on the understanding they'd be back by 8 a.m., then finished reading the briefing papers they'd prepared for her. She touched up her make-up before walking a few blocks south and entering one of the most exclusive clubs in London just as it started to rain. When security waved her through without question, she knew she was expected.

Clad in black marble with gold accents and candles on every table, the Beaufort was somewhere between a Busby Berkeley set and a Prohibition speakeasy. Ingrid made her way through the room, passing between tables where—for the most part—young attractive women in spaghetti-strap dresses sat next to middle-aged men in sober suits. She scanned the room looking for a familiar face. He wasn't there.

She sat at a table as far away from the piano player as she could find and within moments a waiter arrived with an iced glass containing a double measure of vodka and a twist of lime. He set a folded card down next to her drink and retreated with a slight bow. Ingrid picked up the card.

You're late.

She held it above the candle until it caught fire, dropping the charred remains on the table, extinguishing the last of the embers with the condensation from her glass. Only then did she take a sip. And then another. Exactly what she needed.

The piano player announced he was taking a break, and while everyone else in the room greeted this news with polite applause, Ingrid was relieved. It wasn't that the guy couldn't sing—he absolutely could—it was that he'd been singing like it was his last night at Carnegie Hall. Maybe now she could do a little eavesdropping.

The Beaufort had endured a few weeks of lurid headlines earlier in the year when Viktor Bazarov, the owner of a Kazakh mining company, had choked to death—on an olive, if the news reports were to be believed—in one of the club's private booths. A tragic accident, according to the coroner; the work of the SVR, according to almost everyone else. Ingrid had expected to tune into conversations in Russian, or to strain to make out confessions in Ukrainian, but her ears were unwillingly drawn to the tones of a loud American a couple of tables away. The man's slow, Southern drawl made her bristle: he sounded exactly like Marshall Claybourne. She had to twist round and stare hard to make sure her ex-fiancé wasn't in the room.

Satisfied it wasn't him, she took another sip and exhaled deeply.

"You should always wear those clothes." Nick Angelis slid onto the chair next to hers. "Whatever the weather, whatever the occasion. Always. You look wonderful."

Ingrid didn't know what to say.

"Tough day?"

Where did she start? Being drugged? Stabbing someone? Unconscious in the ER? Mistaken for a terrorist on the roof of one of the most heavily armed buildings in Europe? "A bit full-on."

"I was rather hoping you might have been here a little earlier." He was wearing a pressed white shirt, open at the collar, dark denim jeans and a pair of Cuban heels. With his deep tan and firm jaw he resembled a lothario from a Mexican soap opera. It was a look she ought to find repulsive, yet her eyes were drawn to the point where the column of pearlized buttons on his shirt sank beneath the buckle of his belt.

"And yet you waited for me nonetheless. Sweet of you."

"I'm here for work, agent."

"Of course you are." She took another sip, letting the alcohol burn on her tongue before she swallowed. "Do you ever do anything for pleasure?" She regretted the words the moment she said them and could only hope that it was dark enough he wouldn't see she was blushing.

A waiter passed by the table. Ingrid raised her hand.

"You'd like another?" he asked.

She nodded.

"Sir?" he asked Angelis.

"It would be rude not to accompany the lady on her alcoholic voyage. I thought burning the card was a nice touch. Very le Carré."

"As was your text. All you gave me was the name of the venue. No time, no purpose."

"With you, the purpose is always pleasure." He sat a little more upright. "I'm sorry, even for me that was a little..." He struggled to find the right word.

"Sleazy?"

"Can we settle on louche?"

She nodded. "Did you just want to see if I'd come running? Is that it?"

"Heavens, no! I actually have something for you."

She narrowed her eyes.

"Please, I trust that—our recent history not withstanding—you know I am more of a gentleman than to suggest... though of course if you were to suggest the exact same thing..."

"Stop it, Nick." She wasn't going to say it, but she was definitely thinking it. Two consenting adults. No strings. "So what have you got? And why give it to me here?"

The waiter discreetly placed their drinks in front of them and retreated.

"The location is simple enough to explain. After the unfortunate incident earlier this year, Fortnum's now provides security to the Beaufort and, seeing as it is less than five hundred yards from your office, it is practically your local."

"So how many cameras are watching us right now?"

He leaned in. "Precisely? None."

Her surprise quickly waned. It made sense.

"This is one of the few places in London where we guarantee no electronic surveillance. We sweep every four hours for listening devices, and in case someone does attempt to record any activity, there are white-noise screens around the booths and the lighting is at such a frequency that it makes filming problematic. Your average camera phone, or camera pen, doesn't stand a chance. Mobile phone signals are blocked."

The Beaufort was a place where meetings—and murders—could take place in secret. "You would have thought, wouldn't you, that a venue where a prominent man dies in suspicious circumstances would be keen to install the latest surveillance equipment."

He leaned in further, close enough for her to feel his breath on her cheek. "And they have. Sitting over there under the chandelier is Marianne. Igor and Miguel are behind the bar. I believe you passed Channing on the door."

Ingrid scrutinized the personnel as Nick pointed them out.

"I don't suppose you even noticed the operatives we have outside, but as soon as you turned into Waverton Street your arrival here was anticipated."

"Hence the vodka."

"I hope you don't mind."

"You know it's a good choice. So the staff here are all Fortnum's?"

"Almost all. Listening, observing, memorizing. We're like the priestesses at Delphi. We know *everything*."

Very smart. Plenty of private security firms could offer muscle, weaponry and hacked intel from rogue satellites, but few could offer their clients wisdom accrued in the darkest of corners of a venue designed to lure in the world's greatest plotters and schemers.

"Just think, agent, what you could do with that information if you joined us."

She raised an eyebrow. "I think I'm a little overqualified to be a waitress in a club."

"You know how we work. You've been on an operation with me. We'd find something commensurate with your acumen and combat skills." He leaned back to better gauge her reaction.

All Ingrid could think about was the time she had witnessed Nick hold a witness's face underwater until he coughed up the information they needed. Whatever expression that memory produced gave Nick his answer.

"Ah, not yet then," he said. "But one day I hope to persuade you."

She liked accountability. She liked answering to a power she believed in. She liked *being* the law. Clear lines and boundaries suited her.

"We'd have a lot of fun."

"Maybe you can let me moonlight the next time you have an assignment in Paris or Rome."

"Ah, if only. I don't think your employer would approve. Plausible deniability and all that." He maintained eye contact while draining his glass. "With us there's no equivocation. We're like the bloody musketeers. All in. Always." Even he winced at his innuendo.

And yet, rather than being repelled, it occurred to Ingrid that she was—unexpectedly—more comfortable with Nick than she had been with Ralph. Ralph was a good, kind, considerate man, the kind you marry if you want a quiet life. But Ingrid didn't want to get married: she hadn't ended things with Marshall to put another man's ring on her finger.

The combination of ice, fire and lime was waking her up and she'd had just enough vodka to not be embarrassed to stare at Nick. The man was too damn suave for his own good but right now he offered more of what she wanted, more of what she needed. With

Nick, things were transactional, a favor for a favor. She looked up from the open neck of Nick's shirt, lingered on his Adam's apple and then into his eyes. They both knew what the other was thinking.

"So," she said.

"So."

"You said you had some information for me."

"I did?" She had flustered him. She liked that she could do that to him. "Yes I did, didn't I." He picked up his glass. "It's about your boss. Louden."

A well-dressed man in his twenties, a younger version of Nick, approached the table. "Excuse me."

"What is it, Channing?"

"Miss Skyberg's car is here."

"Thank you," she said. "Will you tell him to wait."

"Of course."

She turned her attention to Nick who looked somewhere between surprised and disappointed. "You booked a car?"

"It's work." She finished her vodka in one long burning gulp. She put the glass back down on the table and looked at Nick. "So, do you want to tell me about Louden in the car?"

"Or over breakfast?"

There was no way she was letting him stay the night.

34

The gun felt surprisingly light. It had been so long since Ingrid had got her Glock 23 out of the gun safe at the embassy that she had expected it to feel as heavy as it had the first time her father had put his in her ten-year-old hands. He had needed to leave the farm to renegotiate loans with the bank in Minneapolis and Svetlana had been sick for the first —and only—time Ingrid could remember. Her father, like all farmers, owned several guns but the Glock 23 was the one he kept by his bedside, the one he trusted in the middle of the night. It was the one he wanted her to reach for if anyone broke into the house.

Even at the time Ingrid had thought it was unnecessary: if the feed guy who'd been delivering to the farm for twenty years still had trouble finding the place because it was so remote, there wasn't much chance of an escaped felon breaking in and threatening their welfare. But Hal Skyberg wasn't taking chances. A tall, broad-shouldered man with rosy cheeks and blond hair that never dimmed with age, he had taken her out into the yard and told her to point the gun at a plastic pail twenty yards away. He stood behind her, his huge hands covering hers, as she lined up the sight with the target.

"Check again," he said. "You gotta look real good."

So she did. She adjusted her aim.

"Now straighten your arms. You gotta brace 'em. Lock your elbows."

She followed her gentle father's instructions.

"Now round out your shoulders. That's the thing that makes the difference. You gotta hunch your shoulders like your grand-mama—that way, you can keep 'em still."

By this point, the ten-year-old Ingrid was finding the gun heavy, her aim was dropping.

"You want your legs hip-width apart. That's your stance. That's good Ingrid. Now look again. And when you're ready, you pull on that trigger."

The same gun now seemed so small in her hand, but as she looked down at it lying across her palm, she could still picture that first lesson in the yard and she could feel her father; a physical memory of his proximity.

When she had fired her first bullet, the Glock had bounced right out of her hand and landed in the dirt. The pail was good for fetching water and feed for another decade. But by the time she'd trained with the Jackson County sheriff's office, Deputy Ingrid Skyberg was acing every single practice session.

"Ready?" the instructor asked.

Ingrid nodded and pulled the hearing protectors over her ears. Legs a hip-width apart, shoulders rounded, elbows locked, she braced herself and pulled the trigger, aiming at the center of the target at the other end of the firing range.

The gun still bounced in her hands after every round, but her grip remained secure. Before each shot, she looked again, refocused and pulled the trigger. Aim fast, shoot slow, that was her father's motto. She completed the 'Cop's Dozen'—there were thirteen bullets in the standard-issue magazines—and a second target was lowered from the ceiling twenty yards further away. She changed clips and took aim.

"Ready?" the instructor shouted.

She nodded. Another thirteen bullets, all of them hitting the target. She replaced the clip, ready for the next test.

"OK, miss, that's it," he said.

"Really? No moving targets?"

"No." He looked up at her from his clipboard. "Not today. This was just a preliminary assessment so we can book you in for the course."

"And how did I do?"

"All the Americans we get in here can hit a target—it's the engagement protocols you sometimes struggle with."

She holstered the Glock and checked to see if her new jacket would do up over the weapon. "What? We're all 'shoot first, ask later' and you guys wait until you've had your knee blown off before you open fire?"

"Something like that." He smiled at her for the first time since she'd got there at 8 a.m. "We've had the odd spray and pray."

"I hope any feds you get in here are a little more cautious. We have to account for every bullet."

"Same as us, then." He was a sergeant in the Metropolitan Police's Specialist Firearms Command. He had the calm confidence of a man who could do anything from shearing a sheep, to scaling a vertical cliff face to mixing the perfect martini. The kind of guy you wanted on your team when things got tough.

Ingrid flexed her fingers. In every field office on almost every desk in the FBI you'd find some kind of dense foam toy, or a hand grip, so that agents could keep their trigger finger supple.

"So when can I start the course?"

He looked up from his paperwork. "We run them a couple of times a year, out at our facility in Gravesend."

"A couple times a year? How long will I have to wait?"

"I think you might be in luck. If there's space, you might be able to do it next month. Check with the guy on the desk on your way out, but you'll need a certificate from me first."

"And how do I get that?"

He gave her a smile. "You go and sit in reception, and once I've found someone to countersign it, I'll bring it out to you."

Ingrid looked at the torn and stained couches in the tatty reception area and wondered if she should risk sitting down. It wasn't that she was worried about fleas, more about falling asleep, even with the sound of muffled gunfire coming through the sound-proofed walls. After she had kicked Nick out of her apartment around 2 a.m., she'd had difficulty getting to sleep. She'd lain in bed, going over everything she'd learnt from Olek, the Jupiter Cars chauffeur who had driven them to her place in Maida Vale.

Olek had remembered picking Kristyn up from Wapping very clearly: being eight months pregnant meant she had stuck in his mind. "She was not crying," he kept on repeating when Ingrid had asked if she seemed distressed. His English wasn't great, but he was able to tell her something that she thought might prove useful: he had dropped her off at the Buckingham Palace Road entrance to Victoria station.

"Most people just want the main station," he'd said, "but she asked for it specially. Buck-ing-ham. I remember that." It was how all American tourists pronounced it. It was how Ingrid would have said it once; after all, it is how it's written.

Restless, Ingrid had left her apartment as soon as the sun had come up. She packed her new outfit—it was fast becoming her uniform—into a backpack and ran into Grosvenor Square. By 6:30 a.m. she was showered and at her desk, updating the documents Don and Jennifer had prepared the night before. No reports of pregnant bag-snatchers in the metropolitan area, no unaccompanied teenagers in the maternity units, no sightings of Avery Donaho.

Ingrid yawned. What harm could it do if she sat down for a few minutes? Didn't Confucius say that a smart woman rests when she can, a foolish one when she has to? She went over to one of the couches and took a seat on a thin foam cushion. On a scratched plastic table in front of her was an unappetizing selection of newspapers: the *Daily Mail* and the *Sun*. Ingrid chose the *Mail* on the basis that it was thicker and might actually contain some news. While there was some reporting on the situation in Syria, the first few pages were focused on celebrities she did not recognize, miracle diets and medical breakthroughs. It almost didn't matter what the date was on the cover: the paper could run the same stories on any day of the week.

Her phone rang in her pocket. She looked at who was calling and wasn't particularly surprised to see who it was.

"Agent Skyberg."

"I know who you are. I called you. I presume I don't have to say my name, too? You must have it programed into your phone. Or are the FBI's gadgets so good that you don't just know who I am but where I'm calling from and what I had for breakfast?"

"Yup, Angela, we have breathalyzers in all our devices and I can tell that you had brandy with your coffee this morning."

"You know, you're not far off. Well, what have you got for me?"

Ingrid leaned back against the inadequate couch. "In what way?"

"Well, two days ago you and I made a little agreement, and this morning I find out you haven't been entirely honest with me."

Ingrid flicked through the *Daily Mail* and considered how to respond.

"You told me Truman Cooper's stalker was in London, but I got an email overnight—unhelpful time difference, I would rather not work on a Saturday, at least not this early in the morning—informing me Cooper's stalker is still incarcerated in the Marin County jail."

Ingrid spotted something on page nine that meant she stopped listening: there was a paparazzi picture of Tom Kerrison remonstrating with a uniformed police officer at the side of the road. The headline said 'Fashionably late?'

"Agent? Are you still there?"

"Sure, sorry. Got distracted."

"Now, I've been a good little journalist, keeping quiet until I could safely publish an exclusive, but it turns out there isn't even a bloody story. Quid pro quo, Agent Skyberg."

Ingrid was trying to read the article. It mentioned that the arrest came just weeks after Kerrison's hospitalization for stress. Why hadn't she known he'd been in hospital?

"And do you know what quid pro quo means? It means don't fuck with me. So?"

Ingrid wasn't listening; she was trying to read the article. Kerrison had been stopped for speeding. Yesterday. In the county of Sussex, about fifty miles south of London. Sweat started to dampen Ingrid's palms.

"So," Angela continued, "that got me thinking about why you were really so damn interested in those Heathrow pics, and it's the girl, isn't it? The one in the floral dress."

Ingrid didn't know how to respond.

"Well, she has to be the stalker, doesn't she?" Angela said. "She's not claiming she's carrying Truman Cooper's baby, is she? Because not even my blind grandmother would believe that one."

"Angela?"

"Yes."

"The *Evening News* doesn't print at the weekend, does it?"

"Monday to Friday, three editions a day."

"So, you don't have a deadline until, what, Sunday night?"

"Monday morning, eleven o'clock latest."

"I promise I'll have something for you for Monday's edition."

"And that, Agent Skyberg, is exactly how this sort of arrangement should work. You have a nice day, now," she said, faking an appalling American accent.

Ingrid launched the Google app on her phone. She wanted to know more about Kerrison's arrest for speeding. Truman Cooper had said he was in Italy on business. So what the hell was he doing breaking the speed limit on a country road in Sussex?

35

The other news reports on Tom Kerrison's speeding offense didn't reveal much more than the *Daily Mail* article. The only new information Ingrid uncovered was the location where he had been stopped: a road near a village called South Chailey.

Ingrid phoned Tom Kerrison's number. She had lost count of the number of times she had tried to reach him in the past two days. The phone instantly diverted to voicemail. She was about to hang up when a woman's voice informed her she had reached the publicity department of the House of Versini. Nevertheless, Ingrid left a message asking for him to call her urgently. She dropped her phone onto the torn upholstery and balled her hands into fists, pressing them into her thighs. It was only when the force of the pressure began to hurt that she made herself open her hands, to shake out the tension. But when her eyes drifted back down to page nine of the *Daily Mail*, her shoulder blades moved closer together, her heels pressed harder into the floor and her jaw tightened. She was angry. She had been lied to. But why would Truman Cooper mislead her about Tom's whereabouts? Ingrid got to her feet and started pacing around the reception area. Either Truman had deliberately lied about Tom's whereabouts, or Tom had lied to Truman.

"Can I help?" the police officer on the reception desk asked.

"Thank you. No," Ingrid said, "I'm fine."

But she wasn't fine. She was furious. Her fury, she knew, wasn't for Tom or Truman but for herself. She'd asked for background reports about Oboloyo and Sutcliffe and the Latin Kings, but she'd not done nearly enough research into Tom and Truman. Had she been too impressed with their fame, their house, their money?

She pieced together everything she knew about the two men. One had been as successful as he was beautiful when he was still a teenager, while the other had made ends meet on the streets of Boston and New York until his late thirties. One had spent a lifetime in the closet, the other had never denied his sexuality, trading tricks and favors for a life of parties and glamour. All his adult life, Truman had expected to be successful, but Tom had only ever wanted to earn enough to buy drugs and fun. He was a genius: a fall collection here, an art exhibition there, an award-winning documentary on the side—he excelled at everything without seeming to try, or even care.

Tom Kerrison wasn't a man who anyone told what to do; yet he did whatever Cooper asked of him, including having a child. She wondered how much abuse he had taken over the years, and why he put up with it. Ingrid had a sudden flash of his sculpture of the pregnant woman. The pained expression on her face wasn't anything to do with childbirth: it was how Tom felt about impending parenthood. She shuddered: did he have something to do with Kristyn's disappearance?

Ingrid picked up her phone from the couch and dismissed the twenty per cent battery warning. She wanted to know what Tom Kerrison was doing in South Chailey in Sussex, but when she searched for 'Tom Kerrison Sussex', all the results related to his speeding ticket. She ran a hand through her hair and took a deep breath. She keyed in a different search: 'Truman Cooper Sussex'. She waited for the results to appear on her phone, willing her connection to speed up.

The top link was to a forum asking if *The Belgravia Set* was filmed in Sussex. The next linked to a story of a Sussex eccentric who sported a mustache like the one Cooper's character wore on the show. Ingrid scrolled through a cascade of trivial articles, her disappointment growing with each one.

Google also returned a selection of images relating to Cooper and Sussex. She tapped on one of them. It was a picture of him sitting in a sunny garden drinking a pint of beer. The file name was cooper_sussex12.jpg. Ingrid tapped the 'view page' button. A larger version of the photo appeared on her screen with the caption: 'Truman Cooper enjoys a pint of Harveys in his local pub.' Ingrid zoomed out and scrolled up: it was an article about the movie star swapping the Hollywood Hills for the South Downs. Ingrid swallowed hard: Truman Cooper owned a house in Sussex. She scanned the article looking for a location, her eyes hoping to see the word 'Chailey' but the precise location was not mentioned.

"Are you sure you're OK?" the cop on the desk asked.

Ingrid looked up at him. "Yes. Why?"

"You made a sound. Like you were in pain."

"I did?"

He nodded.

"I'm sorry. I didn't mean to."

"Bad phone reception?" he asked.

"Something like that." It was more the frustration of conducting an investigation via a seven-inch screen and a slow data connection. Ingrid stormed outside into a courtyard that buffered the rifle range from the road and Hyde Park beyond. Heavy traffic noise filled the bright morning air. She called Jennifer.

"Criminal division."

"It's me."

"Where are you?"

"With the Met. Target practice, remember?"

"Sol will be pleased. Louden was in earlier looking for you."

"Louden? On a Saturday?" It was only then that Ingrid remembered what Angelis had said in the Beaufort Club. But then one thing had led to another and the information never got shared. "What did she want?"

"Wouldn't tell me. You want the good news or, like, the bad

news?" Jennifer's sunny California drawl was a contrast to the damp mist that had settled between the trees in the park: fall had arrived. "Well, the good news is that I. Like. just spoke to Gwyneth Jones. I mean literally just got off the phone. And the bad news is that she said she barely spoke to Kate-Lynn, sorry Kristyn, all flight. And I believe her. I totally don't think she's hiding anything."

Ingrid sucked in her cheeks. "That's OK, because I've got another lead."

"You have?"

Ingrid started pacing round the courtyard, like a lone soldier on parade. "I need you to look something up for me. Truman Cooper has a house in Sussex. I need the address."

"OK." Jennifer went quiet while she opened up whichever search engine or database would tell her what she needed to know. In the background, over the sound of traffic and the public address system from a passing open-top bus, Ingrid heard Don say 'good morning'. She didn't feel bad about making them work the weekend: you didn't join the FBI, even as a civilian, if you didn't want to feel the pressure occasionally. "Right," Jennifer said, "I've got something here. The house, oh, wow, that is fancy."

"What is?"

"The house has a name, not an address. It's called Arding Manor."

"And where is it?"

"Um, hold on… near a place called Ditchling. It's a village."

Despite the chill, Ingrid felt flushed and unbelted her jacket. "Now tell me how far this place is from another village called South Chailey."

"How do you spell that?" Ingrid told her, and waited for what felt like minutes for Jennifer to reply. "Six point four miles."

Ingrid gritted her teeth to suppress the 'yes' she wanted to scream into the air. "Next question. How do I get to Ditchling?"

Ingrid started walking toward the gate, her phone clamped to her ear. She unclipped her visitor's pass and handed it to the officer at the barrier and walked out onto a road that ran along the side of the park. She walked quickly to reach her motorcycle, and without thinking broke into a run.

"So, you'd get a train to Brighton from Victoria station and get off at a station called Hassocks. Sounds rude, doesn't it? Um, there's one at 8:51, but you won't get that. The one after that is 9:51... Let's see. It leaves from platform seventeen..." Ingrid was already sprinting by the time Jennifer finished her instructions. "... It says here to use the Buckingham Palace Road entrance, if that means anything to you."

It certainly did.

Ingrid pumped her arms, propelling herself forward, driving her feet into the ground and picking up speed. It was only when she was unlocking the top box and retrieving her helmet that she realized she was still wearing the holster. And it was still holding the Glock 23.

36

Ingrid pulled into the parking lot of The Bull public house in Ditchling at a quarter after ten. She was frozen. Fall had arrived overnight and she'd just been traveling at ninety miles per hour in summer clothing through wind and mist. She pulled off her helmet and gloves and looked at herself in the Triumph's mirrors. She ran her hands through her hair, attempting to give it some shape. There was no way to wear a helmet and have a decent hairstyle, not unless she wanted a buzz cut or a ponytail, neither of which she could ever see herself getting.

The Bull sat at the main intersection in the village. No matter which way she looked she saw something that made her feel she was on the set of a BBC drama. Red mailboxes set inside flint walls, lopsided windows in timber frame cottages, white-painted fingerposts and flower-filled chimney pots standing sentry outside quaint shop doors. All that was missing was a couple of giggling girls in bonnets.

She locked her helmet in the top box and pulled her phone out of her pocket.

"You got that address for me?" she asked Jennifer.

"I'm fine thank you, thanks for asking."

"I'm nearly out of juice, I didn't mean to be rude. I just need to be quick."

"You want me to call your US cell?"

"No point. I left it charging on my desk last night."

"Suppose it seemed like a good idea at the time."

She wasn't helping.

"The address?"

"Well, OK then. I haven't found it yet. It's Saturday. Some places don't open at weekends." Ingrid didn't fill the pause Jennifer had left for effect. "The postal address is just Arding Manor, Ditchling. Nothing helpful in all the usual places; it doesn't appear to be on Google Earth or anywhere so I, like, checked the Ordnance Survey map, and there are three places that could be it. You want me to send you the GPS coordinates?"

"Please."

"And Don wants to know if it's still OK for him to go to Harry Styles's house."

"Tell him he must go. And if he sees a pregnant girl who fits Kristyn's description, he needs to call me right away."

"And if your phone dies?"

"Better call Sol."

Ingrid hung up. Her battery life was down to five per cent. She stared at it as the screen went dark and weighed up the wisdom of turning it off. If she didn't, she risked not being able to make a call in an emergency, but if she did, she might miss a call from Tom Kerrison. It bleeped and immediately lit up. It was the message from Jennifer with the coordinates. Now she was down to four per cent battery. Ingrid pursed her lips and made the decision to power it off.

She tried the door of the pub, but it was locked. She cupped her cold hands round her eyes and peered through the glazed panels: it was dark inside and no one was around. It wasn't yet half past ten: it would be at least another thirty minutes before the place opened.

Across the street was an up-market village store, painted in an understated shade of cream that was probably called 'pebble' or 'chalk' or 'winter sun'. A chalkboard sign advertised artisanal breads, specially imported wines and ten different kinds of olives, not the long-life milk, batteries and frozen microwave meals that—in Ingrid's limited exposure to the English countryside—village stores usually sold.

A bell tinged above her head as she opened the door and she was engulfed by the aroma of baking and freshly brewed coffee. And warmth. Ingrid just wanted to stand there for a few minutes and warm up a little. The store was much bigger than it looked from the outside; the rear half doubled as a café where a small group of moms with babies were enjoying a get-together, while an elderly couple indulged in a particularly unhealthy breakfast of sausage and eggs.

A woman in her early twenties, possibly late teens, stood behind a refrigerated counter. She smiled at Ingrid as if she were an old friend, but didn't say a word.

"Hi, I'm hoping you can help me."

"You're American." She had the self-satisfied tone of someone who had just answered a question correctly on a TV quiz show. Ingrid guessed she was one of many recent graduates who, having racked up a mountain of debt and found the door to the job market slammed shut, had moved back in with her parents and was actually grateful to be working in the local store.

"Correct."

"What can I get you?"

"A little information."

The girl looked worried. "I can try."

Ingrid looked at the selection of Danish pastries displayed in wicker baskets on the countertop. She really should eat something. "Do you do coffee to go?"

"To take away?"

Wasn't that what she had just said? "Yes."

"Of course, what would you like?"

"Americano."

"Milk?"

"No, thanks." She just wanted it to be hot, and to wrap her fingers round it.

"Anything else?"

"I'll take one of those pastries and some directions to a place called Arding Manor. Know how I can get there?"

"Ah." The girl's expression was apologetic. "That I can't do. Let me get Antonia, she makes better coffee than me anyway. It's only my second day."

The girl disappeared through a door into the kitchen at the other end of the counter, leaving Ingrid to ponder if she wanted an apple or apricot pastry. She was so hungry she considered one of each. An older woman with her hair in a bun marched up to the counter.

"Hello," she said, in a voice that was slightly too loud. "You're after directions, I hear."

"And a coffee," Ingrid said. She reached inside her jacket for her wallet and felt the Glock. She instantly pulled her hand back, concerned the woman might see the pistol. "Americano. To go."

"A long black?"

"If that's what you call it."

"One shot or two?"

"Two, thanks."

The woman tamped the ground coffee into the filter and placed two shot glasses on the stainless steel tray of the espresso machine. "Where is it you want to go?"

"Arding Manor."

The woman's eyes narrowed, the skin between her eyebrows puckering like a pastry crust. "Why do you want to know that?"

That wasn't the response Ingrid had expected. "Why wouldn't I want to know that?"

"You know who lives there?"

Ingrid was taken aback by the woman's demeanor. She was starting to remind her of the guards she had encountered during visiting hours at federal penitentiaries. "I do."

"We try to take care of them, you see. They come here for privacy, not to have tourists camp outside the gates."

Carefully, Ingrid reached inside her jacket, angling herself in such a way that the woman would not see what was in the holster, and pulled out her wallet. She selected her embassy ID—her FBI credentials too often made people think she was playing a practical joke—and showed it to the woman. "I'm not a tourist."

The woman peered at Ingrid's card, and then turned back to the coffee machine. "You want milk?"

"No, thanks."

She placed the cardboard cup on the counter. "You know something," her voice was now several decibels quieter. "You're the second American asking for the Manor today."

Goosebumps rippled across Ingrid's skin. Donaho. *Please, God, no.* "Was it a guy?"

"Yes. Anything else?"

Ingrid pointed to the basket. "One of those. Was it tall man, 250 pounds, baseball cap?"

The woman crossed her arms and wrinkled her nose. "No, little fella. Probably should wear a baseball cap, though. Apricot or apple?"

Ingrid trembled with relief as she pulled out a £10 note and placed it on the countertop: Avery Donaho hadn't made it to Ditchling. "Apricot, please. Did you tell him where to find Arding Manor?"

"You know what, I didn't. I took one look at him and thought, 'You're not a fan of the show.' In fact, I'd bet he's never seen it. I didn't like the look of him, so I gave him directions to the A23 instead." She sounded quite pleased with herself.

"Why didn't you like the look of him?"

"Like I say, he should probably wear a hat."

Ingrid didn't know how to respond.

"Well, it's not normal, to cover your entire head in tattoos, is it? Right across the back of his head was a tattoo of a skull, like an X-ray. Only the wrong way round, of course. Two dead eyes in the back of his head. I mean, that's just asking for trouble."

37

Ingrid followed the directions she'd been given to Arding Manor and found herself on a narrow country road tracing the contours of the South Downs. To her right were open fields dotted with sheep, to her left was a long hedge obscuring the houses on the other side from view. In the early morning mist, the place looked almost magical.

The usually reliable Triumph Tiger 800 started to splutter beneath her. She checked she was in the right gear but quickly figured out the problem. She was low on fuel. She leaned forward and turned the petcock to start using the reserve tank. She had enough for another ten miles, fifteen max, before she'd have to fill up. She hoped it wouldn't matter: from the directions she'd been given in the village store, she couldn't be more than a mile away.

Up ahead, Ingrid spotted the landmark she was looking for: a long, low red-brick wall set back from the road. Tall railings were cemented into the wall, and behind the railings was a wooded area. Ingrid slowed to get a better look, but she couldn't see any kind of building beyond the trees. After a couple of hundred yards, she came to a set of iron gates hinged onto weathered stone gateposts, just as the woman in the store had described. She killed the engine and got off the bike. Even with the helmet on, the sound of the birdsong was incredible, like a sound effect from a natural history program.

Beyond the wrought-iron gates a path lined with linden trees curved slightly through the woods and fog toward an unseen destination. Ingrid held onto the gates, pushing her helmet up against the metal in an attempt to see further. It was a pointless exercise: the house would have been bought for its privacy and a curved path deliberately denied prying eyes a view of the residence. It was the perfect place to hide a pregnant woman. Or bury her body. It was only when Ingrid took a step backwards that she noticed the heavy chain on the gates. A rusted chain. And at the base of the gates were tall weeds: they hadn't been opened for years. She spotted messages scrawled in marker pen on the stone gateposts. *I love you Truman. Wanna slow dance with me? Anna, Wisconsin. Japan love you Truman!*

Ingrid pulled her helmet off. This wasn't making sense. Either the woman in the shop had given her—and fans armed with marker pens—false directions, or she had taken a wrong turn. She crossed to the other side of the road to get a bit of perspective. The birdsong was like nothing she'd heard before: the woods were alive with noise, yet she couldn't see a single bird.

She stared at the gates and saw for the first time the way the iron twisted at the top in the middle to form the shape of an A and an M. Arding Manor. *It is the right place.* Either Ingrid had wasted valuable time leaving London, or there was another way in. She got back on the bike and continued on down the narrow road until she reached the end of the red-brick wall. A dirt track left the road at a right angle, running through the woods. The boundary of Arding Manor was now marked by a ten-foot-high chain-link fence.

Ingrid took the turn and after about a hundred and fifty yards she came to a steel gate, solid except for a hatch where a security guard could check your credentials. She killed the engine, put the bike on the stand and looked around. Above the gate were two cameras. A yellow sign had been stuck to the gate to warn trespassers of security patrols. Down the track was a parked car. It had a Hertz sticker in the year window. A rental.

Ingrid stood on tiptoes in an attempt to see through the hatch, but it was too high. Embedded in the gate was an intercom. She pressed the button, but didn't hear a damn thing. She removed her helmet, but still couldn't hear anything. Normally there was a click, or a buzz, but there was just silence, as if it had been disconnected. She waited a minute, then pressed the button again. While she stood waiting for a response, she heard a vehicle drive down the road. It was the first vehicle she had seen or heard since she'd left the village. If Tom and Truman had wanted isolation, they had found it.

Ingrid moved the Triumph out of the way and locked her helmet in its box. She put the bike key in her front pants pocket. In her rear pants pocket was her iPhone. In her jacket was a wallet and a penknife. And the Glock 23. Ten miles' worth of petrol, four minutes of battery life, a little under £20 and thirteen bullets.

If I was in the States, she asked herself, *would I just shoot the damn lock?* Of course not: a tall locked gate was a better challenge than a climbing wall. She placed one hand in the open hatch, the other round the edge of the post, feeling for a hinge or a bolt to grab hold of. Then she bent her knees, pulled them toward her chest like a vertical squat thrust and levered herself to the top of the gate. A flash of the run in Angela Tate's pantyhose slipped into her mind, making her smile. She straddled the cold steel for a few moments to get a view of what lay ahead. Directly beneath her was a muddy clearing rippled with tire tracks left by turning vehicles. Beyond that was a path snaking through the mist-shrouded trees.

She dropped down to the mud, picked herself up and started walking.

38

Ingrid could run faster and further than most humans on the planet. She was fitter and stronger than almost all of the men she'd had to restrain in her career. But there was still something about walking alone through the woods that spooked her. She blamed Little Red Riding Hood.

There was a sudden movement in the trees. She turned.

Ingrid looked through the trunks and thought she saw a branch spring back. Was there a dog? A security patrol? A photographer? She stood stock still, staring into the woods. Her breathing became shallow. Her heart hammered. A breeze rustled through the canopy, sending a gentle shower of leaves down to the mud. She kept her focus fixed on the branch that had moved, aware just how quickly she was drawing breath. There was no one there.

The muddy path—twin tire tracks separated by a ragged stripe of grass—looked well-used. It had rained overnight in London, and by the looks of things it had rained in Sussex too. She couldn't be sure, but one set of tracks appeared to have been created after the rain had fallen. And that meant a car had driven down this path within the past few hours. A big car, possibly the Range Rover she had seen parked in the courtyard of the Wapping warehouse.

The air was cooler in the woods and the morning mist

lingered more densely in patches. Ingrid shivered, but whether from the change in temperature or evolutionary instincts she couldn't be sure. Up ahead, almost silhouetted against the mist, was a large dead tree, its bare branches stretching across the path like witches' fingers. She heard the noise again. A snapping. Something was moving.

Ingrid checked behind her, then craned her neck to see further down the path. She looked left and right into the woods. A large bird flapped its wings above her head. Was that it? Just a bird? Instinctively, Ingrid's right hand reached inside her jacket and felt for her gun. She swallowed hard. What was she thinking? This was England. She withdrew her hand.

The air was sweet, a mix of newly fallen leaves and morning dew with a faint reminder of last night's wood smoke. She filled her lungs, mindful that if she controlled her breathing she would also check her fear. It was just the woods. There were no bears, no poisonous snakes. *This is just a morning walk through the trees.* Her boots squelched into the mud. She didn't want to dwell on how much they had cost.

The path curved away to her right, and the tire tracks deepened where vehicles had been forced to slow and change gear. She looked down, searching for the best footholds, and saw footprints. Fresh footprints. Sneakers. She sensed movement again. She reached in for the gun.

In the middle of the path, staring straight back at her, was a deer. A small female. Neither of them moved. The doe was so small and so beautiful Ingrid didn't want to give her any reason to run off. She didn't even want to blink, just in case it brought their encounter to an end. For a few seconds, maybe a minute, the two of them looked at each other, frozen in time and place.

A sound rumbled through the trees. The deer moved an ear in the direction of the noise then sprang into the undergrowth, darting between the trees. Ingrid stood and watched, hoping for another glimpse, but the animal had merged with the forest. She was gone.

After a few more minutes, Ingrid reached the end of the woods where the muddy path opened out into a yard surrounded by a cluster of small buildings, mostly brick-built with corrugated iron roofs. They looked like garden stores, possibly an office for the estate manager, a couple of garages, and just beyond was a row of large greenhouses. Perhaps if it wasn't the weekend, she thought, there might be somebody working there, but the place was still and silent. The temperature jumped a few degrees in the open, and the weak fall sunshine created shadows across the landscape.

Ingrid followed the tire tracks down a slope and as she turned a bend around a small stand of birch trees, the main house came into view. It looked like something from a history book, the sort of property owned by a duke who had briefly courted Elizabeth I. It wasn't particularly large, but it was grand, with turrets and elaborate brick patterns between the dark timber framework. It had almost as many chimney pots as it did windows.

The track joined the main path from the unused gates, her boots slipping slightly as dirt gave way to gravel. She followed the path through a Moorish carpet of formal gardens and slowly approached the grand entrance. With every step, Ingrid expected to hear an engine as a security patrol approached, or maybe even a gunshot to act as a warning. But all she could hear was her boots crunching on the gravel and a lark singing in the air above.

It took several minutes to reach the front door, which gave her time to come up with a plausible reason for her trespass. She decided that if she was intercepted by a member of staff—and, surely, with such vast grounds and outbuildings, there had to be staff—she would say she was Tom's niece who was visiting for the weekend. If Tom himself answered the door, then she would have to judge her response by how distressed he was to see her.

She rang the bell, a weathered button at the center of an ornate brass disc. She heard the chime resonate within the building and waited for the sound of footsteps. None came. After ringing the bell a second time, she decided to walk round the side of the manor house.

History was not a subject Ingrid knew much about, but she was willing to bet that if she managed to get inside Arding Manor, it would be the oldest building she had ever set foot in.

The stone windowsills drooped with age, the glass inside the leaded panels was rippled and dimpled, made by hand many generations before.

Ingrid flexed her fingers, exposing as much skin as possible to the air to evaporate the dampness of her palms. Beneath her jacket, her cotton jersey started sticking to her underarms. The air was cool, but she was sweating. She peered through each window she passed, and while the low sun made it difficult to always see in, the house appeared to be empty. Where were the gardeners? The housekeeper? Where the hell was Tom Kerrison?

Ingrid reached a smaller doorway that she guessed would have once been—or might still have been—used by servants. Through the glass she saw a large farmhouse kitchen, and on the gravel around the door were several cigarette butts; by the look of them they had been dropped after the last rainfall. That morning. Tom Kerrison had been smoking in the gallery's courtyard the night they met; smoking, and drinking whisky from a flask. Ingrid hadn't seen him smoke since.

There hadn't been any ashtrays in the house in Wapping. He hadn't even smelt of cigarettes. Why? Was it a habit he kept from Truman? After all, wasn't the actor a control freak who needed everything to be perfect? What had his Wikipedia entry said about his participation in *Celebrity MasterChef*? Something about attention to detail and precise presentation. And then there was his fitness obsession. The first time she'd met him he'd had damp hair from a swim. She could easily see he was the sort of person who always performed the same number of lengths, and the same number of strokes per length.

For someone like Truman, a partner who smoked, who willingly let toxins into his body, would be almost impossible to deal with. It barely required any imagination to picture the tantrums he'd throw. He freaked out with the tiniest provocation, like not using filtered water in the coffee machine. She didn't know very much about obsessive compulsive disorder, but she was starting to suspect Truman Cooper's erratic behavior had a medical origin. Having witnessed his outbursts, she could understand why Tom Kerrison might keep secrets. But would he, *could he*, have kept how he felt about fatherhood from Truman?

The article in the *Daily Mail* had mentioned Tom's hospitalization for stress. She was pretty sure that if she asked Angela Tate, the journalist would tell her 'stress' was a code, something agreed between the media and a publicist to obscure the real reason one of the world's most lauded fashion designers had spent a night in hospital. When she thought about the scar she'd seen on Kerrison's wrist, she wondered if the exhibition, the baby and the pressure of running a multinational business had pushed Tom too far. And if he was that unstable, what might he be capable of doing to Kristyn?

Ingrid positioned herself where the smoker had stood so she could have the same view as him. In front of her was a walled kitchen garden with neat rows of ripening squashes and A-frames of climbing beans. It was tempting to indulge herself in thoughts of Merchant Ivory films or Jane Austen novels, but she needed to focus. Something wasn't right. This wasn't the weekend retreat for two middle-aged, enormously successful men. Given their work schedules, it was possible they only made it to Arding Manor a few times a year. They didn't need fifteen squashes in a weekend; they couldn't eat that many beans or lettuces. What was she missing?

Ingrid counted the cigarette butts. Seven. Whoever had smoked them was in distress. She imagined Tom, sitting on the back step, drinking unfiltered coffee and lighting each cigarette from the dying butt of the last. She was starting to see him as he really was—a street hustler, a cowboy who could never quite believe his luck. Despite all his success, Tom Kerrison still didn't think he was worthy of Truman's love. Maybe he didn't think he was worthy of a family either. It explained why he had disappeared: she could only hope to God it didn't explain Kristyn's disappearance too.

Something moved in Ingrid's peripheral vision. She turned, adrenaline surging, ready for confrontation.

"Cully. Hey boy." The good-natured animal walked right up

to her, his pink tongue lolling out of his mouth as he panted. Ingrid patted his head. "Where did you come from?"

Ingrid looked in the direction the dog had come from, expecting to see Tom Kerrison return from an early morning walk. But he didn't come. No one came.

39

"Where did you come from?" Ingrid said again. The dog just carried on wagging his tail, pleased to have found someone to stroke him. He didn't seem distressed, or hungry. "Have you been left in charge?" she said to the dog. "Or have you eaten all of the gardeners?"

Cully's tail started to wag with more enthusiasm.

"You have?"

He let out a sharp, short bark. *One of those dogs that thinks he's human.*

"Come on then, you better show me where you buried the bones."

Ingrid followed a stone path through the vegetable beds to a gap in a clipped yew hedge. She heard a plane overhead and followed it across the sky as it flew over the house. She stared at the rear of the building, making sure she hadn't missed anything. It was three stories high, with the third floor up inside the roof identifiable by a row of small dormer windows. She noted that each window was a slightly different size from its neighbor, a result of repair, or subsidence, or the fact that each frame was made by hand before the *Mayflower* had set sail. She flinched: something moved in one of the top-floor windows. It had probably just been the reflection of the plane.

She followed Cully through the gap in the hedge to a wide

circle of gravel and an open-sided barn that provided covered parking for five cars. In the apex roof of the barn was a row of three skylights: she guessed the loft had been turned into a workshop or a games room, something realtors would describe as a 'man cave'. Two of the parking spaces were occupied, one with a decrepit Land Rover with bricks for tires, the other with a dark green vintage Mercedes Roadster. It was the kind of vehicle a European prince would use to court a Hollywood actress in a 1950s romantic comedy. It was hard to tell with gravel if a car had recently pulled in or out.

Cully trotted up to the garage. The fact that the dog was not showing any signs of distress or neglect suggested Tom was around somewhere. Ingrid felt the hood of the Mercedes. Completely cold. She looked around for any other sign of recent activity. At the far end was a row of trash cans. She lifted the lids one by one, but all were empty. Beyond the trash cans was a door. She tried the handle but it didn't budge.

Ingrid walked around the back of the barn. A garden hoe leaned up against the flint wall, but that was it. She turned to go back, but something made her look again. The wall was wet, like the patch a dog leaves when it urinates. Only the patch was too high. It had been left by a man.

How long would piss take to dry? On a cold misty morning? Fifteen minutes? Thirty, max? A man had been here in the very recent past. A man who presumably couldn't have been Tom, because Tom would have access to a bathroom. Ingrid felt pressure constrict her ribs. She swallowed hard. Or was she just being prudish? All alone on your country estate, would you bother going all the way inside the house to answer the call of nature? The dog barked from the other side of the barn. It wasn't a distressed bark, just a friendly noise to say either 'where are you?' or 'I'm still here, you know'.

Ingrid walked back to the turnaround and noticed that the garage was asymmetrical. The open side didn't run the full length of the barn: the door she had tried had to lead to a stairwell and up to the man cave.

"Hey there boy," she said to the dog. "Who's here with you? Eh?"

The dog's wagging tail was visible above the hood of the Roadster. She walked round the car and saw he was pawing at the bottom of the door. She tried the handle again, then knocked hard.

"Hello!" she shouted. "Anyone up there?"

Ingrid looked at the dog. He really wanted to be let in: there had to be someone upstairs. Someone who wasn't answering. Someone who was hiding.

"Tom? Mr Kerrison?"

She didn't have time to wait until he came down. She barely had a day left to find Kristyn and get her on a plane. Now was not the time for a stake out. She shouldered the door. It didn't budge.

"Stand back, fella," she said to the dog and felt inside her jacket for the Glock. "Seriously, you want to be well away. Shoo!" She kicked the dog gently. The dumb mutt didn't even yelp. "If there's anyone behind this door, you want to step away now. In three seconds I am going to blow the lock off. If you're hiding behind this door, step away." Deep breath. "One. Two. Three."

Ingrid pulled the trigger and fired a bullet into the lock. The dog started to howl. Twelve bullets left. She tried the handle. It still wouldn't budge. "I'm sorry, Cully, but I'm going to have to do that again." She fired again. Down to eleven. Keeping her gun at shoulder level, she kicked the door and it opened.

"Hello?" she said, stepping inside. In front of her was a staircase. There were no other doors, no other possibilities. Just a staircase rising into a darkened room above. "Hello? Tom?"

She thought she heard something.

"Who's there?"

No response. The dog stopped howling. The only sound was her heartbeat, heavy, slow and hard. Ingrid took the first stair. Scuff marks ran the length of the stairwell. There were muddy footprints on the treads. The smell of gasoline told her she was entering a workshop. After another step she stopped and looked up into the void. Keeping the gun at shoulder level, she placed her foot on the next tread.

The dog pushed past her and bounded up the steps, his claws scratching on the bare wood. He reached the top of the stairs, turned right into the room and out of sight. He barked hello to someone.

"Ssshh." A man's voice? A woman's voice? Ingrid couldn't tell.

"I know you're up there," Ingrid said. She looked up at the final four steps. "As you must have heard, I am armed. Do not, I repeat, do not make any sudden moves."

Footsteps. Ingrid moved the gun in a narrow arc, aiming to the right to cover any approach.

A figure appeared tentatively at the top of the stairs. A young woman, hair unwashed, face trembling, eyes wide like the doe on the path, her belly round and taut. Kristyn.

Something leapt inside Ingrid's chest. "It's OK," she said and lowered the Glock.

The girl's eyes darted sideways. Ingrid followed her gaze and saw a shadowy figure standing above the banister. A man. A tattooed man. Holding a wrench. He brought the tool down hard on Ingrid's head, sending her reeling backwards down the stairs, knocking the Glock from her hands.

40

Ingrid's shoulder slammed into the wall as she fell. She extended her right arm, bracing herself, stopping herself from tumbling further. Her heart pounded so hard it hurt. The man rushed down the stairs at her, the wrench still in his hand. *Perfect.* He was going to make it easy for her. He brought his arm down hard, aiming again at Ingrid's head. His momentum and his flailing arm made him top-heavy. All Ingrid had to do was obstruct his ankle and he fell forward, flying down the stairs headfirst.

The man found his feet. The Glock was on the floor next to him. Ingrid leapt down the stairs to kick the gun away, clattering it out onto the concrete floor of the garage. He scrambled up on his haunches, pushed his arms against the wall to lever himself upright. Ingrid raised her knee, jamming it under his jaw as he leaned forward and smashed his head back against the wall. The loud thud his skull made against the brick told her he wouldn't be getting up anytime soon. She stepped out into the garage, scrambled the Glock and holstered it.

The man was slumped at the bottom of the stairs, concussed if not completely knocked out. His skull tattoo was partially visible as his head lolled to one side. Ingrid stepped over him and ran up the stairs, taking them three at a time, racing into the room at the top.

She looked around. A tool bench. Racks of screwdrivers, ratchets and wrenches. An empty desk and a kitchenette with a kettle and a fridge. A tattered couch. Where was Kristyn? Where was the dog? At the other end of the room was a door. Ingrid walked toward it.

"Kristyn? Are you OK?"

There was no answer.

"Kristyn, my name is Ingrid. You're safe now. I promise." Ingrid approached the open doorway. "Kristyn, I'm going to come into the room now."

Kristyn stood opposite the door, wearing a gray tunic dress, a maternity version of something from Manuela's collection, the dog sitting dutifully at her feet. Behind her was a single bed, a metal safe and a wooden chair. She was holding a crowbar that was shaking in her wavering grasp. Ingrid held up her hands in surrender.

"Hi."

"Get away from me." There was steel in her eyes and iron in her voice.

"I'm here to help. I'm from the embassy."

"I know who you are." The bar wobbled in her hands.

"You do?"

"Tom said you might find this place." Kristyn took a step toward Ingrid, holding the crowbar like a baseball player on strike. "Get away. Leave me alone." The dog started to whine. There were heavy footsteps behind and Ingrid turned sharply. The tattooed man staggered toward her, dazed but still dangerous, the wrench in his right hand.

Ingrid stepped toward him and grabbed his right wrist, twisting it outwards until he dropped the weapon. She brought her right hand up under his chin, shoving his head up and back. He was no taller than she was, but he was muscular and strong, a street fighter. She stamped hard on his foot with her heel as he swung an empty right fist at her jaw. The rings on his fingers scratched deep into her cheek.

Ingrid hit his jaw again, slamming his teeth together, slicing his tongue. He grabbed both her shoulders and slammed her against a wall. He brought his head forward and down, jamming his forehead into her temple. She brought a knee up hard and fast, making decisive contact. He lurched backwards, clutching his crotch. Ingrid kicked him in the jaw, aiming for the exact same spot she'd hit before. The toe of her boot rammed up into his chin, snapping his head back and sending him to the floor. This time he was out cold.

Ingrid glanced up at Kristyn, standing on the threshold into the bedroom area, still holding the crowbar.

"You seen any rope in this place?" she asked the girl. Ingrid stepped over the man and rushed to the tool bench. There were a couple of sets of keys, one of which looked like it was attached to a rosary, oil cans and engine parts. "I need to tie him before he wakes."

"There's duct tape," Kristyn said, nodding in the direction of one of the desks.

Ingrid swiped a roll of tape and hurried back to the man. "Who is this guy?" she asked.

Kristyn watched as Ingrid rolled the man over and bound his hands together behind his back. She lowered the crowbar. "He was going to kidnap me."

Ingrid tore the tape between her teeth. "Don't you mean he *did* kidnap you?" Ingrid couldn't work out what was going on. She shoved her arms under his armpits and dragged him across the floor. He was a dead weight and the exertion immediately raised her temperature and heart rate. The dog followed. "Hey there, buddy, keep your distance." Ingrid looked up at Kristyn. "Can you keep a hold of the dog. I don't want him licking this guy awake."

Kristyn dropped the bar onto the couch and lowered herself down. "Come here boy."

"I can't work out if he's one of the smartest dogs I ever met or one of the dumbest," Ingrid said in an attempt to start a conversation. She pushed the man up against the banister and felt inside his jacket. The hilt of a knife. She carefully pulled it from its sheath. A nine-inch blade. A murder weapon-in-waiting. She kicked it across the floor and patted his pockets. A passport, a wallet. She dropped them on the floor and started to run the tape around his chest, through the rails and around his chest again, like a bridegroom tied against a lamppost on a bachelor party prank. Ingrid checked his pulse. Slow but steady. No need to call an ambulance. She bound him at the ankles, knees and feet. Satisfied the man wouldn't be going anywhere anytime soon, she switched her attention to the girl.

Kristyn was still sitting on the couch, one hand stroking the dog's ear, the other her distended belly. She looked bemused rather than scared, stunned more than relieved. The girl winced: she was in pain. Ingrid stayed on her knees next to the man, understanding that the girl needed a bit of space to process, to breathe.

"This was supposed to be my safe house," Kristyn said. Her tone was weary, her voice quiet. "First he shows up, now you. I could have been in the main house."

"Why weren't you?" Ingrid didn't move. She knew how to gain a vulnerable child's trust and invading their personal space was the best way of making them push back. More than anything right now, Ingrid needed Kristyn to trust her.

"Tom said no one comes here. No one has a key even. Except him."

"What is this place?" Ingrid stretched out a hand for the man's passport.

"It's where the driver lives."

"They have a driver?" Ingrid looked at the passport photo, then back at the man. The passport was stolen. One of the advantages of the tattoos, she reasoned. Who could say what this man would look like without them?

"I don't think so. Maybe the people who used to live here had one."

Ingrid opened the wallet. Over £400 and credit cards in several different names. "But it was Tom who brought you here?"

Kristyn shook her head. "He told me to come, gave me keys, but he didn't bring me. I took the train. Tom brought the dog yesterday. To keep me company till he can come back after he's got everything figured out."

Ingrid was confused. "What do you mean, figured out?" She got to her feet, but didn't walk toward the girl.

Kristyn slumped back against the couch and looked up at Ingrid. "Surprised you haven't guessed."

Ingrid bent down and picked up the knife before dropping it into the sink. She exhaled and leaned against the short row of kitchen units. When she ran her fingers through her hair, she felt a bump where the wrench had struck her. Should she say something? No. *Let the girl talk.* If she's talking, just let the words flow, that was how things worked best. The more someone talks to you, the more they come to trust you. The more you talk at them, the more likely it is you'll drive them away. But the girl didn't talk, she just sat on the couch, stroking the obedient dog and staring into the middle distance. Ingrid couldn't risk the silence enduring any longer. She needed to form a bond with the girl.

"Do you need a doctor?" she asked.

Kristyn looked up at her. "No, but you might."

"Why?"

"Your face."

Ingrid felt her cheek and pulled her hand away. Blood. Not too much. "I'll heal. Are you hungry? Thirsty?"

Kristyn shook her head. "No, I feel sick."

"What about Cully? Has he eaten?"

"He got fed this morning. Just before Vinny got here and threw him out."

"Vinny?"

Kristyn indicated the duct tape mummy.

"You *know* him?"

The girl nodded.

"From Aurora?"

Fear flashed across Kristyn's features. It had been the wrong thing to say, Ingrid had shown her cards too soon.

"I'm so sorry about your sister." She took a step toward the girl, sensing now was the time to empathize. She knelt down in front of her. "It must be hard for you right now. You've got so much to deal with."

Kristyn's face was taut. She refused to meet Ingrid's gaze.

"Stop playing nice." The determination had returned to her voice. "I know who you are and I know why you're here."

"You do?"

"You're not from the embassy. Tom said you were FBI. And I'm telling you like I told Vinny: I will not testify."

"Vinny? Why'd he want you to testify?" Ingrid was confused. If he wanted her to testify, then he definitely wasn't working with Avery Donaho.

Kristyn risked a quick glance at Ingrid, disgust evident in her expression. "You people. You think you're the solution, but you're the fucking poison."

"Kristyn, I—"

The girl grabbed the crowbar from the couch next to her and swung her arm in an arc to land a blow across Ingrid's ear, knocking her sideways onto the grubby carpet. The room started to spin. "What the hell?" Ingrid slumped, her body floored by both the impact and the shock.

Kristyn used both arms to haul herself to the edge of the couch. She pushed up with one hand, struggling to get upright. When she had her balance, she stepped over to the work bench, swiped a set of car keys and disappeared down the stairs.

41

Ingrid blinked at the indentation the girl had left on the couch. What just happened? She struggled onto all fours and used the couch to get herself upright.

"Why didn't you stop her?" she said to the dog. "Eh?"

Cully whimpered and cocked his head to one side. *Useless.*

Ingrid staggered across the room to the staircase, regaining increments of balance with each step. Vinny's head lolled to one side and blood dribbled from the corner of his mouth. He looked like a drunk who had passed out but he was breathing fine. Safe to be left. Ingrid made her way slowly down the stairs, stumbling as she reached the bottom, her head still spinning.

Kristyn had somehow squeezed herself in behind the wheel of the Mercedes and was trying the key in the ignition. Ingrid lurched in front of the car, placing both palms flat against the hood.

"Why does Vinny want you to testify? I don't get it. He's not here to stop you?"

The girl didn't make eye contact, focusing intently on the key in the ignition, willing the engine to kick into life.

"Tell me who he is, Kristyn. He's not going to be out cold forever. I can't just leave him like that. Who is he?"

Kristyn tilted her head and stared at Ingrid. "Work. It. Out."

The engine made a slight clinking noise. Either the battery

was dead or it wasn't connected. Ingrid could take her time while Kristyn turned the key fruitlessly. Without the car, the kid had no means of escape. Better for her to realize that than for Ingrid to tell her. The dog appeared at the bottom of the stairs, his front paws on the concrete floor of the garage. He looked at Kristyn, then looked at Ingrid.

"OK, I will work it out… He wants Sutcliffe behind bars, that's got to be it. And he knows your testimony can do that. But you need to know he'd have a helluva fight getting you on a plane right now."

Kristyn didn't look convinced.

"All you'd have to do is tell the check-in desk you're nearly nine months pregnant. Without a doctor's letter they won't let you board. He *can't* make you testify, Kristyn. He's got no power over you."

The girl didn't respond; she didn't even make eye contact. She just stared at the ignition and tried the key again and again, desperately trying to resist the moment when she'd have to admit she wasn't going anywhere.

"I promise you, he can't make you do anything. And besides, *I* won't let him." Ingrid hoped she was gaining the girl's trust. "I promise you."

Kristyn Bowers stopped staring at the key and looked at Ingrid through the windshield. "He says he'll kill Brody if I don't."

Ingrid took a second. "Who's Brody?"

"My sister's little boy."

The hideous details of Kate-Lynn's murder surged into Ingrid's memory. A toddler left alone with his mother's corpse. Ingrid swallowed hard, hoping he'd be too young to remember. She stepped round the hood, opened the driver's door and crouched down. Kristyn looked at her, eyes filled with tears.

"That is one thing I can take care of. Right now," Ingrid said. "One phone call. I can get him into protection. I can make sure he's safe."

"Like Dion? Witness protection didn't exactly work out for him, did it?"

Ingrid carefully placed a hand on Kristyn's knee and was relieved when the girl didn't push it away. "Look, I don't know much about the trial or what happened in Aurora. It's not my case, but I do know your friend Dion must have made a mistake. I read he was killed in Skokie: he shouldn't have been anywhere near Chicago."

Kristyn was listening.

"He must have told someone. I'm not saying witness protection is easy, because it isn't, but it does work. We keep people safe for decades. For the rest of their lives. And it works best for kids. Your nephew will be safe, I can promise you that."

Tears rolled down Kristyn's face. Her hands held the steering wheel like she needed it for support. "But if I do testify," she said, wiping her face, "then Sutcliffe will kill me."

"You can go into witness protection too."

The girl started shaking her head. Her jaw trembled. Her grip loosened on the steering wheel. "You're just saying that because you want me to testify."

Ingrid gently squeezed the girl's knee. "Honestly, Kristyn, right now I don't give a damn about the case. I'd rather a man like Sutcliffe was locked up, but all I care about is you and dealing with that man upstairs. Then I want to get you someplace safe where you can have the baby. I swear."

The girl carried on shaking her head. "I don't believe you."

Ingrid took a deep breath. There was no point saying any more. Deeds were the only thing that could make a difference now. Actions. It didn't matter what Ingrid said; she was going to have to *show* Kristyn she was serious.

"I just want Tom," the girl said. She looked down at her pregnant belly. "He's the only person in this whole fucking mess who doesn't want something from me. I just want Tom."

The dog padded out onto the gravel, as if he was giving the women some privacy. Ingrid's knees were starting to hurt a little from crouching, but she didn't want to stand up. It was important that Kristyn could look down on her slightly. The body language was good: she was demonstrating her subordination.

"Do you know why I'm here?" Ingrid removed her hand,

resting it on the Roadster's chrome foot tread. "I'm here because Truman and Tom asked me to look for you. Did you know that? I'm not here because of Sutcliffe." She paused, hoping to get some kind of reaction from Kristyn. "Now it turns out that Tom's known where you've been all along. He's lied to me—that's fine, I can handle it, the FBI gets lied to for a living—but he's lied to Truman. The guy has been out of his mind, and one word from Tom would have saved him so much pain." She inhaled deeply. Kristyn stared straight ahead through the windshield, watching the dog. "This is the man he loves, and he's lied to him about you, about their baby. So I don't know what plan you and he have been working on, but are you sure he's who you need right now? Are you sure you can trust a man like that?"

Kristyn stopped shaking her head. She didn't move. She was frozen. She didn't even blink.

"Kristyn?"

The girl's jaw started to tremble again.

"Kristyn, what is it?"

"I... I..."

"Yes?"

"I think my water's just broke."

42

"It's going to be OK. *You're* going to be OK."

Kristyn's eyes were wild with fear.

"Let's get you out of there," Ingrid said. "Come on now, nice and gentle." She stood up and offered both hands to Kristyn.

The girl put one foot on the ground and twisted to get her other leg out of the car.

"How on earth did you even get in there?" Ingrid asked.

"I… what if I've…?"

The girl was embarrassed. Old enough to steal a passport and become a surrogate, old enough to cross an ocean, but still worried about the mess she might have made on the upholstery. "It doesn't matter."

The dog padded up to see what was going on. "Hey there boy, give the girl some space." He sniffed at the bullet casings. Kristyn leaned against the car and pulled herself upright.

"How are you feeling? Any pain?"

"A bit." She winced. "A lot. Been going on a while." She reached a hand down and felt the back of her dress.

"Don't worry about it. You're having a baby. It's what happens." Ingrid checked the seat. "It looks fine." She reached under the dash and found the lever that popped the hood.

"What are you doing?" Kristyn asked. She had one hand on

her belly, the other arm was resting on the roof of the car, her face contorted with pain.

"I'm connecting the battery." Ingrid lifted the hood, found the loose wires and attached them to the battery's terminals. "A lot of rich people do it. Makes it harder to steal their half-million-dollar cars."

"A lot of dealers do it too."

Ingrid closed the hood, letting it slam down hard. "All right then, let's find you a hospital."

"What?" Kristyn and the dog were both staring at Ingrid, with almost identical expressions of confusion. "I'm not going to the hospital. You need to call Tom."

"Tom? Why?"

"He's arranging things. Flying a midwife in from Italy, the sister of someone who works for him. Someone untraceable. He said he'd have it all figured out in time."

Now it was Ingrid's turn to look perplexed. "Well, that time is now, kiddo."

"I'm not going to a fucking hospital." Her tone was fierce.

Ingrid rubbed her cheek, only noticing afterwards that she had oil on her fingers. "You can't stay here. What do you think Vinny's going to do? Hold your hand when you start to push? We have to get you out of here. *I* have to get you out of here."

Kristyn shook her head. "Call Tom."

Ingrid thought about her four minutes of battery life. She wasn't going to waste them on Tom Kerrison. "I've called him ten, maybe twenty, times in the past twenty-four hours. I'm guessing when he sees it's my number he doesn't answer. Besides, his phone now diverts to his publicist. You don't have a phone?"

"No. I was supposed to be untraceable." She nodded in the direction of the top of the stairs where Vinny was tied up. "There's got to be someplace else. I can't go to a hospital."

The dog whined and Ingrid crouched down to stroke him. "Why not? Why can't you go?"

Kristyn took a deep intake of breath.

"You OK?"

The color emptied from the girl's face.

"Was that a contraction?"

She winced. "I, er, I think."

"Come on," Ingrid said, getting to her feet. "Let's get you into the passenger seat. You can't stay here."

Ingrid placed both hands on Kristyn's shoulders, hoping to steer her to the other side of the car, but the girl raised her hands and shoved Ingrid away. "No. I won't go."

"You can't have the baby here." Although, if a stable in Palestine was good enough for a teenage mom two thousand years ago, maybe a garage in Sussex wasn't the worst place to start a life?

"I can and I will." Kristyn Bowers was much, much tougher than she looked. "I've been to childbirth classes. I've probably got twenty-four hours of this before the baby comes. Tom will be here by then. He'll bring help. You're not taking me anywhere."

"What about Vinny?"

Kristyn looked at Ingrid. "You've got a gun."

Ingrid was stunned. "This isn't the movies. We don't just shoot people who get in the way."

Kristyn placed her forearms on the roof of the car and rested her head on her hands. She started breathing deeply, her back arching with each inhalation.

"We don't have to go to a hospital," Ingrid said, "but Vinny means you can't stay here. Let me get you to some other place."

Kristyn didn't move. "No. That's not going to happen. I have a deal with Tom. Just call him. Please, call him."

"What kind of deal, Kristyn?" Ingrid couldn't fit the pieces of the puzzle together. "What's the deal?"

Kristyn didn't answer.

"The surrogacy agency were going to pay you twenty-five thousand dollars. What's Tom paying you?"

Kristyn looked up, resting a cheek on her hands. "Twenty-five thousand a year for ten years. He gets the baby, I get the money. So unless you've got a quarter of a million dollars you're not going to tell me what to do. Understood?"

But Ingrid didn't understand. She scratched her head, an action the dog copied. "Hush money?"

Kristyn puffed out her cheeks. "Something like that."

"Why?"

The girl started breathing more rapidly. "I don't know. Not my baby. Not my business." Sweat was glistening at her hairline. "I give him the baby, he sets me up for life." She made eye contact with Ingrid. "I need that deal, lady. You understand? So no hospitals, no 911 calls. I can take Brody. I can get him away. I can start over. No Sutcliffe. No Aurora. A fresh start."

Ingrid stepped out onto the gravel and began to pace. She needed to think. With Vinny upstairs she either had to get Kristyn to a safe place to have the baby, or she had to find a way of dealing with Vinny. If she called the local cops, there would be too many questions to answer. She was trespassing for one thing, and the bullet holes in the door were another. No doubt the nearest station house had someone who was friendly with the local newspaper: anything out of the ordinary at Arding Manor was bound to attract attention.

She shivered. Clouds were gathering and it looked like it was going to rain again.

Ingrid wasn't even sure what crime Vinny could be arrested for apart from trespass, and if he was guilty of that then so was she. He was well tied up: he was a can she could kick down the road for a few hours. Kristyn let out a scream. Ingrid ran back to the garage.

"Come on," she said. "You're getting in the car."

"No."

The dog barked.

"No hospital, I promise. But we can't stay here. When you start to push, you need to be somewhere Vinny can't find you. Come on, take my hand."

Kristyn shook her head slowly. "You must have had medical training. You work for the goddamn FBI."

"I'm pretty good with gunshot wounds, but this is a first birth for both of us."

Kristyn's face twisted in agony.

"You're going to need painkillers." Ingrid thought about the oxycodone in McKittrick's bag and wondered what else the former detective inspector could lay her hands on.

Kristyn puffed out her cheeks and started to blow hard. "OK. But where?"

"I know a place, but first I need to get this car started." Ingrid helped Kristyn to the passenger door. "You said you had Lamaze lessons. What were you told to do right now?"

The girl was bent over like an old lady, one hand staying in contact with the car, the other leaning heavily on Ingrid. "You know what I said about twenty-four hours?"

"Maybe you should be on the back seat? You could lie down if you needed to."

Kristyn nodded.

Ingrid opened the rear door and helped Kristyn onto the cream leather upholstery. "Don't worry about making a mess. I'm sure they can afford to get it detailed."

Kristyn wriggled backward onto the seat.

"Is there anything upstairs you need? A bag? Anything?"

Kristyn nodded. "On the bed."

"I'll grab it."

Ingrid took the stairs three at a time and ran through into the bedroom area. She swiped Kristyn's small canvas backpack from the wooden chair and ran back out into the main room. Vinny had opened his eyes.

"You fucking bitch." A nasty, whiny voice.

"It was a pleasure to meet you, too." Should have taped his mouth.

Ingrid ran down the stairs, threw Kristyn's things onto the passenger seat and climbed behind the wheel.

"What about Cully?" Kristyn said.

Really? The dog?

Ingrid got out and opened the passenger door. "Come on, boy." The dog jumped in and sat on the passenger seat as if that's where dogs always traveled. "Buckle up, boy."

Ingrid pulled the driver's door shut and felt her chest hollow out as she turned the key. *Please, please start.* The engine chugged into life. Relief spread across her skin like electricity. "All right, let's go." She looked in the rearview mirror at Kristyn. "You OK back there?"

"Wherever we're going, we need to get there quick."

Ingrid glanced at the open doorway and wondered how easily Vinny would be able to extricate himself. It was only when the wheels of the Mercedes were spinning on the gravel that she remembered she should have picked up the bullet casings.

43

"I'm sorry," Kristyn said.

"For what?" Ingrid steered the Mercedes onto the drive that led toward the woods and the steel gate.

"For hitting you."

"It's not the first time it's happened. Occupational hazard."

"Did I hurt you?"

"Nothing a couple of Tylenol won't fix," Ingrid lied. The pain on the left side of her head felt like a scalding burn.

The gearbox screeched as Ingrid put the car into fourth. She couldn't remember the last time she'd driven stick. Kristyn's fingers dug in hard to the headrest.

"You see the clock on the dash?" Ingrid said.

"Yes."

"I want you to keep an eye on it and time your contractions."

"OK."

They reached the muddy path that curved through the woods, the 5000cc engine ensuring there was no chance of seeing another deer. Ingrid broke hard as she took a bend, sending the dog flying off the seat and into the footwell.

"Sorry boy." She looked into the rearview mirror. "OK back there?"

"Can't you slow down?"

The steel gate loomed ahead. *Shit.* Ingrid hadn't thought

about how to get it open. There was probably an intercom system. What if the lock could only be opened from the main house? Ingrid slowed, the tires sinking slightly into the dirt. There'd be an exit button. There'd have to be, wouldn't there?

They reached the muddiest section where the path widened in front of the gate. Ingrid put the Mercedes into first gear, then neutral and applied the handbrake. She opened the door and was about to look for a way to release the gate when a loud clunking noise made her jump. It was followed by a squeal. She breathed hard. A few moments later the enormous steel panel began to slide. Number plate recognition system. It was time for something to go her way.

She pulled out of the gate, past her parked Triumph Tiger 800 and turned onto the track that ran alongside the boundary fence. She accelerated toward the road.

"Where are you taking me?" Kristyn asked.

"How close are the contractions?"

"Where are you taking me?" the girl demanded.

"It depends how close together your contractions are. You think you can make it to London? About an hour?"

"I… I don't know."

Ingrid floored the Mercedes, making it bounce wildly over divots and potholes. Ingrid didn't have a clue where they were headed; she just hoped something would present itself through a combination of vigilance and optimism.

They were about a hundred yards from the junction with the road when a car turned off it and headed toward them down the track. *See,* Ingrid said to herself, *I knew something would turn up.* It had to be Tom and the midwife.

"Looks like the cavalry's here." Ingrid brought the car to a halt: the track was too narrow for the cars to pass each other. Tom would realize this, she thought, and he'll reverse.

When the car got closer she saw that it was a Ford Focus. Not a Range Rover or a Maybach or any other kind of rich man's car: Tom Kerrison wouldn't be driving a Ford. And he would be slowing down, she thought. The Ford hurtled toward them, only braking when the driver realized the Mercedes wasn't about to reverse. Ingrid opened the driver's door, ready to tell the other driver he was going to have to make way unless he too was carrying a passenger in labor.

She stepped out and raised her hand at the oncoming vehicle. When the Ford came to a halt she saw who was behind the wheel. Tall, overweight, baseball cap: Mr White Sox. Avery Donaho.

Ingrid swallowed, her mouth suddenly dry.

He placed both hands on the steering wheel and stared at her through the windshield. Had he noticed who was on the back seat? It wouldn't be long before he did. Ingrid got back behind the wheel.

"Plan B," she said and put the car into reverse. "Hold tight."

Ingrid had to get Kristyn away from Donaho. She didn't know what was at the other end of the track. A farm presumably. It didn't look like the kind of route that led to another road. Her choice was a destination she didn't know, or back into Arding Manor where at least she had the advantage of knowing the lay of the land.

"Why didn't he just reverse?" Kristyn said.

There was no need to tell Kristyn the man in the Ford had come to the UK to kill her, but Ingrid couldn't think of a good lie to tell. "Because he's a piece of shit."

The gate clanked open and Ingrid knew there was just no way it would close quickly enough to stop Donaho following in behind them. She swung the rear end in and turned sharply, throwing the dog and the girl. She broke hard, got the car into first gear and pulled away. At least now she was driving forward, and she had more horsepower than whatever Donaho had at his disposal. She liked her chances.

The wheels started to spin in the mud. She swerved to stop them becoming stuck and pulled away down the track through the woods. In the rearview mirror, she saw the Ford turn through the gate. Damn. There had been a slim chance it would have closed in time, with any luck slicing the Ford in half and killing Donaho. But this wasn't the movies.

The dog started to bark. "Not now, Cully."

"Who is he?" Kristyn said again.

Ingrid glanced at the girl in the mirror. Her face was red, her expression fearful. "He's Sutcliffe's man."

Kristyn let out a high-pitched scream. "No, no way."

"I got this covered," Ingrid said. "Like you said, I've got a gun. You're going to be OK. The baby's going to be OK. Even you're going to be OK, Cully."

They were nearing the end of the woods.

"How did he find me?" Kristyn said, her breathing sharp and shallow.

Ingrid didn't have the brain space to reply. She needed all her mental capacity to work out where to head for. Back to the garage wasn't an option: Vinny would find a way out of his restraints eventually. The main house would probably trigger all kinds of alarms if they broke in. The outbuildings near the greenhouses were their best bet. If she could get far enough ahead of Donaho, she could park the car behind one of the brick outhouses, wait until the Ford passed and then find somewhere to hide Kristyn. Ingrid revved the engine.

In the rearview mirror, the Ford was receding. Ingrid was now so far ahead that when they went round a bend Donaho was out of view.

"How did he fucking find me?" Kristyn asked.

"Same way Vinny did, same way I did," Ingrid said, one eye on the track in front, the other on the mirror. They neared the end of the woods. "Now's not the time," Ingrid said, slipping the car back down to third, preparing to turn sharply behind one of the yard buildings. She looked at the path and registered the tire prints in the mud. It was too risky: all Donaho would need to do was follow their tracks.

"Where are you going?" Kristyn asked.

Ingrid had no idea.

44

The path joined the main gravel driveway and Ingrid sped toward the house, looking for a turning or a hiding place. To her right were trees, to her left a rolling lawn. Ahead was the formal garden. There was nowhere.

The wheels spun on the gravel as Ingrid accelerated toward the house. The engine roared as she sped down the driveway, around the side of the Moorish flower beds, behind the enclosed kitchen garden and into the turnaround in front of the garage. Veering off onto the grass and behind the garage might have been an option if it wasn't for the threat of Vinny making an appearance, so Ingrid drove straight past the garage, round the back of the house, and found herself on the wide drive that led to the main gates. She glanced at the fuel gauge. Just under half a tank. *Well, that's something.* She checked her mirrors: Donaho had dropped out of view. It was possible, just possible, that if there was a fork in the driveway she could shake him: tires didn't leave tracks on gravel. But lining both sides of the drive were regimented rows of linden trees. There was no fork, no turning.

The path curved away from the house, through the woods toward the wrought-iron gates. Ingrid pressed down on the accelerator as Kristyn panted loudly in her ear.

"Hang on," Ingrid said. "I'm going to get us out of here."

"How?"

Ingrid headed down a straight stretch of driveway, a couple of hundred yards long, through the trees toward the wrought-iron gates. The wheels spun on the gravel and Ingrid momentarily lost control of the steering before the gates came into view. The same gates that looked like they hadn't been opened in a decade. The dog would not stop barking. Ingrid just kept her eyes front, her hands on the wheel.

"Fuck," Kristyn said. "Fucking hell."

Ingrid put her foot to the floor: if she hit the gates with enough speed, she'd break the lock, then she could turn onto the road and head for safety.

"Fuck," the girl said again. "I think… I think the baby's coming."

Ingrid checked her mirrors. The Ford had turned into the straight path. Donaho was two hundred yards behind.

"Come on." The speedometer nosed up from fifty-five to sixty; the gates were fifty yards away. She aimed at the center, hoping the padlock was so rusted it'd snap on impact.

"Oh dear God, please fucking help me." She sounded desperate.

The dog kept on barking but Ingrid focused on the gates, imagining them flying off their hinges when the car struck them. Then, coming to her senses, she slammed on the brakes, sending the wheels skidding on the gravel.

Kristyn was thrown against the front seats, the dog slid back into the footwell. Ingrid's forehead came within millimeters of the windshield. The Roadster's fender crumpled into the ironwork.

"What the fuck!" Kristyn demanded.

What had she been thinking? This wasn't the goddamn *Dukes of Hazzard*. The gates were heavy iron. They hadn't been moved in years and the Mercedes was an old car, without airbags or crumple zones. *I could have killed us.*

Ingrid's hand was trembling as she opened the door. She got out the car. Donaho was a hundred and fifty yards away. He saw her and slowed to a halt.

"Fuck," Kristyn screamed. "You've got to help me."

I am helping, she wanted to say. *Right now there's just me between you and a man who's been hired to kill you.*

Blood rushed in Ingrid's ears, pumping hard and heavy like a war drum. She stood with her feet hip-width apart and kept her gaze fixed on the Ford. Kristyn screamed from inside the car. Ingrid wanted to help her, to say something at least, but she couldn't take her eyes or her thoughts off Avery Donaho.

His engine was ticking over. His hands were on the steering wheel. He revved hard but the car was not in gear. A roar rather than a bite.

Ingrid could feel the pulse in her neck, the muscles below her ears tightening. She took a step forward, then another. She raised her hands, showing Donaho that she was not carrying a weapon. *Come on, buddy, meet me halfway. My Gary Cooper to your John Wayne.*

Ingrid heard a soft clunk: Donaho had put the car into gear and it started moving slowly down the path toward her. Ingrid's windpipe tightened, her jaw locked. Something moved out of the corner of her eye. It was the dog getting out of the open driver's door. *Not now, boy.* She made eye contact with Donaho, holding his gaze as he moved the Ford slowly down the drive.

Donaho took a hand off the steering wheel. He was changing gear. He was accelerating. He was coming straight for Ingrid, straight for Kristyn. Twenty miles per hour, thirty, forty. He was fifty yards away and still accelerating. Ingrid shoved her hand inside her jacket, pulled out her Glock 23 and took aim at the Ford. She pulled on the trigger and shattered the windshield. Donaho did not swerve.

Aim fast, shoot slow, she heard her father say. She looked again, braced her shoulders. The car was hurtling toward her. She fired again and blood colored the shattered windshield.

The Ford slowed but it was still going to smash into the Mercedes. Ingrid jumped out of the way, shoving the dog into the trees, turning back just as it rammed the Roadster hard against the gates. The airbag blew up inside the Ford, sending Donaho's head back hard against the seat. Kristyn was screaming.

Ingrid holstered the gun. Her mouth hung open. She was

unable to close it. For several moments she simply stood there, listening to Kristyn curse and shout. The dog lay down and whimpered.

Ingrid ran both hands through her hair, letting her palms rest on top of her head. It's happened, she thought. It's finally happened. *I've killed someone.*

"Fucking. Hell." The girl had every reason to scream.

Her jaw still hanging loose, Ingrid approached the driver's door of the Ford Focus. The airbag had started to deflate. Donaho's head was tilted back, his eyes open, part of his skull missing.

Ingrid reached for the door handle and pulled slowly, not wanting Donaho's body to fall out of the car. She stretched in, her face only inches from the man she had just killed, and turned the key in the ignition. The engine stopped. Ingrid withdrew from the vehicle and looked carefully at Donaho. She'd always known this day might come and had often imagined how it would feel.

A hired assassin who was trying to kill her and a pregnant girl? Ingrid thought she'd be able to live with the consequences.

"Oh my fuck."

Ingrid snapped her concentration to Kristyn and rushed over to the Mercedes. Kristyn was lying on the rear seat, one arm clutching onto the driver's headrest, the other digging into her own thigh. The look on her face was pure hatred. "Get this fucking thing out of me!"

Ingrid heard an engine. She stared through the gates as a car passed down the road, oblivious to the drama on the other side. Just an hour or so beforehand she had stood on the roadside, looking in. How long would it be before someone did the same and saw two crashed cars? How long before a *Belgravia Set* fan tweeted a picture? Then how long before the police turned up and found a dead body, killed by an unlicensed gun, on a movie star's driveway? Ingrid's jaw wouldn't stop trembling.

"Oh God, oh God."

If they come, they come. Ingrid climbed inside the car and placed a hand on Kristyn's ankle. "Looks like this is where you're going to have the baby." She removed Kristyn's underwear and helped her get as comfortable as possible. "You make as much noise as you need to."

"Fuck. Off."

And swear as much as you need to. Given how much his father swore, it was something the kid was going to have to get used to.

"OK, I can see the head now. Come on, Kristyn, push."

45

"You don't want to hold him?"

"Keep him away from me."

The boy was crying. A few weeks premature, but he was breathing and he was crying. That was a good sign. Ingrid held him to her chest. "Hey there fella," she said. "One day you're going to have quite a story to tell." Ingrid looked at Kristyn. She was shaking. "Well done. You did great, amazing. You can be really, really proud of yourself, OK?"

The girl nodded. "I don't even want to look at him. That's what they told us at the agency. Don't look, don't hold, don't bond."

"Hey, that's fine, but you know he's kind of attached to you. I can't take him anyplace until we cut the cord. They tell you about the placenta in Lamaze?"

"Uh-huh."

"How long before, you know, before you have to…" Ingrid looked down at the white leather seat. It wasn't very white anymore.

"I feel sick. I'm gonna be sick." Kristyn had turned even paler.

"It's probably just a drop in blood pressure. It'll pass." Ingrid tried to sound authoritative and reassuring, but she was just guessing. It didn't look like Kristyn had lost much blood. "You're probably a little dehydrated. I can go back to the apartment above the garage and find you some water."

The dog pushed his head through the gap between Ingrid's legs and the open door.

"Look who's come to say hello," Ingrid said to the boy. He was going to need feeding. And washing. They were all going to need washing. Her new clothes were ruined. "Hey, stop that!" In the animal kingdom, Ingrid thought, they do eat the afterbirth. Maybe Cully was the best option they had for a clean-up operation. "Shoo."

Ingrid pulled out the penknife from her jacket pocket and started to cut the umbilical cord.

"Stop." Kristyn's voice was breathless and quiet. "Wait. You gotta wait till it stops pulsing."

"They taught you that?"

"Uh-huh."

Ingrid held the boy, wiping his face with the hem of her top. He was mewling rather than crying, but as far as she could tell he seemed like a healthy little boy. If she had to guess, she'd say he was Tom's son: a scrapper, a fighter, a little bit rough round the edges. Something inside her bloomed: whatever the boy needed, she was going to supply it. An evolutionary instinct.

"I think I'm going to pass out."

Ingrid looked over at Kristyn and saw the placenta on the seat. Still holding the baby, she clambered over to Kristyn. The girl was exhausted. "We need to get you a doctor."

"You can't..." Kristyn was too out of breath to finish her sentence. "No ambulance. You promised."

Ingrid didn't remember promising any such thing. "It's OK. I don't want the authorities here any more than you do."

Kristyn looked confused. "You are the authorities."

If only that were true. At that moment, Special Agent Ingrid Skyberg knew she was nothing more than a liability to both the FBI and the State Department. A rogue operative who'd killed an unarmed man with an unlicensed gun. Four bullets to account for.

What the hell have I done?

"Hang in there. I'm going to get this fixed." In the distance she heard a car engine. It wouldn't be long before someone—a dog walker, a tourist or a neighbor—noticed the car crash behind Arding Manor's grand gates. Anywhere else on the estate and she'd have more time. She looked down at the boy; blood was drying on his face. She needed to take him somewhere. Clean him up, get him checked over.

Ingrid pulled the phone out of her jacket pocket and turned it on.

The umbilical cord had stopped pulsing. While her phone booted up, she picked up the penknife and cut it, the unsharpened blade catching on the twisted, slippery fibers. The moment the boy was severed from his life support he started screaming.

"Shhh."

Somewhere in the undergrowth the dog started barking, alarmed at the strange new wailing.

"Shhh. Shhh." Someone was going to hear. Ingrid had to act.

The iPhone screen flickered into life. Three minutes of battery life. She scrambled out of the car, clamping the baby to her chest and tapped open her contacts. There was only one person she could call. She knew it would change everything. That it would be the end of her career. But when she looked at Donaho, the crumpled Mercedes, the exhausted girl and the newborn who needed her protection, she knew she had to make the call. She knew she had to make the sacrifice.

It was the first name on her list. She took a deep breath, closed her eyes and dialed. After two rings, he answered.

"*Dobriy vyecher*, Agent Skyberg. I thought we were keeping things casual." The one thing Ingrid was sure of was that Nick Angelis would always take her calls. Especially after last night.

"Nick, can you track this call?"

"Starting the trace right now." No theatrics: Nick was so good at his job because he understood when things were serious.

"I need a recovery team. A deep clean."

"What are we talking about?"

"One body, two cars." Ingrid paced up and down, trying hard not to look at Donaho's slumped corpse. "And a weapon."

"Is that a baby I can hear?"

"I need a doctor too."

"Give me an hour."

Ingrid exhaled so deeply she almost collapsed. Had she not been holding a baby less than five minutes old, she might well have sunk to her knees. "Shhh," she said, pocketing the phone. "Shh, now." The boy's tiny lungs were reacting angrily to the need to breathe. She needed to get him away from the gates, out of earshot of anyone who might be passing. She licked the knuckle of her little finger and put it in his tiny mouth. He wasn't interested: all he wanted to do was wail.

Ingrid bent down and peered inside the car. "Help is on its way."

Kristyn nodded; she was too weak to be relieved.

"A doctor is going to be here in less than an hour to make sure you're OK and check this guy out."

"And him?" Kristyn said, her head jutting in the direction of the crumpled Ford through the rear window.

Ingrid sighed. "He doesn't need a doctor." The enormity of her actions briefly surged through her body, making her dizzy.

Park it. Box it up. Focus.

"Do you think you can move?"

"I, er... I don't know."

"I'm worried about people passing. Not many cars go along this road, but one of them might be driven by someone slowing down to try and see if Truman Cooper is in residence. You want to try and make it to the house with me?"

Kristyn didn't know what to say. "I, er, oh God."

She was weak. Ingrid didn't want to leave her, but she had to find a way of silencing the baby, and in turn getting the dog to stop barking.

"Do you want to try? You can lean on me."

"I don't think I can. Not yet."

The baby's screaming got louder, tearing at Ingrid's heart. She had to help him. "I think he needs feeding."

Kristyn's face made it clear breastfeeding the boy was not an option. "I... I..."

The girl's head rolled to one side, her eyes tipped backwards. She passed out.

"Kristyn? Kristyn!" Ingrid scrambled across the back seat, clutching the baby to her chest. "Kristyn, come on now. Wake up."

Ingrid tapped the girl's cheeks with her bloodied hand. Her eyes flickered.

"That's it. Come on now."

Kristyn blinked. Her pupils narrowed. She could focus. Ingrid exhaled.

"Listen, you need fluids. I'm going to run to the garage, get you some water." It was three hundred yards to the house, maybe four hundred to the garage. She could be back in a couple of minutes. "Did you have breakfast this morning?"

The girl shook her head.

"I'm going to get you some food. Lie down. I'll be as quick as I can." Ingrid closed the Mercedes' door and looked around for the dog. She did a full three-sixty: he wasn't anywhere. He'd run off into the woods and had disappeared.

Clamping the baby to her chest with both arms she jogged toward the house, away from Kristyn, away from Donaho. The rhythm of her footsteps was matched by the cadence of a phrase that tumbled around in her head: the Lord giveth, and the Lord taketh away. One life exchanged for another.

Leaving Kristyn was a risk, but getting her to testify was now secondary. The girl had just given birth on the back seat of a crashed car and her only company was a corpse. She was tough, tougher than most, and although $25,000 a year would help her live with everything she had been through, it didn't stop Kristyn Bowers being one of the most vulnerable girls Ingrid had ever worked with. She was going to take care of her.

Ingrid reached the main house then ran round the side of the building to the back door, through the kitchen garden and up the path to the garage. The baby was still crying, a primal, hideous sound that scared her. Ingrid bounded up the stairwell to the apartment above the garage. When she neared the top she saw several strands of frayed duct tape dangling from the railing. Vinny was free.

She stopped and looked up. He wasn't looming over her with a wrench, but that didn't mean he wasn't there. She felt inside her jacket for the Glock and proceeded slowly up the remaining steps.

She reached the top, her heart pounding. She scanned the room. She ran into the bedroom area. Not there either. She checked the sink: his nine-inch knife was gone.

Ingrid holstered the gun and knelt down to open the fridge under the kitchen worktop. She was hoping for a bottle of water but found a chocolate bar, TV dinners and a pack of yogurts.

"Shhh, shhh." The baby's cries were sounding increasingly painful. She needed to feed him, she needed to wash and dress him.

She opened the cabinet doors. Just ketchup, broken coffee mugs and a packet of Doritos. She took the chocolate and the chips, and looked for something for Kristyn to drink. But there were no cans of soda, no bottles of juice, nothing she could fill with water from the faucet.

She was going to have to break into the main house.

46

Ingrid didn't want to put the boy down on the gravel. Not without something to wrap him in. His soft sticky pink skin against the hard stones. All Ingrid's instincts told her that was wrong. She slid out of her jacket, one arm at a time so she could keep hold of him, then repeated the maneuver to slip off her holster, dropping both items on the ground. Now she was able to hold the baby to her left-hand side and put herself between him and the kitchen door. She pulled the hammer she'd taken from the tool bench out of her waistband and tapped it against the glass.

The window shattered easily. She checked the boy: no tiny fragments sticking to his skin. Carefully, she knocked out the rest of the pane and reached in to try the lock. She found the catch but turning it did nothing: the door was probably bolted top and bottom. She was going to have to find another way in.

She looked down at the ground: with Vinny on the loose, she couldn't leave her gun where it was. She picked it up and threw it over her shoulder like a tote bag. An unwashed newborn baby and an unregistered Glock 23: 2013's latest accessory trends.

Ingrid came to a set of leadlight double doors that opened into an elegant drawing room. She saw her reflection in one of the panes of glass: her face wasn't any cleaner than the baby's.

Her cotton top was so filthy it looked like she'd completed an assault course.

Making sure her body was between the baby and the glass, she hit the hammer in a short, sharp movement against the lower pane. She tapped out the remaining shards, felt around for a bolt and loosened it. It was only when she had done the same with the top bolt that she considered the noise she was making might attract Vinny's attention.

But he'd have seen the Mercedes was gone, so he'd have left the estate by now. Wouldn't he?

Ingrid bent forward and examined the lock. The doors opened outward, so kicking them in was not an option. Neither was the Glock: it could cause the baby irreparable hearing damage. She reached out for the handle and pressed down, testing to see if there was any give in the mechanism. Then she pulled on the handle and to her surprise the door opened. It hadn't been locked, only bolted.

It shouldn't be this easy. It made her feel like she was walking into a trap. She rushed inside and navigated her way to the kitchen. It was only when she reached it that it dawned on her that she hadn't set off any alarms.

The kitchen looked like something from an interior design magazine. Shaker-style units, a farmhouse table and an Aga range. She dropped the holster onto the table and opened the refrigerator door. An entire regiment of Evian. She grabbed a bottle and turned to run, but something stopped her. Something had changed. It was the baby. He wasn't crying.

"Hey, little one."

Her insides turned to ice.

"Hey, you."

She held him by his shoulders. Had he just fallen asleep? She knew nothing about babies. What was she supposed to do?

Ingrid hugged the child tightly to her chest and kissed his forehead. "Come on, little one. Come on."

She turned on the faucet and while the large ceramic butler sink was filling she opened the first drawer she came to. Cutlery.

The next one was utensils. Eventually she found one storing dish towels and laid several flat on the kitchen table.

She dipped a towel into the water and turned the faucet off with her elbow. She wiped the baby's face and looked at his tiny chest to check he was breathing. He was, but only just. She lowered him into the basin. The instant he touched the water, he opened his mouth and his eyes. Ingrid slumped against the worktop with relief.

"There you go, little one. That's got to feel a bit nicer."

His dark pink arms reached up to her. Evolution, she thought. A baby reaches out for whoever is nearest. And whoever is nearest can't help but reach back.

She wiped him over then placed him on the towels. She had done a terrible job with the umbilical cord. "In a little while, someone who actually knows what they're doing is going to be here."

He began to cry again, but he didn't have the energy to make as much noise as before. He had already exhausted himself. He needed feeding.

Ingrid opened the cabinets to find they were full of Italian olive oil, pomegranate molasses, chocolate truffles and za'atar spice blends: the *MasterChef* winner took his cooking very seriously. But he also, Ingrid remembered, took fatherhood seriously. She thought about the nursery he had made at their house in Wapping, about the stacks of diapers and formula they had ready and waiting.

"I'm willing to bet," Ingrid said to the baby as she wiped her own face with a damp towel, "that your daddy has made a nursery for you here too."

She wrapped the boy in a clean dish towel and scooped him in her arms. After a few false turns, she found a grand mahogany staircase that led up to the second story. Taking the steps two at a time, she bounded past a gallery of portraits of men striking important poses, some in armor, some with dogs. Previous owners of the property she guessed. Or maybe they were props Truman had swiped from a movie set.

She reached the landing and was presented with a long

corridor running in both directions, lined on either side with a succession of doors. She moved down the corridor, trying each handle as she came to it, throwing open the doors to reveal bedrooms with four-poster beds and bathrooms with brass fittings and mottled mirrors. All Arding Manor was missing was a friendly ghost. The floorboards creaked under her feet, adding authentic haunted-house sound effects.

One door opened onto a narrow staircase, presumably leading up to the servants' accommodation. The boy was wailing now, his tiny lungs expelling a piercing sound that reverberated down the corridor. She just wanted to soothe him, to give him comfort.

She came to the final door. It opened out into a large sunny room decorated to look like an aquarium.

"Wow, take a look at this place, little fella. This has got to be your room." It looked like Truman had enlisted the animators from Disney or Pixar to create a scene from *Finding Nemo* or the *Little Mermaid*. The boy's cries told her he wasn't particularly impressed. Ingrid opened a pirate's treasure chest hoping it might be filled with formula, but it was empty.

She pulled out the drawers of a shell-encrusted credenza. "Look, diapers!" Behind a closet door painted to look like the hatch of a submarine, she found enough clothes for an entire kindergarten class.

"Come on." She was getting frustrated. The decoration was so spectacular—the crib was inside a fiberglass clam shell—that it made it harder to find what she was looking for. She stepped into a cave and was relieved to find it led toward what had to be the nanny's room. Ingrid flung open the cabinets and almost whooped when she saw shelf upon shelf of infant formula. Closer inspection showed some of the cartons were ready-mixed and that some of them were suitable for newborns.

"When did they start making *that*? Guess you wouldn't know, huh?"

She grabbed one of the cartons and scanned the instructions. The stuff didn't even have to be heated. She found a baby bottle still wrapped in Cellophane, something she took to be a pretty good sign it was sterile.

"OK, little one. I'm just going to put you down for a second and we're going to get you fixed up. And then we're going to go and help your mom. You OK with that?"

She placed the infant on the bare mattress on the twin bed and winced at referring to Kristyn as his mom. What was the phrase Tom had used? Gestational carrier. *And then some.*

She ripped open the carton of formula, spilling some on the carpet, and then carefully poured the rest into the bottle. She sat down on the bed and picked up the baby.

"Come on. I know this isn't what you want, but you need it. You're kind of tiny and we've got to build you up."

His lips clamped around the rubber teat and he instantly stopped crying.

"That's better." She looked down at him, his eyes a deep ocean blue, and couldn't quite believe what she was doing. *If my mother could see me now.* She sat there for a few moments, then started to wonder how long had it been since she'd spoken to Angelis. Twenty minutes? Fifteen? She looked down at the boy: it had been a lifetime. Ingrid had no idea how much she should let him drink. His stomach couldn't be much bigger than a peanut: he had probably had enough. She pulled the bottle away from his lips and was relieved when he didn't start wailing.

Just a minute. I'll just sit like this for a minute.

She closed her eyes but quickly opened them: Kristyn. How could she have forgotten? She needed to get back to Kristyn.

Ingrid got to her feet. She was going to have to leave the boy, but it would just be for a few minutes. She put him in the crib, tore herself away and stopped at the doorway to check if he was crying. She couldn't hear the baby, but there was another noise. Footsteps.

Someone was upstairs.

47

There was no way whoever was upstairs didn't know she was there: the baby's crying and shattering window panes would have made sure of that. The way Ingrid figured it, there were two pieces of good news: the first was that whoever was upstairs was two floors away from the Glock she'd left on the kitchen table; and the second was that there was only one staircase leading to—or, more pertinently, from—the servants' rooms. And that meant one thing: Vinny was trapped. There would never be a better opportunity to deal with him. This was the kind of situation she was trained for: one combatant, one agent, only one outcome.

She stepped out into the corridor and listened. Apart from the floorboards creaking beneath her feet, the house was as silent as a drafty manor house could be.

A thud. Then another. He was definitely up there.

Ingrid looked around for a weapon. She had to assume Vinny would have his nine-inch knife to hand, if not actually in his hand. What she needed, she told herself, was to be in a *Scooby-Doo* mansion where there were crossed swords above every fireplace, but the best she could find was a small granite sculpture sitting on a console table at the top of the main staircase. She hoped the piece—a twisted infinity symbol made of black polished stone—wasn't too valuable. It reminded her of a propeller, two honed blades radiating from a central shaft. A flash of the Clue board game rippled through her head: Miss Scarlett in the library with the lead piping. She picked it up. It was much heavier than it looked. It was the perfect weapon for knocking Vinny to the floor for a third time.

She crept along the corridor toward the door that led to the secret staircase. Between the sound of her boots on the polished wooden floor and the creaking timber joists, it was impossible not to make a noise. If stealth wasn't an option, then speed was her best bet.

She marched down the corridor, flung open the door and ran up the narrow staircase to reach a miniature version of the floor below: narrower corridor, lower ceiling, smaller doors. She looked around for something to block the staircase and prevent Vinny from escaping. There was no furniture to pull in front of the entrance to the staircase, so she settled for bunching up the threadbare rug in the hope it would trip him and send him flying.

She had a choice: left or right. She went left. Some of the doors were already open, revealing largely empty rooms. One had a few packing crates, another some free weights and a treadmill, a couple had single beds, neither of which looked slept in.

Vinny wasn't in any of them, so she walked back toward the center, minding her feet as she navigated the bunched-up rug, and tried the doors at the other end of the corridor.

Something made her stop in her tracks. Cigarette smoke.

Ingrid stood in front of the door the smell was coming from. There were no footsteps from inside the room, no heavy breathing from the other side of the door. With any luck, he had heard her, lit a cigarette knowing it would be his last for a while and taken a seat.

She examined the door. A handle but no keyhole. That didn't mean there wasn't a latch lock on the other side, or a bolt, or a chair against the handle, but given the age of the door, thick with countless layers of paint, Ingrid assessed it was kick-downable.

The smell of the cigarette got stronger. That was a good sign: if one hand was holding a smoke, that meant he only had one on the knife. Even easier to disarm. Ingrid stepped to the hinge side of the door and reached across to the handle: she was going to try the gentler approach.

She could feel her pulse in her fingers as they gripped the handle and lowered it. The door moved with her touch: no latch, no bolt. She shoved hard, flinging the door against the wall. No knife-wielding maniac lunged at her. She crossed to the far side of the corridor and stared into the room. No one was visible through the doorway.

Gripping the granite sculpture in her right hand, Ingrid swallowed and crossed the threshold. Always the scariest part.

She didn't see the man's face. Only the gun he was holding and pointing straight at her.

48

Tom Kerrison hadn't shaved and he was wearing the same clothes he'd been photographed in when he'd been stopped for speeding. A half-smoked cigarette hung from his lips, a bolt action Ruger carbine at his shoulder. His eyes were bloodshot, his aim wavering.

"Your son is downstairs," Ingrid said. She moved carefully into the room, keeping eye contact with Kerrison. She placed the sculpture down on a washstand: in a game of rock-paper-scissors, a bullet usually wins.

"He's not my son."

"You don't know that."

"Honey," he said, "a guy pretty much knows whether he's jizzed into a yogurt pot or not."

Ingrid pursed her lips, not sure what to make of the picture he'd just painted. "Don't you want to see him?"

Tom shook his head, the Ruger swinging as he did so. "No, he's Truman's. He's got what he wants now. He doesn't need me."

On the small twin bed was a packet of Blazer .38 specials and a length of rope. She looked up: there were exposed rafters. A near-empty bottle of Glenlivet and an overflowing ashtray on the bedside cabinet. Probably someplace else in the house there was a bottle of pills. Ingrid remembered Kerrison's history: drugs, genius, alcohol, risky sex, prison, fast cars. And then there was the scar on his wrist. She finally knew who had left the bullet in the crib.

Ingrid walked very slowly around the perimeter of the small room, turning away from Tom, letting her body language tell him she wasn't afraid or alarmed. "You're paying Kristyn a quarter of a million bucks and you don't even want to see the baby? I don't get it." She reached the window and looked out: it had a view over the yew hedge to the converted garage.

"He wasn't due for another three weeks." He took a hand off the barrel and ran it over the top of his head. "It wasn't meant to happen this way."

"How was it meant to happen, Tom?"

His hands were trembling. She wondered when he had last eaten or drunk anything other than single malt. He was a man in meltdown, on the brink, holding a loaded short-barreled rifle.

"Her and me," he said, "we're not so different."

Ingrid had heard speeches like this before. They were usually delivered as a confession by someone wanting to explain the inexplicable while they still could. The Ruger would end his life as surely as it would the deer's in the woods. Ingrid just needed to make sure he didn't take her with him.

"I figured all the money in one go wouldn't be good for her. She'd blow it or some guy would steal it. But over a decade… it would set her up, just like the guys who helped me with my first store. Payback, you know." He wiped his nose with the back of his hand.

"You wanted to be her lucky break?" Ingrid kept looking out at the garage.

"Something like that."

Ingrid turned and smiled at him. "Do you want to put that down?" One dead body on the estate was enough for one day.

He seemed unsure.

"You can still keep a hold of it, but maybe you could point it at the floor?"

Kerrison lowered the carbine.

"You told me you didn't have a gun license. But then," she

paused, "I'm guessing almost everything you've told me has been a lie."

He shrugged. "It's the groundskeeper's."

Ingrid leaned against the wall opposite him. "I see what Kristyn's getting out of this, but I haven't worked out your angle. You want to keep the baby from Truman but you also want to kill yourself?"

He dropped his cigarette into the ashtray and chewed at his bottom lip. "Something like that."

Ingrid kept her silence.

"He'd be better off without me." Tom slumped down on his haunches. He dropped the Ruger and his head fell into his hands.

Ingrid carefully moved the gun onto the bed and went and sat next to him. Empathic body language. "Want to tell me what the plan was? Because I'm really struggling to make sense of things right now."

Kerrison nodded and wiped away a tear. "Is he OK? The boy?"

"You could go downstairs and see for yourself." She tried to keep any trace of accusation out of her voice. "He's all alone right now."

Kerrison shook his head. "No, it's better he never knows me."

Ingrid was confused. "But I thought... all of this... that you want him to yourself? What am I missing?"

He sighed. "It wasn't meant to be like this."

Ingrid looked into his red-rimmed eyes and tried to understand the pain he was in.

"I was going to get her out of here. Private plane to Milan. She was going to have the baby there, somewhere Truman would never find him. Then... then I was going to set her up in a new life, with her knowing the payments would stop if she ever went to the press."

Ingrid put her hands on her knees. Traces of blood and mucus streaked her forearms. "Sounds like you'd worked it all out. So why are we here? Why aren't we drinking Chianti in Tuscany?"

"It took a little longer to arrange than I thought. With the exhibition, and the new collection... it wasn't something I could get an assistant to handle, you know. I thought she'd be safe here for a few days. I told the staff to go home." He paused. "They probably thought I was going to have a party with rent boys and cocaine."

Ingrid thought she heard something outside. A scrunch of gravel maybe. Could it be Nick and his rescue team? She got up and went over to the window. She couldn't see anyone.

"Why did you put Kristyn out in the garage? Why not treat her to a four-poster bed?"

He sniffed loudly. "Playing it safe. Wasn't sure if she might leave a hair in the sink, something the housekeeper would notice, who'd then say something to Truman. No one ever goes in the garage apartment except me. I'm the only one with the key. Then…" Kerrison punched the floor. "Then this morning this guy turns up. I watched him walking round the gardens, pacing, trying the doors. If it hadn't been for the damn dog."

Ingrid raised an eyebrow. "The dog?"

"Kristyn said she'd be lonely, so when I picked Cully up from the veterinarian I brought him here, you know, to make her feel safe. She let him out for a piss, and the guy spotted him, followed him straight into the garage."

"You saw him?"

"I was standing right where you are now."

"And you didn't try to help her?"

Kerrison was confused. "Help her? He isn't one of yours? He's not FBI?"

"I guess from this height you couldn't make out his tattoos. No, he isn't Bureau, he's a goddamned gangster." Ingrid bit her bottom lip. *And he's out there somewhere.*

"A gangster? I don't get it?"

"Kristyn never told you why she ran away from California?"

He shook his head. "All she said was someone had come to Nuestra Señora asking for Kristyn. Everyone there knew her as Kate-Lynn, so she knew she'd been found, but she never said by who." He paused. "A gangster? I was so sure he was FBI, or from the embassy. I… I thought the game was up. I thought Truman would find out I had never wanted the baby. I knew he'd never forgive me for trying to take away his son, so… so I came up here."

Ingrid looked down at Kerrison. His body had lost all tension; he looked as if he'd been poured onto the floor, his chin resting on his chest. He was beaten. A brilliant artist, a successful man, but a broken human being.

"When I saw you arrive I knew there was only one way out for me. I should have done it weeks ago. I meant to, before the exhibition. Even joked with Truman that the value of all the works would double if I got hit by a falling branch or something..."

Ingrid was sure she could hear someone outside, but there was no sign of Nick or a Fortnum Security SWAT team.

"…and I thought, yeah, double for a tragic accident, quadruple for a suicide."

Ingrid had stopped listening. If Tom Kerrison wanted to kill himself she wasn't going to stop him. He wasn't her priority; Kristyn was. And if someone was walking round outside who wasn't Nick Angelis, she had to go and deal with them.

"Tom?" Her voice was firm.

"Uh-huh?"

"I need you to go and look after your son."

"What? I told you, I don't want him, that's what this is all about, making him disappear. Don't you get that?"

"I don't fucking care." Ingrid picked up the Ruger. "This loaded?"

"Yes."

"Good"

He scrambled onto his knees. "What's happening?"

Ingrid stood in front of him. "The guy you thought was FBI is still on your property and he has plans for Kristyn. I'm going to stop him, you understand?"

He looked at her blankly.

"Your job is simple. You just need to go downstairs and be a father." She marched over to the door.

"And how am I supposed to do that?"

"You know what, Tom, about half an hour ago a teenage girl

figured out how to give birth. I just figured out how to feed a baby. I reckon you'll work it out."

He looked scared.

"He's not even an hour old. Just go to him. Be with him."

Ingrid darted out of the room and down the corridor. When she reached the top of the stairs, she tripped on the rug.

A gunshot reverberated through the house.

49

Ingrid stumbled but found her feet. Clutching the carbine, she reached the main landing when another shot rang out, making the baby cry. Vinny had found her Glock.

She ran down the main staircase, past the dark portraits of long-dead men, to the ground floor. She stopped and listened. Nothing. That wasn't a good sign. What she wanted was Vinny shouting his head off, making demands for Kristyn to be brought to him or else.

Then she heard something: rapid, light footsteps on the flagstone floor. The dog.

Ingrid hadn't fired a carbine in over a decade. They'd been useful on the farm but they were no good for combat, and almost useless against a Glock. But it looked impressive. It was intimidating. Ingrid figured it might buy her a few seconds. She shouldered it and walked toward the kitchen.

The dog barked. Not an angry bark, or a distressed bark, more of a 'hi, over here' bark. She had a vision of Cully sitting at the feet of a man with a gun, wagging his tail and hoping for a biscuit.

Ingrid took long, deliberate strides. Careful, considered movement lowered the heart rate, improved decision-making. She stopped every couple of paces to listen.

When she was close to the kitchen she thought she could hear heavy breathing. After another few paces she thought the breaths had become sobs. She walked forward, waiting at the doorway before taking a deep, steadying breath and stepping inside.

Slumped against the refrigerator door was Kristyn. Her numb, unseeing eyes stared straight ahead, oblivious to the dog whimpering at her side. Ingrid followed Kristyn's gaze toward the supine figure of Vinny, sprawled on the limestone slabs, his head lying in an expanding pool of blood.

Ingrid placed the Ruger on the kitchen table and knelt down next to Kristyn. She could see without touching that there was a strong pulse in the girl's neck. Then she blinked.

Ingrid placed a hand on the girl's knee. "Hey."

Kristyn looked at her, with the swimming eyes of a drunk, someone so inebriated they were liable to pass out. Her clothes were covered in blood. Drying blood. From giving birth, not a gunshot.

The girl moved her lips, but no words came. Lying on the stone floor next to her right hand was the Glock. Ingrid leapt up, grabbed a tumbler from a cabinet and filled it from the faucet. She held the glass to Kristyn's lips. "Drink. You need to drink something."

Kristyn's lips feebly held onto the rim of the glass, though most of the water dribbled down her chin.

"A doctor is coming. Are you in pain?"

Kristyn's head shook by the tiniest of increments. "Hungry."

Ingrid hoped the girl had a taste for gourmet chocolates and artisan breadsticks. She raided the cabinets and brought her a selection of snacks. Ingrid opened the packets then set them down on the floor and crouched beside her. The girl was exhausted, like a marathon runner who'd hit the wall.

How many women, Ingrid wondered, in the history of mankind, have given birth and killed someone within an hour? Her heart ached for the girl.

"Here, let me help." Ingrid unwrapped a chocolate truffle and popped it in Kristyn's mouth. "Better?"

The girl nodded, then a tear fell down her cheek. Ingrid

reached an arm round her shoulders and pulled the girl toward her, holding her as she began to sob.

How many women, Ingrid wondered, in the history of mankind, will have embraced after both killing a man within an hour of each other?

Ingrid felt her own eyes prickle with tears. Vinny and Donaho might have been gangsters—they had probably always known their lives would be ended by a bullet—but neither of them had got up that morning and thought it would be their final day.

Ingrid stroked Kristyn's hair and kissed the top of her head. "It's OK, you've not done anything wrong. I promise you, this is going to be OK."

The dog sat obediently in front of them, whimpering slightly. Ingrid supposed it wouldn't do him any harm: she unwrapped a bread stick and held it out for him.

"Good boy."

Ingrid started to tremble. Adrenaline was leaving her system. The threat was over. Her body was entering a correction phase, also known as the what-the-hell-have-I-done phase. Ingrid knew many of her colleagues had taken a life and had always wondered how they coped. She feared the guilt might extract a price she would be unable to pay. There was no getting round it: she had taken a man's life. And in doing so she had forfeited her career. She was going to have to leave the FBI: it would be the minimum payment Angelis would require to clean up her mess.

"I…" Kristyn's voice was faint, "I had no choice."

Neither did I.

"In a little while, when the doctor gets here, a team of people is going to come in and take care of this. No one will ever find out. You're not going to go to jail, or spend the next twenty-four hours in a custody suite."

Kristyn pulled away from her. "Why? I killed him, didn't I? Just like someone killed my sister. Isn't…" She reached out and took a sip of water. "Isn't somebody going to want justice for him? Like I want justice for Kate-Lynn?"

Ingrid pushed Kristyn's dirtied hair from her face and looked into the girl's steely blue eyes. Kristyn Bowers was possibly the toughest woman she'd ever met, tougher than Svetlana, tougher than any of her Quantico instructors. Maybe even tougher than she was. After everything Kristyn had been through in her seventeen years, and after everything the past few days had thrown at her, she still wanted justice for her sister. Ingrid's admiration for the girl was boundless.

"You know, there are a lot people who'll say Vinny just got justice."

Kristyn nodded. "But, still..."

"No one's even going to report him missing. You know that if he'd died in Aurora, he'd be in a dump truck, or under concrete on a building site. This is what happens to men who lead lives like that." Now wasn't the time to tell her the best way to get the justice she sought was to testify. The conversation about returning to Chicago could wait: she had twenty-four hours before she needed to put Kristyn on a plane.

"How's the baby?" Kristyn asked, wiping away a tear.

Ingrid looked in the direction of the hallway. "I'm guessing that the fact we can't hear anything is a good sign. Tom is with him."

Evolution. She knew it would work. You can't hold a newborn and not feel something. You just can't.

Kristyn flinched. "What's that?"

The dog ran to the back door and started barking at the noise of a helicopter coming in to land.

Ingrid took the deepest of breaths. "That's the cavalry."

She slid her arm out from behind Kristyn and held the girl's shoulders firmly. The two women stared at each other, both blinking back tears.

"I'll be OK," the girl said. "Go."

Ingrid slowly got to her feet and shakily stepped out into the garden. She followed the sound of the rotors and reached Arding Manor's broad, sweeping lawn just as the Sikorsky six-seater made contact with the ground. The blades pounded the air with such force she felt they might blow the dried blood from her skin. The door slid open and a tall, muscular man in black fatigues jumped down.

"You Skyberg?" he said, though the rotors drowned out his voice.

"Yes." She was shaking.

"Ambrose." Behind him, three operatives in Tyvek suits began unloading a series of flight-cases from the helicopter. "A truck is on its way to remove the vehicles. Angelis said there was a body—"

"There are now two."

He nodded, as if that was a perfectly normal confession.

"Which one of you is the doctor?"

"That's me," Ambrose said.

"It's this way."

As they ran toward the house it occurred to Ingrid that not hearing a sound from Tom or the baby wasn't a good sign after all. In fact, it might be an extremely bad one.

50

Three days later, Ingrid was standing outside the entrance to St Thomas' Hospital Accident and Emergency department. She had one finger in her ear to block out the sound of the driving rain and tried to listen to Sol on a temperamental line.

"Yup, Kristyn testified, we did our bit," she said, hoping her reply made sense as she hadn't properly made out what her boss had said.

"Now we have to hope the jury does theirs."

An ambulance siren crescendoed, making it even harder to have a conversation. "I should go."

"You must be tired," he said.

It was 11 p.m. or thereabouts and she was exhausted. The flight back from Chicago had been delayed by four hours and all Ingrid wanted to do was climb into bed and sleep for a week. "I'm OK."

"Good, because you really ought to be in early tomorrow."

"Why?" The ambulance turned into the parking lot, its blue lights flashing against an eggplant sky. Ingrid winced until the driver turned the siren off.

"Louden's replacement is starting."

"That was quick."

"They obviously don't trust me to hold the fort."

Ingrid thought better of telling Sol over the phone that it didn't matter whether or not she made a good impression with the new boss, because the first thing she had to do in the morning was tender her resignation. She watched the EMTs open the back of the ambulance and lower a gurney onto the wet blacktop. The ambulance was parked under an awning, but the wind whipped the rain under the cover and onto the patient. Ingrid took a slow, purposeful breath, steeling herself for whatever lay inside. "I better go," she said. "This is a crappy line and I'm getting wet."

"OK, see you in the morning. Bright and early." He hung up.

The sliding doors opened automatically and Ingrid walked up to the reception desk, dragging her flight-case behind her. The floor was wet with muddied footprints: how many people had fallen over and broken a bone *after* they'd made it to the ER?

There was a line of people at the reception desk. An LED display announced the average waiting time to be seen by a doctor was three hours and twelve minutes, and the counter staff were getting a hard time from impatient relatives and patient casualties.

How many days had it been since she had been admitted here? Was it really only four days ago? That seemed impossible, as if someone had invented a time-bending machine and used her without consent in an experiment. She counted the days: today, fly back from Chicago; yesterday, escort Kristyn to court; Sunday, fly to Chicago; Saturday, killed a man; Friday, stabbed a man, got drugged and woke up in this very hospital. Just four days. Impossible. Ninety-six hours and she'd barely slept: closing her eyes was like loading a cassette of her firing a gun at a speeding car and pressing replay. She knew she hadn't had a choice, but that did nothing to put her at ease with what she'd done.

"Hi," Ingrid said when she made it to the counter. She pushed her wet hair off her face. "I'm here to visit Natasha McKittrick. She was brought in earlier today."

The receptionist, a stocky man with thick-rimmed glasses and a plaid shirt, looked at his computer screen. He said something to her, but she was too embarrassed to ask him to repeat it. He had a thick accent, sub-Saharan Africa was as specific as she could pinpoint, and she could not understand him. She waited until he repeated himself.

"It is on the third floor," he said.

"What is?" she asked.

"ICU." So that's what he'd said.

"She's in intensive care?" It was only when she spoke the words out loud that Ingrid felt the full horror they represented.

"Third floor," the man repeated, and pointed in the direction of a bank of elevators.

Ralph had meant it when he'd said to get there quickly. Intensive care?

The elevator doors closed and Ingrid looked at herself in the mirror. She had gotten drenched just walking from the taxi to the hospital and her hair was plastered flat against her scalp. She wasn't wearing any make-up; there was no barrier between her puffy under-slept eyes and the scrutiny of the world. Or the scrutiny of Ralph Mills.

The doors opened and Ingrid followed the signs to the ICU, the wheels of her case rattling noisily on the tiled floor. She hoped she wasn't disturbing patients. The corridors were surprisingly quiet: visitors had gone home to be replaced by a skeleton night shift. She pushed through a set of double doors into the ICU reception area. There was no one behind the desk, but Ralph was sitting alone on the visitor chairs.

"I came straight here," Ingrid said. "You didn't say she was in ICU."

He stood up and embraced her. She could tell he'd been crying.

"She wasn't when I called, but she had some kind of seizure, a stroke they think, and so they brought her here."

Ingrid's mouth fell open. "A stroke? Is she going to be OK?"

Ralph bit his bottom lip and took hold of Ingrid's hands. "I don't know."

Ingrid's jet-lagged brain tried to compute the new information. "Who's in there with her? Is Marcus here?"

"Who's Marcus?" So Ingrid wasn't the only one who didn't

know. "I don't really know her family. She's the boss, right? Or she was. Oh, God, I don't mean past tense because... but, you know, the misconduct thing... oh shit, I'm really useless at this sort of thing." Mr Sensitive. It wasn't without appeal, but it wasn't for Ingrid. She knew that now. She just had to find a way of telling him.

"Do you know what happened?"

He grabbed the handle of Ingrid's sodden case and wheeled it over to the seating area. "Multiple stab wounds to the abdomen."

Ingrid shivered. Liquid nitrogen replaced the blood in her veins. She was too stunned to say anything.

"Then internal bleeding." Ralph sat down and pushed the hair off his face. "When I first got the call I thought it had to be revenge, you know, for the case we're working."

Ingrid sat beside him. "She mentioned it. Some random stabbing outside a pub."

He shook his head. "I mean, what are the odds? She's investigating a shanking, a case of mistaken identity, and the moment she gets taken off the case she becomes the victim of a copycat crime."

"She was stabbed in a pub?"

He rested his hands on his knees and leaned forward. "You know that pub I told you about? The Queen Mary? The one in Pimlico?"

Ingrid's face went novocaine numb. "What?"

"I mean, what the hell was she doing in there?"

Her jaw moved but words wouldn't come out.

"What is it?" he said. "What's wrong?"

Could he see her guilt? Was it that obvious? "She was there for me," she managed. "I asked her to look into something. Thought it would keep her occupied, keep her mind off the misconduct thing." Her head slumped into her hands but the second she closed her eyes an instant replay of the Arding Manor driveway knifed its way through her head. The spray of Donaho's blood on the other side of the windshield was stained into her retinas.

A set of double doors opened at the far side of the reception area. Two orderlies wedged open the doors and wheeled a gurney through. Neither Ingrid nor Ralph commented on the strapped and shrouded corpse they were taking to the hospital's mortuary. Ingrid pictured Donaho and Vinny's bodies being zipped into bags and loaded onto the back of a white truck. Angelis said they'd be wrapped in concrete and dropped somewhere over the English Channel. The image was quickly replaced by one of Megan's coffin being lowered into the ground. Ingrid shivered. Not enough sleep, not enough food, too many memories. When the orderlies had pushed through another set of doors, the reception area returned to stillness, the quiet punctuated with occasional electronic bleeps from distant machinery and the whirr of a coffee vending machine.

Ralph reached out and put a hand on her shoulder. "Hey, you couldn't have known."

Oh, but she did. She had absolutely known how dangerous that pub was, and yet she'd still asked McKittrick to find out what had happened to the man she'd assaulted. It was a copycat crime all right. Ingrid didn't know how much more she could cope with. It gave her some solace to know the new role at Fortnum's would afford her alternative ways of delivering justice for her friend.

The door from the ward pushed open and a nurse in scrubs smiled at them.

"Are you here for Natasha?"

Ingrid stood up. "Yes?"

"You can go in and see her if you like."

51

There was a line of vehicles waiting to get into the embassy's underground parking garage. It was September 11th and security were doing a thorough job. Which was fine for everyone in a car, but there was only so much water Ingrid's rain gear could repel. She imagined having to rewrite her resignation letter because the ink had run.

"I need you to take your helmet off," the security guard said from inside his booth.

"But you know it's me, Steve."

"I'm sorry. Just for today."

Ingrid pulled off her helmet, tilted her head in the direction of the security camera above the entrance and smiled as the rain got in her eyes and plastered her hair against her scalp.

"Thank you," Steve said.

Ingrid put her helmet back on and kicked the bike into gear.

"And happy birthday," Steve added as she rode down the tunnel into the garage.

How does he know it's my birthday? She guessed her entire record flashed on his computer every time the cameras registered her presence.

She pulled round a corner to her usual parking space and was annoyed to see another bike parked where hers should rightfully be. She pulled alongside, wondering if both bikes could fit in the narrow space and saw that tucked inside the leather strap over the seat was an envelope labeled 'Agent Skyberg'. Ingrid looked again at the bike. It was a Triumph Thunderbird. It was Truman Cooper's Triumph Thunderbird.

Ingrid turned her engine off and put her bike on its stand. She pulled off her helmet and gloves, reached for the envelope and read the note inside.

Agent,

Truman asked me to give you this as a way of saying thank you for your help. He says that now he's a father he can't possibly take any risks. He and I both know that's utter crap—he never used the thing anyway—but I guess he just wanted you to know how much he appreciates your efforts. And I do too: it's good to have you working here.

FBW

Inside the envelope were the ownership documents and two sets of keys. Ingrid took a step back and admired her new bike. Midnight blue, blazing chrome and a cream leather seat. An absolute beauty. She allowed herself a smile. On any other day, on any other birthday, it would be an amazing gift: but the ambassador's note made handing in her resignation even harder.

Ingrid peeled off her waterproofs to discover the rain had penetrated where the fabric had bunched up, which was right around the crotch. She looked like she'd wet herself. Her fabulous new clothes were at the dry cleaner's in the hope of being rescued, so not only was she back wearing her frumpy suit, but it was clinging to her where it was wet. Perfect for meeting the new boss.

Ingrid hung up the rain jacket, took her bag from the Tiger's top box and walked toward the elevator. Normally, she'd take the stairs to the third floor, but she wanted to look in the mirror and see if there was anything she could do with her wet hair.

She was impatient waiting for the elevator. There was no cell phone reception underground and she wanted to know if there was an update from Ralph on McKittrick's recovery. She was also eager to get to the office and find out just what had happened to Louden. Sol had sketched the outline of the situation on the phone the previous night, but she had been preoccupied about Natasha.

The doors finally opened, revealing an elevator full of people who had got in on the ground floor and were annoyed the car had gone down instead of up. Ingrid pushed her way in, her suit pressing against someone else's raincoat. Drips from a folded umbrella ran down her pants leg.

Ingrid wasn't sure if she would need to be interviewed about Louden. After all, it was her emails she had been monitoring. When Louden had found out Ingrid was working on the Sutcliffe case, she had done a favor for an old Chicago colleague, an old and corrupt colleague who wanted to keep Sutcliffe on the streets so he could continue taking a slice of the Kings' profits. In all likelihood, Louden's intel had led Donaho to Arding Manor.

The moment the elevator doors opened, she checked her phone to see if Ralph had called. No messages. Ingrid entered the criminal division office and was surprised to see Sol sitting at her desk. She had prepared what she was going to say. No small talk. Just do the deed. Tender resignation. Work out the notice. And leave. But she'd imagined giving her speech in Sol's office, not hers.

"Agent." Sol smiled. "You seen this?" He pointed to the previous day's edition of the *Evening News* and a piece by Angela Tate. Above a photo of Tom, Truman and baby Francis was the headline: 'Truman Cooper All Set For Family Life.'

"I saw it in the departure lounge yesterday," Ingrid said. "The same photo was on the cover of *People*." This wasn't the conversation with Sol she had rehearsed.

He got to his feet, scratched his beard and leaned in. "Listen." His body language and his tone weren't encouraging. "I thought I better wait for you. Wanted to make sure I saw you before the new Deputy Special Agent in Charge starts his rounds."

He looked so serious that Ingrid thought he'd found out. Had Angelis' deep clean left a speck of dust? Oh God. She wasn't going to resign. She was going to get fired. She looked down and noticed for the first time the wet patch the umbrella from the elevator had left on her trousers. It had been so crowded she didn't get a chance to look at herself in the mirror. She reached up and felt her hair, plastered flat against her scalp. No doubt her make-up would have run too.

"Really? Why?"

Sol looked reluctant to answer. Her phone rang. It was Ralph. "I absolutely have to take this."

Sol nodded his consent and walked over to the open office door, keeping lookout over the bullpen.

"Hi. How is she?" Ingrid's throat hurt it was so tight.

"Awake. Did you ever meet my colleague Cath?"

"Yes, I think so."

"She's with her now. They're transferring her to a recovery ward. It's sounding good."

Ingrid stumbled a little, holding onto the back of her chair for support. She inhaled deeply, as if more air would somehow allow her to absorb what Ralph was saying.

"That's... that's wonderful."

Sol glanced nervously in Ingrid's direction. Something was obviously going on out in the bullpen, but she didn't give a damn what it was.

"So, I'll see you there again tonight? Perhaps we could meet for a drink beforehand? Or afterwards?"

"Ralph, look..." She didn't know what to say.

"It's OK. I get it. We had our moment."

"And it was a nice moment..."

Out in the bullpen, Ingrid heard a familiar voice. A Southern voice. Oh, please, no. *Not him.*

Her heart began to beat heavily and Sol stepped to one side, allowing the primped and pompous Marshall Claybourne to enter the room.

"I tried to warn you," Sol said, taking a step back. "Meet the new DSAC."

Ingrid dropped the phone onto her desk without hanging up. She could hear Ralph's voice asking if she was still there.

Marshall ran a manicured hand through his pomaded blond hair. "Hey, sweetie." He smiled broadly. It was a smile that said he knew precisely how much his appointment would unsettle her.

"Really?" Ingrid said, uncomfortably aware of her tired, wet suit, puffy face and slicked down hair. Not the way she'd hoped she'd look when she saw him again. "You?"

He shoved his hands in his pockets and leaned back against the doorframe. The cocksure bastard had got himself yet another promotion.

"Thought I'd swing by, wish you a happy birthday and all. I know it's not easy, what with it being today of all days."

Ingrid hated that Marshall knew it was her birthday. She hated that she could smell his cologne. How dare he come to London. How *dare* he.

"Well, let me tell you something." Ingrid was in no mood to play nice. "That is absolutely the last time you call me 'sweetie'. You say it again and I will shove a harassment case so far up your greasy pole it'll break your teeth. Got it?"

Ralph's tinny voice applauded down the phone line. Sol smiled at her admiringly.

"Is that a threat, agent? Because there are procedures for agents who cannot handle authority." His smile broadened. "Disciplinary procedures. Redeployment. Demotion."

Marshall Claybourne had come to London to get revenge, to make her life hell.

"Well, I've got a lot of folk to introduce myself to. I'll be seeing you," he said to Sol. Marshall turned on his heels, rotated against the doorframe into the bullpen and out of sight.

She couldn't resign now. Everyone would think it was

because of Marshall. She was just going to have to find some other way of repaying Nick Angelis.

Don't forget to find out what happens when Nick Angelis calls in the debt in BELOW ZERO, the fifth Ingrid Skyberg Thriller.

Available in paperback and ebook.

BELOW ZERO

AN INGRID SKYBERG THRILLER BOOK 5

Stockholm is under siege. A bomb has gone off, a series of high profile people have been kidnapped, and the city is in lockdown. Unfortunately for Special Agent Ingrid Skyberg, everything is kicking off on the same day she is in town to complete a dangerous assignment that is so secret, and so illegal, that neither the FBI or the US government can ever know about it. Her instructions are simple: no ID, no credit cards, no trace. If she ends up in jail, or floating face down in the harbor, there can be no way of identifying her.

No badge, no gun, no back-up: this time Ingrid is on her own.

Available in paperback and ebook.

EVA HUDSON

THE INGRID SKYBERG THRILLERS

Run Girl - Prequel (A novella)

In Europe to help broker a peace deal between warring African nations, Secretary of State Jayne Whitticker is in the middle of delicate negotiations when her favorite grandchild disappears from Paris.

Special Agent Ingrid Skyberg is hauled out of her FBI training session at Scotland Yard to head the hunt for the eighteen-year-old girl, who the FBI believe is now in London. Will she succeed in her unexpected mission? Or will her failure lead to the collapse of the crucial peace talks?

Fresh Doubt - Book One

A story of lies, secrets and deadly mind games. Brilliant American psychology student, Madison Faber, is in police custody—a potential murder suspect. Two hours ago she found her roommate lying in a pool of blood. Only FBI agent Ingrid Skyberg can save her.

Kill Plan - Book Two

An American trader is found fatally poisoned in his office in the City of London. Two days later, a Latvian immigrant is discovered floating face down in the River Thames, brutally murdered.

When Special Agent Ingrid Skyberg starts investigating, she soon becomes the target of a vengeful serial killer.

Deep Hurt - Book Three

In a seedy hotel in central London, the baby daughter of a US Air Force pilot lies lifeless in his wife's arms. Accused of killing the fourteen-month-old in an uncontrolled rage, Kyle Foster flees, taking his eight-year-old son with him.

Will Ingrid find Foster before he hurts anyone else? Or will she succumb to the old demons she's been trying to escape for the last eighteen years?

Shoot First - Book Four

A teenage girl disappears after witnessing a gangland murder in Chicago. Nine months later, and heavily pregnant, she arrives in London only to disappear again.

Special Agent Ingrid Skyberg has just two days to find the girl and get her to testify or else a brutal killer walks free. But Ingrid isn't the only person looking for the girl, and a war that started on the streets of Chicago is about to explode in the peaceful English countryside.

Below Zero - Book Five

Stockholm is under siege. A bomb has gone off, a series of high profile people have been kidnapped, and the city is in lockdown. Unfortunately for Special Agent Ingrid Skyberg, everything is kicking off on the same day she is in town to complete a dangerous assignment that is so secret, and so illegal, that neither the FBI or the US government know about it. Her instructions are simple: no ID, no credit cards, no trace. If she ends up in jail, or floating face down in the harbor, there can be no way of identifying her.

No badge, no gun, no back-up: this time Ingrid is on her own.

Final Offer - Book Six

One man wants to buy the presidency. One woman stands in his way.

A shadowy UK-based group has been trying to hack the US elections. When Special Agent Ingrid Skyberg is assigned to find out who's funding the hackers, she finds herself up against an invisible enemy who is extremely powerful and utterly ruthless.

To bring them to justice, Ingrid must go undercover and infiltrate the world of super-rich Russian oligarchs. But money buys all kinds of protection and Ingrid soon realises that by taking on this battle she's putting everything on the line – her career, her future, her life.

GET AN EXCLUSIVE SKYBERG NOVELLA

Want to read more about Ingrid Skyberg? For FREE? Join Eva's mailing list at evahudson.com and receive RUN GIRL, a novella featuring Ingrid Skyberg's first assignment in London for free. You'll also get news be kept up-to-date when new books in the series are released.

Visit evahudson.com.

ABOUT THE AUTHOR

Eva was born and raised in London. She worked as a local government worker, web editor, dot com entrepreneur, portrait artist and singer. In 2011, Eva won the inaugural Lucy Cavendish Prize for Fiction for her first novel, *The Loyal Servant.* The book was also shortlisted for ITV's People's Novelist Award.

In 2013, Eva published the first Ingrid Skyberg Thriller and never looked back.

To find out more about Eva or Ingrid, please visit evahudson.com. You can get the latest on all things Skyberg by following Eva on Twitter at twitter.com/eva_hudson and Facebook at facebook.com/evahudsoncrimewriter.

Printed in Great Britain
by Amazon

81961170R00202